TOTALLY SPIRITUAL
BOOK ONE

TOTALLY SPIRITUAL

BOOK ONE

Quinn Rivers

Podium

Podium

TOTALLY SPIRITUAL
BOOK ONE

CHAPTER ONE

A Regular Day

No, I swear, people these days just don't *get* cinema anymore!"

An obnoxiously loud voice carried through the already busy café, just as it had been for the past five uninterrupted minutes. It was as though the man that it belonged to was in some kind of competition to see who could be the most annoying and socially unaware. Meanwhile, the young woman across from him seemed to try and hide her face between her own shoulders to avoid the glares from the other people around. As though her silence was an invitation for him to continue, the man once more opened his mouth. "You can't blame them, though. The trash they show these days—"

"An iced caramel cappuccino for you, and a simple black coffee for you." With a smile on his face, the young server placed two cups onto the table in front of these two customers, interrupting the "conversation." Staring up at him, the man clicked his tongue, then quickly turned back to the woman across from him, but the server wasn't quite done yet.

"And it would be much appreciated if you could lower your voice. You are disturbing the other customers," he quickly added, wearing a professional smile on his face. The man scoffed and shook his head, as if he had just heard a distasteful joke.

"This is a public place! What, we can't even have a conversation in public anymore?"

"Actually, Café Runic is a privately owned business, so if you're not willing to quiet your voice, we reserve the right to remove you from the property," the server retorted before the customer even closed his mouth again.

With a click of his tongue, the customer glared back. But, he also started to notice the server tapping the wooden serving platter with his finger very obviously, basically wanting to drag attention toward it. And at the base of that finger, the server's red and recently bruised knuckles became apparent. As the man looked back up, seeing that customer-service smile combined with a pair of unamused eyes, he meekly shrank back. Figuring that the problem was solved for the time being, the server looked at the woman seated at the table, giving her an encouraging wink before turning back around and heading toward the counter.

"Ah, how little I miss having to deal with that myself," the man lazily leaning onto the counter said with a reminiscent smile, but the server just rolled his eyes in response.

"You're the owner. I'd actually appreciate it if you did 'deal with that' every once in a while."

"And what, take away my little knight's job? I wouldn't dare!"

"Don't call me that."

As if hurt by the blunt rejection, the owner touched his hand to his chest. "What, your mother can call you that, but I can't?"

"Yes, actually," the server sighed loudly, glancing past the man in front of him, "Runar."

"Ryan," the owner, Runar, replied with a puzzled expression, but Ryan just shook his head.

"No, the milk is bubbling over."

As the confusion on Runar's face was replaced with panic, he turned around, seeing that he had left the hose of the milk frother inside the pitcher and hadn't fully closed the valve again. As he hurried to clean up after himself, Ryan heard the café's bell ring as another customer entered through the door. The customer looked around a little nervously before spotting the counter with Ryan standing in front of it and quickly approached him.

"Welcome! How can I help you?" Ryan asked, returning back to his customer-service mode, and the young man kept glancing around the space.

"Uhm, do you guys maybe have another door somewhere? My girlfriend can't get through your main entrance . . ."

With a raised brow, Ryan looked past the worried young man, spotting a figure standing in front of the door outside. Smiling, since this wasn't the first time this happened, he motioned for the young man to follow him and walked over to the door. He pulled it open and stepped through, quickly looking up at the person in question, her single large eye starting to well up with embarrassed tears.

"Hey, it's all good, nothing to worry about!" Ryan said with a smile, trying to calm her down as he pulled the door shut behind him. He then quickly stepped aside to make some space. "Just give it a try, reach out to the door."

A bit confused, the young cyclops girl did as told, pushing her hand toward the door handle. As she did so, with a quiet sound of stone rubbing against stone, the bricks around the frame shifted aside to make way for the expanding wooden door.

"We've got an adaptive doorway. Cyclops, minotaur, giant; as long as you fit into our main space, the door will work," Ryan explained, looking up at the surprised expressions of the two customers. "We're still trying to figure out how to make that more obvious. If you have any friends that also belong to larger species and enjoy some good coffee, feel free to let them know that our door opens for anyone."

Excitedly, the young woman walked through the door, which had now grown enough to let her pass through. Ryan followed behind and glanced at the door that returned back to its standard size, and guided the couple toward a table that could accommodate them both. And after taking their order, Ryan returned to the counter to pass it on to Runar.

"Seriously, can't we just put a sign out front? You know everyone's always confused about that," Ryan complained, but Runar just groaned as he started working on the orders.

"I know, I know, you've been annoying me about that for a few weeks. I'm working on it, okay?"

"Why'd you even have to go with that kind of thing? That can't have been cheap."

"A friend offered to install it for free when I opened the place. And it's much better than having three different doors or something, like some places do," Runar complained. "And if we don't do that, it would have to be a single massive door, but a door for a three-and-a-half-meter cyclops is going to be annoying for, like, a one-meter gnome to open. And I swear to the gods I refuse to get one of those stupid motion-sensor sliding doors."

"What's your issue with those anyway?"

"They fucking ignore me all the time." Runar clicked his tongue, putting the finished orders onto the counter in front of Ryan. "When you're done with that, go ahead and call it a day. You started early today, anyway."

A bit surprised, Ryan looked back at Runar. "You sure? I don't mind working a little longer. It's pretty busy, y'know?"

Runar locked eyes with Ryan, holding up his finger and pointing at him like a warning. "Don't make me repeat myself. There's some packages for you anyway, go take care of those. I don't like the clutter."

"I've seen your bedroom, dude."

"Point taken. Now shut up and get going already."

Ryan smiled lightly, choosing not to fight against it. After bringing the ordered coffee and pastries to the young human-cyclops couple, he made his way to the back of the café. He quickly hung up his apron, unlocked the door next to him, and walked up the stairs into the flat above the café, then grabbed the two cardboard boxes from the hallway on the way to his room.

Ryan pushed the door shut with his foot and placed the boxes down on his desk, and then looked around for something to open them with. His eyes landed on his X-Acto knife and he quickly ran it through the tape holding the cardboard box shut. As he opened it up, a broad smile formed on Ryan's face.

"Oh hell yeah," he let out as he pulled the contents out of the box; it was a model kit, depicting an old, and probably historically inaccurate, orcish armor. The box art was colorful and exaggerated, and an orc's dark green skin peeked out underneath the armor's cracks as the warrior prepared himself for battle.

With a happy hum, Ryan threw the now-empty cardboard box onto the pile next to his door. "I thought it was only going to arrive on Thursday."

He placed the kit onto his desk and then glanced over at the other box. It was a lot heavier than the kit, and the name written at the top of the return address stuck out. MARY LOCKE.

He used the X-Acto knife to open this one up as well, and the first thing he saw was an old T-shirt that he specifically said he didn't need anymore. With a sigh, he threw it onto his bed to put away later. The rest of the box was filled with bags of homemade cookies, some of Ryan's favorite snacks, and a few nonperishables.

He pulled out his phone and looked at his recent call list, then dialed one of the numbers toward the top before he put his phone on speaker. As the call went through, Ryan put the box onto the ground and started to open the model kit, pulling his small toolbox over toward him.

With a slight crackling, the call connected.

"Hey, Mom," Ryan quickly said. "How are you?"

"I'm well, honey, I just got home!" Ryan's mother replied with a happy voice. "How was work?"

"Well, slow, nothing big happened. Someone still keeps stealing Janice's lunch, and we think maybe it's Sandra again, but we don't know for sure," she replied, updating Ryan on matters related to people he never met and was never going to meet, as Mary usually did. "How are you doing, though, how is school going?"

"School's fine; exam season's over, so things are pretty chill right now. I've been working more, and hanging out with Silvia and Modak and stuff," Ryan replied, as he started removing his new model's individual pieces from the plastic frames with his clippers, before he put them into different sorting boxes to keep track of them.

"That sounds nice. How are they doing? Oh, and how is your uncle?"

"Silvia and Modak are fine—they're also just happy not to have to study all the time anymore. And Runar, he . . . well, he seems to be doing alright. Not any worse than he always does, at least," Ryan pointed out, lightly scoffing. "Honestly, I've got no idea how he's been managing without me, though. The café is pretty popular, and Runar is . . . well, Runar."

"Be nice to him! He's letting you live with him rent free and even pays you for any work you do," Ryan's mother replied, but he couldn't help himself.

"Yeah of course, I'm super grateful, but the guy never seems to sleep and is constantly walking around with circles under his eyes that make him look like an undead."

For a few moments, the person on the other side of the call was silent, before quietly agreeing, ". . . Well, that's also true."

Ryan laughed silently as he continued clipping the pieces, a sound that became clearer to Mary during this quiet moment.

"Oh, are you doing another one of those toy model things?"

Ryan stopped for a moment, trying to consider if it was worth it to correct her on the "toy" part of what she said. It wasn't. It wouldn't have been the first time anyway. "Yup, just got a new one. It's apparently inspired by this 300 CE armor from the orcish independence war, but I think the word *inspired* is carrying a lot of weight here."

"Well, as long as it looks nice!"

"I guess so."

"That reminds me, though, did my care package get there?" Mary asked, and Ryan quickly glanced over at the box next to him.

"Yup, thanks again, by the way. You don't always have to send me so much stuff. My shelf is filled with so many cans I'm starting to look like a prepper," Ryan pointed out awkwardly. He was happy to get packages from his mom so often, but at the same time, the guilt of having her do so much was something that he couldn't help but feel just as strongly every time.

"Nonsense! Better a prepper than starving!" With an immediate reply, Mary shut down any further complaints from Ryan. "But anyway, there should also be a small box at the bottom there. I found it in your dad's old stuff. It has a bunch of those toy model tools, so I figured you might have a better use for them than I do."

Surprised, Ryan raised a brow. He thought that at this point, they knew about all of his father's stuff, so hearing his mom say that she "found it" was surprising. "I'll take a look later and see what I can use. Thanks. But how are things on your side—you said there was another small street fest thing happening before?"

"Oh yes, right!" Mary replied in an upbeat, excited voice. "I nearly forgot, but I met Johnny's mother there, and apparently Johnny awakened recently! I think she said it was some sort of physical class, something like an Enhancer? Apparently he's starting a business now!"

Ryan held back his desire to sigh at that information. Johnny was a good guy for sure, so if anyone deserved to awaken, he did. Especially with the fame and flashiness that usually came with being an Enhancer, it was better for a guy like him to get that class. At the same time, Ryan hadn't spoken more than a sentence at a time with Johnny since eighth grade, so he couldn't say that he particularly cared all that much. Though, maybe there were some slightly jealous undertones to that.

The conversation continued like that, speaking of relatively mundane matters for around twenty more minutes. By the time the call was over, Ryan had removed all the model's individual pieces and had even started flipping through the model's guide to double-check that he had the right idea about all the pieces.

"Make sure to eat well," Mary said, a smile audibly on her face.

"I will. You as well, Mom."

"Of course. Love you, my little knight."

"I love you too, Mom. Talk to you later," Ryan said, as he reached over toward his phone, then ended the call. He twisted his chair around and leaned forward for the care package his mother had sent, then shuffled through the items inside. And just as she had said, at the bottom of the box, Mary had hidden another small wooden box. He was surprised to see something as intricate as it was, considering how long it must have been stowed away and hidden. It didn't seem like something that you would keep in an inconspicuous place. He pushed the latch to the side, and quickly revealed the objects within.

Some clippers, a metal file, a couple of brushes, as well as needles and thread, and even a small handkerchief. It seemed to basically be a random assortment of stuff, but it was still pretty high-quality, even if at least two decades old. Not that he figured he would have any use for these. The tools that he had were newer, and in a clearly much better state. The ones in the box were all quite pretty, though, with intricate patterns on their surfaces, so Ryan might clean them up and display them with his models.

As he pushed everything in the box around, he noticed something glistening in response to the rays shining into it from the window. A thin red layer of light filled the box completely. It was a gemstone, neatly cut into shape. Not large by any means, barely half as big as his thumb, but it wasn't something that he expected in here. Though, Ryan also didn't expect a silk handkerchief, but something about that gemstone stuck out, as if it didn't belong.

He reached his hand into the box and picked up the red gem, the refracted light now covering his fingertips. Or at least, Ryan assumed that it was refracted light, but the shine was far too strong for just that. It was glowing, not through the sunlight, but through its own power.

Ryan's eyes focused on the stone, enthralled, then he felt a sharp stinging, as if someone had stuck a needle into his eye from outside his periphery. But it didn't really hurt either. It was intense and focused, but not painful. And as the feeling subsided, something entered his view.

[Congratulations! You have awakened as a Spirit Keeper!]

CHAPTER TWO

The Spirit Keeper

[Congratulations! You have awakened as a Spirit Keeper!]

Ryan's mind was filled with incoherent thoughts. A storm of words and ideas all climbing on top of each other, fighting for the spot at the front of his focus. Was he hallucinating? Was it some sort of elaborate prank? Or, was it possibly that somehow, maybe, he actually awakened?

But, if that were the case, then his class was one that he had never heard of, which immediately made his heart skip a beat. It wasn't something that he would admit to others, but even at his age he was still obsessed with the Awakened. He spent a lot of time on the different forums and wikis talking about news or updates on different Awakened, and even more embarrassingly, he had basically every publicly known class memorized. So, either the only people that awakened as a Spirit Keeper were those who felt like they needed to keep it a secret, or he was the first one who had ever awakened as one. Of course, either of those seemed more than just unlikely, so maybe Ryan had simply overlooked it. It could be a class that was so mundane and boring that nobody paid it any attention, and even Ryan had skipped past it.

None of that really mattered in this moment, though. Ryan had awakened. Once he managed to collect his thoughts, his heart beating so loud that it drowned out the noise from the café right below his feet, and even that of the cars driving by and honking in this terribly loud city. Then he did what everyone did when they first awakened. He thought of the command prompt, and before he even consciously formed the words in his mind, the floating, vaguely translucent window appeared in his view.

[Ryan Aglecard] [Age - 19]
[Spirit Keeper | Level - 1]

[MP - 18]
[Stats]
-[Dexterity - 1.12]
-[Intuition - 1.01]
-[Mana - 0.56]
-[Sociability - 0.98]
-[Spirituality - 0.47]
[Skills]
-[Spirit Construction | Level - 1]
-[Spirit Domain | Level - 1]
-[Spirit Link | Level - 1]

". . . What?" Ryan let out in disbelief. Mana, intuition, and spirituality . . . he awakened as a magical class. Ryan Aglecard, who had never really shown even a hint of magical talent. Hell, he wasn't even particularly interested in magic beyond what he saw on TV as a kid. His lowest stats were quite literally the two most important stats for a magic user; mana and spirituality. And it wasn't even a contest.

"There's something . . . something wrong, right?" he muttered to himself. "I know that people awaken talents they didn't know they had, but . . . seriously, a fucking magic class?"

If he had known this was going to happen, then he would have taken magical theory instead of physics in high school. But that wasn't what was important right now. Ryan looked down at his hand and the red gemstone still held between his fingers.

A mysteriously glowing gem he had never seen before, as well as a sudden awakening as a magical class he never heard of before. This was obviously connected somehow.

Ryan took in a deep breath as he collected his thoughts. Keeping the gemstone in his hand, refusing to let it go for now, he walked over to his desk and picked up his phone. With a few quick motions, he pulled up a group chat and dialed. As usual, it didn't take long for someone to pick up.

"Yo, what's up?" a deep and immensely tired voice asked, its owner seemingly distracted, and Ryan didn't even hesitate to respond.

"Modak, I need you and Silvia to come over, right now."

"It's like 5 p.m., the subway's gonna be hell," Modak replied with a loud groan. "It's not something we can talk about like this?"

"No, it's not, I—" Ryan started trying to explain, when the sound of another person joining the call interrupted him, and Ryan instinctively pulled the phone away from his ear in preparation for what was about to happen.

"Hey, hey, hey, how's it going?!" Silvia, the third of the group, energetically yelled, as she always did when answering a call.

"Ryan wants us to come over."

"What? Do you know what time it is? The subway is going to be hell."

"That's what I said," Modak immediately replied, happy to hear his opinion seconded.

"Who gives a shit. This is important, so please come over," Ryan practically pleaded. His confusion and excitement were mixing into a mass of constantly whirring, storm-like thoughts that had him basically petrified at trying to figure out what he was supposed to do.

The other sides of the call were silent for a few moments as Modak and Silvia worried about their friend. "Are you alright? What happened?" Modak quickly asked, though Ryan could already hear footsteps and doors being pulled open as his two friends already got moving.

"I'm fine, I . . . I awakened," Ryan said bluntly, and the voices of his friends immediately died down. The only thing that Ryan could hear was the yelling of Modak's younger siblings, echoing through their flat. It came to the point that Ryan wasn't sure if something was wrong on the others' sides, then Silvia broke the silence.

"Holy fucking—give me thirty minutes, I'll be right on my—" she yelled out, hanging up mid-sentence as she hurried to get ready.

"Wait, are you serious? You awakened?" Modak questioned, clearly unsure if he heard right. At that point, three or four other voices popped up in the background of Modak's call.

". . . Wait, who awakened?" a woman, probably Modak's mother or maybe his sister, asked, quickly parroted by the young voices of two of his younger brothers.

"Someone awakened??"

"Who did?"

Modak let out a loud groan as he tried to focus back onto Ryan for a moment.

"Yes, I really, seriously awakened," Ryan once more announced with a smile on his face, and Modak immediately replied to him.

"Alright, I'll be right there."

With a deep sigh of relief, Ryan dropped down onto the edge of his bed. "Thanks, man. See you in a bit."

As the call disconnected, Ryan placed his phone to the side, looking back down at the gemstone in his hand. His fingers rubbed over its surface, looking at it a bit more closely. If this gem was related to his awakening, then he should take care of it well. And as if it was responding right to Ryan's thoughts, the soft glow, which had disappeared once Ryan took it out of the box, seemed to come back as a slow pulse. The light dyed his fingertips red, and a shiver ran over Ryan's body as he noticed new windows pop up in front of him.

[You have received a new Quest!]

[Maximus's Request]
[The noble Spirit Maximus is trapped in an ethereal form.
Construct him a vessel so that he may protect the world once more.]
[Conditions – Construct Maximus's Body with the provided materials]
[On Success – Maximus's Gratitude]
[On Failure – Maximus's Disdain]

"Maximus?" Ryan read as he looked over the quest information. He wasn't even surprised that he got a quest in the first place; at this point, any more surprise felt almost forced out of him. But what did worry him was that there was basically no real explanation, and he had no idea who the quest-giver was supposed to be. And then, there was something else important he couldn't figure out.

"What materials?" Perplexed, Ryan looked back down at the gemstone, but as he moved his head, he noticed something out of the corner of his eye. Wisps of red light, the exact same color as the light coming from the gemstone, were floating over his desk. They were gathering together, forming a shape; some kind of box.

Ryan jumped up and walked over. These were the "materials," then? Carefully, Ryan held out his hand toward the mass of light, holding his breath nervously. And then, the moment the tip of his finger touched it, the light scattered like a bunch of flies that had gathered on rotting fruit. And what was left behind in the light's stead was a familiar-looking box, which quickly fell onto Ryan's desk with a loud slam. The box fell right on top of the model pieces that Ryan had prepared during his call with his mom, flinging them all across the room. If his mind hadn't gone completely blank at the sight of the object that appeared in front of him, he would have been pissed, but right now, he didn't even care about those pieces.

Because on the desk in front of him, he had a whole new model. A classic box with bright art on it, depicting a suit of armor in the middle of swinging his sword at some kind of training dummy. That's what the light had given to him.

These were the materials he was supposed to use to "construct a vessel."

Maybe Ryan really did go insane after all, since there was no way this was what he thought; it was probably just the appearance of the box. Carefully, Ryan pulled open the box. Inside of it, neatly stacked on top of each other, were a number of frames holding a number of small model pieces. He rubbed his eyes in disbelief.

"What the actual fuck is going on?" Ryan let out involuntarily. "What the . . . I . . . what?!"

Ryan reached into the open box and pulled out the frames. They were definitely real. He could feel them press up against his skin, and he could feel their weight. Their . . . surprising weight. As Ryan pulled the frames out, they were way too heavy. The pieces and the frame holding them were made of actual metal, instead of the hard plastic they were usually made of. Tucked in between the frames were thin sheets of leather and finely woven fabric, each also prepared in a way to allow for smaller pieces to be cut out from them. Ryan dropped down onto his chair, unsure what to think.

"I guess I'll just get started?" he muttered, reaching out to his clippers, placing them against the edge of the first piece attached to the metal frame, and trying to cut through it. Just as he thought, it wouldn't budge; it was metal, after all. Since he would prefer not to damage the clippers, he put them to the side, grabbing his X-Acto knife to get started with the leather. After placing it onto his cutting mat, he tried to cut through the thin strip keeping the leather piece in place, but even then, he wasn't able to cut through it.

"Huh?" Ryan muttered, pulling over a piece of paper he had laying on his desk, and the knife cut through it with ease. But the leather didn't even have a mark on it. And when he tried the same with the fabric, it didn't work either. No imprint, nothing at all to even hint at the fact that Ryan was pushing down onto it with as much strength as he could. If he pressed it down any harder, he was worried the knife was going to break in his hand. Clearly, this wasn't something normal. At least there was that, and his class wasn't just related to building regular old models.

Ryan glanced to his side at his status window that was still open. His eyes landed at the bottom of the window. There were three skills: Spirit Construction, Spirit Domain, and Spirit Link. Just from the names, he figured the first of those three would be the one he needed right now. And as he focused on it, another window popped up in front of his face.

[Spirit Construction]
[Level - 1] [Proficiency – 0%]
[Allows the user to construct the Spirits' physical bodies.]
[Effect – Spirit Construction for 20 Minutes]
[Cost – 10 MP] [Cooldown – 1 Hour]

"That's . . . not a very helpful description," Ryan muttered, annoyed. Clearly it was the right skill, but he didn't want to use it without thinking about it first, so Ryan quickly pushed the pieces to the side. He turned on his computer and quickly opened a browser, making his way to one of the sites saved to his quick-access, AWKND, an all-round wiki about the Awakened, skills, classes, and anything related.

The first thing he did was search for the name of his class, "Spirit Keeper." No direct results, but there were a few entries about other spirit-related classes.

"Spirit Summoner," "Spirit Whisperer" . . . even a class called "Spirit Killer." He remembered this one pretty well. A couple years ago, it made headlines because someone went around killing all the nature spirits that he could find, and then ended up awakening as that class. But even then, there was nothing about his class, and none of his skills showed up in the skill search either. At least Ryan had regular stats, so he knew what they were all about already.

Even when searching the keywords separately and looking into the keywords "Spirits" and "Keeper," he couldn't find anything that helped him directly. So, he moved on to a separate site and looked up some things about spirits themselves.

A spirit is a being called into existence through a concentration of magic that has attained a sense of self. Due to their nature, spirits are aligned with certain specific concepts and essences related to the area and magic they were born from, such as Rivers, particularly old Trees, and even sites of worship have been known to produce spirits over time. They . . .

So, what? Did that mean that this model kit was so old that it suddenly turned into a spirit? Ryan sighed and leaned forward, continuing to read through the whole article. And toward the end, he came to a simple conclusion.

"I don't get any of this shit," he groaned to himself. At this point, he had no other choice. If he couldn't find any information about it online, then he just had to use this "Spirit Construction" skill. It didn't seem like anything harmful, and if it only used "10 MP," it should be fine. If he remembered right, even the most basic mage spells used 20 MP, so the effect couldn't be anything dangerous.

Slowly, Ryan concentrated on the skill, and his mind was filled with a cloud of information. Of concepts that he hadn't known about before. He had heard this described before, but it was really just as weird a feeling as every other Awakened claimed. While he didn't get any particular details, Ryan simply understood how to activate the skill, as if he was gifted with some kind of muscle memory. As he tried to make use of it, something welled up in Ryan's chest for the first time in his life. It felt like that warm feeling spreading through your body after drinking something hot on a freezing cold day. That feeling started in his chest and slowly moved down his arms and into his hands.

For a moment, he could swear that his fingertips let off a slight glow, but he couldn't actually see anything. Now that the skill was active, Ryan reached out to the metal model frame, tugging on one of the pieces. It felt . . . different, but he still wasn't able to detach it from the frame. As Ryan once more reached out to his clippers to give them another try, his eyes landed on that box filled with his dad's old stuff.

That gemstone was in there, so maybe the tools were related as well. He reached out to them, carefully grabbing the old, seemingly blunt clippers. He felt the warmth flow from his fingers into the tool, and on its metal parts, small runes and patterns began to glow. Immediately, Ryan knew that he had been right.

He brought the clippers to the metal frame, and tried to cut through the thin connection holding one of the pieces in place. As if he were cutting through a thin thread, the metal was cut through. For a moment, Ryan thought he had somehow missed, but he very clearly saw the narrow gap where there wasn't one before. After he did the same two more times, the first piece fell onto Ryan's cutting mat, and as he looked at the smooth edges of the piece, a heat grew in his chest.

It wasn't that same magical warmth that he felt when activating his skill just now. It was the heat of excitement that made Ryan's heart beat loud enough that he was sure Runar could hear it from downstairs. Without a moment's hesitation, Ryan grabbed the piece organizer that was still holding a few plastic pieces of that orc armor model that hadn't been flung around the room earlier, and emptied it out onto the edge of his desk.

Immediately, Ryan started removing all the small metal parts from the frames.

CHAPTER THREE

Spirit Construction

The old wooden door shot open too fast to even begin to creak. The first to step into the room was a young elven woman, followed by a hulking figure of an orc that ducked slightly as he entered through the doorway.

As the two entered, they saw Ryan sitting at his desk, carefully working on something. Taken aback, Silvia stepped closer to him. "Seriously? You've got the nerves to work on a model right now?"

Ryan turned around, looking at his friends with a broad, awkward grin on his face. The kind that Ryan wasn't able to stop himself from showing in weird or uncomfortable situations. "Yeah, so, this whole thing is part of it, actually . . ."

"Part of what?" Silvia raised a brow, looking at the desk. Spread out there were just some regular pieces of one of the models that Ryan would build all the time. It didn't look any different from the ones that were set up on the shelves, or the ones that Silvia had painted together with Ryan at some point. However, what *did* stick out to her was something else entirely. The tools that Ryan was holding— the small clippers and the metal file he was using to clean up the edges of the individual pieces—were letting off a faint glow.

"Holy shit, is that magic?" Silvia asked excitedly, and Ryan looked up with a smug nod.

"I think so, yeah. It lets me actually cut out the parts of the model."

". . . What?"

In the background, Modak had squatted down after stepping onto a small piece that had been thrown across the room. There were a lot that were scattered around, but the one he was now holding in his hand was different. It was the face of the one the model was depicting, the green plastic being just a couple shades darker than Modak's own skin.

"I'm gonna try not to get offended at this being on the ground," he sighed loudly, standing back up before walking over to Ryan's desk to get a look at everything himself.

Ryan, seeing that his friends were both watching, quickly picked up the single frame that was still laying on the desk, and it had just a single piece that was attached in a single spot. "I'll explain in a second, but the activation period for the skill is over soon, so I'm going to show it to you first, since . . . honestly, I thought I was going crazy earlier, so I wouldn't blame you if you—"

"Oh, just do what you were gonna do already." Silvia lightly slapped Ryan's back to prompt him to keep going. With a quiet grumble, Ryan picked up the clippers and put them up against the single last connection, and with a single quick motion, the last piece fell onto the cutting mat underneath. But the moment that the last connection was gone, the frame that Ryan was holding simply fell apart into that same red light that had formed the box earlier, scattering away into nothingness before everyone's eyes.

The plastic orc head that Modak was still holding in his hand until now quickly fell to the ground as he stared at Ryan's desk. And then at Silvia, and then at Ryan himself, and then back at the desk.

"Your class is related to model building?" Modak asked, as Ryan turned around in his chair. He could feel the magic that had been gathered at his fingertips slowly disappear as the skill was deactivated and the one-hour cooldown started. And at the same time, another translucent window appeared in front of his eyes.

[The -Spirit Construction- Skill has leveled up!]

With a curious expression, Ryan focused on the name of his skill, and its information window quickly appeared.

[Spirit Construction]
[Level - 2] [Proficiency – 3%]
[Allows the user to construct the Spirits' physical bodies.]
[Effect – Spirit Construction for 21 Minutes]
[Cost – 10.5 MP] [Cooldown – 1 Hour]

Ryan took mental note of the changes to the skill. It was going to be active for one more minute, but at the same time, the skill now cost half a point more mana. At some point, the cooldown would probably start increasing as well, but for now those were the only changes. The skill would be on cooldown for another forty minutes; cooldowns started once the skill was first used, not when it ended.

And Ryan could subconsciously feel exactly how much time was left until he could use it again, down to the exact second.

Whichever was the case, Ryan now had the time that he needed to properly explain what had happened to his friends. He started right where he needed to; opening the box that his mom had sent him, saying it was his dad's old stuff. That he then found that glowing red gemstone at the bottom, which his mom had apparently overlooked. And of course, that Ryan awakened the moment he held that gem in his hand.

Once Ryan was done telling them his story, the three stayed quiet for a while. Ryan was nervous and felt the awkward silence press down on his body, making his heart beat faster and faster. And that was exactly when Modak broke through that silence.

With an almost childlike curiosity that stood in stark contrast to his usual demeanor, not to mention his sheer size, Modak leaned forward. "How does it feel?" he asked, his deep black eyes practically radiating toward Ryan.

"I . . ." he replied slowly, looking down at his hands, "I don't really *feel* any different, I guess? It's weird. I thought I would be overcome with this strength, this immense power, but I just . . . I don't know, I feel like I always do."

"Tired, bored, and with an underlying sense of anxiety?"

Ryan looked over at Silvia and narrowed his gaze. "I told you that in confidence."

"No, guys, I . . . I mean . . ." Modak stuttered. "How does it feel to use . . . magic?"

A bit surprised, Ryan raised a brow. "Well, it's not like I cast a spell or anything, and the skill only cost me 10 MP, so it really was nothing special or anything. It was just like warm water running down my arms, washing away the gunk and stuff that's been covering my fingers until now. If that makes any sense."

Modak seemed only somewhat satisfied with that answer. Ryan could tell that he had a lot more things he wanted to ask, but it wasn't like Ryan knew anything in particular about magic. Not more than anyone else, at least, and he awakened not even an hour ago, so he didn't have the time to collect his thoughts yet either. Rather, maybe Silvia would be able to explain things a bit better. Elves generally tended to have a slightly better connection to magic than orcs and humans. Though, then again, Silvia never showed any particular interest in it either.

"But seriously . . . *you* of all people got a magical class? I'd have thought you'd be, I don't know, a Brawler or something?" Silvia pointed out with a somewhat puzzled expression, and Ryan could do nothing but shrug in response.

"It's not like I expected this either. I know they're not really accurate or anything, but literally every single quiz I'd take online said I'd get a physical class if I awakened," Ryan sighed. "Though, it's not like I awakened under normal circumstances either. I'm pretty sure most people don't awaken by touching a glowing gem."

"Right," Silvia started, leaning back as she raised a brow. "Does that mean your father was also a 'Spirit Keeper'? If that was in his stuff, then he must've been, right?"

Ryan looked back at Silvia with a scoff. "Dude, my dad was an accountant. My mom said he was a massive history buff, though, and got really into model building too. He probably just bought that stuff somewhere and didn't have a chance to take a closer look at it."

Both Silvia and Modak looked at Ryan with deep stares, until their friend quickly buckled: "Fucking—fine, I'll talk to Runar about him later. Happy?"

"Yup," Silvia replied immediately, glancing down at the gemstone that Ryan was once more clutching in his hand. "So . . . that's a spirit core, then?"

"A spirit core?" Ryan repeated. It wasn't the first time he heard about it, but since he never looked into it all that much, he thought it was more of a metaphorical thing. Not that it was an actual physical object.

"Right, of course! A spirit core is basically a spirit's heart, the thing that their magic and essence is focused into. It pushes their magic around like blood, basically," Modak quickly explained. "If you had the predisposition to become a 'Spirit Keeper,' actually making contact with a spirit could make that happen, right?"

Ryan looked down at the gemstone, and carefully placed it onto his desk. "Uhm . . . sorry about that, Maximus, I didn't know that I was holding your heart."

"Maximus?" Silvia laughed quietly. "What kinda name is that supposed to be?"

"I didn't come up with it!" Ryan retorted defensively. "That's the name it said on the quest. If I'm building a body for a spirit, and this gem is that spirit, then this gem is Maximus . . . right?"

"Speaking of." Silvia stood up from the ground and walked over to Ryan's desk, looking over at the sorting box set at the center. "That's a lot more pieces than normal, right? And you don't have a guide or anything?"

"About two, or three times as many, I guess? But they're also a lot smaller, so it's probably gonna be the regular one-tenth scale?" Ryan suggested, "And I guess it would've been too easy if there had been a guide . . . but at least my Spirit Construction skill makes it a *bit* easier, still."

Ryan picked up a small metal piece. Or rather, a section that had already been built. Something like a deep crack was on its surface, separating two pieces. "I was wondering how to put it together, 'cause they didn't have things I could just click together like with regular models, but if I push two pieces against each other with that skill active, they just fuse into each other."

He held the piece up to the others. "I think the crack here means that it's wrong, telling me I need to put something else there. Because the other section here is also *two* pieces, and not one, but they just fit together perfectly. So I think that part happened to be right."

Silvia and Modak came to take a closer look. Just as Ryan said, there wasn't a slightest hint of another piece having been fitted onto it, like they had always been just a single piece. But of course, that wasn't the case with that other, extra part. It very obviously didn't fit there, and that wasn't just because of the crack that made it seem like you could separate the parts just by holding them wrong; it was very obviously not the right piece.

"So it's a puzzle, then?"

"I guess so," Ryan replied, turning back toward the box with those dozens and dozens of pieces with an annoyed expression. "Except this is going to take forever at this rate . . . I can only work about twenty-one minutes at a time, and then have to wait another thirty-nine minutes until I can keep going."

"Then maybe we can try and arrange them first," Modak suggested. "That way you can put it together faster when the skill cools down."

"Huh. I guess so. Ah, hold on." Ryan quickly got up and left his room. But he returned just a few moments later with two more chairs in tow that he had grabbed from the dining table, quickly placing them down in front of his desk next to his own.

"If you guys are up for it, let's just get started."

Silvia and Modak didn't hesitate for a moment as they sat down on the chairs. Of course, Silvia took the comfortable, well-cushioned office chair that Ryan had been sitting in earlier.

"Only because you're doing me a favor here." Ryan clicked his tongue with a playful glare, sitting down on one of the hard wooden chairs, while Modak looked at the two of them with an awkward sigh.

"And what do I get, then?"

Ryan looked up at his friend and thought for a moment. "Hm . . . my undying love and appreciation?"

Modak contemplated it for a few seconds, and then nodded while sitting down. "I can live with that."

And without further ado, the three got started. They sorted through the different pieces, which Ryan had already divided up as best as he could. Of course, it wasn't all too easy to get every part of it figured out, though some areas were easier than others. The hands and feet, and of course the helmet—these were parts of the model that were more obvious. Parts of the metal had been dyed red, seemingly being some sort of detail on the larger armor. Since there were less of them and they had complex, thin shapes, they simply put them aside for now and would have Ryan test them out later. If they at least had the art on the box to reference, this wouldn't be as big an issue, but the moment that Ryan had started taking the first pieces out of the frames, it fell apart and disappeared into that magical red light as well.

The parts that were rather simple were actually the leather and cloth parts. Silvia quickly recognized different sections to be the same shape as what regular clothes were sewn from, so she could reference what she already knew about that and had them sorted out quickly.

Out of everything, though, the pieces that surprised and confused Ryan, Modak, and Silvia the most were the thin, curved pieces of wood. These in particular were as thin as twigs, seeming to be roots that were supposed to grow all over the final armor, above and under the different plates, as though holding it all together.

Of course, the moment that Ryan's skill cooled down, he would immediately activate it again. At least his mana recovery was only a little lower than 10 MP every hour, so he was able to activate it multiple times in a row without waiting for his mana to recover above ten points. Of course, the skill leveled up one more time too, so things became a little more annoying, but since the amount of time he could work in a row increased a little as well, he couldn't complain. And then, once the skill was active again, Ryan would simply push the pieces against each other, and they would fuse together as if they were a single part in the first place. If something was wrong, he simply had to tug at it and could pull it off, like removing a chunk of soft clay.

But even with the three of them working together, because of the limited amount of time that Ryan's skill was active at a time, it took until 11 p.m. for the final model to be completed. The last thing that Ryan now had to do was take the red gemstone and place it into the chest cavity of the model armor. Those thin roots that were growing all over the armor, stretching onto its limbs and climbing in between the metal plates, formed a solid bed for the gem to fit perfectly into.

Modak and Silvia silently watched on as Ryan pushed the gem inside, the small roots almost wrapping themselves around it, trying to pull it into their embrace the moment it came close. As the gem's soft, dim red light began to shine from its center, the roots absorbed it, making the magical essence pulse through to the roots' tips. Somewhat nervously, Ryan hurried to place the chest-plate, which he had removed to allow him to put the gem inside, back onto the rest of the armor. And then, he just sat there, his hands pulled away from the small model armor to make sure he didn't accidentally break anything. The room was silent, and the light flowing out to the ends of the roots dyed Ryan's whole desk in a deep red.

"How long is it supposed to—" Silvia asked, glancing over at Ryan.

In the middle of her sentence, the armor twitched. Like a wave of spasms and cramps flowing through the spirit's new body. The leather gloves making up its fingers bent in a way that made Ryan fear he put it together wrong, as the metal let out creaks that you would rather expect from a large construct settling into place. And then, all at once . . . the armor went limp. Not the stiffness that it had when it was first put together, but completely limp, like someone was now within the armor's formerly hollow interior, sleeping.

And then, that someone woke up. The small model carefully sat up on the cutting mat, pushing itself up. For a few moments, it seemed unstable on its new legs, but before anyone could have even realized, it moved more confidently.

The Knight looked around for a few moments, as if getting used to the ability to actually *see* things again, and before long, its sight landed on Ryan. Without a moment's hesitation, the Knight dropped onto its knee, lowering its head.

[You have completed the Quest -Maximus's Request-]

CHAPTER FOUR

Knight Spirit Maximus

Ryan looked at the small, twenty-centimeter figure stood on his desk. The spirit "Maximus" had just shown his gratitude to Ryan, or at least that's what the quest "reward" would make him assume. But before he could even try to think about it more, two messages appeared in front of his eyes.

**[You have become the Keeper of the
Knight Spirit Maximus.]**

[A new domain has become available.]

"So, what now? Can it do tricks?" Silvia wondered curiously, and Ryan laughed, his nervous tension disappearing immediately.

"He's not a dog," Ryan protested, looking back at the spirit, concentrating on Maximus as a whole as if he was pulling up his own status window. "Though, I do wonder, can I maybe see anything about him?"

Just like Ryan hoped, another window appeared.

[Maximus]
[Knight | Level - 1]
[AP - 18]
[Stats]
-[Aura - 0.56]
-[Strength - 0.79]
-[Stamina - 0.71]
-[Resistance - 0.86]
-[Physicality - 0.81]

[Skills]
-[Knight's Attack | Level - 1]
-[Knight's Guard | Level - 1]
-[Knight's Martial Knowledge | Level - 1]

"That . . . hold on . . ." Ryan muttered, confused. "That's just the actual Knight class, and a regular . . . huh?"

"You okay? What's going on?" Modak asked with a worried expression, and Ryan quickly nodded.

"Yeah, yeah, I'm fine . . . But . . . do you guys remember learning about awakened Knights in history class or something?"

"Uhh . . . vaguely?" Silvia replied. "What about it?"

"So, Maximus just has a regular status window. I don't know much about spirits, but I do know that's not normal. He has a class and all, and that's the 'Knight' class . . . Here, hold on," Ryan said, reaching past Maximus to get to his computer's mouse. He opened a text editor and quickly typed everything out for Silvia and Modak, since they couldn't see the system windows.

"Huh . . . those stats are kind of low, right?" Modak asked. "Yours are a bit higher than that, right?"

"Well, yeah, but you've got to consider that he's basically a ninth of my height . . . for that, he's pretty strong," Ryan quickly explained. "And we don't know a ton about Knight skills, but they sound decent enough too."

Ryan quickly pulled up the information on Maximus's three skills, copying them over for Silvia and Modak as well. During that whole process, Maximus himself was just staring at that massive window of light in front of him, with nearly childlike curiosity.

[Knight's Attack]
[Level - 1] [Proficiency – 0%]
[An offensive aura envelops your weapon.]
[Effect – +10% Damage for 1 Minute]
[Cost – 10 AP] [Cooldown – 2 Minutes]

[Knight's Guard]
[Level - 1] [Proficiency – 0%]
[A protective aura envelops your body]
[Effect – +10% Resistance for 1 Minute]
[Cost – 10 AP] [Cooldown – 2 Minutes]

[Knight's Martial Knowledge]
[Level - 1] [Proficiency – 0%]

**[The deep and extensive knowledge of a Knight,
allowing the skilled use of a large variety of weapons.]
[Effect – Increased proficiency with all weapons]**

"Yeah, these are just regular skills. If he weren't tiny, there'd be nothing hinting at Maximus being a spirit," Ryan pointed out, and Silvia placed her chin onto the desk, taking a closer look at Maximus.

"So he's literally a spirit of Knighthood?"

Ryan slowly nodded his head. "I guess so. I mean, are those a thing?"

"Well," Modak started, contemplating it for a moment, "I haven't heard of that before, but Kars and Mila are the Great Spirits of Technology and Agriculture, so a concept like 'Knighthood' doesn't seem impossible."

"I guess it doesn't matter, really. He seems pretty cool either way," Ryan pointed out, a smile on his face. "I'll have to figure out a way to see what he can actually do, though. And test out my other skills a bit."

As if remembering something, Modak raised a brow. "Right, speaking of things you've got to do . . . Are you going to register soon?"

"I mean, I have to. It's not like I can just be an unregistered Awakened. I don't plan on keeping it a secret either, so I don't want to deal with any fines or anything," Ryan pointed out, looking over at Silvia. "Though, do you think I could maybe talk to your sister about some stuff? Dealing with all that bureaucracy on my own sounds . . . rough."

"Huh? Oh, yeah, I'll ask her. But Yanna's been pretty busy since she awakened, so don't count on it too much," Silvia pointed out, her eyes deeply focused on Maximus as if she was looking for something.

"Is everything alright?" Modak asked, and Silvia slowly nodded. She raised her head and pointed at the screen where Ryan had written down the skill information.

"Yeah, just like . . . the skills say a lot about weapons here, right?"

"Yeah?" Ryan replied, not sure where she was going with that. "What about it?"

Silvia looked back down at Maximus, and pointed something out that Ryan himself hadn't realized until now.

"He doesn't have any weapons."

Ryan was left alone in his room with Maximus. Silvia and Modak headed home for the time being, since it was getting a bit too late. Of course, they would meet up again soon; they practically hung out every night anyway. But for now, Ryan had a lot of things to think about on his own.

Maximus stood on the desk and looked up at Ryan, who was tapping his finger on the tabletop. "Okay, so . . . Why don't you have any weapons?" he wondered out loud. "You're a knight, and what's a knight without a sword?"

Seeing Ryan's confusion, Maximus tilted his head to the side.

With a slight laugh, Ryan shook his head and scooted closer to his desk, then quickly turned toward his monitor, navigating to his browser that was still opened to the Awakened wiki, and quickly opened a new tab. In the top bar, Ryan typed out a name.

"Hayden Aglecard." His father's name. The first few results were social media profiles of people named something similar to "Aglecard," or other people named "Hayden." Though, there didn't seem to be a lot of people actually called "Aglecard."

However, after the social media sites came some news sites, and the headlines surprised him.

*- **Aglecard** Charity Auction Raises 50,000,000 Gild*
*- 20,000 Homes Built Throughout Riveria by the **Aglecard** Charity*
*- **Aglecard** Charity Donates Ancient Artefacts to the*
Riverian National History Museum
- Thousands of Centurean Refugees Find Employment
*Through the **Aglecard** Charity*
*- The **Aglecard** Charity . . .*
- . . .

Ryan stared at the screen, a little taken aback. Literally every single article mentioning the name "Aglecard" talked about some kind of massive charity. If it was like that, then he wouldn't be able to find a lot about his father through the internet. Everything would be drowned out by things related to this charity instead, so talking to Runar in the morning would be a lot easier.

But even so, since he was already at it, Ryan decided to look up some things about spirits. While he would have much preferred a physical class, now that he awakened as this Spirit Keeper class, he had to make this work. Of course, there were ways to get a different class; it was vastly expensive and incredibly exploitative, but there was a company that dealt with the trading of classes. Not that Ryan was interested in that; he had way too many questions about this class to just get another one.

While Ryan was distracted, looking up a lot of different things on the internet, Maximus had started searching the desk, pushing things around as if trying to look for something. By the time Ryan noticed that something was going on, Maximus had already picked up the X-Acto knife and removed the safety cap.

"This is so weird," Ryan muttered with an awkward smile, and as he finished speaking, Maximus began to swing the knife around. It was almost too fast for Ryan to see, until Maximus suddenly stopped. And then, he began to stab the knife forward a few times. Overall, it really just seemed like he was trying to get used to it.

"Damn. If I need you to fight a cardboard monster for me, I'll let you know, bud." Ryan stood up and walked toward his door. It was pretty late, so he figured he should just get ready for bed right now. Then an idea popped up in Ryan's head. "Hold on . . . does that actually count as, like, a weapon for you? It just said 'weapon,' but . . . I guess that's kind of a spear for you . . . so . . . Do you want to try to use your . . . uhm, Knight's Attack skill?"

As though waiting for that suggestion, Maximus slammed the flat bottom of the improvised X-Acto spear onto the desk. And that exact moment, a wave of red light streamed through the roots covering Maximus's armor, flowing right into the knife. The edge of the blade was soon covered in a glowing red edge as Maximus's aura strengthened it.

"No fucking way . . ." A smile formed on Ryan's face, and he rushed over to his shelf, where an empty energy drink can was waiting to be recycled. Immediately, Ryan placed it onto the desk, which was just a little shorter than Maximus himself, and clearly the small Knight understood why the can was there.

Maximus swung the X-Acto spear to the side, moving it in sharp angles. At the last motion, Maximus stabbed it forward and pierced the side of the can, pulling the upper half off, leaving it stuck to the blade. But the part where the can was connected up until a few moments ago now had sharp triangles sticking out, each the exact same size as every other one. It took Maximus just a second to do this.

". . . Huh." A broad grin formed on Ryan's face. If Maximus could use something like an X-Acto knife as a proper weapon, then maybe he could also use other things. Either way . . . there were a lot of things to try out. But at this point, Ryan was seriously just exhausted. The adrenaline from awakening was all used up, and he was ready to crash into bed. But before then, there was one more thing Ryan had to try out.

Ever since one of the system messages he got earlier, he could feel something in the back of his mind. Something like a mental image that was trying to push itself to the front. Ryan was pretty sure that it was related to one of his skills; the Spirit Domain.

[Spirit Domain]
[Level - 1] [Proficiency – 0%]
[Allows the Spirits to enter a space of their own,
where they can live, train, and keep their belongings.]
[Effect – Grants access to the Spirits' domain]

It was a skill without any sort of cost or cooldown connected to it; a passive skill. So it was constantly active.

Ryan looked at Maximus curiously. "Can you get into your domain?" he asked, and without hesitation, Maximus nodded his head.

He placed the safety cap back onto the X-Acto knife and placed it down on the cutting mat. The knight bowed down slightly in front of Ryan, and his body fell apart into those red wisps of light that were starting to become so familiar. However, instead of disappearing into thin air, they flowed toward Ryan as if carried by some nonexistent wind, clinging to his skin.

After the wisps of light disappeared in Ryan's body, that mental image in the back of his mind became more clear. Ryan was able to see a space. A cube. Ten, by ten, by ten meters. At the base of that cube was a meter's worth of dirt and gravel. In the corner was a small wooden hut, though most of it seemed to be cut off by the cube's planes. The only thing inside was a single bed, and there really wasn't enough space for anything else. If the door opened inward, it wouldn't be able to open fully either.

But most of the space in the cube was taken up by that patch of dirt and gravel outside, with a single straw training dummy propped up on an old wooden stick. As Ryan could feel the warmth of the red light flow through his body, that light began to gather in the center of the cube, coming together to form Maximus.

The late-night subway car was mostly empty, just a few drunken, midweek partygoers sitting around and feeling the train's deep buzz travel through their bodies. At one end of that car sat a young orc with thick headphones pulled over his ears.

Modak glanced down at his phone, checking the time as he slowly sat up with a tired groan. He caught himself on one of the vertical metal bars as the train came to a halt. As the train pulled away from him again, Modak slowed down for a moment and turned around. Instead of leaving through the exit right by his place, he would take the one on the other end, taking the opportunity to check something. And the moment that his head peeked out over the stairs leading up to the street, Modak let out a deep sigh, seeing the lit windows of the nearby building. There was a large sign at the front. BROG'S GARAGE.

"Not again . . ." he muttered to himself as he approached the door next to the main garage. The smell of dust and oil immediately attacked Modak's nose, and even through his headphones, the loud, twenty-year-old rock music drowned out every other sound. Without a moment's hesitation, Modak grabbed the phone laying in between the speakers and paused the music.

And immediately, a large head with half-gray hair peeked out from behind the car standing in the center of the garage. "What the—" the man, Brog, said with an annoyed expression, before seeing who it was.

"Modak! What're you doin' here?"

"No, Dad, what are *you* doing here? It's like 1 a.m., you promised not to do this anymore."

"Oh come on, now." Modak's father shook his head with a loud groan, then wiped the black oil from his hands as he moved around the car to take a look at the clock. "Huh, I guess you're right . . ."

"What is it this time? Why are you still working?" Modak asked, not in the mood to play around right now. His father turned back toward the car; an older model, but in pretty decent condition overall.

"Well, the owner's comin' tomorrow, I've gotta get this done. Not like I can just give 'im back a broken car!"

"That car's been here for a week, Dad. Wasn't Paul supposed to work on that one?"

"Paul . . . he's been a bit busy recently, so he . . ."

"Just fire him already. He's been slacking off for months, Dad," Modak sighed, but Brog shook his head immediately.

"No, no, I can't do that to 'im. He's about to have a kid." Brog looked at his son with a somewhat awkward expression. Modak wasn't particularly happy with that excuse, but he didn't want to tell his father what to do either. It was his business, so it was his responsibility.

With a click of his tongue, Modak put his bag on the ground and took off his jacket, which he then carefully hung on the rusty hook near the door.

Confused, Brog looked at him. "What are you doing?"

Modak walked over to the edge of the car lift, hitting the button to make the hydraulics raise it up a bit more so he could take a closer look at it from underneath.

"Not like we can give back a broken car, right?"

Lying in bed, Ryan looked up at his ceiling. Today was an interesting day, to say the least. He wanted to deny it, but there had to be something up with his father; why else would he have a spirit in a random toolbox? There were some rare cases where classes could be inherited, but those were all things established hundreds of years ago at the dawn of the system.

"He was . . . an accountant," Ryan muttered quietly, holding his hands to his face with a loud groan. He was still far too awake to actually sleep right now. Even Maximus, in his domain, was still awake, just seated on the edge of his bed.

Ryan grabbed the phone laying on the corner of his bed. It probably wouldn't help him fall asleep, but he might as well scroll through his Loop feed for a bit. The app opened up with an excited young woman pointing at the green-screened image behind her: *Ten must-go places in New Riverside during Spirit Week this year!"*

"Oh, right . . ." Ryan raised a brow. It was going to be his first Spirit Week here in the city soon. It was already a big deal in his small hometown, but he heard that everything was at a whole other level here in New Riverside. For now, Ryan saved the video and kept scrolling.

"New suspected dungeon formation in—" Ryan instinctively scrolled past the video. New dungeons popped up every week or so.

"An animal disappeared from New Riverside Zoo!" As Ryan kept scrolling, he noticed something off, though. Not right in front of him, but in the back of his mind, Maximus suddenly stood up within his domain, staring Ryan down.

"Uhm . . . are you alright, dude?" he asked, concerned, and Maximus quickly shook his head, and then started pointing up. Not sure if he understood correctly, Ryan slowly scrolled back up to the video he just interrupted.

"New suspected dungeon formation in an abandoned factory in Copperbeach! After this copper foundry first went out of use more than a decade ago, it has been locked off from public entry. But when some urban explorers found themselves exploring the premises, they noticed the telltale signs of a new dungeon and quickly reported it to the authorities. It has been classified as a Low danger level and—" Ryan watched through the video, a bit bored. These never showed what the actual dungeon was or revealed any useful info, so he preferred watching longer deep-dive videos on Klicks instead.

However, Maximus seemed to be more than just curious. As Ryan looked inward into the domain, he noticed the Knight standing in the center of the space. Ryan could tell that Maximus wasn't looking at him right now, but past him, as if watching the world through his eyes. And Ryan didn't know why he could tell; it was just like a gut feeling, considering that Maximus stood there as he always did. He didn't even have a face that could be expressive. But Ryan could tell that Maximus was . . . angry. As if that realization triggered something, a message popped up in front of him.

[You have received a new Quest!]

CHAPTER FIVE

Awakened Registration

Modak woke up to the incessant ringing of his phone. The sunlight was shining through the cracks between his blinds, and an involuntary groan escaped his mouth. Modak grabbed his phone and turned off the alarm, before swinging his feet over the edge of his bed. His body felt heavy, but he still had to get up.

He moved his hair out of his eyes and sluggishly walked past his desk, still covered in tiny screws, pieces of plastic, wires, and circuit boards. They'd been laying there for a week now, gathering dust. But Modak hadn't really had the time and nerve to keep working on them. For now, he made his way to the small bathroom across the hallway to brush his teeth. As Modak did that boring, rhythmic motion, his green-brown fingers stuck out to him. He had stood here for fifteen minutes last night trying to scrub off as much of the motor oil as he could, but it just stained his skin like hell, so he couldn't get any more off. At least it should be enough not to taste it if he accidentally touched his lip, so it could be worse. By the time Modak moved on to brushing his tusks, he noticed how quiet it was in the flat. The only thing that he could hear was the sizzling of oil coming from the kitchen.

Modak rinsed off his tusks, trying to ignore the deep, dark circles under his eyes, and then took a turn to the left as he stepped out of the bathroom. He pushed open the next door, seeing two young boys still dead-asleep in their beds. Rolling his eyes, he scooped up one of the backpacks off the ground with his foot and kicked it onto the closest bed. With a startled yelp, the young boy shot up.

"Huh, what?!"

"Get up already," Modak said, watching his other brother slowly rise from his bed as well.

"Oh come on . . . just five more minutes . . ."

"Zigg, don't make me pull you out of bed again." Tapping his foot on the ground, Modak looked straight into the tired boy's eyes.

Groaning loudly, the boy pulled back and responded, "I'm not Zigg, I'm Mogh . . ."

"No, you're not. Now get up already."

"How would you know?"

Modak left the room and shook his head, annoyed, yelling toward the boys as he walked down the hallway, "For the last time, you're fraternal!"

As Modak entered the combined kitchen and living room, he saw his mother put down a plate of eggs and sausages on the table.

"Morning, honey," she said, smiling lightly. "Thanks for taking the boys to school today."

"Of course," Modak yawned. "Their school's on my way to the store anyway."

As he sat down at the table, he quickly started to eat. Before long, his siblings streamed into the kitchen, sitting down at the table as well. Even Zigg and Mogh managed to roll out of bed. Once Modak was done with his food, he glanced over to one of his brothers, seeing massive cracks on the screen of his phone. "Oh come on, Pock, what happened?"

"What? Nothing," Pock replied defensively, pushing his phone under the table to hide it.

"He fell off a skateboard while trying to impress his *girlfriend*," Gilik, another one of Modak's brothers, said with a broad, teasing grin on his face.

As his face quickly turned a dark green, Pock stuttered out, "She—She's not my girlfriend!"

Gilik grinned at his older brother and was about to make another retort, but his mother quickly gave him a light, playful tap to the back of the head. "Stop messing with your brother."

Modak raised a brow and held out his hand toward his brother. With a grumble, Pock revealed his phone again and placed it in Modak's hand, and Modak quickly took a look. There were some pixel errors and the touch screen didn't work that well anymore either.

"Hm . . . alright, I'll swap the screen out later. But seriously, I've told you a thousand times, just put a damn screen protector on it already," Modak said, giving the phone back to Pock, who just silently stared down at the table, his face still dyed by that dark blush. Modak glanced down at his brother's leg. "Did you hurt yourself when you fell?"

After a few moments, Pock shook his head. With a smile, Modak got up and grabbed his plate; he roughed up Pock's hair while walking over to the sink, then put the plate inside. He looked at his mother. "Do you need me to drop off something from the store later?"

After a few moments of thinking, she nodded her head. "If you could grab some pickled mandrake, and maybe some more flour, that would be great."

"Of course." Modak smiled, then slowly walked back to his room while making a note on his phone to buy eggs and look into a replacement phone screen. Right before he could walk through his door, his sister Kora walked down the hallway, scratching her belly while still half asleep. Modak raised a brow. "Up already?"

Glaring daggers at Modak, Kora replied, "How can I not with how much you're yelling. Pretty energetic for someone who came home like three hours ago."

". . . I was helping out Dad," Modak replied, but Kora raised a brow, confused.

"Wait, I thought you went over to Ryan's place."

"Yeah, but when I came home, I saw that Dad was still at the garage, so . . . what was I supposed to do?"

"He's a grown ass man, Modak," Kora sighed. "It's not your job to pick up after Dad."

"It's fine, it wasn't that big a deal. We managed to finish pretty quickly anyway," Modak replied, stepping into his room.

Kora looked at her younger brother with a concerned smile. "Just . . . take it easy, alright? You're looking really tired these days."

"I'm fine, but . . . thanks for worrying," Modak replied, and slowly closed his door. With a longing glance at his bed, he walked over to his closet, then grabbed the first thing he saw to change into. As he was changing, though, his phone started buzzing.

Picking it up, his trousers in his other hand, Modak saw a text that he didn't expect.

Ryan
Yo, who wants to go shopping with me? Going to a dungeon soon

Silvia
Wtf you awakened like yesterday

Ryan
Yeah and I'm itching to go already

You
Don't you have to register to go to dungeons?

Ryan
_ya_
already getting ready to go to the awakened center rn
Yanna sent me some stuff to prep me beforehand

Silvia
but why do you want to go to dungeons anyway? They're so icky

Ryan
I was watching a video about a dungeon that formed in town recently, and Maximus gave me a quest to go take a look
so I figured I might as well
it's a low danger dungeon so yk

Silvia
ooh damn, another quest?
sounds fun then
count me in! When are we meeting?

You
I'll join too, but I've got an early shift so it would have to be after.
Why are you guys even awake already? It's 6:30.

Silvia
never went to bed in the first place <3

Ryan
same lol
*@**Modak** when are you off work today? Let's just meet at the store at the end of your shift, there's some stuff I want to get from there anyway*

You
I'll be done at 4pm

Modak tossed his phone onto his bed and finished getting dressed. At least buying stuff shouldn't take Ryan too long later, so Modak should be able to come home and just go into a coma without any trouble.

Once he was fully dressed, Modak waited for Zigg and Mogh to finish getting ready and walked with them to the nearby subway station. As usual, they were messing around, so Modak had to walk behind them to keep them in line. He pushed them forward a bit as he wrangled them into the train car, making sure he always had them in his sight amidst the crowd that flowed into the train. It would take a while for them to get to their station, so Modak pulled the small book out of his bag and started to read.

"Ew." Zigg stared up at his brother, past the book's edge. "Why'd you read on the subway?"

"Because it's the only place where you two can't run off while I'm not look-ing," Modak replied, his eyes flowing over the pages.

"We're not dogs, ya know?" Mogh scoffed, but Modak just rolled his eyes with a slight sigh.

"Yup. Nine-year-old *dogs* tend to actually listen."

"Whatever," Zigg replied, already moving on. "Can you help us with our homework again tonight?"

". . . You don't even know what homework you're getting today. Try to do it on your own first, and if you don't understand something, I'll help you out. Deal?"

"Fiiine . . ." Zigg groaned. The rest of the train ride was a lot more quiet, at least in regard to the twins. Once they reached their station, Modak pushed the boys out of the train, and the three walked up to the street level. They followed the crowd of other kids walking to school, and before long, they split up. After Modak made sure that the twins were actually inside of the building, he started to walk to his part-time job.

Since university was on break, he was trying to work as much as he could to make some extra money, which meant getting up early every day. It was just a nice feeling to have some spending money when he went out with Ryan and Silvia, and being able to support his parents a bit more was nice too, of course.

The walk to the store Modak worked at took another fifteen minutes. It was originally a specialty store with foods from different cultures outside of Riveria, and they carried a lot of very specific foods for species with more specific food requirements as well. They even sold some specially produced stones for some avian species to keep in their gizzards. Generally, his work was fine, though dealing with customers was sometimes a bit awkward and uncomfortable. But since Modak was a bit more on the taller, stronger side of the spectrum, he worked in the warehouse and item-sorting section most of the time. His man-ager was fairly relaxed as well, so as long as it didn't negatively influence his work, he was allowed to listen to music or, what he did most of the time, listen to some audiobooks. It was actually a decent opportunity to catch up on some stuff he had pushed back.

But work itself was really quite monotonous, and eight hours would pass by agonizingly slowly. Though, Modak was sure it was a lot better than what Ryan was dealing with right now.

A long yawn escaped Ryan's mouth as he stepped into the Awakened Center. It was a large clean space that allowed any Awakened to get the support they needed. Depending on the direction that the Awakened wanted to go, they also offered classes for specific licenses, an emergency room that was capable of dealing with an Awakened's strengthened body, as well as training rooms that could be rented. Though, the training rooms didn't seem to be used that often.

Also, compared to other bureaucratic and government buildings, it was so much less busy. Compared to the ten million people living in New Riverside, there were only about forty thousand Awakened spread all throughout, so that made sense. There was a reason why Ryan's tiny hometown didn't even have one of these; awakening was so rare that it wouldn't make sense.

There were a couple more people in here, but considering its size, it might as well have been empty. Ryan walked up to one of the counters. The clerk was a strigan woman with pure white feathers, looking at him with a gleeful chirp.

"Good morning, my name is Aurora Carlyle. How can I help you today?" she asked in a happy voice that seemed to practically invite Ryan in. He quickly replied, though he was nervous about what was going to happen today. Yanna told him that he would probably end up having to fill up a ton of documents and even go through some tests since he had a unique class, so he really wasn't all too excited about that. But if he wanted to go to a dungeon, he had to deal with it. Not having to pay a hundred-Gild fine for not registering in time was also a pretty good incentive, of course.

"Good morning! I'm here to register, I awakened yesterday."

Aurora clapped the small talons at the ends of her wings together with a quiet hoot. "Congratulations! In that case, please follow me to a private room where we can complete the registration." Aurora quickly stepped up from behind the counter and led Ryan to one of the elevators, which they took to the fourth floor together. Once there, Ryan was brought to a small office. The desk had a small name sign reading AURORA CARLYLE on it.

"Alright, in that case, let us get started. First, we need some generic information: name, age, place of residence, contact methods, and so on." As she explained, Aurora pushed a keyboard over to Ryan and turned the monitor toward him so that he could quickly fill the standard information out.

Simultaneously, she seemed to be typing in some things on a separate computer, and once Ryan was done, she took a look at the basic information.

"Perfect. So, Mr. Aglecard, what is your class?"

Ryan let out a nervous sigh. "So, yeah . . . it's called 'Spirit Keeper'? I couldn't find any info about it online, so I think it might be a unique class?"

Aurora tilted her head to the side for a moment, and then quickly snapped her sight back to her screen, as though she wanted to hurriedly check something. "I assume that is s-p-i-r-i-t, space, k-e-e-p-e-r?"

"Yes, exactly."

After checking things for a few more moments, Aurora turned back toward Ryan. "We will be verifying this information later anyway, but this is completely accurate?"

"Uhm, yeah, of course . . . Is there a problem?" Ryan asked nervously. If this class really did turn out to be a dangerous class that only psychopaths could get . . .

maybe he would be locked up right away? Of course, that was ridiculous, but considering Aurora's shocked expression, that might as well have been the case.

"No problem at all! Once again, congratulations on attaining a unique class! At least as far as our database is concerned." Aurora didn't look away from the screen, hurriedly typing and opening tons of documents. "However, this being the case, the process will be a little different today."

"How different, exactly? My friend has a decently rare class, and she told me that she had to take a bunch of tests . . . will that be the case?" Ryan wondered, and Aurora slowly looked over.

"Yes, and no. The tests that we will be taking are different depending on the actual specs of the class and the specific circumstances. Now, especially for unique classes, while we would like to learn as much as we can, anything beyond the basic information is a voluntary process. That means we will record the exact stats you automatically gained access to as well as your skill information. The only part that is slightly different is that, because we are lacking that data, we would like to ask that you periodically give us information on your current stats, levels, skills, et cetera," Aurora explained, and Ryan raised his brow, a bit surprised.

"I don't need to show you my skills?"

"If you would like to, of course. However, as you have a class that has not yet been recorded otherwise, we have to act under the assumption that your class is tied very closely to your individuality. As such, even more so than for other classes, it is considered protected information. So, we will only proceed with any tests beyond the basic information as long as you agree."

As Ryan took a moment to think about it, Aurora moved some more documents over to the screen in front of Ryan.

"Please just fill these out and then we will head back out for the tests."

As Ryan looked over the documents, he quickly glanced back at Aurora. "Oh, and I would like to apply for a Dungeoneering license as well, if I can."

"Of course! Though, that does require you to pass a simple test so we can make sure you know the rules and regulations surrounding dungeons, together with a small fee."

Ryan stopped for a moment, looking at the woman in front of him nervously. "How much would that fee be?"

"That would be a hundred Gild total, including the processing fee as well as the printing fee for the actual physical license."

". . . Sounds about right . . ."

CHAPTER SIX

The Channel

Ryan stepped through the large doors of the Awakened Center. In his hand, he was holding a small metal card, his Awakened license. On it was his name, date of birth, class, and a small symbol that showed that he passed the test for the additional Dungeoneering license. And though the process wasn't particularly easy, he actually expected a *lot* worse.

He did have to take a few tests where his current stats were evaluated, not just the ones that he actually unlocked but also the more common physical stats like strength, physicality, agility, and so on. However, besides that, it was all actually pretty chill. Ryan wasn't aware, but there seemed to be some laws that had been specifically put into place to protect the privacy of the most rare classes that existed, such as unique or bloodline classes. That was why he didn't actually *have* to tell them anything beyond the most basic information, as Aurora had explained to him.

And considering that Ryan had no idea what the deal with his class was yet, he was quite happy about it too. That being the case, the process still took until 1 p.m., especially the Dungeoneering test at the end of it all. Luckily he knew a lot about this sort of thing already, so after taking a look at some of the practice materials that Aurora had given to him, he just tried the test out and passed with an almost perfect score.

"Let's just go grab some lunch." Ryan stretched lightly and quickly pulled up a map on his phone. Just looking around, he was intimidated. Since there weren't that many Awakened in the city, there was only a single Awakened Center. At least public transport was great to the Channel, though, something that Ryan didn't really expect initially.

Most of New Riverside was encased by a fork and confluence in the Galerian River and was split up into multiple boroughs. In the encased center was Upstream, the part of town where Ryan, Modak, and Silvia lived, and the oldest part of the city. There was also Copperbeach, a mostly industrial borough, as well as Lakeview, which included the parts of town that were submersed in the Galerian Lake that formed in this part of the river. At some point, the city spread beyond the western branch toward the mountains, creating the two boroughs of the Falls and Rapids due to the nature of the river adjacent to them, as well as beyond the eastern branch toward the forests, aptly named Eastbanks.

And then, in the western branch, there was another island holding the smallest borough, the Channel. Even though it was the smallest, it was by far the richest part of the city, and it was clearly visible too. Compared to the old, historic buildings that Ryan was used to in Upstream, everything here was so new and simply massive. The skyline of this part of town was visible from literally everywhere in New Riverside, but being here, looking up at the skyscrapers from the street level was just ridiculous.

"Fucking hell, man . . . this is crazy," Ryan muttered, starting to walk around to follow the direction his map sent him, and soon enough he was sent into what, at first glance, looked like some kind of mall. There were shops all over the place, but just glancing at them, Ryan knew for a fact that he couldn't even afford socks from any of them.

Either way, this place wasn't even his final destination yet; he wanted to go to this noodle place that he heard about on Loop that looked pretty decent, and for some reason it sent him through here. And then, after turning around the corner, Ryan saw the escalators that seemed to reach upward for miles. He wasn't totally sure, but he figured he might as well take a look, and quickly stepped on the escalator.

It wasn't necessarily fast, but it was a lot better than having to walk up this far. And then, once he reached the top, Ryan stepped out of the building and was once more on street level. A bit taken aback and confused, he looked around to figure out what was going on. This was clearly a pedestrian zone, but he was walking by one of those earlier as well, and that was before going up what felt like ten miles on that escalator. Curious, Ryan kept walking around and soon noticed some railings at the edge of an open area, and quickly walked up to it. As he looked down, he saw nothing but a massive drop to the roads below.

"Huh . . ." Ryan muttered, surprised. He didn't expect things to be like this here in the Channel. It was a whole different world compared to what he was used to. Though, whatever the case, Ryan was hungry. After enjoying the view for another few moments, he turned back around and kept following the map to the restaurant. It was a small hole-in-the-wall place that seemed almost out of place in this neighborhood, though maybe that was the intention behind it. The old wood, the Shimarian style and décor, and the lovely, inviting vibe. Everything else in this part of town was so cold that Ryan felt almost unsettled, so this was a nice change.

He stepped into the shop and took a seat at the counter before his order was quickly taken as well. Ryan watched curiously as the chef expertly used his four muscular arms to prepare the food just a few steps away from him. The smell of the broth and the braised pork practically made him salivate.

When the bowl was finally placed in front of him and the steam of the soup heated up his face, Ryan couldn't wait to dig in. Though, of course, he took a quick picture first and sent it to his group chat.

You sure you don't want anything? Ryan thought, inwardly looking at Maximus, though he just replied with a single short nod. . . . *Do you at least want to come out or something? I feel awkward enjoying myself while you're stuck in there. You didn't want to come out during any of the tests either.*

For a few moments, Maximus seemed to be in contemplation as Ryan started to eat, when he reacted in a way that just seemed off to Ryan. He stopped what he was doing, jumping up to his feet, staring into empty space. Though, Ryan could tell that he wasn't looking into "empty space," but outside of the domain, as if looking at something beyond Ryan's body. And Maximus seemed tense.

"Mr. Aglecard, I'm very sorry to disturb you. Could I have a moment of your time?" As Ryan turned his head, he saw an elven man standing right in front of him wearing a dark suit. There was a small, light-blue sparrow pin attached on the left side of his chest.

Ryan swallowed the food in his mouth, looking back at the man with a frown. He was covered in a cloud of disgustingly potent cologne, and Ryan was worried that the man's greased-back hair was about to catch fire from the kitchen's open flames.

"Uhm . . . Do I know you?"

"Not yet, but it would be a pleasure to change that," the man said, pulling a white business card from his jacket's inner pocket, practically forcing it into Ryan's hand. "Simon Grand, of Bluesky Industries. We heard that you just registered your class with the Awakened Center. Congratulations on that, first and foremost."

Ryan stared at the man confused. It hadn't even been thirty minutes since he left from there. "How did you—"

"It's all public record, Mr. Aglecard. As you must know, every Awakened and the name of their class is placed into the database for every Riverian citizen to view."

"Right, fair enough. Though that doesn't explain how you fucking know where I went to get lunch," Ryan replied. The vibes he got from this guy weren't particularly comfortable.

For a while, Simon Grand just stared at Ryan with a soft business smile plastered on his lips, before turning over toward the chef. "Coffee, please. Black."

"Don't got coffee," the chef replied, unamused. "Ya can have tea if ya want. Green."

"Then I will take that, thank you very much," Simon replied, and slowly turned back toward Ryan. "Mr. Aglecard, are you aware of what we do at Bluesky Industries?"

"Vaguely, I guess?" That was a lie. Anyone even a fraction as interested in Awakened knew about Bluesky Industries. They dealt with anything related to the system, producing a ton of technology that interfaced with it. A lot of the scanners that Ryan had just used at the Awakened Center were made by them, as were most workout machines for the Awakened. They also made plenty of weapons, tools, and any other items that different Awakened might need. And, over the past few years, after a certain breakthrough, they started dealing in a whole other matter as well.

"Well, to give you a brief explanation, we have dedicated ourselves to making the lives of all Awakened easier and better. And we are especially concerned when it comes to people like you, who have attained unique classes."

Ryan continued eating, listening to Simon yap on. If he just played along, this guy would hopefully leave soon enough. Though, he was pretty worried about Maximus's intense stare that was aimed right at Simon.

The man continued, "People with unique classes face many, many challenges that are often simply not worth the trouble. As you must know, the rarity of a class has no influence over that class's inherent power, so many unique class holders fall behind their contemporaries. Without the lengthy analyses and growth strategies that have been created for more common classes, in our day and age, having a wholly unique class comes with truly nothing but downsides."

Ryan glanced away from his food. He knew it. It was going *that* way.

"So?" he asked, and Simon's smile grew a bit broader than it had been before, as though he was happy with the flow of this one-sided conversation.

"Wouldn't it be much nicer to have a class that you can grow properly in with the assistance of your peers? Not one that was decided for you by the world, but one that *you* decided on." Simon pulled the business card that he had placed next to Ryan back toward himself, taking out a pen. He wrote a number on it.

Three hundred thousand Riverian Gild.

"This is how much we're willing to pay for your unique class. And in addition, we're willing to let you choose any class from our existing catalogue."

Looking at the number on the business card, Ryan had to swallow in contemplation for just a second. That much money would be enough to buy his mom a house. Maybe not a mansion or anything like that, but it would be enough for her to live peacefully without having to deal with that shitty landlord anymore. Ryan's heart beat heavily in his chest at the mention of that much money. However . . .

"I'm not selling my class, sorry," he replied, though it did hurt him a bit. His class was clearly somehow related to his father, and until he knew more about that, he refused to even let others besides the people he trusted most know too much about it all. Not to mention, his class was the one that gave Maximus a body. If he sold the class, would he be selling Maximus as well? Or would Maximus be forced to once more return to that spirit core form for an indefinite amount of time? Frankly, Ryan didn't know which one would be worse. Either way, no matter how good of a deal that much money would be, he didn't want to sell.

"Now, now, don't be like that, Mr. Aglecard. I know that your family is quite wealthy, but three million Gild is not a number to scoff at," Simon pointed out with a slight smile, and Ryan looked back at him, confused. His eyes gazed back at the business card, and his heart dropped. It almost felt like he had a heart attack. Ryan had missed a zero.

For a moment, Ryan buried his face in his hands. That was a truly life-changing amount of money. His mother would never have to work for the rest of her life, and Ryan would be set up just amazingly for the future as well. That number made refusing just harder. Not to mention, "What do you mean, 'your family is quite wealthy'?"

Taken aback, Simon looked at Ryan with a puzzled expression. "You are a son of the Aglecard family, correct? Of the Aglecard Foundation?"

Is that why he offered that much? Ryan wondered. It made sense, though. Within New Riverside, that charity foundation seemed to be a pretty big deal, so after seeing his last name, this guy must have thought that Ryan was part of them. "Aglecard" was an otherwise pretty rare last name, after all. Though, since Ryan wasn't planning on selling either way, no matter how big the number got, he figured he might as well try to play around a bit.

"Well, who knows? But what makes you think I'd sell for three million?" Ryan asked, smiling lightly. This being the first smile that Simon saw from him, he seemed to become a bit more confident.

"I see. Considering your status, three million might sound like a bit of a joke to you. Let me tell you what, I'll talk to my supervisors and see if I can get you a bit of a better deal. Though, remember that this offer only exists before you reach level 10. After that, class exchanges become impossible, even for us." Simon stood up from his seat, never even having touched the green tea that the chef had placed in front of him. But even so, he took out a wallet and procured a hundred-Gild bill, then quickly handed it to the chef. "This is for Mr. Aglecard's food as well."

The chef took the money without another word, just slowly nodding at Ryan. Simon turned toward the young man and smiled. "We will reach out to you with a new offer soon, Mr. Aglecard. Until then, please take the time to contemplate what your class is truly worth to you."

And without further ado, Simon Grand turned around and left the restaurant, leaving Ryan stunned. He took another look at the business card still laying on the counter, breathing out a heavy sigh.

"An Aglecard, huh? Didn't expect ta have such a high-class customer today," the chef pointed out, grabbing the untouched cup of tea to just drink it himself, since Simon didn't. But Ryan, once he made sure that Simon wouldn't be in earshot, just let out a laugh.

"Man, do I really look that posh to you? Fuck no, I just have the same name. But if letting that guy misunderstand that for a little while gets me my lunch paid for, why not play along a bit?" Ryan grinned lightly as he looked back at his food, finally continuing to eat. The chef let out a loud laugh, and the hands that had never stopped moving around ever since Ryan came in here were practically stunned.

"That's hilarious. So even those sparrow bastards can be wrong, huh?" he asked rhetorically, before looking at Ryan with a big smirk. "Though, I don't wanna be you when they find out ya don't have a unique class."

"Hm? Oh, no, that part's true," Ryan replied. "As he said, it's all public record anyway, so I'd be surprised if they were wrong about that."

The chef raised his brows curiously. "That so, huh? Well, congrats, anyway. Looks like you're gonna be coming into some big cash soon."

"Nah, I'm not selling. The class is too important to me for that." Ryan picked up the bowl in front of him and quickly drank the rest of the broth left in it. As he placed it back down and wiped his mouth, he saw the surprise on the chef's face.

"Didn't expect a kid your age ta have that kinda foresight. I'm impressed," the chef smiled, holding one of his hands forward to Ryan. "Chantora Basir, Chef. The awakened kind."

Ryan looked back surprised, shaking Chantora's hand. "Holy shit, no wonder this food was as good as it was. Sure earned yourself that, what, six hundred percent tip?"

"Sure like to think so."

"Well, either way, I'm Ryan Aglecard. No affiliation, obviously. And I'm a 'Spirit Keeper.' Also the awakened kind."

"Spirit Keeper, huh? What's that let you do?" Chantora asked curiously, and Ryan looked around for a moment. This restaurant wasn't actually all that busy. It *was* quite out of the way and in some side road, but considering how big that video on Loop was, he expected a bit more. Though, right now it was quite useful. Looking inward, it seemed that Maximus was quite happy about coming out now. With how he had reacted to Simon's presence, Ryan didn't hesitate to trust Maximus's gut feelings for this.

Ryan slowly held his hand toward the counter as Maximus stepped out of him. The red wisps quickly formed his body, and the small knight looked up at Chantora, whose four eyes curiously stared at him.

CHAPTER SEVEN

Shopping Spree

Silvia sat on the couch, sketching something on her tablet, as a towering figure suddenly stood over her from behind. Leaning forward, he placed his fur-covered hands onto her shoulders and glanced at the screen.

"Well, well, well, who is that supposed to be for? Doesn't look quite so practical in day-to-day life," the man said with a booming voice, and Silvia slightly turned her head and looked up at the minotaur standing behind her as she took out her earbuds.

"Dad? Didn't even hear you come in. I thought you were already on your way to that conference." Silvia smiled broadly, as her father, Dimos, walked around the couch and sat down on the dark brown armchair a few steps away. His round belly pressed up against the white button-up shirt, and his hooves pressed into the carpet.

"I'm carpooling with Jamal, but he had something important to take care of. I will go to pick him up in . . ." he explained, looking down at the watch on his wrist, ". . . about thirty minutes."

"Ah, okay, okay. So, anyway, you know about Ryan, right?" Silvia asked, and Dimos quickly nodded his head.

"Of course I do—you, him, and that Modak boy spend a lot of time together, right? You talk about them a lot."

"Right, they're both awesome! Anyway, turns out, Ryan awakened, like, yesterday."

Dimos's eyes widened slightly. "Oh, is that so? Well, that sounds quite wonderful. Do you know what his plans are from now on?"

"Well"—Silvia thought about it for a moment—"he's got a magic class, but he's not really the 'classic' magic type? That would actually be more like Modak's deal . . . but because of his class, I guess he can't get into Awakened sports like Yanna. He said he wants to give Dungeoneering a try, so maybe that's where he'll go?"

Dimos raised his brow. "Dungeoneering? And his parents are fine with that?"

"His family situation's a bit complicated, I think, but his mom sounds very supportive. Anyway, that's like, his deal to figure out, but I thought I'd help in another way."

"I see, now." Leaning slightly forward to the table, Dimos grabbed a small candy and popped it into his mouth. "So you're designing him something for his dungeon adventures?"

"That's the plan! I'm very happy with how it's looking right now. We're meeting up to buy some stuff for his first dungeon trip anyway, so I figured we can drop by the fabric store, the one in Driftwood that I really like, and then tonight I can get started!"

"Okay, well, don't overwork yourself. You already got home quite late last night, didn't you?"

"I guess so." Silvia leaned back on the couch. She *was* pretty tired still, but nothing she couldn't deal with. Luckily elves only needed four to five hours of sleep anyway, so she should be able to catch up pretty easily. "But I'll be fine, don't worry."

"If you say so, I know you can handle yourself," Dimos said with a smile on his face, as the door leading downstairs to the basement and garage opened up. Through it stepped a tall minotaurean woman carrying three large bags.

"Oh?" Athina let out, looking at Dimos. "Honey, you're still here? I thought you should already be on your way."

"I will head out soon to pick up Jamal and then we will be on our way," Dimos explained, pushing himself off his armchair. He walked over to his wife and gave her a quick kiss.

"Is his husband acting up again?"

"I didn't want to pry, but it's possible. We have been going to a lot of conferences recently, so I couldn't blame him," Dimos pointed out, helping Athina unpack the groceries.

"That may be true, but you don't see me get that upset every time. You and Jamal are psychiatrists. Doctors. It's part of the deal." Athina let out a long sigh, looking at some of the groceries now on the counter. "Oh, but do you want me to make you something for the trip? Since you have the time now."

"I do feel a little peckish. It would be lovely if you would, my dear."

"Oh, you little suck-up." With a scoff, Athina gave Dimos a small love tap with the back of her hand as she turned toward the living room again. "Sweet pea, do you want to eat something as well?"

Silvia thought about it for a moment but just shook her head in response, glancing at the empty bowl on the table in front of her. "No thanks, I just had some cereal earlier."

"In the middle of the day again? I thought I told you to eat a bit better," Athina sighed, looking at her daughter with a raised brow. "That reminds me, didn't you also promise to go running with me last night?"

"Well, sure, but there was a bit of an emergency."

"What kind of emergency? Is everything alright?" Athina asked with a concerned expression, looking over at Dimos.

He shook his head and explained, "Her friend Ryan awakened yesterday."

"Oh? Well congratulations to him, then. He's a pretty . . . rowdy kid, right? Did he get a physical class, then?" Athina asked, as Silvia got up from the couch.

"Nah, a magical class. A summoning class, at that," she replied, walking up to the kitchen island.

Athina raised her brow. "Ryan was the one that caused that whole mess during your orientation week, right? Or was that Modak?"

"Nope, that was Ryan. He doesn't know why he got a magical class either, but he doesn't seem super upset with it. We're going out to buy some stuff that he needs later. Actually . . ." Silvia explained, glancing at her phone, "I should get ready to head out in a bit."

"Hold on, what kind of mess did he cause?" Dimos asked, confused, but Silvia just waved the question away.

"Just some accident, that's all."

"An accident that ended up with a broken nose, multiple fractured ribs, and a massive scandal, if I remember correctly?" Athina scoffed, looking at her daughter with a hand on her hip.

Dimos looked around, confused, as Silvia shrugged. "Yeah, Ryan *accidentally* beat up a creep that was trying to harass some of the freshman girls."

"Pretty sure I remember there being a bit more to it than that, but fair enough," Athina replied, looking over at Dimos whose expression was already showing his confusion and worry about what kind of person his daughters were friends with. "I'll explain it to you later, it's a long story. But he's a good kid, don't worry."

"If you say so . . ." Dimos muttered quietly as Silvia walked up to him, giving him a hug.

"I'll go get ready now, have a safe trip."

"Thank you very much. You have fun with your . . . 'rowdy' friend," Dimos replied, as Silvia let go and made her way upstairs.

The metal locker closed with a creak as Modak threw his backpack over his shoulder. With his headphones on his head, he walked out of the break room, to the front of the store. And as he walked to the entrance, he spotted two people standing there, already waiting for him.

"Yo, how are you doing, man?" Ryan asked as he gave Modak a hug, quickly followed by Silvia who did the same.

"Tired. Ready to drop into a coma. Only slept for like one or two hours last night," Modak pointed out, suppressing a yawn.

"Hah, still more than the two of us," Silvia scoffed with her arms crossed, and Modak just stared back.

"Elves should sleep for four hours, humans for seven, and orcs for nine. And I'm barely getting a good five on the regular." Modak pointed at the dark circles under his eyes as he looked at Ryan. "So, what did you want to get here? Lunch? Does Maximus have a special diet or something?"

Ryan shook his head. "It doesn't look like he eats at all. Spirits are sustained by magic, right? But no, basically, I'm looking to buy him some weapons."

". . . This is a grocery store."

"To be exact, a grocery store that targets species with specific needs. Which means that you sell knives, tenderizers, pots, all that stuff at a dozen different sizes," Ryan explained, starting to walk into the store as he grabbed one of the red baskets by the entrance.

Curiously, Silvia walked up next to him. "What, he's going to fight using kitchen utensils?"

"Yep. Last night after you guys left, I gave him my X-Acto knife. His skills worked on it, insanely well. But considering that an X-Acto knife isn't particularly strong, I figured equipping him with some more sturdy things wouldn't be a bad idea. And, you know, Awakened stores don't really sell things that work for him," Ryan explained, as Modak quickly took the lead.

"That sounds incredibly reasonable. So what kind of stuff are you looking for? You mentioned knives, tenderizers, and . . . pots?" Modak stopped at the aisle that the three were looking for, and Ryan shrugged.

"More like, lids, I guess. I was thinking they might make good shields?"

"Clever, clever." Silvia squatted down, taking a look at the items on the lower shelves. "So, whatcha thinkin'?"

"Actually"—Ryan held forward his hand as a flood of red wisps poured out of his fingertips, and Maximus appeared on his palm—"I was thinking we'd pick together. I explained the plan to him already, and he seemed up for it."

Modak looked around at the shelves, picking up a few of the packages. The one he was holding now was a kitchen knife. "So what about things like this? The handles for most of these are way too big for him."

"A lot of the time those are just screwed and glued on, so we could pry them off and put new ones on?"

Modak thought about Silvia's suggestion, then nodded his head as he turned to Ryan. "Right, that could work. Silvia, do you think you could . . ."

"Yes, obviously I can. Got all I need at home," Silvia replied, excited.

Ryan looked at his friends with a broad smile, happy to be getting their help. As she grabbed one of the knives and held it up to Maximus, Silvia tried to compare the sizes between the knife and the knight. "What about the size of these things in general? Can he even carry a knife that's as big as him?"

Ryan nodded immediately. "Oh yeah, for sure he can. I showed you his stats. Despite his size he has the physical strength of a fourteen- or fifteen-year-old. And that's just at level 1."

As the Knight looked around the new space that he found himself in, his eyes seemed to land on a few different things. He looked at the knife that Silvia was still holding next to him and nodded his head.

"Seems like he's into it." Silvia smiled, putting it into the basket Ryan was holding on to.

"So what kind of weapons would he need?" Modak questioned. "He's got a knife, so that's basically like a sword, right?"

"True, but I was thinking we could get a few different ones so he can fight in different ways. Like a cleaver, a serrated knife, one of those small cheese knives. But none of those will work against the monsters in the dungeon we're going to; some blunt weapons would be better. So some metal meat tenderizers, and anything else that could work against stone. Though, since we're here, I'd like to get anything I can get my hands on. I saved up a good chunk by now so I should be able to afford whatever I need."

And with that, the four got to work. Silvia and Modak picked out whatever they thought could be useful, and if Maximus agreed, it would go into the basket. At the same time, Ryan would show Maximus around the aisle to see if there was anything that stuck out to him. If they found something that seemed like a better fit than what they already had, they would replace what was in the basket, and if it was cheap enough, they would get multiple. In the end, they got their hands on a decent selection of things.

Some different knives, a few forks as well as spoons, though Ryan didn't know why Maximus wanted spoons. Silvia suggested a set of metal chopsticks, and that she could probably file down and sharpen one pair. Not only that, but a pair of meat tenderizers, small pans, like those for single eggs, small metal rolling pins, as well as a pair of scissors and the metal pestle of a mortar-and-pestle set. For shields, they picked out some small pot lids and cutting boards, though for the latter it was hard to find one that was small enough for Maximus, and that didn't even account for the fact that it didn't have any comfortable way to hold it. But once again, Silvia said she would take care of it and figure something out.

"So . . . where are we going next? You're gonna need more than just some stuff for Maximus, right?" As the group waited at the checkout register, Silvia looked at the items on the conveyor belt. All of it was really just for Maximus, not for Ryan.

"For now, I'll just get things for the dungeon I'll be going to. The Awakened Center had a computer where I could log into Awakened-exclusive forums. It's super fucking cool, by the way, so much sick stuff on there, but they had some info on the dungeon itself. The monsters in there are made of stone and metal, so next I'll try to buy a sledgehammer and a pickax at that home improvement store a few blocks down," Ryan explained, looking at the list that he had written down on his phone.

Modak glanced at the list for a moment and curiously looked at his friend. "Why a home improvement store? Wouldn't a weapon store be a bit better? Since you've registered, you should have access to those now, right?"

"Well, yes, but everything in there is super expensive. And while I was having lunch in the Channel earlier, I met this guy, an Awakened Chef, and he told me that there's really not a massive difference between tools for Awakened and non-Awakened. He said he was using the same knives he's used since before he awakened."

"Then why are those Awakened stores even a thing?" Silvia asked, confused, and Ryan quickly glanced at her as he paid for everything with his phone.

"I mean, there's a difference when you get to higher tiers, apparently. A regular joe isn't gonna need some highly enchanted pickaxe, so those aren't sold in regular stores. They're pretty expensive to make too. Not to mention things made of mithril or adamantine. Also, they sell swords, bows, axes, guns, and whatever else some classes depend on that are too dangerous to just be sold elsewhere. Though you'll need licenses for a lot of specific types of weapons anyway. The Awakened Center apparently offers a bunch of courses for that."

The group made their way out of the grocery store, then quickly walked to their next destination, when Modak was reminded of something else. "By the way, won't you need something like armor as well? It sounds kind of dangerous to go without any kind of protection."

"I've got that one covered too," Silvia pointed out smugly. "Once we're done here, we'll head down to Driftwood to the fabric store I usually go to. They sell a ton of stuff, including some materials for basic armor."

Ryan smiled a bit awkwardly at Silvia before turning back toward Modak. "Yeah, she told me about that earlier while we were waiting for you to finish. Said she wouldn't let me pay for it either . . ."

". . . Aren't materials like that pretty expensive? And hard to work with? Will you be fine?" Modak questioned, just as confused as Ryan was when Silvia mentioned it to him earlier.

"I love giving gifts to my friends, so what? And you know I've got the money to spare."

"Right, I keep forgetting that you're actually already a professional . . . why are you going to uni, by the way?"

"The fine arts course at New Riverside University is pretty good, and one of my professors is actually an Awakened with the Painter class. I figured it'd be helpful," Silvia explained with a broad grin on her face. "Plus, because of my history, I was able to get a special admission to the school where I'm allowed to take some classes in other courses, like fashion design, architecture, stuff like that. It's pretty neat."

Modak sighed deeply as he looked down at the ground. "Can we count that as nepotism, somehow? So unfair . . ."

Ryan scoffed, "Dude, you serious? One of your mechanical engineering profs went to *you* for your opinion on his work. You're not really one to talk here."

"Says the most famous first-year student in the history of our school, our knight in scuffed-up armor," Silvia pointed out, but Ryan just looked at her as he tried to hide his reddening cheeks.

"Please don't call me that . . . Also, that doesn't help me with any of my classes, just makes people either scared of me, or hit on me. Though that last part is pretty nice . . ."

"You bet it is. Oh, that reminds me, that really cute changeling girl invited us all to some club, right? When was that again?" Silvia thought, and Ryan let out a long sigh, as though he had only just remembered.

"I forgot about that with everything that's going on . . . It was this Saturday, actually . . . I might skip out on it this time, honestly. You guys feel free to go without me, though."

"Seriously? You're the one that drags us out to pubs every other night," Modak complained.

"And again, we were invited by a really cute changeling girl," Silvia emphasized, but Ryan shook his head.

"The dungeon stuff is more important right now. Depending on when I go, I might join, but no promises. Also, Silvia, she might have invited us through me, but she's clearly super into you. And from the sound of it, that goes both ways."

". . . Shut up, just come join!"

"Seriously, I don't want to be the third wheel all night," Modak sighed loudly, but Silvia immediately turned to him with a raised brow.

"In that case, if Ryan can't come, I could invite Yanna," she pointed out, watching Modak's face turn a dark green.

Ryan grinned with a chuckle. "In that case, it might really be better if I don't come, huh?"

". . . Le-Let's just talk about this later, alright?" As he stuttered, Modak picked up the pace so that his friends wouldn't see his face. Though of course, they both knew exactly what expression he was making.

CHAPTER EIGHT

Dungeon Air

Ryan wiped the last of the tables clean, getting ready to open the café for the day, glancing over toward his uncle stood behind the counter.

"You know . . ." he said, feeling a little awkward. "What was my dad like? From your perspective?"

Runar snapped his head around in surprise. "Uhh . . . Where's that coming from?"

"I'm just curious . . . Mom sent me some of his old stuff the other day, and I realized that I don't really know that much about him beside what mom told me, and she . . . doesn't talk about him that much," Ryan explained, not fully turning toward his uncle.

"I mean . . . what do you want to know? There's a lot to say about him. He was always honest, helped those around him whenever he could . . . got in trouble with our father a lot." Runar leaned onto the counter in contemplation, a small, bitter smile on his face. Ryan didn't see him like that a lot.

"Why did he get in trouble?"

"Ah . . . Our father . . ." Runar sighed, as the topic moved to a direction he didn't particularly seem to like, but he still explained as best he could. "He was very traditional, I guess? He put a lot of pressure and expectations on Hayden, wanting to turn him into something that he just . . . wasn't. And Hayden would not stay quiet about the fact it *really* wasn't what he wanted. And then, when our father died, he . . . he left. Moved somewhere quiet, away from the rest of our family, met your mom and . . . you know the rest of the story."

Ryan looked back at Runar with a frown. "And just left you alone?"

"Oh, I mean, it was fine, I wasn't like, *alone*. Our mom was still around back then, our cousins and friends supported us a lot . . . I guess I was mad at him for a while, though. I was fifteen, so obviously, you know? But there was also a ten-year age gap between us, so we hadn't been super close until later anyway.

We only reconnected about a year before he passed," Runar explained, even if he seemed a little nervous. But seeing Ryan's expression, he quickly tried to clarify, "There's no hard feelings or anything. I get why he left, and honestly, it was the right decision for him. Things worked out really well, and if he had stayed . . . he wouldn't have been happy. And that's what really matters in the end."

Ryan looked at the ground, trying to figure out how to word his next question properly. "Okay, this is gonna sound weird, but was he interested in magic at all? Like, spirits or something, maybe?"

Runar froze up for a moment, something that didn't get past Ryan, but he soon shook his head and replied, "Not that I know . . . But it's possible, obviously. You never really know. Why?" he asked with a slight frown.

Ryan slowly held forward his hand. "I found something in his things when Mom sent them to me, and when I grabbed it, well . . ."

Red wisps of light started to flow out of Ryan's fingertips, gathering on the table in front of him. And soon, the light itself dimmed, revealing a small model-sized knight.

"I awakened," Ryan started. "This is Maximus, a spirit. He . . . well, his core was with dad's stuff, so . . . I figured maybe you'd know something about it."

When Ryan looked back up away from Maximus, for a fraction of a second, he spotted an expression of shock on Runar's face that Ryan wasn't able to pin down exactly. But just a moment later, Runar himself seemed to realize, and relaxed his face into a smile. "Holy shit, that's . . . that's fucking amazing! But a . . . a magic class, huh?"

"Yeah, I know, I know . . ." Ryan replied, smiling awkwardly as he looked down at Maximus. "I had hoped for some kind of a physical class, but this one seems pretty fun too, I guess. I mean, it's really not easy to get disappointed by awakening, so I really can't complain."

Runar stared at Maximus, not averting his gaze as he spoke, "So, you found that spirit's core, and that made you awaken? And you're sure it was with your dad's stuff?"

"Yeah, I'm sure. It was with some model-building stuff."

". . . Right . . . And this happened the other day?" Runar asked. His eyes were still stuck on Maximus, and Ryan really didn't know what was going on, but it was freaking him out.

"Yeah, on Tuesday, after my shift. I went out to get it registered yesterday in the morning, and then Silvia, Modak, and I went—"

"Wait, you registered already?" Runar asked, his face even more pale than usual.

"Yes? Was I not supposed to?" Confused at his uncle's sudden worry, Ryan just stood there, unsure what was going on. "If you're mad that I didn't tell you beforehand, I'm sorry. But yesterday was one of your random 'break days.' I tried telling you on Tuesday already but you weren't in your room, you wouldn't reply to my texts, and the basement was locked, as always. What did you want me to do?"

". . . What about your mom—does she know?"

"Of course she knows. I talked with her for like three hours last night about what my plans are and how this changes things. She trusts me to do the right thing, so why are you acting so weird?"

Runar kept staring at Maximus, something that the Knight continued to reciprocate. In the end, Runar just let out a long sigh. "I'm sorry, I just . . . I've seen a lot of people's lives changed by awakening, and not just for the better. I'm the only family you have here in the city, so I want to make sure that you'll be alright."

Ryan sighed deeply. Until now, Runar mostly acted like a friend, taking on more of an older brother position. Seeing him this worried was unusual, especially considering his normal demeanor.

"And I appreciate that, I really do. If I need your help with anything, I'll tell you, but I know what I'm doing. It's not the class that I expected, but I'm pretty happy with it. Maximus is great, and man, it's a unique class! I'm so curious to see what's gonna happen if I keep growing this."

Runar looked at Ryan, still clearly concerned. "Just tell me if you need help with anything. I've got some friends that know a thing or two about spirits, so I can ask them. And text me some updates on big stuff that happens, alright?"

"Right, of course. Well, right now, the only thing you've gotta know is that I'm going to a dungeon tomorrow, and someone from Bluesky tried to buy my class yesterday. That guy might come here too, so just tell him I'm not interested if he does. Oh, but if you want, just use this whole thing to get some free stuff."

". . . Text me this kind of stuff right away from now on."

Ryan stood in front of the factory. He was wearing the clothes that Silvia had specifically designed for him. On it were specific hooks and pockets to hold all the makeshift weapons that Ryan had bought for Maximus, so that Ryan could easily give Maximus whatever he could need. Of course, at the same time, it was all positioned and attached in ways that allowed Ryan to move without constraints so that he could fight as well.

On Ryan's legs and torso, hard protective pads were attached as armor, and Silvia had even customized the helmet that Ryan bought. She even borrowed Ryan's backpack and added some loops to them that could hold the hammer and pickaxe for the dungeon.

"That girl's fucking insane," Ryan muttered to himself with a grin on his face. Silvia had done all this in just two days. Though, Ryan didn't even want to think about how much all these materials were worth . . . if he got his hands on some item drops in the dungeon, he definitely had to buy her something. But that wasn't what he had to concentrate on right now.

Ryan looked at the checkpoint that had been set up just a few steps behind the old, rusted entrance, stepping up to the reinforced entry gate. He held his Awakened license up to the scanner at his side, and a green light quickly lit up in front of him as the gate opened up, allowing him to step inside. Once he was through, he could feel the quality of the air change considerably. Not that it was worse, just *different*. Ryan heard about this tons of times before. "Dungeon air." Due to the high concentration of mana, there was a tangible difference in the quality. This presence of mana emanating from the dungeon's heart was what caused the "dungeonification" of the surrounding area, and if regular people lived in this ambience for a long time, they would end up with "mana sickness." If you had generally high aptitude for magic or awakened, getting mana sickness was a lot harder, though still possible. For high-risk dungeons with particularly high concentrations of mana, even an Awakened would collapse and vomit within minutes.

To protect the surrounding areas, and to prevent the dungeon from evolving into Stage 3—the point where it affected the areas adjacent to the original structures—once a dungeon was found, a barrier with limited entry points would be placed around it. Ryan had just stepped through one of those entry points. Turning around, Ryan noticed the refracting light on the surface of the barrier, like that shifting rainbow hue you would see on soap bubbles.

Ryan placed his backpack onto the ground, first grabbing the pickaxe. He needed to try out both, but using this initially seemed a bit safer. From inside of his bag, he grabbed a few things. A pair of gloves, an energy drink, and a protein bar. He put on the well-fitted gloves with rubber pads on the palm and fingers. Hopefully, these should improve the grip he had on the pickaxe and hammer, and also make the whole thing a bit easier on his hands in general. Depending on how long he was going to be here today, his hands could suffer quite a bit. Ryan was confident in his stamina, but things like this always took more than you would expect.

With a wave of his hand, a flow of red wisps flowed out from Ryan's arm and hands, and Maximus appeared next to him. Ryan handed him one of the hammers, formerly a spiked meat tenderizer, and then leaned back against the brick wall next to him. Silvia had pried off the old handle and then wrapped the metal rod that acted as the handle's core in some fabric. Since Maximus's hands were gloved anyway, it didn't need to be super comfortable. Maximus seemed quite happy with it as well, especially since he could wrap both his hands around it well enough. Silvia had really outdone herself, again.

"We'll head inside in a bit. I just need to get used to this air first . . ." Ryan explained to him, and Maximus replied with a slow nod. Taking a deep breath that left his throat weirdly warm, Ryan pulled on the energy drink's tab and drank a mouthful. He tore off the protein bar's wrapper with his teeth and quickly took a bite. Maximus was watching this intensely.

"Hm? What, you want one as well?"

Maximus slowly shook his head, and Ryan raised his brow for a moment. It didn't take him long to understand why Maximus seemed confused. "Right, sorry. So basically, a ton of Dungeoneers suggest this before you head into a dungeon, especially for beginners. These don't really do much once your physical stats get high enough, but for me right now, the extra energy won't hurt, at least."

As though he agreed, Maximus nodded his head in understanding, and then slowly turned toward the dungeon itself. It was a large run-down factory that clearly hadn't been used in a while. Though, it wasn't a terrible sight, and Ryan understood why urban explorers came here; the whole plot was filled completely with wildflowers. The factory's brick walls, as well as its smokestacks, were covered in vines and ivy. Quite impressed by the view, Ryan pulled out his phone. The gloves he bought could be used with touch screens, luckily. He pulled up the camera and tried to take a picture of the building, but the photo ended up somewhat distorted. Dungeon air tended to do that to regular cameras, and Ryan didn't care enough about taking pictures to buy a phone with a mana-sensitive camera, so this would have to do. Though, these distorted pictures also had their own charm to them.

He continued to take long, deep breaths until he seemed to get adjusted to the dungeon air.

"You remember the signs we agreed on?" Ryan asked, and Maximus nodded his head. Since Maximus wasn't able to talk, and Ryan could only really understand rough ideas when interacting with the spirit, they agreed on some very simple hand signs that Maximus would show to Ryan if he wanted to swap to a different weapon. Similarly, Ryan had a hand sign that he would show to Maximus for a single specific reason.

To let Maximus know that he was about to activate the Spirit Link skill, usually he would just tell him, but it would be a lot safer to be quiet inside of the dungeon whenever possible.

Over the past few days, Ryan had used the Spirit Link skill a few times in preparation for today.

Though it was mostly useful for a few specific circumstances, this skill would be very important for today.

"And remember, just use your skills at your own discretion, don't wait for my signal. I trust your judgement," Ryan reminded Maximus as he slowly stepped away from the wall. He tightened his grip around the pickaxe's handle with a smile, leaning down one more time to pick up Maximus.

"You ready?"

Maximus replied with a quick nod, and the two made their way toward the large door that was the factory's entrance. Squatting down next to the door, Ryan carefully pushed it open and peeked inside. There was nothing there, so he carefully made his way inside while glancing at his phone screen. He had opened the Awakened Forum app, specifically the page for this dungeon. There was a rudimentary map on here spanning about five hundred by seven hundred meters, though of course that probably wasn't the full extent of the dungeon's interior.

A dungeon, once it reached Stage 2, would start distorting the space of the structure it infested. While it also changed the outside, to an extent, most of the change happened within the physical space in the dungeon. Most of the time, especially for dungeons like this that were still fairly young within Stage 2, the original structure's spaces would be repeated and folded upon each other, almost as if seen through a broken kaleidoscope.

The worst part was that they could change over time, though at least not without warning. This map should still be fine for now. If Ryan had better funds, he could have bought a dungeon-mapper. Though, it might be worth investing in if he ended up going into dungeons more anyway. Depending on how much you mapped out, you could get a decent chunk of money from the DMB, the Dungeon Management Bureau.

Ryan stepped farther into the building, keeping low as he did. Soon, he came by some rails on the ground. After glancing over at Maximus, who was also looking back at him, Ryan slowly and quietly moved forward. Luckily, the ground was covered in grass, weeds, and moss, so his footsteps were almost completely silent.

However, it didn't take long for him to hear a sound from a whole other source. Rusted metal scratching against even more rusted metal, and the reverberating sound of rocks being hit against steel repeatedly. Ryan peered around the corner, and spotted the first monster he had ever seen. His heart was almost ready to jump out through his throat as he looked at the back of that figure.

It was a person made completely out of stone, as if someone took a pile of bricks and molded it into the shape of something that should resemble what seemed like a dwarf. It was trying to push a minecart filled with the green of deeply oxidized copper, but it seemed like something was blocking its way along the rails. Looking around, Ryan spotted a piece of ore that had probably dropped out of that very cart just earlier, and picked it up.

He looked over at Maximus, who nodded his head. Carefully, Ryan moved farther around the corner, and threw the piece of ore at the back of the stone monster. Almost instantly, the monster turned around. Its legs were in the same position as before but its back twisted around 180 degrees, until it was looking straight at Ryan, who was squatting just barely in view. Once its legs and feet caught up to the rotation, the monster started running at Ryan; not particularly fast, but considering it was a dwarf-sized mass of stone, it was still pretty terrifying.

While its heavy footsteps approached, Ryan and Maximus retreated into the area they were in before, where it seemed a safer to fight this monster. Ryan tightened his grip on the pickaxe, but he wasn't the one that was going to fight.

Maximus grasped the former meat tenderizer, now an improvised war hammer, with both of his hands, and Ryan could see a thin red light envelop the weapon and Maximus's Knight's Attack skill was activated.

CHAPTER NINE

First Takedown

Maximus ran at the approaching stone dwarf, both hands holding tightly on to the improvised war hammer's handle. The hammer impacted on the monster's ankle, and splinters of the brick that made up its whole body were flung into every direction. The hammer itself was swung back after the impact as the monster was momentarily stunned, though not for all too long.

Taking the opportunity, Maximus jumped backward slightly while the monster stomped its injured foot down at the small Knight. The moment of the impact that Maximus had skillfully dodged, the hammer was once more swung at the exact same spot as earlier. A flurry of attacks started to unfold as Maximus used the strength and expertise that filled that small body of his. And before long, the stone was damaged too much to carry the monster's weight, and its ankle fully cracked and it fell to its knee. From where he was standing, Ryan was able to see everything unfold, ready to intervene with his pickaxe should he ever need to. However, there was a very important reason why he wasn't doing so right away.

While Ryan's main purpose for coming here was to complete the quest that Maximus had given him, he thought that it was the best opportunity he was going to get to let Maximus level up. Every class had different ways of leveling up, adhering to the "purpose" of the class. Combat classes did so by fighting, and in particular a Knight leveled up by "vanquishing evil." Though Ryan wasn't a big fan of the idea of assigning the concept of "evil" to anything, he knew that hunting dungeon monsters was one of the best ways of leveling up the Knight class. And since Ryan's class wasn't a direct combat one, he most likely wouldn't see a massive amount of growth from fighting directly.

If he had to guess, considering that his class was completely built around supporting spirits, at least thus far, his class would most likely grow if he did exactly that: act in a way that allowed Maximus to do what he did best.

And to do that, Ryan was currently looking out for the way to kill this monster. He spotted roots slithering around the crevices of the monster's stone body, as if those were the thing holding it all together. They were also already growing and trying to pick up the parts that splintered off through Maximus's attack, most likely to repair itself.

However, as he looked around, there was one part of this plant that was actually exposed. A small, faint red bud that had yet to bloom, just barely peeking out from the bricks right where this thing's ear should be.

"Maximus," Ryan said, trying to stay just under yelling volume so that his voice would echo as little as possible. He had purposefully moved to a place where Maximus could look at him without leaving himself open, as he pointed to his ear. The knight replied with a quick nod as he ran around the monster's body, which twisted around to continue keeping track of its tiny opponent. If it kept doing this, then Maximus wouldn't be able to properly attack the bud, so Ryan quickly ran in and kicked away the monster's foot, purposefully crushing the plant's roots under his boot.

The monster quickly turned its attention toward Ryan and reached out to him, grabbing the end of the pickaxe's handle. However, before Ryan even needed to do anything like pry the tool away, Maximus jumped up.

With the physical strength he had combined with the low weight of his body, Maximus should be able to jump right onto Ryan's head with ease, so reaching a kneeling dwarf's ear was an easy matter.

Maximus swung his hammer straight at the bud, angling it just right so that the unprotected, juvenile flower was torn off. The moment that this happened, Ryan could see the roots within the monster's body wither away, leaving only a pile of bricks behind.

[Maximus has killed a Level 1 -Dungeon Monster-]

As the system message appeared, Ryan experienced something he hadn't noticed before.

Small particles of dim light, so dim that it would be impossible to spot if it weren't for the shadows of this ruined structure, surrounded Maximus like a cloud of dust releasing from a surface all at once, before soon flowing back inside of the armor. But it wasn't just Maximus; as he looked down at his hand, Ryan spotted similar grains of dimly glowing dust surround him for a brief instant. It felt both warm and cold, almost like frostbite, just without any sort of pain connected to it. He had gathered some "experience." It seemed like he was on the right track; simply supporting Maximus was going to let him level up.

And now that he properly realized this, he could recognize this sensation from when he was actually building Maximus's body. He had been feeling a lot of new things then, since he had been using magic for the first time, but he most likely gained some experience then as well. That being the case, Ryan did wonder how close he had been to leveling up.

He stepped over to the pile of bricks and picked one of them up. It was a lot lighter than it should be. Curiously, Ryan tightened his grip on the brick and watched it crumble away like it was made of foam. These bricks had been created by the dungeon specifically for this monster, and now that it was "dead," it was reclaiming the materials it used, which was making it as weak as foam. It should take a few more minutes until it was fully gone, but Ryan didn't want to wait that long. He took the bricks and placed them on a pile next to him, searching through the monster's stone remains. And then, on the ground below them, amongst some crumbs of that foam-brick, Ryan found what he was looking for.

Some . . . seeds? Those are the drops . . . ? Ryan thought to himself, though he wasn't sure what he was expecting. A monster like this wouldn't drop anything special. Though he doubted he could sell these seeds to anyone for more than some spare change, maybe he could try planting them in some pots on the balcony. Runar did love plants, so maybe this was going to help smooth things over with him.

Ryan opened up the small pouch hanging off his belt and placed all of the tiny seeds inside. He stood back up and wiped the dust off his gloves, looking back over at Maximus. "Good to go?"

The Knight nodded his head, and Ryan and Maximus continued on through the dungeon. Though, it didn't take long until they ended up in a slightly worrisome situation. Just behind the minecart that the monster had been trying to push forward was a door that seemed to lead into a larger hall. According to the map, this was one of the rooms corresponding to the part of the old foundry where the metal was actually smelted down and cast into ingots. Ryan could hear some footsteps beyond the door. So, he had two options.

One, turn around and go to another part of the dungeon that was easier to look over. However, avoiding spaces like this didn't seem like a good option at all. The quest that Maximus gave him was to investigate this place, and staying in the safe parts wouldn't really make for a great investigation. He needed to go to places where things were actually happening.

So, number two it was. Ryan looked over at Maximus and gave him the hand sign they had decided on, before the knight quickly nodded his head. And so, Ryan activated one of his skills, Spirit Link.

[Spirit Link]
[Level - 3] [Proficiency – 56%]
[Allows for the user to mentally link with the target Spirit, guiding their actions. During the activation period, the user has an extremely strong understanding of the target Spirit's body and the effect of their skills.]

[Effect – Spirit Link for 10 Minutes 40 Seconds]
[Cost – 10.5 MP] [Cooldown – 40 Minutes 20 Seconds]

It was already at 56 percent, so it might level up today, depending on how much he was going to end up needing to use it. He concentrated on the skill's effect and watched as those red wisps of magic flowed out from his chest and over to Maximus. They thinned out and flowed around each other, slowly forming a thread as thin as spider's silk.

The moment that the thread fully formed, Ryan felt a wave of dizziness come over him. He didn't exactly share Maximus's senses now, but he simply "knew" what it was that the spirit was seeing and hearing. As if the processed information that you would gather by looking at things was simply given to him. It was a bit awkward to keep track of, but that was the main thing that Ryan and Maximus had been practicing so that Ryan could actually make use of this skill decently.

There were some other effects, like allowing Maximus to copy Ryan's movement almost perfectly, but there wasn't a real use for that right now. Maximus was more than skilled at fighting on his own. However, due to the way that senses were shared, this skill could be used in a very specific way.

Maximus walked through the small gap in the ajar door, quickly rushing over to one of the rusted minecarts that had been left standing nearby. Using it as cover, he moved around it and then made his way to one of the other pieces of machinery within this large room, until he positioned himself in a way where he could safely see the area around the door that he had just left. Seeing that there was no monster nearby, Ryan slowly pushed open the door, waited a second, and, while crouched, rushed toward the minecart. Like this, the two continued making their way through the room. And it didn't take long until a few of the monsters popped up, walking through the rows between the heavy machinery and broken-down carts. And whenever they did, Maximus would look for them, taking advantage of his small size, and Ryan would use the information given to him through Spirit Link to navigate safely. However, the skill effect only lasted for a bit more than ten minutes.

Luckily, there was a catwalk nearby, and the stairway was positioned so that Ryan was able to make his way up there without being spotted. There were some other monsters on the catwalk in other parts of the room, but there were plenty of crates to allow Ryan to hide himself without being spotted, and most of the monsters were over by the crucible anyway, and not back here where Ryan and Maximus were hiding out.

Ryan carefully sneaked over the catwalk, trying to get to a better position to see what was going on. All the monsters were walking around that massive crucible on the other side of the room. The heat in here was already unbearable, but it was clearly a lot worse right over there. Ryan was able to see the monsters carry the heavily oxidized copper to the top of the crucible, throwing it into the red-hot liquid inside. And now that he was here, Ryan could actually see the differences in the monsters; they weren't all dwarves, at least.

Some looked more like humans or elves in their stature, others a bit more bulky and muscular like orcs. And there was a single one that was far taller than the rest, a cyclops. Though cyclopes were a species that was in the vast minority here in this country, making up only about a percent of all people in all of Riveria, they made up a significant portion of workers during the era of industrialization, and, to this day, could be seen in construction and these sorts of factories. However, right now, seeing a four-meter cyclops made of stone was quite terrifying, and the fact that these "worker" monsters were replications of the people that used to work in this factory quickly became quite annoying. Ryan frowned lightly as he stared at the crucible. It was nearly filled to the top.

Since this is a fairly new dungeon, there wasn't too much information about this place yet beyond some basic maps that were created using special tools, as well as the general appearance of the monsters. So far, three monsters had been found.

The first, most common, and weakest; the worker. The ones that were currently swarming the dungeon. The second had been dubbed the foreman, which seemed quite similar in general, but the gaps in between bricks were filled completely with copper, and there were certain areas completely covered in copper as well. The last kind, the manager, was even more enhanced, but Ryan did hope that he didn't have to encounter one of those today. However, as he looked around, Ryan thought this was too good of an opportunity to simply pass up.

He looked at one of the sheaths attached to his pants, detaching the scissors from it. Silvia had sharpened these a ton apparently, creating a second edge on each of the scissor blades, meaning that Ryan had to be really careful with this. But this seemed like the best tool for the job.

"Ready to nip some buds?" Ryan whispered, and Maximus immediately nodded his head. He held the hammer back toward Ryan and then swapped it for the scissors. Maximus opened them wide, and when they were opened to their limit, the piece that was keeping them together in the middle released with a click, and the knight was now holding dual blades.

Ryan carefully picked up Maximus and continued moving forward in a crouch. Soon, they got close to one of the workers that was up here on the catwalk with them. It was walking toward one of the sets of stairs, but looking around, this seemed like probably the best time to attack. Ryan looked for the flower bud, but it wasn't by the ear this time. Instead, it was on the left of where a belly button would be. Right now, the two were hidden behind on of the old, half-rotten crates, and the monster would be walking right past them.

It was about five steps away when Ryan got ready. Maximus carefully held the scissor blades while hanging on to Ryan's hands; Ryan was holding the knight in front of his chin, getting ready to toss him forward.

Once it was three steps away, Ryan could feel his heart pound in his chest, almost drowning out the sound of the monster's footsteps on the metal surface. Maximus activated his Knight's Attack skill.

When it was just a single step away, Ryan slightly pulled Maximus back the moment that the monster stepped into sight, and Maximus's blades were fully enveloped in that soft red light.

Maximus was thrown forward, passing right in front of the worker's belly. With a skillful, quick motion, the soft pink flower bud was cut apart. The monster seemed to react for just a moment, but immediately fell forward onto its knees as the roots holding its body together were rotting away.

The sound was quite loud from where Ryan was standing, since it was right in front of him, but considering the general volume in the room, it didn't seem like any of the other workers heard it. Or if they did, they didn't seem to care to investigate, simply continuing on with their work without batting an eye. Though, they didn't have eyes to begin with.

Ryan grinned lightly as he dismissed the kill message in front of him, as Maximus carefully landed on the branching catwalk that Ryan had been facing. This seemed like a fairly simple tactic of fighting these things, at least as long as Ryan knew where the bud was and the monster didn't see them beforehand. So while it did require a few things to fall into place, it still seemed effective. Just knowing for sure that the flower bud was the weakness of all these guys was already good enough for Ryan to figure something out for the others. Having such a basic, fragile, and clearly exposed weakness would definitely make this a lot easier.

Ryan could once more feel that wave of experience come over him, and carefully started putting the monster's bricks to the side. Once again, only seeds were dropped. Ryan carefully picked up as many of them as he could and placed them into his pouch.

Though, as he did, a red window popped up in front of him. From the color, he could tell that it was a notification relating to Maximus.

[The -Knight's Attack- Skill has leveled up]

Already? So it's level 4 now, Ryan thought. It was the highest skill either he or Maximus had so far. The Spirit Link and Spirit Construction skills were the next in line, each being at level 3. Though, as Ryan looked at the skill's effect, he couldn't help but be impressed with that level of growth.

[Knight's Attack]
[Level - 4] [Proficiency – 2%]
[An offensive aura envelops your weapon.]
[Effect – +17.5% Damage for 1 Minute]
[Cost – 13 AP] [Cooldown – 2 Minutes]

At level 1, the skill only gave a 10 percent damage boost. If it kept growing like this, this would clearly be a ridiculous skill, though with the AP cost rising alongside the damage, it would also get quite expensive over time. Luckily, it was apparently possible to use a skill at a lower level than what one actually reached, though it would yield much less proficiency. It was something that usually only the cream of the crop were able to do, but seeing how Maximus moved, Ryan was confident that he would be able to do it at some point.

Whichever the case, Ryan looked around at the other parts of the catwalk. There were more monsters here. Maybe if they took all these down, it would be enough to earn either Maximus or himself a level-up.

CHAPTER TEN

Level Up

Ryan sneaked around the wooden crate, getting dangerously close to that humanoid figure made of brick, held together by a flower's roots. And then, he finally found the bud of that flower; it was hidden at its side, covered by its arm most of the time. This was going to be a bit rougher to deal with, but he and Maximus really did have to take this one down. It stood in the way of where they needed to go; a door leading to another room via these catwalks.

However, Ryan had an idea. He locked eyes with Maximus and carefully placed the knight down onto the front of his left boot, where Maximus held on to the laces. Slowly, Ryan moved forward toward the back of the monster, tightening his grip on his pickaxe. He had practiced with this plenty yesterday, so he had a pretty good feeling of the range of this thing. But it was also going to be his first time actually swinging it at one of the monsters in this dungeon.

Ryan suppressed his breath, trying to be as quiet as he could be, as he stood up and straightened his back. He pulled the pickaxe back and, with a swift motion, swung it right at the monster's underarm. The pickaxe was lodged between the bricks as fragments were flung around. Keeping the pickaxe pushed in so it wouldn't dislodge, Ryan leaned his whole upper body backward while shifting his weight onto his right leg, pushing his other foot into the monster's hip, or where its hip would be, as though he was trying to tear its arm off. With this, before the monster was even able to properly react, Maximus was delivered right to the flower bud and was able to quickly cut through it. Immediately, Ryan could feel the resistance of the bricks disappear, and quickly twisted his body around so that he wouldn't be thrown backward.

The monster fell apart into a pile of bricks as the roots that supported its body disappeared, and Maximus glanced up at Ryan, who wasn't able to hide the broad grin on his face. Doing things like this, fighting freely without restraint, was just exciting beyond belief. It made Ryan feel a bit of regret at not having gotten a physical class that would allow him to train his combat abilities much more easily, but at the same time, fighting alongside Maximus was a unique experience as well. Not to mention, he had grown quite attached to Maximus, so he wouldn't trade this class for anything. Not even that massive, life-changing amount of money that Bluesky was offering to buy his class.

Ryan squatted down in front of the pile of bricks, pushing it all to the side to look for the seeds, when two windows appeared in front of Ryan. One was white and mostly transparent, like the ones that always popped up in front of Ryan when he was checking his own skills. And one was a deep red, belonging to Maximus.

[Maximus has leveled up!]

[You have leveled up!]

Ryan's heart pounded in his chest. If he didn't know any better, he would swear that others would be able to see his chest rapidly pop up and down, and a broad grin appeared on his face.

Immediately, Ryan pulled up his and Maximus's status windows.

[Ryan Aglecard] [Age - 19]
[Spirit Keeper | Level - 2 (+1)]
[MP - 21 (+3)]
[Stats]
-[Dexterity - 1.17 (+0.05)]
-[Intuition - 1.1 (+0.09)]
-[Mana - 0.62 (+0.06)]
-[Sociability - 1.06 (+0.08)]
-[Spirituality - 0.55 (+0.08)]
[Skills]
-[Spirit Construction | Level - 3]
-[Spirit Domain | Level - 1]
-[Spirit Link | Level - 3]

[Maximus]
[Knight | Level - 2 (+1)]
[AP - 23 (+5)]
[Stats]
-[Aura - 0.66 (+0.1)]
-[Strength - 0.87 (+0.08)]
-[Stamina - 0.77 (+0.06)]

-[Resistance - 0.92 (+0.06)]
-[Physicality - 0.9 (+0.09)]
[Skills]
-[Knight's Attack | Level - 4]
-[Knight's Guard | Level - 2]
-[Knight's Martial Knowledge | Level - 2]

Ryan looked at the increases within the knight's as well as his own statuses, and was more than just happy with it. Both his and Maximus's five base stats increased by more than 0.3 total each, which was actually slightly above the average. Especially Maximus—his stats increased by nearly 0.4.

While Ryan couldn't feel a massive difference just yet, there was definitely something tangibly different than it had been just a minute ago. Whether it was his senses or that subtle heat flowing through his body; it all just became clearer. Though, the kinds of stats that Ryan had were a bit harder to really notice in the first place. He should really start working out with Yanna so that he could unlock some physical stats beyond dexterity. Those wouldn't automatically increase by leveling up, but training was usually considered a more effective method of increasing your stats anyway.

That was, if you weren't Maximus. He was training like a madman whenever he was in the domain, but his stats never increased. Which, to an extent, made sense. His body was something that was "built" by Ryan, after all. It most likely wouldn't be able to increase in strength that easily. Though, Maximus didn't seem to care that his stats didn't increase through training, at least when Ryan asked him about it. Maybe that training was just some kind of habit that had formed, like something to let off steam.

For a short moment, Ryan looked over at Maximus, who was seemingly hoping to quickly move on. He was right; Ryan could geek out over all of this later when there wasn't a constant threat of being attacked. After getting rid of the system windows, Ryan quickly picked up the seeds that the monster dropped and then grabbed Maximus. The two quickly hurried over to the doorway that this worker had blocked. When they peeked through, it seemed to be completely empty. It seemed like some kind of break room, with old tables set up in rows for the factory workers to eat their lunch at.

Since this place was empty right now, Ryan took the opportunity to check his phone. There was a specific place that he was looking for: the office.

When you looked at the factory's original blueprint and compared it to the map of the dungeon, the only room that seemingly wasn't copied over was the elevated office space overseeing the main foundry hall. Of course, a dungeon's layout usually didn't adhere to what it was before. For example, this break room was originally near the entrance and on the ground floor, not here on this elevated level you could only access through the catwalks. However, it was unusual for a space to be completely missing from the dungeon.

That was, unless it was done deliberately. Maybe the dungeon was initially born within the office space, so it was treating that area as a bit more "special," turning it into either a unique or a much rarer occurrence. That was Ryan's current theory, at least. And if that was the case, whatever it was that pulled Maximus to this dungeon would probably be in there. He didn't even bat an eye at anything else in the dungeon so far, after all.

He looked at the map provided on the Awakened Forum's page for this dungeon, trying to figure it out somehow. But if the dungeon could purposefully hide away the offices, then it probably had a fairly high connectivity to the space itself, so there should be some kind of pattern there. Because the monsters were acting in very specific ways, Ryan guessed that this dungeon might already be a lot more intelligent than you would think.

And then, Ryan noticed it. At the edge of the currently explored dungeon was an empty space on the map. It wasn't particularly large; actually, it was quite small, so it was easy for him to overlook it until now. Adjacent to that empty space were hallways as well as one of these production halls that Ryan was in just now. Initially he thought that it would just be a space that the dungeon hadn't taken into account, but looking at the rest of the map, it was all fitting together like a perfect puzzle. Having that kind of space just left open like that without any kind of entrance was far too suspicious. However, it was pretty deep into the dungeon, so Ryan would have to be careful on his way there.

Just as he was thinking that, Ryan heard heavy footsteps outside in the large hall. He peeked up and looked out of the door leading back. There wasn't a monster there, so he carefully stepped out, and saw that something was going on at the crucible. It was overflowing now, with splatters of molten copper hitting the ground. But right in front of it, where the molds would usually be placed, stood one of the workers. The cyclops-shaped monster was holding on to the edge of the crucible, and carefully tipped it over. A flood of red-hot liquid metal flowed over the worker. That whole massive crucible was emptied on top of it, but there was barely a puddle forming at its feet, as though its body was soaking up all the metal like a sponge.

It didn't take long for the metal to seemingly cool down; it happened much faster than normal, but this wasn't quite the usual process anyway, so Ryan dismissed the dungeon's logic. All that copper was created by the dungeon in the first place, so it could do whatever it wanted with it. Either way, once the metal had cooled down, Ryan saw the second type of monster for the first time.

The newly created foreman took a step forward. The flower bud that had been growing on its chest had now bloomed into a metallic copper flower, and the gaps between the bricks were completely filled in with metal as well. Nonetheless, it seemed to be moving perfectly fine.

Without hesitation, the foreman walked over to a nearby pile of copper ore that hadn't been thrown into the crucible yet, picking up a piece of the oxidized, green ore before holding it up to the flower on its chest. Like a ball of hair sucked in by a vacuum, the copper was quickly devoured. The foreman did so with all of the remaining copper that was laying there, and when it was finally done, a small area of copper had formed around its chest, now covering the bricks, as metallic tendrils started to spread over its body starting at the flower's base.

So that's how they transform . . . Ryan thought to himself. If he could report that later on, he might actually be able to get a bit of money from the DMB. Unless someone else already reported this, of course.

Ryan carefully stepped back into the break room. Now that a foreman was in this hall together with all the workers, Ryan really didn't want to take any risks. There was another exit on the other side of the break room.

Ryan rushed through the space, carefully peering through the doorway. It was another catwalk in some kind of storage room. Looking around, there weren't that many workers in here, and only one or two on the catwalk network up here. Down below was a massive pile of raw copper ore, which different workers were shoveling into the minecarts so that another worker could start bringing it away. Though, the rails were leading away from the room that Ryan was just in. If the dungeon wanted to create more foremen, then it would've been a lot easier to just connect this storage room to the adjacent room with the crucible.

Maybe there's something about the ritual of bringing the ore through the rest of the building, Ryan thought to himself. Most dungeons worked in that kind of way, following arbitrary rules that it imposed on itself. Whichever the case, Ryan didn't really have the time to think about that right now. He slowly continued on, trying to get an overview of the space and the monsters within it. Before long, he figured out a good moment to try and get out, and quietly rushed down the catwalk's stairs. He turned around the corner into the hallway, trying to remember the map in his mind.

One right, two lefts, straight, and then right and left again . . . he repeated in his mind over and over again. Luckily, by now the Spirit Link skill had cooled down, so he was able to use it again and send Maximus ahead for scouting. Even when he was sprinting, Maximus didn't make any noise due to his low weight, so the knight was running a bit of a distance ahead of Ryan, checking out the hallways and spaces that they had to go through to get to their destination.

Now that they had a clue about where they had to go, that was their focus instead of trying to keep taking down more workers. They could do that later on their way back, where they would end up closer to the dungeon's entrance in case something went wrong.

The way they were moving, it didn't take the pair all too long to get to their destination, and they were soon just a little bit away from the space that Ryan guessed to be the office. Maximus seemed to be getting more motivated to continue on as well, as if he was sensing what it was that made him want to come here in the first place.

However, there was an issue. There was a monster walking through that hallway, and if it had just been a worker, that wouldn't have been an issue. But it was a foreman. Those metallic flowers that sprouted from the buds couldn't just be cut apart, so they would probably have to be destroyed otherwise, and the foremen definitely wouldn't go down with just a single attack either.

But that wasn't even the worst part. The foreman was based on a cyclops. A three-meter mountain of bricks and metal. Copper tendrils were covering nearly its whole body, with reddish-brown buds carefully sprouting along them. This was clearly a more advanced version of the foreman, and Ryan didn't know if that already made it stronger than others.

He thought for a moment. It would be too risky to just face the foreman, and due to the position of the metal flower that they had to destroy, the difficulty was raised even more. It was right in the center of its face, where its eye would usually be. He tapped his foot on the ground nervously, trying to come up with a solution. If there were just some kind of entrance to the office already, this wouldn't be much of a problem. He could probably just sneak past the foreman somehow. But there wasn't; Ryan would need to try and break through the wall somehow. And that would not only take time, but also make plenty of noise; it was not the kind of thing he could do sneakily.

But then, an idea came to him. Maybe he could lure the foreman away after all. He pulled out his phone and double-checked the map, looking for a good spot to execute the idea. Ryan used one of the entrances leading away from the foreman and sneaked through the foundry, soon finding the rails that he was looking for. If he followed these rails, then he would end up in one of the storage rooms with those massive piles of ore. He slowly made his way down the rails toward a specific area where he could hide out and wait for an opportunity. And it didn't take long for a worker with a cart to come by either.

Since Maximus and Ryan already had some practice with these guys, it wasn't particularly hard to take the worker down. And once he did, he took his pickaxe and lodged it under the wheel, trying to tip the cart over somehow. Luckily, the handle of the pickaxe was also made of metal and was well reinforced, so there was no threat of breaking it. Though, Ryan had to shovel parts of the ore out of the cart first to make it a bit lighter, but soon managed to finally tip the whole thing over.

Immediately, Ryan picked up as much of the ore as he could possibly carry, creating small mounds of it at regular distances leading back to the tipped-over minecart. He was creating a trail for the foreman to follow right back to the minecart filled to the brim with ore.

As he was making his way here, he had spotted two other foremen that he had been able to avoid easily enough. But each of them was picking up any copper that was left behind on the ground, ignoring the carts and storage rooms completely, so Ryan figured they only "cleaned up" any ore that wasn't going to be directly used to create more foremen. And by tipping over that cart, Ryan hoped that it would count in the same way, and would keep the cyclops foreman distracted for long enough.

Ryan turned around the corner, placing down the last small pile, holding one of the clumps of ore in his hand, getting ready to bolt down the hallway in the other direction. He could see the foreman in the distance, its back turned to him right now. Ryan took a deep breath, and threw the ore into the hallway, specifically aiming for a spot without grass or moss. But before it even landed, Ryan was around the corner and rushing toward one of the nearby doorways, as he heard the footsteps of the massive monster come closer to the corner. They stopped for a while, then moved on. Then stopped for a while, and moved on. It seemed to be working.

Now, he just had to get back to that hallway.

CHAPTER ELEVEN

The Core Room

Ryan carefully peered into the hallway. The foreman was gone; he could now try to break through the wall into the hidden office space. However, he still had to be careful; he had no idea if that monster would come back, or if another one would come around the corner any moment now. Just in case, Maximus would stand in a position where he could see if anything was approaching so that he could warn Ryan.

But first, he had to take a look around to see if there was any spot that he could break down more easily than others. After all, at the end of the day, a dungeon was created as a reflection of the space it infested, and the rules of the space before did usually influence the dungeon itself. And a simple rule of buildings like this was that every room needed a door. Of course, if Ryan was right about this, then the dungeon was already smart enough to hide the office away, but he doubted that a young dungeon like this could just ignore rules like that. If it could, it would be able to close off whole corridors that would lead to this space instead of just hiding away the room itself.

And as Ryan made a loop around that closed-off room, he found what he was looking for. The outline of what seemed to be an old doorway. You saw this kind of thing often when the area around an old brick house was reconstructed; shapes that were clearly once doors but were turned into walls by simply filling in the doorway.

Right now, it was also covered in layers of moss and ivy, as if the dungeon was trying everything it could to hide it away. Ryan took the serrated knife that was originally part of Maximus's arsenal and started to cut away the ivy while tearing off as much of the moss and the rest of the plants as he possibly could. It didn't take long until Ryan had exposed nearly the full doorway, and it became even more clear that the dungeon was trying to hide something behind here. The ivy and moss was growing back rapidly over the doorway. Well, rapidly compared to normal plants, at least.

He could see them wriggle and move, but it would take a while for them to be able to cover the whole thing again. By then, Ryan would hopefully be done.

After putting away the serrated knife again, Ryan grabbed his pickaxe, and didn't hesitate to swing it at the filled-in doorway, specifically aiming at the gaps between the bricks. The sharp tip dug into the mortar, and as he kept going, he could tell that the wall was getting weaker. He did have to hide a few times while some workers walked past, but it seemed that overall, the noise that he was making wasn't actually too much of a bother. It didn't take long until the first bricks were quite loose, so Ryan pulled off his backpack, reattaching the pickaxe to swap it for the sledgehammer he had been carrying with him as well. All this stuff he was carrying with him was super heavy, but also clearly worth it.

Ryan grabbed the hammer and swung it at the loosened bricks. The first seemed to fall into the space beyond, and Ryan's motivation only rose. Hit after hit, the door opened up more and more, until it was large enough for Ryan to squeeze through. Maximus came running over, and the two stepped into the dark space together. Ryan reached backward and grabbed the torch hanging on the side of his backpack. The moment he pressed the button to turn it on, the thick dust in the room was illuminated.

As he moved the light of the torch around, Ryan was left just a little confused. There was nothing here. Of course, he did end up finding the office, but that was really all it was. An old, dusty office with a single desk in it. Piles of boxes with paper that had already turned back into pulp, and rusted filing cabinets. Nothing but a trashed and ravaged room that you could find in any building that's been left abandoned and rediscovered by bored teens.

Ryan let out a deep sigh, shaking his head a bit annoyed. Did he go through all of that for nothing? Was that just a false lead from Maximus?

However, as Ryan took a breath in again, he could feel an incomparable dizziness come over him. It was like when he first stepped into the barrier surrounding the dungeon, just a lot more intense. The amount of mana in this room was completely oppressive. That could only really mean one thing. Why didn't he realize when he noticed that the office was this hidden away?

This was the core room.

"Shouldn't it be way harder to get to this place . . . ? Core rooms should be far better protected than this . . . !" Ryan muttered with an awkward expression. He thought that there would be more office spaces scattered about, and that there was just going to be some special item or something in here. That's what was usually supposed to happen in dungeons like this. This was bad. Really, really bad.

When a dungeon's core room was invaded, it would go on high alert. When a dungeon was more advanced, it would have an extremely powerful monster within the core room, but this one was clearly too young for that, and made do with a cyclops foreman. If that was the case, it had to be on its way right now.

Ryan picked up Maximus off the ground and rushed back to the hole in the wall that he had created, but it was too late. Heavy footsteps approached as the already dim light from the hallway was completely blocked. A large head with a metallic flower in its center stared in through the hole, and the monster quickly pushed its arm through, tearing at the loosened bricks to expand the opening so that it could step through as well.

"Fuck, fuck, fuck!" Ryan's heart pounded heavily. This was a massive mistake. There was nowhere for him to run. It was only a matter of time before the foreman made its way inside.

"Think, Ryan, think! You finally awakened, there's no way you're going to go out at level fucking 2!" His teeth were being pressed together so hard that Ryan was almost worried they were about to crack, but the adrenaline being pumped through his veins didn't let him keep an all too clear mind.

There was a reason why the core room was protected in every dungeon; it was the only place that a dungeon could be killed, or "closed" from. Of course, Ryan had no clue how to do that. It was a complex process where the mana of the space was interfered with in some very particular ways. The DMB had specific task forces for this, since it was a dangerous process.

However, there was something that Ryan could do. Every dungeon had a "heart." In advanced dungeons, it would often turn into a sort of monster itself, but at this stage, it could only be something in the form of a small object, hiding out somewhere in here. If Ryan could destroy that object, he could at least make the dungeon go to sleep for a while. It wasn't the same thing, but it was something like a "temporary closure," since the dungeon's mana wasn't able to spread any further during this process, and monsters would be strongly weakened until the dungeon was able to form a new heart.

"Maximus, do you have any idea what it could be? You're the one that wanted to come here in the first place," Ryan pointed out, nervously glancing down at the small knight, who just shook his head in response, even if he was clearly looking around in search of a clue.

But it was too late. The foreman was pushing its way into the office. However, even when it came inside, different to what Ryan expected, it didn't attack immediately. Rather, it seemed like the foreman was going to try and catch him.

"So you can't be too reckless in here either?" he guessed, a slight grin forming on his face. The foreman was extremely large. It seemed to have grown a bit in size compared to before. And this office was extremely narrow; if the monster just recklessly attacked him, it was possible that it was going to damage or destroy the dungeon heart on its own. That did make things a little easier.

Ryan pushed his hand behind him and grabbed the drawer of one of the filing cabinets. He quickly pulled it out and threw it at the monster. As it raised its arm to block the throw, lumps of old paper flinging around, Ryan was able to focus a bit more on the monster's appearance. It wasn't just taller; it looked completely different.

It no longer had those flower buds growing all over its body; instead, they had all blossomed and it was covered in what was basically a field of copper wildflowers. And the core that had grown on its head changed quite a bit as well. The monster's head had basically been fully replaced by a large flower, its glistening petals protecting it. It had gone a step further, and had become the last monster that had apparently been observed in here.

On the forums, it had been dubbed the "manager." Honestly, Ryan didn't care much for the names, especially not right now. If this was really the monster's next stage, then being grazed by it could be a death sentence. Those flowers' petals were supposed to be extremely sharp, so Ryan could end up in pieces instead of being crushed by a pile of bricks.

"Maximus, I have an idea, and it might be reckless, but—" Ryan started to say, but the knight was just staring back intensely. Even though he wasn't actually saying anything, Ryan somehow could tell that Maximus was fine with whatever he had planned.

As he moved around the room, Ryan pulled another one of Maximus's weapons off; the pestle. It seemed like the best blunt weapon for restricted spaces, since Maximus would just be able to slam it straight down. He gave it to the knight, and then threw him up toward the flower that had replaced the monster's head. Luckily Ryan used to play basketball all the time, because the knight descended perfectly into the flower. While the monster was still trying to reach out to Ryan, Maximus started his attack on whatever was contained within those petals. The monster grasped at its head, trying to get Maximus out. But at the same time, this sudden invasion made it a lot more reckless. It moved around, bumping into the shelves and desk, and crushing some of the random objects scattered on the ground under its immense weight.

Of course, Ryan wasn't protected from this chaos either. As the monster flailed around, it just grazed his shoulder and he was thrown into the cabinets behind him. The air was pushed out of his lungs as his back hit the rusted metal, despite the backpack acting as a buffer. He fell to the ground, struggling to breathe in again.

But then, Ryan noticed something on the ground. It had fallen out from his jacket's pocket just now; his phone, the screen illuminating his face. And that was when an idea crossed Ryan's mind. Without even being able to breathe properly yet, he picked up his phone and shakily navigated to the camera. He reached out for the high-power torch laying nearby on the ground, and held both forward.

"Dungeon air," or rather, the mana within that air, heavily distorted the images of regular cameras. And that distortion effect became stronger the more concentrated the mana was. And since all of it originated from the dungeon's heart, it had to be the most dense right around it. Ryan looked around the room, barely able to see anything beyond the heavily distorted image and the bad lighting. The flailing metallic cyclops in the room didn't make it any easier either.

However, just a moment later, Ryan found it. A spot that was far more distorted than any of the others. It was a classic location as well. The painting on the wall, though the canvas itself was heavily damaged already. Ryan forced himself off the ground, though his right arm didn't let him put any pressure on it. He stumbled over the trash on the ground and moved behind the desk. Ryan tore the painting off the wall, revealing an old, rusted safe. Roots and ivy were growing out through the ajar door. After pulling the safe open, Ryan almost wanted to vomit as a thick wave of mana flowed right into his face. But he pushed through, grabbing the object in the center. It was an intricate copper brooch depicting a bouquet of wildflowers. His hand burned as he touched it, despite his gloves, like he was trying to pick up red-hot metal. But it was better than dying.

Ryan dropped the brooch onto the desk. His hammer was somewhere in the rubble, so Ryan pulled the pickaxe off his bag. He felt a searing pain in his right shoulder as he tried, but it was too dark to see what was going on, so he simply pushed through, soon holding the pickaxe tightly in both his hands.

He raised it high over his head and, without hesitation, swung it down at the piece of metal. The moment the pointed tip dug into the metal flowers, a flood of mana once more poured out against Ryan. He felt dizzy and fell to the ground. This time, he couldn't hold back his nausea and vomited. A system window popped up in front of him, but his sight was too blurry to read what it said on it.

However, he clearly wasn't the only one that was affected by the destruction of the dungeon heart. The "manager" monster fell to its knees as well. The copper petals that were reflecting the light of Ryan's torch were practically wilting, until it finally fell forward. Maximus climbed out of the monster's flower-head, dragging the scratched-up and dented steel pestle behind him. Ryan carefully got off the ground. Right now, the most important thing was to just leave this room. The mana would grow weaker as the dungeon entered hibernation, so they could just wait things out for a little while.

Carefully, Ryan climbed over the monster's slowly crumbling body and stepped out of the office. Once he was finally outside in the hallway again, he dropped down onto the ground. The air here was already so much better, and as if that fact triggered something in him, he felt massive, searing pain in his hand and shoulder. He tore the glove off his hand. It was bright red, but not just from the heat that the brooch had produced while practically melting away the glove, but also from a thin layer of blood that was dripping down his arm.

Glancing over at his shoulder, Ryan saw that his jacket and shirt had been cleanly cut apart, right next to where the armor pads had been placed, and were soaked in a deep red as well. Trying to not hurt himself even more, Ryan let his backpack slide off his shoulders, trying to carefully open his jacket. But before he could do it himself, Maximus jumped in, having thrown the pestle to the side, so that he could help Ryan. Luckily, with the knight's strength, it was an easy job, though Ryan still cramped up a bit in the process. The whole right side of Ryan's chest was covered in blood, and it was continuing to drip down his arm.

"The . . . the flask at the top in my bag, grab it," Ryan stuttered, and Maximus didn't hesitate for even a moment. He pulled open the backpack and pulled out a thin metal flask. "Also grab the tube there. Yeah, that one, exactly. And gauzes and—" Before Ryan could even finish, the knight had grabbed everything that they were going to need.

Using his already ruined shirt, Ryan patted off as much of the blood as he could, then opened the flask and poured water onto the wound to clean it out. As he dropped the flask to the side, Maximus already approached with a prepared gauze, having spread a layer of the gel in that tube on it. Hesitating for just a moment, Ryan ground his teeth together and pressed the gauze onto his wound. His whole body tensed up as the healing gel was pressed onto the wound. But at least it was supposed to be pretty effective.

"This shit better work. It cost a fortune . . ." Ryan clicked his tongue, as he tried to grab the roll of bandages from Maximus, but the knight shook his head. Instead, he just had Ryan hold the end of the bandage while applying the rest himself. It was a bit awkward, but at least it was all properly held together. Now, the special healing gel could just do its job . . . it would keep bleeding for a little bit, but the wound would quickly close up. He still had to go to the hospital later to get some proper care for this, but it would do for now. The gel was also numbing, so the pain was going to fade away soon, hopefully.

Now that his shoulder was done, Ryan got started with his hand, using that same gel on his burnt palm. Luckily it wasn't as bad as it could have been; the glove did block some of the heat. When he was done, Ryan leaned back against the wall. Maximus was holding a protein bar toward him to get him to eat something, and as he indulged, Ryan finally glanced at the system windows that had popped up.

CHAPTER TWELVE

Fragment

Ryan leaned against the wall, biting into the protein bar. He was freaking out too much to look at them earlier, but a few system windows had popped up in front of him.

[You have temporarily closed the -Abandoned Copper Foundry- Dungeon]

[Maximus has killed a Level 3 -Dungeon Monster-]

[Maximus has leveled up!]

[The -Knight's Martial Knowledge- Skill has leveled up]

Ryan sighed in relief. It seemed that everything worked properly. Small dungeons like this would take a while to heal from their hearts being destroyed, so if Ryan reported this to the Dungeon Management Bureau, they would probably send out some people to permanently close it. Some dungeons were kept up if they could be managed properly or had some kind of benefit. Some dungeons produced structures and dropped items that could be useful for research, or some were safe enough that they could be used to, at least temporarily, protect civilians during emergencies. There was also the rare case where a dungeon was showing levels of sapience and deals could be struck with them, but Ryan only knew about one or two like that in history.

Whatever the case, that other message was a lot more imminently important. Another level-up. Not his own level, of course; the window was Maximus's red, so killing that manager was enough to justify another level.

"Hah . . . I put you together on Tuesday, and you're already level 3? Good job, little dude." Ryan smiled, holding his left fist toward the small knight. A bit confused, Maximus tilted his head to the side. Ryan laughed slightly. "Just bump my fist with yours."

Hesitant, Maximus did as Ryan said, carefully hitting his fist with Ryan's.

"Don't look at me like that, this is a normal thing. Like a . . . small celebration, you know?" Ryan explained, as he concentrated on Maximus's status for a second to make the window pop up.

[Maximus]
[Knight | Level - 3 (+1)]
[AP - 27.5 (+4.5)]
[Stats]
-[Aura - 0.75 (+0.09)]
-[Strength - 0.96 (+0.09)]
-[Stamina - 0.84 (+0.07)]
-[Resistance - 1.0 (+0.08)]
-[Physicality - 0.96 (+0.06)]
[Skills]
-[Knight's Attack | Level - 4]
-[Knight's Guard | Level - 2]
-[Knight's Martial Knowledge | Level - 3 (+1)]

"Damn, at this rate you'll be way stronger than me soon . . ." Ryan sighed lightly. Though, at least he could get stronger through training, and it didn't look like Maximus would be able to do that. That considered, Maximus might end up falling behind in the higher levels.

Ryan leaned his head against the wall behind him. He could feel the uncomfortable wriggling on his shoulder as the healing gel did its job. He should probably try and wait for a while until he could make sure that the monsters wouldn't be a danger anymore before heading back outside.

Should only take like half an hour . . . I hope, he thought. And even if they were still active, their bodies should be weak and crumble with just a single attack from Maximus, especially since he did get a bit stronger now. Though, when Ryan looked at the spirit, he did get a little concerned.

". . . You're also pretty banged up, right? Are you going to be fine?"

Maximus looked down at himself, at the dents and scratches covering his armor, but just replied with a single quick nod.

"If you say so. I'll take a look later and see if I can at least get rid of the dents later." With a loud groan, Ryan pushed himself off the ground. "But now, let's just finish your quest already."

Truthfully, that was what Ryan had hoped to see earlier when looking at those system windows; a message saying something like "You have completed the quest," but in the end, it didn't come yet. That meant that whatever it was that Maximus wanted to find here was still inside of the office. At least, now that the dungeon heart was destroyed, the mana inside of the room should have dissipated a little bit. And he could take his time searching through it now as well, so that was a good thing too. Ryan carefully climbed through the hole in the wall. The air in here was still densely filled with mana, but it wasn't nearly as bad as it was earlier. Either that, or the pain from his shoulder and hand was distracting Ryan enough.

He walked over to the torch still lying on the ground near the desk, shining it around the room. The first thing that he noticed was that the manager was still in the middle of being broken down. There were still parts that you could recognize as a humanoid form, but for the most part, it was just bare metal plates that were crumbling into dust. He took a step closer toward it and squatted down, putting the torch into his mouth as he used his healthy hand to push some of the metal pieces to the side. He was still wearing gloves, so he wasn't super worried about cutting himself as long as he didn't shove his hand onto these petals recklessly.

When he started, Maximus quickly rushed over and started to help, pushing aside the parts of the monster that seemed to be breaking down. Underneath, there were actually a few item drops. Usually, monsters didn't drop anything when they were killed after a dungeon heart was destroyed, but maybe since it died so quickly after that happened, it still left some things behind.

Most of the drops were just seeds again. However, instead of being regular seeds like the ones from before, they were metallic copper seeds at different stages of rust and decay. These especially seemed quite interesting, so Ryan and Maximus quickly gathered them up and put them into the pouch with the others. Once they got everything, Ryan slowly stood up again and continued to look around.

First, he took a step closer to the desk. "Do you still not know what we're looking for?" Ryan wondered, looking over as the knight jumped onto the table. However, he didn't respond, and slowly approached the hole in the desk that had been created when Ryan swung the pickaxe to destroy the brooch. The pickaxe itself had fallen onto the ground, but the remnants of the brooch still seemed to be there, slowly crumbling apart.

But as Ryan shone the light onto it, a small glimmer of green was reflected back at him. "Maximus?"

The knight nodded his head. He had been aiming for the brooch in the first place. Ryan watched as Maximus pushed aside the metal pieces leftover from the brooch. He seemed to be pulling a layer of metal off something, a small green gemstone. The hair on Ryan's neck stood up as he leaned forward.

"Wait, is that what I think it is? This is why we came here?" Unable to hide his puzzled expression, Ryan watched as Maximus took out the small spirit core from the crumbling metal shell.

How did Maximus know that this was here? Or rather, why the hell was this here in the first place? Were spirits somehow related to dungeons, or was this a special case? Ryan showed Maximus some videos of other dungeons beside this one, and he didn't seem to react at all. This just didn't make sense . . . Why was the same thing that Ryan had found in his dead father's stuff *inside* of a dungeon heart?

But seeing Maximus stand there, with that gemstone in his hands, Ryan realized that it didn't even matter right now. Maximus was . . . sad. And that was when Ryan realized. This core wasn't just a lot smaller than Maximus's; it was fractured. This was just a piece of a full core. Maximus solemnly held the fragment up to his forehead, for just a few moments, and then looked back at Ryan. He gave a single quick nod.

**[You have completed the Quest
-Abandoned Copper Foundry Investigation-]**

Ryan was happy that he completed the quest, but he couldn't help but feel a bit weird about it all. Especially after seeing how Maximus was acting, he wasn't able to just be happy right now. As he stood there, thinking, another message appeared in front of him.

**[You have attained a new Expansion kit for
the Maximus Series - Crusader Model]**

With a raised brow, Ryan looked at the message, and soon felt something form in the back of his mind, as if a memory was being pushed into his head from outside. It was similar to how he saw Maximus's domain, just that it was instead a small cardboard box like the one that Maximus's original pieces appeared in. But he would take a look at that later, as the small knight was holding the spirit core's fragment toward him. Nervous, Ryan put the torch back into his mouth, and held his hand forward.

The spirit dropped the fragment onto his palm, and shivers ran over his body like when he first held Maximus's core. A dim light shone through the gemstone, but it wasn't nearly as strong as what Ryan had seen before. It was weak, as though whatever was inside of it was just barely holding on.

[You have found a Fragment of Gaia (1/3)]

[You have become the Keeper of the Garden Golem Spirit Gaia]

[A new domain has become available]

Ryan watched as the fragment of the gemstone fell apart into green threads that burrowed into his palm, flowing through his veins. Once more, Ryan could feel something expand in the back of his mind. It was a new domain, but it was nothing but a blank white space. The fragment carefully floated in its center.

". . . Is this what this class is?" Ryan asked, glancing past the system windows at Maximus. "I kind of figured, but . . . I'm supposed to help and guide and . . . protect you guys?"

While he seemed a bit hesitant, it didn't take long until Maximus nodded his head. With a long sigh, Ryan looked up at the ceiling. It wasn't quite what he had expected, but just looking at it from that point of view, he did understand why this had become his class. He had always wanted to help and protect others some-how. First his mom, then his friends. Then other kids at school, and then com-plete strangers that he saw out on the street. And if this is how that desire manifested . . . Ryan really didn't mind.

"Alright . . . So . . . Gaia then, huh? And a Garden Golem Spirit? I guess I can see the connection . . . with the monsters in here made from stone and all. They were basically a kind of golem, but what the hell is a 'Garden Golem'?" Ryan mut-tered, puzzled. "Do you have any idea where the other two fragments are?"

Maximus quickly shook his head, and Ryan started tapping his foot on the ground. "Alright, I'll look into it. You should be able to tell if we're onto some-thing, right?"

After Maximus's nod, Ryan smiled and started walking back out of the office. Now that this was dealt with, there was no reason to stay in there. Of course, Maximus followed behind as well. However, as the two were walking back out into the hallway, Ryan could feel his body be surrounded by that thin cloud of glowing dust. He *did* just find another spirit, so that made sense.

[The -Spirit Domain- Skill has leveled up]

[You have leveled up!]

Ryan stared at the system windows. Leveling up a skill was one thing, but . . . leveling up himself? Again? Twice in a day? Sure, he was just level 3, but it still felt . . . fast.

"Holy fucking—" Ryan let out involuntarily, as he immediately pulled up his status window.

[Ryan Aglecard] [Age - 19]
[Spirit Keeper | Level - 3 (+1)]
[MP - 23.5 (+2.5)]
[Stats]

-[Dexterity - 1.23 (+0.06)]
-[Intuition - 1.2 (+0.1)]
-[Mana - 0.67 (+0.05)]
-[Sociability - 1.15 (+0.09)]
-[Spirituality - 0.61 (+0.06)]
[Skills]
-[Spirit Construction | Level - 3]
-[Spirit Domain | Level - 2 (+1)]
-[Spirit Link | Level - 3]

A broad grin appeared on Ryan's face as he saw the stat improvements. Sure, his mana and spirituality were still super low, but his dexterity, intuition, and sociability were rising particularly quickly. The increase in sociability was actually particularly nice, since the higher that stat was, the easier it should be for him to communicate with Maximus, as well as Gaia once Ryan found the other two fragments.

The effects for the intuition stat were the most unclear to Ryan so far, though; it was often described as a sort of "sixth sense," but Ryan didn't really know what that was supposed to mean. Every stat presented itself slightly different in each person. Less so in physical stats like strength, for example, but even so, some people felt the stat affect their arms more than their legs, or vice versa. And for mental stats, that kind of thing was far more common, so Ryan had no idea what kind of change he had to expect. Though, it wasn't anything that Ryan would mind; he just had no idea why it increased the most out of all his other stats. Stat increases weren't technically *completely* random, after all.

But well, Ryan could try and figure all that out once he left the dungeon, anyway. Modak and Silvia wouldn't believe it when he told them that he was already level 3, and he was more than excited to see their expressions.

"Though, they might get a bit mad as well . . ." Ryan pointed out with a nervous sigh, looking down at his clothes. His shirt was completely ruined now, since he used it to wipe away his blood, but the jacket still seemed fine for now. Despite the large slit in the shoulder, it was better than walking around without anything on, especially since he didn't really want anyone to see his back.

Carefully, Ryan picked up the jacket and pushed his arm through, clenching his teeth as the weight settled on his shoulder. He then squatted down and put as much of the items attached to that jacket into his backpack, and reattached the hammer and pickaxe to it too, throwing it all over his healthy shoulder.

"Let's go." Ryan started walking and Maximus quickly followed. Actually, Maximus was walking ahead so that he could take care of any monsters that might still be walking around. Ryan was navigating with the map on his phone, and since there was less of a need to be quiet compared to before, it didn't take long until the pair made their way out of the dungeon. Seeing the rainbow hue of the barrier above him was a massive relief, and he was barely able to stop his hand from shaking as he held his Awakened license against the scanner, watching as the reinforced gate opened up.

Ryan stepped out into the road in front of the dungeon. Usually, the air in this part of town would never be something he happily breathed in, but compared to the mana-filled dungeon air, it was almost like being back home.

Immediately, Ryan dropped onto the low, knee-height brick wall at the edge of the road. Maximus jumped up next to him, as Ryan let out a long sigh of relief.

"That was way, way too close for comfort. Next time, we'll prepare longer than a few days . . . alright?" Ryan suggested, looking over at Maximus as he pulled his phone back out. He quickly dialed a number that he saved in his phone just the other day, then held the phone to his ear. It only took two rings for someone to respond.

"This is Aurora Carlyle speaking. How can I help you, Mr. Aglecard?" the chirped voice asked from the other side of the speaker, and Ryan quickly explained the situation.

"Yeah, so, I went to my first dungeon today, and I have a few things to report. You told me that I should call you for that, right?"

"Yes, of course. The Awakened Center and the Dungeon Management Bureau are part of the same larger organization, so I am your go-to person for every Awakened matter. Was there any trouble in the dungeon?" Aurora asked, and Ryan could hear some typing in the background of the call.

"No, nothing like that . . . well, actually, kind of, I guess? Long story short, I found the core room and ended up destroying the dungeon heart. The dungeon was marked for closure, so I figured I should let you guys know so that you can make that happen?" he quickly explained, as the typing on the other side of the call disappeared.

". . . Are you positive that you destroyed the dungeon heart?"

"Yep, I got the notification and everything," Ryan replied. "On the way back outside, it seemed like most of the monsters were already too weak to even move, so I guess it's the best time to make it all happen."

"Mr. Aglecard, did you bring any anti-mana measures with you to the dungeon?"

"Uhm . . . no? Not really . . . is there a problem?"

"It was the 'Abandoned Copper Foundry' dungeon, correct? I will be requesting the DMB's assistance immediately; they should send out a response and first aid team shortly. You only just left the dungeon a minute ago, correct? Please stay nearby and try to avoid moving too much. I will keep you updated on the arrival time of the response team."

Ryan looked at the dungeon's entrance with a light sigh. Maybe he did have a reason to be worried after all.

CHAPTER THIRTEEN

Emergency Care

Ryan kept his eyes closed for a while, just taking in the "fresh" air of this industrial neighborhood. But his serene peace was then interrupted by the sound of screeching tires as a number of cars pulled around the corner, stopping right in front of the dungeon's entrance. A person quickly jumped out from one of the cars; Aurora.

She rushed over toward Ryan and looked him up and down. "Mr. Aglecard, are you alright? Are you feeling dizzy? Nauseous?"

"I'm fine. I felt a bit sick earlier, but now that I'm back outside, it's all good." Ryan tried to stand up to properly greet her, but he was pushed down by the man that followed her.

"Just in case, stay still," he said, taking out a small light out of his pocket and shining it into his eyes. "Follow the light, please."

Ryan was confused, but he did as told. While he was doing so, someone else came up to him, grabbing his wrist. They slapped a thin metal bracelet onto it and started typing something on a tablet. The man, a paramedic even if his clothes didn't match the part, glanced at Ryan's right hand. "What happened? Are you injured?"

Somewhat awkwardly, Ryan nodded his head. "Yeah, I did get hurt in there, hold on," he replied, slowly slipping his jacket off his right shoulder. He looked around nervously to make sure nobody was behind him first, though, and tried to keep the jacket hanging over him as much as he could. "My shoulder was cut by a monster inside, the 'manager,' or something. The metal on its body was super sharp, so it was a clean cut, at least. I used some healing gel on the gauze, and the bleeding stopped. I also ended up . . . touching the dungeon heart, and it gave off this ridiculous heat, but only once I touched it. Used that same gel on my palm. The tube is in my backpack, I can take it out for you if you want."

The paramedic glanced over at Aurora. "Didn't you say he awakened just the other day?"

". . . Yes, only last Tuesday. Mr. Aglecard, you say you faced a manager?"

Ryan nodded. He was going to need to report this all to the DMB in a bit anyway. The response team was seemingly getting ready to head inside, just waiting for the paramedic to be done with Ryan so that they could talk to him. Though, seeing that Ryan was about to explain the situation more closely, Aurora called over the person leading the response team; a gnomish woman carrying an intricately crafted cane. She didn't seem to need it to walk, so she was probably a mage.

And so, Ryan quickly started to retell everything that he had done in the dungeon, including how he saw the foremen being created, the drops he got, and how he made his way into the offices. "And then, I broke the dungeon heart with the pickaxe, and a bunch of mana was shot into my face. I felt sick for a bit, but when I left the core room, I was alright again."

The gnome, holding a voice recorder toward Ryan, frowned lightly. "I see, and why exactly did you search out the core room again?"

"I didn't directly look for the core room, I just remembered that the office wasn't found anywhere yet, and then I found that weird space on the map. I thought it would be an . . . I don't know, like a puzzle or treasure room or something. And I know that you get a good chunk of money for that kind of information, so I figured, why not check it out? If I had known it was straight up the core room, I wouldn't have done that. There're a lot easier ways to commit suicide," Ryan scoffed, slowly shaking his head. Though, seeing the faces of the people in front of him, it seemed like he was the only one who found that funny. "Uhm . . . sorry."

Ryan wasn't totally lying either. Obviously he didn't expect it to be the core room, and he wouldn't have gone in there as recklessly if he had known. But he didn't really care that much about the money that came with finding spaces like that, though it was an incentive that didn't necessarily prevent him from looking for that space either. He just didn't feel like explaining the quest, nor did he want to explain that there was a fractured spirit core inside of the dungeon heart either. Worst case, they might try to take Gaia from him, and that was a risk he wasn't willing to take.

"I see. Well, you certainly earned yourself quite the reward now. Since you told us right away, we should be able to close the dungeon permanently soon, so you should get a hefty sum from that. We'll let you know through Miss Carlyle. Do you remember the location of the core room?" the gnome woman asked, holding a tablet in front of Ryan. It was a seemingly more detailed map of the dungeon than what was on the Awakened Forum, though it of course still marked the core room as an empty space.

Ryan quickly nodded, tapping at the location. "It's right here, should be easy enough to find. The route wasn't that complicated. Took me like twenty-ish minutes to get out?"

"Perfect. Thank you for the assistance, Mr. Aglecard. We'll be headed right in." The gnome nodded, satisfied, and turned around without another word.

Before she could fully leave, Aurora turned to the gnome. "Thanks for coming so quickly, Melanie."

". . . Don't mention it," she replied, quickly heading back over to her team. Overhearing the short exchange, Ryan stared at the paramedic that was still checking on him, now holding the tablet that his colleague had connected to that thin wristband they slapped onto him.

"Wait, was that Melanie Rodriguez?" Ryan stared at the gnome's back in disbelief, and the paramedic scoffed with a nod.

"That's her, alright. Why, you know her?"

"You kidding? Of course I know about her, who doesn't? She's like . . . *the* Terramancer, you know? Man, I would've asked her for an autograph if I'd known . . . Though that's probably a bit awkward when you're in the middle of work, right?" Dejected, Ryan watched as Melanie and her team entered the dungeon's barrier, completely getting rid of his chance. Seeing his expression, the paramedic just let out a laugh.

"Seriously? For someone who should have severe mana poisoning, you're pretty energetic."

". . . Mana poisoning? Isn't that, like . . . really serious?"

"It sure as hell is, but you seem pretty fine . . . guess you got pretty lucky, huh? I mean, sure, you've got extremely elevated mana right now. If you were a bit higher leveled, I'd have suggested you purge it somehow, but I doubt it even shows up in your status. It's all in your muscles and blood right now, and basically fully avoided your magic circuits," the paramedic explained. "Though . . . your SvMax levels are a bit high too . . . I'm guessing you leveled up in there?"

"Ah, yeah, twice actually. Got pretty lucky, I guess," Ryan explained. While it was something to brag about, now that he was actually in a situation where that was a choice, he did feel a bit too awkward about it.

Aurora, overhearing this, stepped closer again. "You leveled up twice? In your first week? That is quite impressive, Mr. Aglecard. Congratulations!"

"Thanks, I'm pretty—" As Ryan spoke, he once more heard the sound of screeching tires. But this time, accompanied by another sound that he recognized quite well. The confused voice of his uncle.

"Ryan? Ryan! What the hell is going on?" Runar yelled out, barely remembering to park his run-down old car before jumping out of it as he came sprinting over. Aurora tried to block him, but seeing Ryan's expression, she decided to let him through.

"'Sup, Runar. Some . . . stuff happened," Ryan said with a nervous smile. He could see how concerned his uncle was, so he felt pretty bad. Runar had already closed the shop today so that he could stay here to wait for him.

"I barely went out to grab some food for thirty minutes, then got a call from you that you're back outside, and I come back to this? What the hell is— Wait, is that blood? Are you hurt? Do I need to call an ambulance?" Runar's gaze darted around the area, but he clearly didn't take all too much information in yet.

The paramedic currently taking a look at Ryan scoffed quietly, "The ambulance is here already. Don't worry, he's . . . well, he's not fine, directly, but way better than he should be, all things considered."

Runar stared at his nephew with a deep glare, forcing Ryan to turn his head away nervously. "Godsdammit, don't scare me like that . . . So he's going to be fine?" Runar asked, carefully stepping behind Ryan, placing his hand onto his left shoulder. His hand was shaking, almost as much as Ryan's.

The paramedic nodded. "Yeah, I'd say so," he said, starting to carefully unwrap the bandages around Ryan's shoulder and hand. "We were mostly worried about his mana exposure, and he still needs to keep it low for a while, but he'll be fine. Otherwise, there's his shoulder, but it doesn't seem to be that—"

As the paramedic pulled away the gauze, he froze up for a moment. He stared at the wound on Ryan's shoulder, which had only barely stopped bleeding, and involuntarily swore, "What the fu—How the hell are you this calm right now? Aren't you in pain?"

Ryan shrugged, or at least he would have, if his shoulder weren't as numb as it was. "Obviously, but what am I supposed to do? Cry about it? In public? Fuck no. Way too sober for that."

". . . Are you sure about that? Are you on any pain meds? Alcohol? Drugs?"

"You've got a full list of everything in my body there, right? You know I'm not," Ryan replied, and the paramedic slowly turned toward his colleague, locking eyes with them for a moment.

"Alright, well . . . in that case, you're a hell of a man," he laughed, carefully rubbing his hands together while stretching his neck. "Now, this isn't going to hurt, but it might be a bit uncomfortable, so to avoid any movement, I'll be numbing your shoulder anyway, alright?"

After Ryan approved, the paramedic held his hand over the wound. Ryan felt a slight wave of warmth cover his shoulder, before an immediate numbness came over his whole arm as it slumped down a bit. And then, the paramedic got to work. A slightly translucent white needle appeared in his fingers that he pressed into Ryan's skin, pulling a similarly translucent thread behind it. This was a Medic skill. Ryan didn't know what he expected, but it definitely wasn't being treated by an Awakened paramedic outside of a dungeon.

The whole time this was happening, Runar kept standing behind Ryan, as if covering his back from DMB employees that were walking around him. And of course, Maximus was inside of his domain during all of this. He had gone inside once the first cars arrived, by Ryan's request.

"All done," the paramedic said with a smile, as the needle from his skill disappeared. "Your shoulder will stay numb for a while, and I'll send a prescription to your insurance card for painkillers. Basically, if you're in pain, take one, but at most two a day, at least six hours apart. Keep applying that healing gel with bandages every day, and swap out the bandages every morning until the wound looks decently healed. And obviously, don't overdo it, alright?"

"Of course. You said I'm supposed to come up for a checkup in a couple days?" Ryan quickly asked, as the paramedic applied a fresh bandage to his shoulder.

"Just come to the Awakened Center's medical office during regular business hours at the start of next week. I'll usually be there."

"Alright, I'll—"

"I'll be driving you there next week," Runar said from behind Ryan. Now that he saw that Ryan was doing a bit better, Runar's grip on his nephew's shoulder was growing quite a bit stronger.

". . . Right, thanks. What about my hand? How's that doing?"

The paramedic glanced down at Ryan's palm. "Honestly, that's not looking so bad, probably hurts like a bitch, though. Just keep your palm wrapped up with healing gel for the weekend. Once the redness is gone and it stops hurting, you're fine."

As the other paramedic quickly took the wristband off Ryan's arm, Aurora stepped back up toward him, nervously hooting, "Mr. Aglecard, in the future, please do be more careful. We at the Awakened Center have high hopes for you. And even if it all somehow worked out today, it could have very easily gone very badly."

Noticing the squeeze in his left shoulder, Ryan carefully nodded. "I know, I'll be taking it a bit more slow, I think. Might do a bit of training for the time being."

The paramedic raised his brow. "Did you not hear what I said about taking it easy?"

"I'm a magical class. I'm not gonna be doing anything that hurts my shoulder."

"Yeah, but you also very barely avoided severe mana poisoning, so seriously, just take it slow. Read a bit or something, but don't do any major mana exercises for now."

Ryan sighed lightly. Though that did make things a bit more annoying, realistically he wouldn't be able to do any of those "major mana exercises" anytime soon anyway. He'd have to head to the university library and read up on some magic theory for now. For now, though, he just put his jacket back on properly, and reached out for his backpack, which was snatched up by Runar before he could grab it.

Still trying to avoid his uncle's stare, Ryan turned back to Aurora and the paramedic. "Is there anything else right now? I'd like to go home and just rest a bit."

Aurora slowly shook her head. "We will keep you updated on the progress of the dungeon closure. If the DMB has any more questions, you might have to go to them sometime next week, but this case actually seems pretty straightforward. So yes, please go ahead, rest and heal up, Mr. Aglecard."

". . . Ryan is fine, by the way," he replied, feeling awkward about constantly being called "Mr. Aglecard." It felt so stiff and formal and he didn't like it at all.

Aurora hooted quietly, "Then, Ryan, have a good weekend and take care of yourself well."

"I will. Thanks." Ryan smiled and stood up, then followed his uncle to his car. After dropping into the passenger seat, Ryan leaned back into the cushions and let out a long, deep groan.

"You better shut your mouth." As he slammed the door shut behind himself, Runar practically growled at his nephew, "What the fuck were you thinking? You promised me you'd try to be safe, and what, you ended up destroying a dungeon heart?"

"I just—"

"Are you seriously in that much need of money? Did you get caught up with the wrong crowd? Is someone extorting you or—"

"No, dude, calm down," Ryan interrupted his uncle when he could finally get a word in, but he really didn't know what to say, ". . . I can trust you, right? Even if you acted like a fucking maniac when I told you I awakened?"

"M-Maniac?" Runar stuttered out. "I was just surprised, that's all . . . But yes, of course you can trust me. It's just . . . you're my family, Ryan. Every time I look at you, I see your father when we were growing up. I'm scared something is going to happen to you too, so I don't want you to get caught up in this whole mess. I adore you, man . . . seeing you like this breaks my heart, seriously."

Ryan sat there in silence for a few moments. He really didn't know what he was supposed to say to that. As the car started rumbling, Runar started driving down the road. No matter how weird Ryan felt about how Runar reacted, he still trusted him probably more than anyone in the world. Runar had always been there for him and his mom, even after his father died, and throughout every bad choice they made afterward. Even when Ryan did briefly get caught up with the wrong crowd in school, Runar was the one that helped him through it all.

". . . Maximus gave me a quest to go to the dungeon," Ryan explained, and Runar turned to him, startled.

"What? Why would he . . ."

"I guess he sensed that something, or someone, was in there. When I destroyed the dungeon heart, I found something inside of it, another spirit core, but it was fractured. It belongs to this spirit called Gaia."

CHAPTER FOURTEEN

A Night Out

Ryan stepped into his room, his wet hair clinging to his back. He stepped up to the mirror, taking a closer look at his shoulder. It did look pretty gnarly. Though the healing gel suppressed the swelling, it was still pretty red. But the stitches looked quite nice, so it at least wouldn't leave an ugly scar. Ryan had enough of those anyway, so he would prefer if he didn't get too many more.

He sat down in his chair and took the gauzes and healing gel that he had laid on his desk earlier, then quickly applied a fresh bandage to his shoulder and palm before tapping his finger on the desk. ". . . I can just take a look, right? Doesn't mean I have to build it?" Ryan said, inwardly looking at Maximus, who was enjoying his newly enlarged domain. After it leveled up, it seemed to have expanded about a quarter of a meter in every direction. Not a massive amount, but still noticeable overall.

Realizing what Ryan was talking about, Maximus stepped out from the domain, his body quickly forming from red wisps of mana. Standing on the desk, he stared up at Ryan.

"Don't look at me like that, I'm fine, seriously. And again, just looking at it doesn't mean I have to build it," Ryan pointed out, and though Maximus kept staring, he was quickly ignored.

Ryan held forward his hand, and red wisps of light flowed out from his fingertips, forming a small cardboard box. On its front, it said MAXIMUS SERIES - CRUSADER MODEL - RIGHT ARM, and, as it said, a right arm was displayed on the front. Though it was still made from the same materials as Maximus's body, it did look a bit different. Bulkier.

Ryan grabbed his X-Acto knife, then carefully cut the cardboard box open before pulling out the frames. Just like before, there were some metal frames, one red and one that gray steel color, as well as a sheet of leather and a frame made of wood that held those roots that grew all over Maximus's body. Once he took them all out, the cardboard box fell apart into mana again.

"This really isn't that much . . ." Ryan pointed out, glancing over at Maximus. "I mean, I wouldn't need to use my right hand all too much . . ."

Maximus continued to stare up at Ryan intensely.

". . . And the skill uses so little mana it barely counts, right?"

The knight slowly shook his head, as if disappointed by Ryan's logic.

"Oh come on, you know you want me to build this too, so just be quiet." Ryan immediately reached out for the wooden box on his table, then quickly opened it up to pull out those special clippers. Without even glancing at Maximus again, Ryan activated his Spirit Construction skill as the patterns on the clippers lit up. He didn't even hesitate and started to get to work, quickly removing the individual pieces from the frames and putting them into one of his small kit-sorting boxes. Similarly to how he had done it when Silvia and Modak were here, he was going to cut out all the pieces as quickly as he could, sort and align them during the cooldown, and then start putting them together during the next activation period.

But as he moved his fingers around, even though he was using his left hand, he managed to do it all insanely fast, at least what he was used to. He'd been building these models since he was a kid, so it was easy for him to tell the sudden difference.

"Dexterity sure is useful, huh?" Ryan grinned lightly. Frankly, even if it just helped him with his hobby, it still was exhilarating to see himself grow and change. Literally just this morning, he wouldn't have been able to do any of this.

And due to how fast he ended up being at taking the pieces out of the frames, he was able to start some trial and error by pressing some of the pieces together. He actually got surprisingly far when his skill's effect ended. After the cooldown, he was able to continue putting everything together, and it didn't take long until the full limb was done.

"Alright, I've got two more minutes on my skill's effect . . . Maximus, come here," Ryan said excitedly, and Maximus carefully stepped toward him. At this point, since he knew that Ryan was going to do whatever he wanted anyway, Maximus didn't hold back either. Clearly, he wanted to give the new arm a try as well.

Ryan carefully grabbed Maximus's shoulder, and the limb popped out with ease. Maximus stood there, now missing an arm. It was a bit creepy, but Ryan had no right to complain, anyway. He quickly took the new arm and pressed it against the knight's shoulder, and it attached itself immediately.

Maximus stretched out his fingers and twisted his arm around a bit. While it was the same length as before, it just had a ton of bulk to it. In general, while it still had the same overall style, the different plates were more angular.

"So . . . what does that do now?" Ryan wondered curiously, and prompted by Maximus, the knight's status window appeared.

[Maximus]
[Knight | Level - 3]
[AP - 28 (+0.5)]
[Stats]
-[Aura - 0.76 (+0.1)]
-[Strength - 0.99 (+0.03)]
-[Stamina - 0.85 (+0.01)]
-[Resistance - 0.98 (-0.02)]
-[Physicality - 0.96]
[Skills]
-[Knight's Attack | Level - 4]
-[Knight's Guard | Level - 2]
-[Knight's Martial Knowledge | Level - 3]

"Oh! Wow, that's . . . huh," Ryan muttered quietly. "It's . . . better than before. I mean, you've got less resistance, but you've got more aura, strength, and stamina in exchange. Not massively different yet, but . . . if you use the full Crusader model, it would be worth a lot, right? I guess it might make up for the fact you can't train, but . . ."

After a bit of thought, Ryan leaned backward in his chair. He didn't know why, but his gut was telling him something.

"Could it be that one of my skills will let me strengthen you otherwise? Like, I could upgrade your stats or something," Ryan suggested, just saying it into the room. Maximus didn't seem to react to it all that much, but Ryan felt something a little off about the way that he was staring up at him.

But before he was able to think about it anymore, Ryan's phone rang.

"You sure you're allowed to drink? Aren't you on painkillers?" Modak asked nervously, his eyes darting around the table.

"I'm not on painkillers . . . Just didn't take them today," Ryan replied with a grin, holding up his beer into the middle of the table. "Come on, man, my wallet's five thousand Gild overweight—help me out here!"

"Cheers to that," Silvia replied, clinking her glass against Ryan's before the two looked at the orc sitting next to them. A bit hesitant, Modak held up his glass, clinking it against his friends', before the three of them each took a large swig.

"Oh gods, that's so good." Ryan smiled broadly, staring at the foam in his glass.

Silvia let out a loud scoff. "You sound like you haven't had a drink in years. We were here literally two weeks ago."

"Yes, two horrible, horrible weeks."

"So . . . how're you doing? I know you've been keeping us updated, but you literally didn't leave your place since you got back from the dungeon," Modak pointed out, concerned.

"That's totally not true! I've been on the balcony."

"Which counts as your place," Silvia added. "And you were only out there to plan out that planter you ordered, right?"

"Well sure, but still. Fresh air." With a smile, Ryan started tapping his finger on the table. "I've just been looking into a lot of stuff. Mostly, general mana theory for toddlers. Also been trying to look into any possible dungeons I could."

Modak and Silvia looked at each other for a moment. "You're not seriously planning on going to another one, right?"

"I mean, at some point, but not right away, no."

"Dude, are you insane?" the orc let out, puzzled by his friend's words. Ryan had nearly just died not even a week ago, and he was already talking about going to another dungeon? But Ryan didn't seem to be joking about it either.

"Dungeons are the only clue I've got right now, alright? I've got to keep looking for 'that,' so I've got no choice," Ryan explained. Obviously, he was scared of going back to dungeons right away too, but he just didn't know what else he should do. What if the rest of Gaia's fragments were stuck in other places, and someone else came along and closed the dungeon? He couldn't just walk up to that person and ask for the thing that dropped from the dungeon heart; only an insane person would do that.

Silvia started resting her chin on her palm. "So Maximus doesn't have any other ideas either? He knew that something was up with that dungeon, so wouldn't he know other things?"

"He doesn't know either, no. He said he basically just knew that something was in there, but he didn't know it was 'that.' So he doesn't know where the rest is. But he figures he'll know when we get to it."

"He said that? Seriously? I thought he's mute or something, but he told you that?"

"No, obviously he didn't speak. It's just through 'yes or no' questions," Ryan pointed out, sighing deeply as he leaned back in his chair. "But seriously, can we not talk about this stuff? At least not in the middle of a fuckin' pub. We're here to celebrate and have a good time, alright? Speaking of, how was the club on Saturday?"

Silvia slightly flinched at the mention as a broad grin formed on Modak's face. "Oh it was fun, alright. For some of us more than for others."

Picking up on the vibe that his friends were giving off, Ryan immediately stared at Silvia. "Did you . . . ?"

". . . Yes."

"With that changeling girl?"

"Yes."

"Looks like we've got more to celebrate than I thought," Ryan laughed as he took another swig of his beer, but Silvia was ready to protest.

She glared at her friends, mostly Modak. "It wasn't anything special, just a kiss . . . we got along well, but I don't know if there's anything there . . . we were both pretty drunk."

"Oh come on, how could she not like you? You're amazing." Though he was sad that he wasn't able to be there to witness this in person, Ryan wanted to be supportive without showing his FOMO too much.

". . . Well, but she's . . . she's just so cool, you know? She's saving up money right now with her friends to found an art collective, and they're doing this exhibit, and they're renting the old train station for it! Isn't that sick? And she's got those super cool patterns and tattoos on her arm that she designed herself and they're literally moving and dancing around, and just . . ." Burying her face in her hands, Silvia let out a loud groan, but Ryan couldn't help himself but laugh.

"Silvia, don't you have like a yearly exhibit literally in the middle of the Easel?" Ryan asked, and Modak nodded his head immediately.

"Yeah, my school took a trip to one of them before because they heard someone our age made everything there. Like, come on, now."

"But that's . . . different," Silvia protested quietly, only slightly looking up from behind her hands. "My dad used to have a bunch of clients from the Channel, so that was the only reason I got in there."

"I'm not sure that's . . ." Ryan wasn't sure what to say. Frankly, he had no idea about how that sort of art culture really worked. The only "gallery" in his hometown was the small section in the corner of the public library, and those paintings were made by kindergarten and elementary school kids. He hadn't even been to a museum before Silvia started dragging him and Modak to them after they all met.

But Modak seemed to have an idea, at least. "Well, we can ask Fae herself what she thinks."

"What—"

Modak raised his hand up and waved toward the door. Silvia immediately snapped her whole body around, and after seeing the changeling in question stepping into the pub with her friends, she turned back around and tried to hide herself in her own shadow. "Oh no, oh no . . ."

However, to Silvia's dismay, it seemed that Modak was able to get Fae's attention. She excused herself from her friends and quickly stepped over. Ryan and Modak quickly stood up and greeted her with a hug. Silvia, though reluctant and nervous, also stood up to say hello.

"How're you doing?" Modak asked. "I didn't know you guys come here too."

Fae smiled broadly with a quick nod. "Yeah, we usually go to this other pub a bit farther out, but Kit was told about the Sunken Ship so we decided to come here tonight," she explained, as Ryan pulled up another chair from an empty table and added it to their own, and they all sat back down.

"Good choice, this is our go-to. My uncle told me about it; we live like five minutes down the road," Ryan explained, unable to stop himself from glancing down at Fae's arms to see what Silvia was talking about. On her quite literally paper-white skin, splotches of bright colors were moving around. It looked like when you dropped paint into water—just vibrant clouds that seemed to respond to touch, lingering around her bracelet and rings, all originating somewhere under her clothes and just flooding out toward her hands.

"Oh? You live nearby? It's such a nice neighborhood, all the old buildings here," Fae replied surprised, and Ryan nodded his head, almost with pride.

"Yeah, I live above Café Runic, I'm not sure if you know it. My uncle owns it, and I just moved in with him when I started uni."

"I think I've walked by there a couple times. I'll come drop in next time!"

"Please do! He doesn't look like much, but my uncle makes amazing coffee. Don't tell him I said that."

As Fae and Ryan were talking, Silvia and Modak were having their own silent conversation. While Modak was trying to urge the elven girl in front of him to talk to Fae, Silvia was clearly nervous and doing whatever she could to avoid it. But in the end, she wasn't able to beat Modak and his deep, deep stare.

"Do you, uhm . . . want anything to drink?" Silvia asked, awkwardly holding her glass in Fae's direction. The changeling looked at her with a broad, excited smile, but slowly shook her head.

"I think the others are ordering some for me already. And I'm not really a big fan of dark beer," she explained, and Modak let out a loud scoff.

"Shouldn't have said that one in front of Ryan."

"No, no, it's all good. I'm in a good mood, plus I owe her for not showing up to the club on Saturday, so I'll let it pass just this once," Ryan sighed loudly, not hiding his playful disappointment in Fae.

Now that it was finally brought up, as though she had been waiting for it, Fae quickly turned to Ryan. "Right, so . . . why didn't you come on Saturday? Are clubs not your vibe?"

"Oh, it's not that. I mean, I guess I do prefer a pub, but we do go out to clubs sometimes. But no I just wasn't able to come, I hurt my shoulder pretty badly."

Fae glanced at Ryan's right shoulder that he had just pointed at. "Awe, I'm sorry . . . are you feeling better now? What happened?"

"I'm a bit better yeah. And well . . . it's a bit complicated, but . . ."

"He was pummeled by a dungeon monster," Silvia explained, seeing that Ryan was tripping over his words. Plus, she wanted to somehow integrate herself into the conversation anyway.

"Wait, what?" Fae asked, confused. She looked back and forth between Ryan and Silvia, unsure what to say.

Ryan sighed deeply, starting to explain, "I awakened recently, so on Friday, I went to a dungeon, and it didn't end amazingly."

"I mean, it ended alright, all things considered," Modak pointed out. "He was level 1 when he went in, destroyed a dungeon heart—which led to the full closure—leveled up two whole times, and only came out with a burn on his hand and a cut on his shoulder."

". . . When you say it that way, I guess it did end pretty good."

Silvia threw a deep glare at Ryan after hearing the tone of his voice. "Seriously, don't you dare. Just let your shoulder heal."

Fae laughed slightly. "Isn't it fine? Don't physical Awakened heal pretty quickly anyway?"

Immediately, Silvia and Modak let out quiet laughs, and the orc looked at their friend with a grin. "Yep, *physical* Awakened definitely do."

Confused at what they were laughing about, Fae glanced around the table, looking at Ryan for context. He just let out a long, deep sigh. "I'm a magic type."

CHAPTER FIFTEEN

The Library

Deep into the night, the group stepped out of the pub into the open air. Ryan took a deep breath, stepping to the side to make room for the others stumbling around behind him.

"You guys gonna be fine?" Ryan asked, looking at Modak and Silvia. The orc scoffed and nodded his head immediately.

"What do you take me for? Tonight was nothin' to me!"

Ryan laughed slightly. "Sure, sure. Text me tomorrow morning and tell me how you feel then."

"Whatever," Modak grumbled, quickly stepping forward to give Ryan a big hug. "Love you, man, I'm glad you're alright."

"Sh-Shoulder, shoulder! I'm not *that* fine yet!" Ryan flinched with a nervous laugh as Modak pulled back. "But thanks, dude. Love you too. And be careful on your way home, alright?"

"Of cooourse! Nobody's gonna mess with me!" With a smug expression, Modak crossed his arms, clearly flexing his arms.

Meanwhile, Silvia was practically the opposite; rubbing her eyes, yawning, and clearly ready to drop into bed once she got home. Frankly, Ryan was a lot more worried about her than Modak. If she didn't have such a straightforward way home, he would be concerned she'd get lost at this rate. But something good did come out of this. As tired as she was, she was leaning onto Fae without realizing. When, or if, she remembered this tomorrow, Ryan would have to turn his phone on mute, or else her texts would cause an earthquake in his room.

"Come on, guys, you've gotta hurry to catch your train," Ryan pointed out, glancing at the time on his phone, and Silvia tiredly nodded her head. She hugged Fae and Ryan, even giving the changeling a kiss on the cheek, and then she and Modak started walking down the road toward the nearby subway station.

Ryan turned toward Fae, who stood there still a bit taken aback. Her face, usually a blank white, was covered in a wave of colors; tones of blue and pink and red and orange, swirling around her cheek where Silvia had kissed her.

With a grin and a chuckle, Ryan apologized, "Sorry about that, they just get like that when they've had too much to drink."

"I-It's fine," Fae stuttered out, before she just stood there silently for a bit.

"Uhm . . . you gonna be good on your way home?" Ryan asked, trying to break the silence, and Fae quickly nodded.

"Yes! Of course, some of us live in the dorm fifteen minutes away, so we'll just be walking back together," she replied quickly.

"Well alright, get home safe, then." Ryan smiled as he stepped closer to give Fae a goodbye hug, but she held up her hand to block him.

"A-Actually . . . there's something I wanted to talk to you about first . . . if that's fine?" she explained, and Ryan raised his brow confused.

"Uhm . . . sure? What's up?" His heart beating anxiously as he thought about what Fae wanted to discuss, Ryan watched the colors all over Fae's body nervously spark up. She pulled Ryan a few steps away, out of earshot of her friends, and took a few deep breaths. At this point, if he hadn't seen how head over heels she was for Silvia all night, Ryan would have thought Fae was about to ask him out. But that made him even more worried; he had no idea what this was about.

However, Fae slowly built up to it. "I just . . . wanted to thank you."

"Huh?" Ryan looked back at her, confused. "For what? Did I do anything for you?"

"I . . . uhm . . . During that party at the end of orientation week, I was one of the girls that . . . you know . . ." Fae anxiously turned her head away, and Ryan finally realized. He only vaguely remembered the girls from that night. It was dark, and Fae probably switched up her appearance a lot anyway, as changelings tended to do. And really, those girls weren't his focus anyway.

"Oh, I didn't realize," he replied, "but there's nothing to thank me for. I saw a very pushy guy hovering over some girls in an alley. I said something, and then . . . you know the rest."

"Well . . . yeah, but you weren't the only one that saw it," Fae pointed out. "And . . . he was a professor. I didn't expect anyone to even say something, and especially not someone to just jump into the alley like that."

Ryan didn't know what to say. He had always been impulsive like that. It didn't matter what it was, but he always had a big mouth when he saw people in trouble, and had a tendency to go all out when things got violent. It didn't always turn out as well for him as it did that time.

"Seriously, don't . . . you don't need to force yourself to thank me. The guy swung at me once, and I beat him hospital-ready. I saw your expression afterward;

you know I way overdid it. If the situation hadn't been as serious as it was, I would've been kicked out as well."

"I . . . I mean, I . . . was just a bit shocked. There was so much going on, and I . . . I just really wanted to thank you for helping after, but I . . ."

"But it took you five months to finally muster up the courage to come talk to me," Ryan added, saying what was written between the lines. "You don't need to force yourself to be my friend, I know that the way I act sometimes is way over the top, and I get if you're . . . scared of me."

"No, th-that's not—"

"But I think you and Silvia are really cute together. I can tell how much you like her, and obviously she really likes you too, so I don't want to be an obstacle and—"

"Seriously, stop!" Fae loudly interrupted Ryan, almost surprising herself. "Yes, I was a bit scared of you after that, and I wasn't sure what kind of person you were. But then I came to talk to you, and you were just so bright and warm and that just immediately disappeared. Especially after tonight, there's no way I would still be even slightly scared of you. Just give yourself some credit, man."

Ryan smiled lightly. He was glad to hear that, though of course being practically scolded like that felt a bit weird.

Fae continued, "Everyone at school knows how good of a guy you are, alright? Seriously, if *anyone* was to awaken, I'm just *so* glad it was you," she pointed out, before a laugh left her mouth. "I mean, I didn't know you were that kind of nerd, though. A magic class?"

Ryan laughed slightly as well. "It's not that kind of magic class. It's a summoner thing. Turns out, it actually suits me pretty well."

"I'm really glad to hear that. And now, to the important part . . ." The colorful patterns on Fae's skin once more started flaring up as she stared at the ground, fiddling with her hands while trying to hide her smirk. "You really think Silvia likes me?"

Modak's head felt ready to break apart. Daggers and needles might as well be stabbed in and out of his skull, and maggots seemed to be roaming through his innards.

Modak was hungover.

He carefully rolled to his side, grabbing the phone that was laying on his bedside.

You
help
call an amilanve

> *anbulance*
> *ambulance*
> *I will never drink ever again.*

<u>*Ryan*</u>
lmfao

With a loud groan, Modak looked at the time. It was already close to noon. He swung his feet over the edge of his bed, carefully staring down his legs at his feet.

"How am I in my underwear, but still wearing boots . . . ? These aren't even the ones I was wearing last night, what the fuck?" Modak pushed the boots off his feet and carefully stood up, then held his forehead as he stepped out of his bedroom to wash up.

"Ew." Kora walked down the hallway, putting in her earrings. "Wear some pants."

"Okay. Go to work," Modak suggested in response, but Kora just turned back to him and sighed.

"I'm about to. Are you blind?" she asked. Now that she mentioned it, Modak noticed that she was wearing a dark gray pant suit. She looked totally different now than she did in her time off. And then, he remembered.

"Ah . . . you're headed out to Orianda till tomorrow or something, right?"

"Yup. Was already on my way, but I forgot something," Kora explained briefly as she walked to the living room, grabbing her bag from the chair next to the dining table. "Now seriously, wear some pants."

Modak quickly rushed over her, intercepting his sister before she could leave out the door. "Does that mean you've got that fancy company car standing downstairs?"

". . . Yeah? Why?"

"You think you can drop me off at uni on the way? I wanted to go to the library for something," Modak explained in a pleading voice, but Kora just scoffed.

"Why? You got a cute little study date?"

". . . Have you never heard of NRU's library before? That's the most horrifying place for a date ever. No, I'm looking up some stuff for Ryan."

"Why, can't he read?"

"No, he can, obviously. But he's still hurt, and I want to do something to help him out. Plus, he paid for all my drinks last night so I owe him one."

"Ahh, that's why you smell like a liquor cabinet," Kora sighed, looking up at her brother with a raised brow. ". . . You've got thirty minutes, exactly. If you're not here and ready to go by then, I'm leaving without you? You hear?"

With a broad smile, Modak rushed back toward the bathroom. "Thanks, you're the best! Love you!" he exclaimed, making a small heart with his index finger and thumb while Kora just sat down on the couch.

"You bet I am."

And so, Modak rushed through getting ready, jumping into the shower and scrubbing his body down as quickly as he could. Afterward, as he ran into his bedroom with a toothbrush in his mouth, he looked around to decide on what he would need to bring with him today. With foam at the edges of his mouth, he got dressed and glanced at his clock, then quickly jumped back into the bathroom to spit out the toothpaste. And in record pace, despite his immense headache that threatened to stop him every step of the way, Modak ran back toward the living room, where Kora was already waiting by the door.

She looked at the watch on her wrist. "You ready to go?"

"Yup."

"You don't need breakfast?"

"There's a bakery out front by the library, I'll get something there," he explained, and Kora shrugged as she pulled the door open.

"Fine by me," she said, as Modak followed her out and pulled the door shut behind them. And as promised, Kora quickly dropped him off near the university library, and Modak swiftly stepped out of the car.

"You'll be back tomorrow evening, right?"

"Yeah, around seven or eight if things go well. Will you be at work then?"

"Sadly. Got late shifts today and tomorrow."

"Alright, don't overdo it at the library, then. Take some breaks. And get yourself something to eat, alright?"

"Of course. Drive safe." Modak smiled, shutting the car door. Kora pulled out of the parking space and drove off as the young orc let out a slight sigh. Of course, as promised, he headed into the bakery and got some sandwiches, but he was still feeling a bit too sick to eat anything right now, so he just put what he bought into his backpack for the time being.

And then, it didn't take long for Modak to navigate the campus and make his way to the library. As he stepped inside, he took in that pleasant smell of paper together with a big cloud of dust. The tower-like bookshelves stretched out toward the ceiling. Modak walked around the many rows and looked up, searching for a certain individual.

"Mr. . . . Stonebreaker . . . How can I . . . help you?" a voice asked from above him. Its owner descended from the ceiling via thread. Her mandibles rubbed against each other as she formed her words.

"Oh, hello . . . how are you?" Modak asked, a bit taken aback. Arachnids were usually quite particular, but Aranea was probably the most sociable amongst the librarians, who were all scuttering about. They were sorting and retrieving the books, repairing them, and otherwise assisting the university's students, professors, and researchers.

Aranea's mandibles rubbed against each other. "How can I . . . help you . . . Mr. Stonebreaker?" she repeated herself, and Modak slowly collected his thoughts.

"Right. Sorry. I'm looking for information on a few things. The awakened class 'Knight,' the class 'Spirit Keeper,' spirits belonging to the concept of 'Knighthood,'" Modak quickly explained. Being straightforward with the librarians was usually the best idea. Aranea began to flick the thread she was hanging from with two of her legs in a specific pattern.

"Spot . . . Twenty-one . . . TI . . . K," Aranea replied, turning around before climbing back up her threads. Modak made his way through the library, finding his row and the seat that had been assigned to him. He sat down on the chair and waited for a few moments, though it really didn't take long for Aranea to arrive. Though, that didn't seem like a good sign. Usually another librarian would come down to bring the actual books.

Aranea quickly placed down an old leather-bound book in front of Modak. It was always quite a sight to see the librarians carry them, as their whole bodies were barely larger than the books themselves, so their eight thin legs were clutching them tightly. Though, there were a few librarians that were bigger, so they would bring the larger books when needed. But Aranea would only come out when the librarians had to talk to others; either to hear what books needed, or to tell them about some issue related to those books.

"Nothing about . . . Spirit Keeper or . . . Knighthood Spirit," Aranea explained, her eight deep black eyes staring into Modak's. He already guessed that there would be nothing about Spirit Keepers here. Otherwise it would be a surprise that the Awakened Center didn't know about them, but it was still worth a try.

"I see . . . then do you have a catalogue of different known spirits and their concepts?"

Immediately, Aranea pulled her body up by the thread again, without responding. A few moments later, before Modak could open the book he already had in front of him, one of the other librarians came down and placed a second book on Modak's desk, and then disappeared a moment later.

Modak pushed his hand into his backpack and pulled out his laptop, already a few years too old, and placed it on the desk as well so that he could take notes to show to Ryan later. The fact that there weren't any books on Spirit Keepers and Spirits of Knighthood was a bit annoying, but he really wasn't expecting much in the first place. However, the books he did have seemed interesting enough.

One of them was a collection of different classes that had been noted down a few hundred years ago, and the other one was *Spirituologist's Journal* as the author communed with a number of different spirits to properly categorize their magics and concepts. Of course, they were just copies of the original texts that were created by the different librarians over time. Original copies of a certain age and fragility were probably kept in a completely separate place. Either way, they were the exact books that Modak needed.

He got as much information out of these as he could get, and then flicked the thread connected to the corner of the desk. In response, Aranea would come over as soon as she could, and Modak could request new books while the others were brought away.

"Hm . . ." Modak muttered to himself. There were some more specific insights on the Knight class than there were online, so that was definitely worth it. In regard to other spirits, he wrote down whatever he could find about the ones with more unique concepts connected to them. A lot of spirits were more based around magic- or nature-based concepts, but there were spirits of specific types of magic or even spirits of specific kinds of combat, but nothing that really seemed to be related to knights or knighthood. That didn't mean they didn't exist, of course; rather, Modak knew they existed since Maximus was a thing. It just meant that they hadn't been encountered often enough for that information to be noted down.

As Modak was flipping through the pages of the book, he felt a tap on his elbow. Startled, he turned around and looked down at the perpetrator; a gnome.

"Oh, Richie, how's it going?" Modak asked in a low voice, and the fellow student across from him smiled.

"It's . . . going. You know how it is. What're you reading up on?" Richie asked curiously, standing on his tiptoes to try and get a look at what the books Modak had actually were. Seeing this, Modak quickly closed the books and held them over toward Richie.

"Just some stuff about spirits."

"And . . . medieval classes? What, did you awaken?" Richie wondered with a raised brow.

Modak sighed lightly, "Well, not me, but a friend of mine."

"Huh . . . interesting. So it's a really old-generation class, then? Those don't pop up that often anymore."

"Right, you are a . . . Technomancer? That's the youngest generation, is it?"

Richie quickly nodded with a smug expression. "Yup, yup. A result of the digital age!"

"I guess you don't know a lot about older gens, then?"

"Nope, sorry. Don't really care too much about that," Richie replied apologetically, and Modak let out a slight sigh as he leaned back into his chair.

"Well, it was worth a try. So, what are you doing here? Doesn't really seem like your . . . scene," Modak pointed out. Technomancers tended to really be all about the newest tech and all that. That didn't mean they didn't read, of course. They were still a type of knowledge-hungry mage after all, but most of the time they would read through their phones or tables.

"Ah," Richie said, pointing behind himself toward the book-return box set up nearby. "I was bringing back a schematic book that I borrowed for reference."

With a raised brow, Modak looked down at Richie, an inkling of something coming to him. "For the robotics club, or just exam stuff?"

"Robotics club. Our project the past semester was making robots for Power Duels," Richie explained smugly, looking up at Modak with a slight grin. "Why? You interested in joining after all?"

Modak sighed and shook his head, "Sorry, man. I really don't have the time. But . . . Power Duels, that was that thing where you fight with miniature robots, right? Like on TV?"

"Yup, we're doing our final showcase this weekend. Well, it's really just a small tournament, but both can be true."

A slight smile formed on Modak's face. Power Duels were pretty popular a while ago, which meant some decades earlier. There was even a whole TV show about them, and even some cartoons where the kids fought far too extreme duels with those robots. But the way Power Duels worked gave Modak a certain idea. Seeing the orc's expression, Richie was a bit confused. But Modak quickly revealed why he was smiling with a certain question.

"Richie, do you think you could do me a favor?"

CHAPTER SIXTEEN

Power Duels

Alright, so, what's happening?" Ryan asked, following his friends down the hallway.

"Just calm down already," Modak replied. "You're so impatient."

"Dude, you texted us, told us to come to uni, and literally said nothing else. You expect me to not be curious? Do you know what this is about?" Ryan turned toward Silvia, who simply shrugged in response.

"How would I? I got here like a minute before you."

Modak stopped in front of a door: The sign hanging on it simply read ROBOTICS CLUB.

". . . You're bringing us to meet your nerd friends?" Ryan asked with a raised brow.

Modak scoffed and pulled the door open. "You've got a magical class, bud. You're one of the nerds."

Ryan looked down at his hands, his eyes quivering in shock. "What have I become . . . ?"

"Just shut up already." Modak pushed Ryan into the room, and the three friends quickly stepped into the robotics clubroom. It was a fairly open space, and about half a dozen people were currently working on something or another. However, the center of the room was suspiciously open. Tables and shelves had been pushed to the side against each other to make space, and broad white tape sectioned off a square area. One of the people on the other side of the room quickly perked up as the door opened, and pulled the large headphones off his ears.

"Oh, already here? That was quick," Richie pointed out, pushing himself off his chair and moving over to the three guests, wiping his hands with a small towel hanging over his shoulder. He quickly stretched out his hand toward Ryan and Silvia.

"Richard Snappertie, at your service!"

Ryan raised his brow, shaking Richie's hand. "Ryan Aglecard . . . sorry, but Snappertie, that's . . . you're the Technomancer, right?"

"Yup, that's me," Richie replied, glancing over at Ryan as he shook Silvia's hand as well.

"Silvia Redhorn," she introduced herself, and Richie looked up at her with a curious expression.

"Redhorn? Are you somehow related to Yanna Redhorn?"

"Yup," Silvia replied with a smug grin, "she's my older sister."

Surprised, Richie looked over at Modak and Ryan to see if he heard right, just getting a slight nod from each of them. Figuring that he shouldn't press about this kind of thing, Richie quickly moved on, "Alright, so which of you two awakened?"

Ryan raised his hand with a brief wave. "That'd be me," he said, looking over at Modak. "Now, why are we here? Am I supposed to learn how to use magic from him or something?"

"No, no, it wasn't anything like that. The robotics club is working on—"

"Hold on," Richie interrupted Modak, looking at Ryan with narrowed eyes. "Magic? You . . . you awakened with a magical class? Ryan Aglecard, the guy that not even people from the martial arts clubs mess with . . . that Ryan Aglecard awakened with a magical class?"

Silvia chuckled with a nod of her head. "You're just as surprised as the rest of us."

"Shut up." Ryan glared at Silvia briefly, before looking back down at Richie. "You know me?"

"Of course I know you. I doubt there's anyone at this school that hasn't heard some rumor or two about you at this point. Gods, you made a hell of a mess during your orientation week." Richie laughed, but Ryan quickly interrupted him.

"I get it, I get it . . . but yeah, it's a summoner-type class, basically. I didn't expect it either, trust me, but . . . it's pretty neat."

A broad, curious grin formed on Richie's face as he put everything together. "Oh, okay, I see where this is going. Let me guess, whatever it is you summon, it's a . . ." Richie held his hand over one another, about twenty to thirty centimeters away from each other, ". . . yay tall physical combat summon?"

"That . . . yeah, that's exactly right." Ryan glanced over at Modak, who was just standing there with a smile on his face.

Exactly then, Richie stretched his hand out toward the table that he was sitting at earlier. For just a moment, his eyes seemed to give off sparks of soft blue light, which quickly traveled through Richie's arm like a current. An arc of electricity shot outward from his finger to the table, connecting with something there. Before that arc of energy even settled down, some quiet metallic thumps could be heard. A small figure leapt off the table and came running over to the group, quickly jumping up onto Richie's arm.

"Meet R.0.X.13. Or, well . . . Roxie," Richie said proudly, showing off the small humanoid robot stood on his shoulder. Roxie had a vaguely feminine, stylized form with thick arms and legs. The two antennae on top of its head, combined with the hexagonal compound eyes and some other design features, made it very clear that Roxie was borrowing a lot of traits from ants.

"Wait, is this a Power Duel robot?" Ryan asked immediately, leaning slightly forward with a broad smile on his face. "Holy shit, I watched that show every week as a kid, that's so cool!"

Silvia pushed forward and took a close look at the robot as well. "I think I've still got all the *Power Duels* comics at home, I've never seen a real Duelist! I mean, I've got some of the toys, but it's not the same thing."

"Heh, well, Roxie here is a state-of-the-art model that I myself built." With a smug grin, Richie glanced at the robot, before looking at Ryan. "So, are we doing this or not?"

Ryan looked at Modak, not sure if he was understanding everything correctly, but seeing his friend's excited smile, he let out a sigh. "Honestly, you could have explained it beforehand, man."

As he held forward his hand, a flow of red wisps appeared from Ryan's arm and hand, gathering on the ground until they formed the body of Maximus. As Richie placed Roxie down onto the ground, he took a closer look at the small knight.

"Oh wow, that . . . what kind of summon is it?"

"He's a type of spirit. Maximus the Knight."

Richie raised his brow curiously. "Huh, alright. I wonder how a spirit compares to my cute little Roxie, then."

"Great, can we start right away, then?" Ryan asked, just as curious about that as Richie seemed to be. However, the gnome quickly shook his head.

"Oh gods no, we need to do a bunch of tests first." With a scoff, Richie walked over to his table, grabbing a tablet that was laying on it. He moved some things around opened some kind of data-entry program. "All of our robots are installed with full-body sensors. You know, to track the damage points and stuff. But obviously, your spirit doesn't have that, so we've got to figure out how to track all that. And since armor doesn't exactly have stats in the same way, I—"

"Actually, that armor is his body, so I can actually tell you what his resistance stat is," Ryan pointed out, and Richie raised a brow curiously.

"Is that so? Well, that does indeed make things a little easier. Here, can you fill this out real quick? I've made some stat approximations for Roxie, so with that I should be able to calculate the damage received based on the amount of force that Roxie uses at any specific moment together with the counter-impact that's measured with any attack," Richie explained, handing the tablet over to Ryan, who quickly entered the stats that the input fields were asking for. When he was done, he quickly handed the tablet back, and Richie looked it over for a moment.

"Huh, that's pretty high, considering its size . . . but it doesn't have the agility stat, so I guess it's really more of a strength-tanker?" Richie asked, and Ryan nodded with a slight shrug.

"Basically, from what I gathered," he replied, looking down at Roxie somewhat curiously. "So, that robot can put up with his stats?"

"Stats aren't everything, so yes." With a smug grin, Richie crossed his arms. "You're at the NRU robotics club right now, bud. Our Duelists would kick the butts of the ones from the original series. The original series is also about thirty years old, but that's not important. The fact that we've got state-of-the-art magical engineering resources helps too, I guess. Oh, but we'll be balancing some of the point values to make up for the stat difference to a certain degree. I hope you don't mind."

"Nah, go ahead."

Richie walked over to one end of the square area sectioned off through tape. He snapped his finger, and a spark of electric blue magic arced between the tablet in his hand and the monitor set up at the side of the makeshift "arena." There were now two numbers displayed on the screen, one labeled, "Roxie," the other "Maximus."

"Each side has a hundred points. It's basically their health, and every attack will reduce the opponent's, of course. I mean, you've played games before, right? You know how it works."

Ryan scoffed and nodded his head immediately. "Yeah, don't worry. I get the gist. But . . . sorry, can I have a quick moment?"

"Sure, take your time."

Ryan slowly squatted down and picked up Maximus off the ground, approaching the door. Modak and Silvia looked at him with concern, before the latter quickly asked, "Is everything alright?"

"I'm good, don't worry. I just need to talk to Maximus real quick," Ryan replied, then pushed open the large door and closed it behind himself again as he stepped out. Modak stared at Silvia with a worried expression.

"Should I have talked to him about this first?"

Silvia smiled and shook her head. "You're fine, don't worry. He's probably just nervous? I mean, he's been in plenty of fights before, but this is a little different. And by the way"—Silvia looked over at Richie curiously—"you guys are just spending your time reenacting old game-shows-turned-cartoon-turned-cultural-phenomenon?"

"Not all of our time. Just a lot of it."

Outside the door, Ryan looked at Maximus who stood on his palm. "Before this starts, I feel like I should ask, but . . . you're fine with that, right? To fight that robot?"

Maximus stared back at Ryan for a few moments, before giving him a single slow, but very deliberate, nod.

"It's not like this is just for fun either, you know . . . ? I mean, sure, it does sound fun and all, but I mean . . . you're a Knight; this is like the perfect environment for us to practice the Spirit Link skill, right? It doesn't hurt anymore, but the doc said I shouldn't put too much pressure on my shoulder yet. My mana's still out of whack too, but skills are fairly harmless in that sense."

Once more, Maximus replied with a single nod.

". . . Am I way overthinking this?"

Another nod from Maximus quickly followed. Ryan let out a slight scoff. "Alright, if you say so. So, when we use Spirit Link, how are we doing this? Do you want to try out my style of fighting for a bit? Or do you just want me to nudge you in certain directions? I'll be able to see the whole thing, after all. Might have a better overview."

Maximus seemed to think for a moment. But it didn't take him long to come to a decision, holding up one finger.

"Alright. Then let's do this." With a grin, Ryan nodded his head. "Guess it's a good opportunity to try out that new arm of yours too, huh?"

With an excited smile, Ryan stepped back into the room, then placed Maximus down on the ground on the opposite site of the arena to where Richie was waiting.

"You okay?" Modak was worried after Ryan left the room so suddenly a minute ago. But Ryan quickly turned around toward him, and all the concern he had was immediately washed away. There was a broad smile plastered all over his friend's face.

"Couldn't be better." Ryan took a few steps back until he was outside of the makeshift arena. By now, the other robotics club members had also gathered around and were eagerly awaiting the start of the Power Duel. Having one of their creations fight against a spirit certainly was a rare opportunity.

"Can we get started?" Richie asked, pulling some gloves over his hands. They were covered in circuit-like patterns that immediately lit up the moment Richie fully wore them.

Ryan raised his brow curiously. "What are those for?"

"Hm? Oh, these are just a tool to give me finer control over my magic. You don't have anything like that?"

"Not yet at least. I've got a pretty rare class, so there's no equipment made for it."

"Gotta get it custom-made, then. I can send you the name of a place I like," he suggested, and Ryan didn't hesitate to accept the offer.

Richie quickly clapped his hands together with a broad grin on his face. On the monitor that was displaying the "health" of each Roxie and Maximus, a ten-second countdown started. "Alright, get ready. Now."

As Richie said so, and as the timer kept counting down, Ryan activated the Spirit Link. He closed his eyes for just a moment, and as he opened them again, his irises were glowing in a bright red. The red wisps of magic flowed out from his hands, forming a connecting thread between himself and Maximus, so thin that it was hard to see it.

Soon, Ryan was overcome with new sensations; Maximus's sensations. The weight of his armor, the things that he could hear and see. All the information was simply put straight into Ryan's head. He wasn't sure if he could ever get used to this. It just always felt so foreign to him.

Ryan held his hand slightly forward, clenching his hand into a fist. And right then, Maximus did the same thing, as if mimicking Ryan's movements perfectly.

Richie seemed to have noticed this as well, but wasn't able to properly register it before the countdown hit zero. The moment that a buzzer signaled the start of the fight, Maximus ran forward. It was a weird sensation to Ryan; he wasn't controlling Maximus directly, but it was a sort of "suggestion." Ryan and Maximus were working together almost perfectly, as Ryan, who had an over-view over the arena, guided Maximus's movements as much as the knight was allowing him to.

Maximus closed the distance to Roxie in not even a second, at which point, Ryan swung his fist forward as he would in a normal fight. He felt a pressure stop his arm as Maximus's fist impacted on Roxie's body. Ryan glanced to the side; that punch was worth fifteen damage points.

As he looked back at Richie, the first thing Ryan noticed were the gnome's bright white teeth pressed against each other for a massive, excited smile. Richie held his hands forward, as though he were placing his fingers onto some kind of keyboard or controller as his fingers started moving faster than Ryan could keep track of. Roxie slid past Maximus to move the fight closer to the center of the arena, and the knight quickly followed.

Ryan did a sweeping motion with his leg, which was quickly mimicked by Maximus. And as Roxie jumped out of the way, Maximus jumped toward the robot. He reached out, and while Roxie entered a guard stance to protect its face, the knight's hands wrapped around the back of its head, grasping it tightly.

As the body of Maximus crunched together, forcing Roxie's head down with his whole upper body, his knee rocketed right through the robot Duelist's defense. Immediately after the full impact, Maximus let go and stretched out the leg he used to attack just now, kicking Roxie away. The robot now only had forty-one points left.

"Gods . . . so that's how you fight?" Richie asked with a nervous smile on his face. "Remind me to never mess with you . . ."

"Hah, don't worry." Ryan laughed slightly. "You seem like a good guy, so I doubt it would come to that."

"Right . . . well, anyway . . . it was a bit surprising, but nothing I can't handle."

Ryan raised a brow at what Richie said, focusing on the arena again. Roxie was running toward Maximus, and Ryan pushed forward his arm for another punch. But just before Maximus's fist was supposed to touch the robot, Roxie just stopped moving altogether. As if someone had pressed "pause" on a video, it just froze mid-motion, interrupting any sort of momentum. Taken aback and unsure what was going on, Ryan hesitated. And in that moment of hesitation, Roxie's momentum returned.

With almost the same speed as before, the small robot moved forward and swung at Maximus. But the moment that Roxie's jab touched the knight's armor, sparks of electricity flew outward. Ryan could feel the heat and impact on his chest as the bright light of the sparks blinded Maximus's view. It was truly an overwhelming "stun." From the corner of his eye, Ryan saw Maximus's points.

Fifty-six. That single punch took nearly half the points off, and if he hadn't experienced the sensation of that punch himself, Ryan would have thought that Richie was cheating. But it wasn't really like Ryan had the time to think about it all too much. Before the sparks of electricity even disappeared, Roxie attacked again.

Its arm shot forward for another jab, as the robot started to move around skillfully like a trained martial artist. Meanwhile, Richie's fingers were moving around midair like he was playing a complex piece on an invisible piano. But that skillful and fast movement wasn't really what Ryan and Maximus were struggling with the most. It was the fact that at seemingly random points, Roxie's momentum was just canceled or paused, or whatever it was that was going on.

Sometimes it would continue, as though Roxie was unpaused, but at other times, it just started moving in a completely different way, as if it was restarting its movement from zero. Like that momentum from before was just thrown away; discarded. Though, there was one thing that did seem to keep building up.

Throughout these erratic and hard-to-predict motions, it was hard for Ryan to keep track of it all, and Roxie kept getting hits in. Sometimes, there were more sparks, and sometimes, there weren't. Either way, it didn't take long before Ryan and Maximus's first Power Duel was over.

Roxie - 41 Points | Maximus - 0 Points

CHAPTER SEVENTEEN

Power Source

Ryan and Maximus hadn't gotten a single point in after Richie and Roxie got serious.

"What . . ." Ryan looked at the gnome across from him in disbelief, as Richie carefully picked up the robot to look it over and make sure nothing was broken or too scratched up. ". . . what the hell was that?"

Modak and Silvia also quickly approached. "How did you do that?" Silvia questioned, just as puzzled as Ryan. But Modak seemed to have some kind of idea.

"Was that an Energy Transmutor?"

"An Energy what, now?" Ryan asked, and Richie quickly explained with a proud grin on his face.

"An Energy Transmutor. It can take one form of energy and turn it into another directly. In this case, it can access and transmute kinetic, electrical, and magical energies into each other."

As he picked up Maximus off the ground as well, Ryan looked at Richie confused. "So what, you just turned Roxie's momentum into electricity for those sparks?"

"Basically. It's a relatively new technology, so it's not perfectly efficient. The only reason I can do it is because I can supplement some of the energy loss through my magic. The others had to come up with their own gimmicks, though."

Ryan looked around at the other club members, who were all excitedly agreeing.

"Do you think . . . Maximus and I could fight the others as well? For practice, I mean," Ryan asked, not even hesitating. Maximus was a knight, a physical combat class. And after the end of the battle, Ryan noticed not only himself, but Maximus be surrounded by a particularly thin layer of that glowing dust representing a growth in experience. Of course, the others couldn't see it, but Ryan could. While these battles were basically nothing but spars, they still allowed for Maximus to grow.

He had no idea why he hadn't thought about it before; a large portion of martial-arts-based Awakened ended up in combat sports, rather than actual "classic" combat scenarios. While they tended to level up slower than people that were active in Dungeon Diving or Heroics, they still leveled up.

Ryan wasn't necessarily expecting a full level-up, but just bringing them closer to the next one would just be great. Plus, the sooner Ryan reached level 10, the sooner he could get the Bluesky guys off his back. They kept calling and showing up at the café. Luckily Runar managed to intercept them most of the time, but until Ryan reached level 10, the point at which the trading of classes became impossible even with whatever methods Bluesky had found, they clearly had no intention of letting up. Not to mention, leveling up and strengthening their skills would make finding the rest of Gaia's fragments just that much easier.

So, in order to level up as soon as possible, Ryan and Maximus would make use of whatever they could. They needed to fight. And doing it here, in such a safe environment, only brought benefits. And if all the Duelists were as unique as Roxie, then this would not only be useful to grow stronger . . . but it would also just be a lot of fun. However, it wasn't just Richie's own choice to be made.

The gnome looked around the room, trying to gauge the opinions of the other club members. Seeing that they were all curious and interested, the gnome replied with a nod, "Sure, as far as I'm concerned at least. I'll run it by the other members properly first, though. Ah, but obviously it can't happen right now either; we're all still working on the finishing touches. This whole Power Duel thing is part of our main project for the semester, so we're doing our final test run this Friday afternoon. You can come by if you want, I'm sure the others will be happy to have the data from fighting a spirit."

With a grin, Ryan looked at Maximus as he stood on his palms. "Are you alright with that as well?"

Ryan didn't even have to wait for an answer; before he was able to even finish the question, Maximus nodded enthusiastically.

"Looks like we're set, then," Ryan replied, already getting excited. But Modak was more curious about something else.

"So, you said you're doing a test run? Are you guys going to be presenting this to anyone?"

Richie looked at him with a raised brow. "Of course. We've got a whole fair thing going on this weekend, where we'll present our work to some companies and organizations as a thing to sort of sell ourselves. It's a great way to get a couple job offers for after uni," Richie explained. "We've got some big shots coming this time around, actually."

Modak looked around the room at the other members, almost regretting that he didn't join this club after all. But he simply didn't have the time to spend on this. Honestly, he barely had the time to be here right now.

Richie took out his phone and held it toward Ryan. "Here, give me your number. I'll text you the time and let you know if the plan changes or anything."

Ryan quickly entered his phone number and returned it. And then, without further ado, Ryan, Modak, and Silvia left the club room.

". . . That was so cool." Silvia let out after the door closed behind her. "Can we join you on Friday? I loved *Power Duels* so much as a kid, please!"

Ryan laughed slightly and nodded. "Obviously, come join. Literally don't know what I'd do without you two at this point."

He looked at his friends for a moment as Maximus was starting to be taken apart, flowing into Ryan's palms to take a break in the domain. He was seriously insanely grateful for everything they'd done for him. Not only did they make his life here in the city amazing, but after he awakened, they went full-force in supporting him through it all. He really—

"Sorry, coming through." A young woman pushed through the small group. They were standing in the middle of the hallway, so she really had no choice but to go right through them. A young hobgoblin, carrying a cardboard box filled with bits of metal, tools, screws, wires, and most importantly, a partially constructed Duelist robot. She rushed through the hallway and pushed down the door handle with her elbow, carefully making her way into the room.

Taking some deep breaths, the girl put the cardboard box onto a free table on the other side of the room. While taking everything out of the box, she was approached from the side.

"Vanda, you alright? Didn't expect to see you here today." Richie came up to her with a smile, "You missed a pretty good show just now."

"Hm? Oh sorry, yeah, I was busy with work and then my little sister was suspended from school for a while. I-I'm trying to finish this in time, I'm so sorry . . ." Vanda replied nervously. Her hands were shaking and her clawlike fingernails were digging into her skin as she tried to calm herself down. Seeing how she was acting, Richie shook his head and started helping her unpack the cardboard box.

"Why are you even apologizing? This isn't a job; you're supposed to be here to have fun. I mean, yeah, a lot of us use it as jumping-off points, but if we can't have fun with all of this stuff now, how can we later?" Richie explained his stance, and Vanda slowly looked at the gnome next to her.

". . . Right . . . sorry."

Richie looked at the current state of Vanda's work, raising his brows in curiosity. "Oh? That looks like a pretty interesting strengthening method."

As if a switch was flipped, Vanda snapped her head toward him. "Right? The power output was plateauing, and then I remembered this documentary about Enhancers that I watched a while ago. I spent days just looking into specific documents about the unique flow of mana through an Enhancer's body!" she explained, seemingly starting to look for something specific in her tools and materials. "Did you know that they're one of the few physical-class Awakened that use a combination of aura and mana to strengthen themselves? They let the two different energies intertwine in these rhythmic pulses. The aura is the base for the strength and then the specific application of mana refines it into the specific type of strengthening that the Enhancer needs."

"Oh? I think I've heard that before . . ." Richie muttered, cupping his chin in thought when he finally realized, "Wait, are you using both magical and electrical applications? At the same time? How does that even work? Is it really giving the same effects as an Enhancer's abilities? And your Duelist is so small, how did you . . ."

An awkward laugh left the corner of Vanda's mouth. "Well, it's actually a bit of a glass cannon . . . it's very easy for it to get damaged, and kind of complicated to repair. But when I did some tests, I was able to boost the strength by a whole extra 34.7 percent! And that was only when using a really basic energy pattern!"

It wasn't just Richie that was shocked by this revelation. The other club members that managed to overhear what Vanda was talking about all came closer to take a look.

"By that much? Seriously? Weren't the baseline stats of your Duelist pretty decent in the first place?" Richie asked, not sure if he heard right. "That's ridiculous, just . . . wow . . . How's the energy efficiency looking?"

Immediately, it was clear that Richie hit a sore spot. "So, that's actually one of the things I'm struggling with . . . on the electrical side, things are fine, but the mana output is still far too high because no matter what I do, I can't get the precision I need into the mana patterns . . . So what I'm mostly working on right now is trying to fine-tune things. The voltage is fine, but the amperage is too weak, no matter what I do. Because I need two power sources, I just can't seem to find any mana sources that give me what I need . . ."

A bit in thought, Richie let out a groan. "I see the problem. That kind of thing can be solved when you scale it up for industrial solutions, but since our presentation methods are Duelists, that's a bit of a struggle . . . You think you'll be fine until Friday? A first-year that awakened recently is going to do some Power Duels against us. He's a summoner, and he summons a Duelist-scale fighter. They're pretty skilled too, so it should make for some great data if you're interested," Richie explained. "Frankly, the companies that show up might always be interested in Awakened, but they sometimes seem even more interested in technology that can match up to Awakened. Especially since your approach is Enhancer inspired, I think you have a really good shot at making something work this weekend."

Vanda's heart beat loudly in her chest, as if threatening to jump out through her throat. Hearing that from Richie was basically a dream. Not only was he the top of all his classes in the magic engineering program, but he was even a

Technomancer! There wasn't anyone in the robotics club that didn't take his opinion about things like this as fact.

"Th-Thank you!" Vanda forced out anxiously. "That means a lot!"

"Let me know if you need help with anything, alright? We're all here to support each other."

"Of course!" Looking at Richie's back as he moved back to his own table, Vanda couldn't help but smile broadly. She looked at the bottom of the cardboard box, where she was keeping something wrapped up. After carefully taking it out, Vanda unwrapped what she assumed to be the solution to all her problems.

Vanda quickly grabbed one of her tools and removed one of the plates covering her Duelist's back. As she had a lot of things relying on the presentation working out this weekend, Vanda was concentrating deeply on finding a way to make this happen. She pulled an old mana battery out of the small robot in front of her, and then grabbed the wrapped-up object. A small glass cylinder with metallic plates at the top and bottom.

And inside of the cylinder was a single object, a crystal that could act as an immense source of mana that she had managed to harness. "Let's hope this one works . . . I really owe Christopher for getting me this . . ." She smiled as the small green stone illuminated her fingertips.

Ryan, Modak, and Silvia stepped out of the university's science building, and the orc looked down at his clock with an annoyed expression.

"Urgh . . . Sorry, guys, I've got to go or I'll end up being late for my shift." Modak let out a loud sigh, tiredly rubbing the bridge of his nose.

Ryan raised his brow surprised. "Wait, you've got work today? And you spent the time that you should've been recovering from your hangover in the library for me? Seriously?" he asked, feeling even worse for relying on his friends so much.

"The library's the perfect place for that, don't worry. It's quiet and nobody can bother me there for too long if they don't want to deal with Aranea."

With a shudder, Ryan nodded. "Don't remind me . . . the first time I went there, I nearly shat myself . . ."

"That's what you get for dropping one of Aranea's precious books," Silvia laughed, barely glancing up from her phone. Curiously, Ryan took a step closer.

"You texting Fae?"

Silvia's cheeks quickly turned a bright red. "No! I mean, yes, generally, but not right now! I'm texting Yanna. She asked me if I want to wait for her to finish her workout. Ryan, you had some stuff you still wanted to ask her, right?"

Ryan thought about it for a moment, and when he remembered what exactly it was, he excitedly nodded. "Right, yes! I wanted to talk to her about the best approach for unlocking some physical stats."

"Ah . . ." Modak nervously looked at his friends, stumbling over his words. "I guess say 'hi' to Yanna for me?" the orc asked, as Ryan and Silvia both looked at each other, trying to hide their smirks.

"Yes, Modak, we'll say 'hi' to Yanna for you," Ryan laughed quietly, patting his friend on the shoulder.

"You know, she'll be pretty disappointed you're not doing it yourself. You sure you don't want to come along for a little bit? Probably won't take too long." Teasingly, Silvia pointed down in the direction of the building that Yanna was working out at.

Modak seemed to actually consider it for a moment, but then just shook his head. "I seriously have to get going. I might already have to run to catch my train . . . maybe next time."

"Boo!" Silvia held forward her hands and gave Modak two thumbs-down.

"Fuck off," Modak scoffed as he gave his friends a hug. He then quickly turned around, heading out toward the subway station. "Talk to you guys later!" He waved the two goodbye again as he headed down the path in the opposite direction of his friends.

As they were walking, Silvia rushed ahead a bit, forcing Ryan to pick up the pace as well. Before long, the two reached the buildings at the edge of the campus, belonging to New Riverside University's sports faculty. Right behind the building they stood in front of, a couple dozen students were running on the tracks. Meanwhile, inside of the gymnasiums in front of them, people were either practicing their martial arts or simply doing muscle training. And there was a reason why this school had the most Awakened students in the whole country.

No matter the faculty, the school provided as much support as possible to their efforts, and that included the sports faculty. Silvia and Ryan entered the gym for Awakened students. Everywhere they looked, heavy machinery was set up in rows that allowed for any Awakened to train using weights unsuited for any regular gym. If Ryan remembered correctly what he heard during the tour in orientation week, the strongest machine supported up to two tons of weight, even if just theoretically.

Ryan couldn't wait to train here once he properly spoke to the university's administration about his awakening. He really wanted to open up some physical stats besides dexterity.

"Hey, you kids," a gruff voiced yelled out from across the room, as a mountain of a man approached the pair. The grooves of his muscular arms and upper body were practically filled in with heaps of sweat that was dripping on the ground as he walked.

Since the man was more than a meter taller than he was, Ryan instinctively took a step back to not get rained on.

"This place is only for Awakened."

A little ticked off, Ryan raised his brow. "Excuse me?"

"I'm just sayin', if ya ain't an Awakened, ya can't use this place, so get outta here already." The troll in front of the two looked down at them, sighing lightly.

Ryan looked up at the man in front of him, his brows furrowed into a frown. "For your information, I am an Awakened, not that it matters to you. Yes, non-Awakened students aren't allowed to use the machines for their own safety, but they're allowed to be in here like any other student. So how about you calm down for a second and let us wait for our friend in peace?"

Not sure what exactly to say, the man glanced back and forth between Ryan and Silvia. "I, uhm . . . I . . ."

Before he could continue talking, or at least attempt to, the loud slam of a magic-supported barbell hitting the ground made all three of them flinch for a moment. As Ryan looked past the living wall in front of him, he spotted the person who created that sound. A young minotaur, drenched in water that pressed her short-buzzed fur against her densely muscle-packed skin, making it cling to the base of her horns. While she was shorter than the troll in front of Ryan and Silvia, she was still much taller than either of them. As she approached, her hooves clopped on the gym's floor while she pulled her headphones out of her ears.

CHAPTER EIGHTEEN

Yanna Redhorn

Silvia, Ryan? Sorry, I didn't expect you guys to get here so quickly," the minotaur said with a surprised smile on her face. "I'll take a quick shower and get dried off, and then I'll be right out."

"Wait, you know these guys?" the troll asked with a slight frown, and the minotaur looked up at him with a confused expression.

"Laram, that's my sister. I literally showed you a picture of her before. Did he say something to you guys?" Yanna asked with a concerned expression. Clearly, this wasn't the first time that Laram acted as he did.

"No, no, all good, he was just saying hello." Silvia looked up at the minotaur with a smile, but Laram couldn't even react to what the young woman had said.

"That wasn't a joke? I mean, she's an . . . elf, you know?"

"She's adopted, dumbass." With a sigh that made her septum piercing rattle slightly, Yanna looked back at Ryan and Silvia. "I'll be right back! Just ten minutes!"

And with that, the young minotaur rushed through the gym to the locker rooms. Nervously, Laram scratched his cheek. "Sorry, I didn't know you were here for Yanna . . ."

"Don't worry about it, man," Ryan replied, slowly turning around. "We'll just wait for her outside."

The troll watched the two visitors leave, making their way outside.

After a few moments of silence between the two, Ryan looked over at Silvia. "What?"

"I didn't say anything."

"Yeah, exactly. That's pretty unusual," Ryan replied, and Silvia raised her brow.

"I just think you don't have to play into how other people act all the time. If you just try to calm them down a bit, you wouldn't end up in so many fights."

"Come on, what was I supposed to do? He was clearly out for a fight. I'm not gonna act like a wuss in front of someone like that."

"Ryan, that was Laram Oggberg, he was just scouted for the Awakened League."

"Yes, I know that. Which also means that I know it never would have led to anything physical. But if he comes to us and acts like a dick, I won't just let him do what he wants. Being an Awakened doesn't mean you can push everyone else around." Ryan sat down on the bench near the entrance, crossing his legs with a click of his tongue.

Silvia sat down as well, smiling lightly. "You know, it's kind of a shame you don't want to get into Heroics."

". . . I just don't think it'd be good for me," Ryan pointed out. "It's the most dangerous field an Awakened can get into, and I'm not . . . I don't know, I just don't think I would be good at it. Not to mention, I would just be putting Maximus in danger with that, and I don't want that."

"And what, Dungeon Diving is better? Safer?" Silvia asked, staring daggers into Ryan's shoulder.

". . . I mean, statistically, yeah. If I prepare a bit better next time, don't take the same kinds of risks, and have some other people join me, I think it's really not that bad. I'd also still be helping people without having to deal with literal psychopathic maniacs every day. Have you seen what kind of criminals are running around in this city?" Ryan let out a loud scoff. "And I know these kinds of things don't happen often, but there's a guy that shrank down a whole bus of people and kept them on his necklace for a week. Like what the fuck am I supposed to do against that shit?"

Silvia looked up, slouching down on the bench. "You could also do something else entirely. Frankly, even if you might not be able to join something like the Awakened League or someplace where you need to be super strong, if you open up some other stats and train them up a bit, you could basically pick whatever regular job you want. Any company would go crazy to say they have an Awakened on staff."

Ryan scoffed as he shook his head, immediately denying that option. "And what, become a mascot? Nah, if I'm going into a non-Awakened field, I won't let myself be used for publicity. I really don't want that kind of attention."

"You're already pretty famous around uni, though."

"Does it look like I'm enjoying that? It's uncomfortable. You saw it earlier. Richie already acted like he knew everything he needed to know about me, and that was the first time I even spoke to the guy. And everyone keeps acting that way. If I were to get into some shit like Heroics, that would get even worse."

Silvia let out a deep, disappointed sigh. "Damn . . . I would have loved to design your outfit."

"You already made me one . . ."

"That was just some boring utility gear, I'm talking about a real recognizable thing. Something that looks just super cool, like you'd see in a game or a comic or something."

Ryan sighed loudly, looking at his friend. She really just loved making things, whether she was good in that specific field or not. But the thing was that she dove so deeply into any topic she was interested in that she ended up becoming an expert in it within a few weeks. Granted, that was only related to things that made her creative veins pop up, but still.

She's the one that convinced Ryan to get more into model customization rather than just building the ones straight out of the box, and even though she never did it before either, within a few days she basically knew more about model building than Ryan. Similarly, she was working on some things with Modak, repairing and customizing old tech together, like that cassette player that Silvia always carried with her, attached to her hip, painted in fashionable colors that always seemed to match her outfits. She always did that kind of thing, and when she had her mind set to it, she would try to get it done, no matter what. Though it could get exhausting sometimes, that was probably one of the things that Ryan respected and loved most about her.

Knowing that he wouldn't be able to stop her anyway, Ryan conceded, "Fine. Just don't give me body-tight spandex. Make it fit my vibe."

Excitedly, Silvia clapped her hands together, as though she really only needed to get the go-ahead. "The pact has been sealed, you shall not be allowed to change your mind now."

". . . Godsdammit . . . But I'll be paying for whatever you make from now on. You convinced me last time, but now that I got the reward money from the DMB, there's no way I'm letting you work for free."

"I really don't need the money, you know?"

"It's about the principle."

Ryan and Silvia sat there for a little while longer, chatting away for a while. At some point, Ryan had wanted to get out Maximus, but he seemed to be in the middle of something. He was seated on the edge of his bed, his hands clasped together in front of his face, clearly thinking about something. Ryan would ask him about it later, but right now he figured it was better to leave him be.

And then, before long, Yanna stepped out through the gym's main entrance, her fur still slightly wet but starting to get frizzy. "Thanks for waiting."

Silvia jumped up from the bench and gave Yanna a hug. "No worries, it wasn't that long."

While Silvia was still hugging her sister, Ryan noticed Yanna glancing around, as if looking for something. Or someone. With a slight grin on his face, Ryan looked over at her. "Modak went home already."

"Hm?" As if startled, Yanna looked back at Ryan, nervously stuttering out a response, "Oh no, I-I wasn't—I just thought since Silvia said you three were together earlier that he would . . . be here too . . ."

Silvia finally let go of her sister and took a step back, the same grin on her face. "If you want to see him so bad, we can go by his work in a bit."

Yanna stood there somewhat hesitantly, as though she was considering the offer for a few moments, but finally shook her head. "No, it's better if we don't. I doubt he'd like being bothered at work . . ."

"Fiiine," Silvia replied disappointedly, and Yanna quickly looked over at Ryan, hoping to change the topic.

"Silvia said you want some advice about stats? What exactly do you want to know?" she asked curiously.

"So, the only physical stat I have is dexterity. I'd love to get strength, agility, and maybe even resistance? But I heard that one's pretty hard to train even if it's one of your base stats . . ." Ryan explained, and Silvia nodded with a shiver.

"Yeah . . . I don't have resistance personally, but Laram's been pushing me to train for it . . . There's a few methods, but the most common one is to just get beat by others repeatedly."

". . . Huh. Yeah, let's not . . . What about strength and agility? Oh, and stamina would be great too, actually, now that I think about it. I'd love any physical stat besides just dexterity, to be honest . . ." Ryan tried to hide his disappointment, though he probably wasn't very good at it. Again, he ended up really liking his class, but in his mind, he always imagined himself getting super-strength or -speed if he ever awakened. But now, that probably wouldn't really happen.

Yanna looked down at the watch on her wrist, which she seemed to have used to track her workout earlier. "You know what, should we go back to our place and talk there? My coach actually gave me a bunch of booklets about common industry-standard training methods for stats. You can look up a lot of it online, but you never know what's true and what's bullshit some self-proclaimed expert came up with on the spot."

Ryan turned toward Silvia, who also quickly nodded her head a few times to show that she would be happy to have him.

"Alright, sure. That sounds pretty amazing, actually. I'll be happy to get anything I can. Though in the first place, training physical stats is just so much more straightforward anyway . . ." Ryan sighed, as the three started walking toward the nearby parking lot together. "Like, how the hell am I supposed to train my sociability?"

"I'm glad I don't have to deal with that kind of thing," Yanna pointed out in relief, before actually thinking about Ryan's mostly rhetorical question. "But, I guess you could act more like Silvia?"

Ryan scoffed, shaking his head, "Yeah, sorry, but that's not going to happen. I have, like, five friends. Two of them are here, and one of them is my uncle. Not that I can't make friends, I just don't really care to. I'm happy with how things are. But Silvia is friends with like half the fucking uni at this point; I was shocked she had to introduce herself to the guys at the robotics club."

Silvia just shrugged in response. "I don't hang around the science building that much. I think I've seen Richie around before. I just never spoke to him."

Trying to catch up to the conversation a bit more, Yanna curiously looked at the two of them. "You were at the robotics club?"

"Ah, yeah, do you remember Power Duels? They made their own robots for that, and Modak arranged it so I could join in with Maximus."

"Maximus?"

"Right, sorry," Ryan replied, looking into the Knight Spirit's domain. The Knight didn't seem to be as deep in thought as he was earlier, and seemed to be paying attention to what Ryan was doing. Noticing that he was about to be called out of the domain, Maximus just gave a quick nod, showing that he was ready. A moment later, he appeared on Ryan's hand.

Seeing Yanna, and understanding she was a friend, Maximus slightly bowed forward as a greeting, and so Ryan introduced, "This is Maximus the Knight Spirit."

Yanna leaned forward to take a closer look. "Wow! You're saying it's a Knight? I didn't know spirits like that even existed."

"Apparently they really don't," Silvia pointed out. "Modak said he was looking around the library and he checked out some catalogues of known spirit concepts, and there was nothing related to Knights or anything."

"Interesting . . . I know this girl that works for the Magic Tower that I could ask about it. If anyone would know, it's them, right?"

Surprised, Silvia looked up at her sister. "How'd you meet someone from the Magic Tower?"

"She awakened around the same time I did, so we met at this event for newly awakened people," Yanna explained, looking over at Ryan. "You'll probably get an invitation to one of those in the mail too."

"And a newly awakened girl got a job at the Magic Tower?" Ryan raised a brow. That didn't sound necessarily promising and just another case of nepotism, but if she awakened into a class that was deemed useful by the Magic Tower, she would probably still be able to help Ryan out somehow. "I mean, if you could ask her, that would be great, thank you so much."

"Yeah of course, no worries!" Yanna smiled with a slight huff as she unlocked her car.

The group pulled into the garage of the townhouse, and the sisters' eyes landed on the car parked at the leftmost spot. Silvia turned to Yanna. "Wait, was Dad supposed to come back today?"

"I don't think so. I thought he was supposed to come back on the weekend."

Yanna parked the car, then Silvia stepped out. Ryan got out from the back seat as well, following behind his friends to make his way up the stairs into the spaces above. Hearing that Silvia and Yanna's father was home made him pretty nervous; he had met their mother before, and she was already quite intimidating. At least Ryan knew where the sisters got their energy from. But even so, imagining what their father was like made him nervous.

As they stepped into the living room, Ryan spotted the man in question. Seated on a large armchair was a large figure who then stood up the moment he saw his daughters enter. He opened his arms wide, revealing a large round belly pressing up against a suit's button-up shirt. Gray hair was sprinkled all over the areas of fur that were openly visible.

"Welcome back!" Silvia said with a broad smile on her face, hugging her father. As he rubbed his hand over her back, nearly covering it completely with his palm, that massive man, even larger than Yanna, replied.

"I'm glad to be home, honey," a calm, smooth voice replied, as he let go of Silvia and gave a hug to Yanna as well. Ryan was a bit relieved by how approachable he seemed.

When the man released Yanna, Ryan stepped forward, holding out his hand. "Nice to meet you, Mr. Redhorn. I'm Ryan, a friend of Silvia and Yanna from uni."

With a smile on his face, the man clasped Ryan's hand. He expected him to practically crush his hand, especially considering how much larger the minotaur's hand was than Ryan's, but it was just as gentle as his overall appearance. "It's a pleasure to finally meet you, Ryan. I've heard a lot about you. And please, just call me Dimos."

Yanna soon started walking toward the stairs, then turned around with a hoof on the first step. "We're just grabbing some stuff for Ryan. You know, the booklets I was given about stats training."

Dimos raised his brows, quickly turning back to the human in front of him. "Oh, right! Silvia told me that you awakened, congratulations!"

Ryan laughed nervously. Being congratulated for it always felt a bit awkward, but he appreciated it nonetheless. "Thanks. But yeah, it's a magic class, and I'd like to open up some physical stats that I can train."

"Of course, that is very reasonable. You should try to cover all your bases, especially if you plan on becoming a Dungeoneer," Dimos agreed. "Do you already have plans for your first dungeon trip?"

"Actually, I already went last Friday," Ryan explained, seeing Yanna's expression from the stairway. He guessed that it would be better not to mention that he got pretty hurt.

"I see! I'm glad to see you in good health, then." With a laugh, Dimos patted Ryan's shoulder. Luckily, it was his healthy one.

"Yeah, but it was a bit rougher than I had hoped, so before I go to the next one, I'll train myself up a bit."

"Very smart. Well, I will not hold you up, then." Dimos smiled, slowly turning around to take a seat on his armchair again. He sat back down on his armchair, watching as his daughters and their friend made their way upstairs. But Dimos himself was just nervously picking at his fur, sinking into his seat.

He looked at the note in his hand, and read through it again and again.

"I wish I didn't have to tell her about this . . ." Dimos sighed quietly, looking up at the stairs.

CHAPTER NINETEEN

Wildflower Planting

I t was very nice to meet you, Ryan," Dimos said with a smile as he stood by the door leading down to the basement and garage, and Ryan nodded his head, holding the pamphlets and booklets that Yanna had given him.

"Likewise! I hope you have a good rest of your night," he replied, stepping through the door.

Dimos looked at his eldest daughter. "Drive safe."

"Of course. We'll drop by Moondust and grab some coffee on the way home—do you want anything?" Yanna asked, and Dimos raised a brow.

"Coffee? At this hour?" With a deep sigh and a shake of his head, Dimos slowly turned his head toward Silvia. "But actually, could you maybe stay behind? There is something I would like to talk to you about."

A bit surprised, Silvia looked at her father's expression. He usually didn't pull her aside to talk to her specifically, so it must be something serious. She quickly looked at Ryan.

"Sorry about that. Talk to you tomorrow?"

"Yeah, you got it. Thanks for the help today," Ryan said, quickly giving his friend a hug to say goodbye, and Silvia turned to her sister.

"Can you pick me up a—"

"Caramel frappe, you got it," Yanna replied with a thumbs-up as she made her way down the stairs, followed by Ryan who just gave another quick wave as he stepped down the stairs after Yanna.

"You know what that's about?" he wondered out loud, but Yanna quickly shook her head.

"Nope. Maybe it's about her grades or something? Or someone wanting to buy something that she made. Mom and Dad sort of act as semi-managers for all her art stuff," Yanna explained, unlocking her car. Ryan got in on the passenger side, and it didn't take long until the pair pulled out of the garage.

While driving, Yanna glanced over toward the young man sat next to her. "So, you know which stat you're gonna try to open first?"

After thinking about it for a while, looking down at the booklet on his lap, Ryan just slightly shrugged. "Not totally sure. But I guess I'll go for stamina and agility first. My shoulder's still too bruised up to do any proper strength training. But once I can, I guess I'll also try to go for strength and physicality."

"So the whole deal, huh?" Yanna replied with a laugh. "Well, don't overdo it, though. Especially when it comes to opening new stats, you'll have a pretty rough time. And new stats you open grow slower than your base stats anyway. And level-up improvements don't happen either, so it's even worse."

"I know, I know," Ryan replied with a sigh. It was pretty annoying, but it wasn't the end of the world. Frankly, he would have been able to lead a happy life without awakening. He was happy with his stamina or strength, so anything on top of that was just a bonus. The only issue would come if Ryan continued going to dungeons. He would have to figure out some ways to support Maximus better, because it wouldn't take long until he couldn't do anything against monsters. At least, if he wanted to fight against anything but the lowest level of dungeon monsters.

"What about you? Did you open any other stats?"

Yanna quickly shook her head. "Not yet, no. I've been more focused on training up my main stats."

"That was . . . agility, aura, strength, physicality, stamina, and perception?"

With a surprised scoff, the minotaur looked at Ryan. "You have the Mountain Archer class memorized?"

A little embarrassed, Ryan nodded as he turned his sight away. "I've got most cool classes half memorized. And when you awakened, I had to learn more about your class."

"Awe, how cute," Yanna replied with a grin. "But yeah, that's the ones. Perception is really, really annoying to train up. Seriously, I wish having more main stats meant you'd have more total growth, but it's just . . . it's just more things to train. My training results for my strength training have been really lagging behind, it's pretty annoying . . ."

Ryan looked over at Yanna with a slight smile. "I mean, yeah, but it all balances out. You're still low level, but your stat growth per level has actually been pretty good, right? What was it, around 0.39 total growth per level? That's more than my average."

"Well . . . I guess you're right. But, dude, have you seen the kind of arrows that's normal for Mountain Archers to shoot? They're as thick as your arm. Do you have any idea what kind of draw weight my training bow has?"

"Yeah, but you also only awakened a couple months ago. You're at a pretty good pace, right?"

Yanna stared at Ryan from the corner of her eye. "I don't want to hear that from someone who leveled up twice in a single day."

"Don't blame the player, blame the game."

"You suck."

"You don't mean that," Ryan replied with a grin, looking at the minotaur smugly.

Yanna sighed, shaking her head, "Whatever."

Ryan stepped out onto the surprisingly spacious balcony of this small building with Maximus on his hand, taking in the evening sun with a satisfied smile. It was starting to heat up a little recently, and it was getting right to that wonderful midpoint of being warm enough to spend the day outside to relax in the sun, while not being so hot that you would end up drenching your shirt in sweat. Around this time of year, you also started seeing cold-blooded species out and about more often, making the city just that much busier and more diverse. Compared to what Ryan was used to in his hometown where 90 percent of people were humans, this sight alone was wonderfully exciting.

However, he didn't come out here to people-watch. He came out here to work; he glanced over at the large flat planter that had recently been built here. Runar didn't let him help out, whether it was constructing the planter or filling it with soil. Since Runar was actually pretty interested in plants, he was able to help Ryan out with everything, including preparing mana-rich compost.

Rather, up until now, Ryan hadn't done anything for this yet, besides gathering the original seeds. He let out a light sigh and placed Maximus down on the edge of the planter, then opened the small pouch in his hand. Inside were a number of wild-flower seeds, some of which were made of copper, at different stages of rust and decay.

Frankly, he didn't even know if these seeds would end up sprouting, but Runar told him to just give it a shot. Even the metallic seeds. At the end of the day, they were items dropped from a dungeon, and the only thing left from the Abandoned Copper Foundry. After the dungeon had been closed, the mana started to dissipate and the structure returned to its former, empty state. And considering that item drops were the only things from a dungeon that could be taken out of it, Ryan felt like he had to give it a try. Especially since these seeds were basically worthless.

Very rarely, dungeon monsters could produce items that were useful or rare, but these were really just seeds with a surprising amount of mana. Though, surprising considering their size, nothing extraordinary at the end of the day. He showed them to Aurora when he went to the Awakened Center for his checkup, but she said they were only worth a few Gild at most.

So, Ryan did the only thing he could do now; sprinkling them over the soil. He grabbed the small gardening shovel shoved into the bucket next to the planter, and covered the seeds in a thin layer of soil-and-compost mixture. Ryan then grabbed the watering can, also conveniently prepared by Runar for him, to quickly water the seeds, and then . . . just stood there. Staring at wet dirt. Sure, plants with higher mana concentration tended to grow faster, but not to the point where he would be able to see them grow in front of his eyes.

Ryan clapped his hands together, rubbing the small bits of soil off them, nodding, satisfied. "Well. I think we deserve a break, don't you?" he asked, looking at the Knight who had watched the whole ordeal curiously.

Maximus replied with a nod, before showing a time-out sign with his hands.

Laughing slightly, Ryan reached out to Maximus as the latter stepped back into the domain. Usually, while at home, Maximus was outside a fair amount. Even when Ryan was working sometimes, he would stay upstairs in the flat and do his own thing, just enjoying having a body. But when he felt like taking a break in the domain, he would show Ryan the time-out sign, and he would make it happen. Ryan needed to be close enough to physically pick Maximus up for him to move into the domain, after all.

Ready to grab himself a drink from the café, Ryan went back inside and made his way downstairs, but as he stepped out from the back behind the counter, Runar snapped his head toward him.

"Oh gods, finally! My savior! I need you to take over!" he yelled out. "Just for like ten minutes!"

With a slight sigh, Ryan nodded his head. "Just hire more people, you cheap bastard."

"It's hard to find good employees! I'm already wasting money on one with a massive attitude."

"Well, if you think paying yourself is a waste of money, you don't have to." Ryan turned and entered the back room to quickly wash his hands, getting rid of the rest of the soil. He grabbed his apron and the bandana he usually wore to keep his hair up during work, and stepped back out behind the counter as he finished tying it up.

"Thanks, you're a lifesaver. Got an urgent call I've put on hold for like an hour," Runar explained, quickly taking out his phone and dialing a number.

Ryan waved him off and sighed, "Then just go and take care of it, I'll be fine. Take your time."

Without further ado, Runar ran off, leaving Ryan in charge. Luckily there wasn't anyone at the counter just yet, so he had the time to properly get ready and clean up after some of the mess that Runar left behind.

As he was wiping the counter clean, the door opened up and a customer came slithering in. A large black-scaled lamia. He was wearing a short-sleeved shirt that displayed the intricate white-ink tattoos all over his dark brown skin.

"Welcome! How can I help you?" Ryan asked, quickly putting on his customer-service smile.

"Could I have an iced latte? Oat milk, please," the lamia replied, placing his hands onto the counter with a slight smile on his face.

"Yeah, of course, just a minute," Ryan replied, quickly getting to work. He scooped up some ground coffee into a sieve and twisted it into the espresso machine. As he waited for the water to heat up, Ryan pulled open the ice drawer and filled the cup. But while he was moving around, the incessant stare of the customer was digging into his skin. Lamias couldn't even blink, so Ryan felt like every tiny motion of his was being surveyed.

As the feeling kept creeping up on him, something else popped into Ryan's mind. "Hold on, don't I know you from somewhere?" he asked with a slightly curious expression. "Do you go to NRU?"

The lamia perked up and quickly nodded his head. "Yes, I do! It was Ryan, right?"

"Yeah, that's me. And you were . . . something with a *C*?" Ryan replied, already feeling awkward about not remembering his name. He had a pretty unique appearance, so it was surprising Ryan hadn't remembered him right when he entered in the first place.

"Christopher, yes. With a *C*."

"Sorry about that, man. I'm really bad with names," Ryan replied, as he got the espresso ready. He turned his head back to Christopher with a raised brow. "Love the tattoos, by the way."

Raising his brow, Christopher smiled, this time a bit broader than before. The corners of his mouth almost stretched up to his ears, even though it was just a light grin. "Thank you. They're pretty special to me," he explained, the bass of his voice pushing itself deep into Ryan's head. "Do you have any tattoos of your own?"

Ryan quickly shook his head. "Nothing yet. I just moved here from this super small town, and my mom isn't the biggest fan of tattoos anyway, so I figured I'd just wait until I moved out. Not like they're cheap either, right?"

As Ryan poured the espresso over the ice in the cup, Christopher nodded his head. "I was quite lucky. My cousin is a tattoo artist, so I got a discount."

"Got any tips for a tattoo newbie, then?" Ryan stirred the cup around and filled the rest with chilled oat milk.

Christopher seemed to think for a while, and quickly came up with something. "Just make sure to be aware of the permanence. The choices we make can't always be too easily undone."

Ryan laughed and nodded. "Yeah, you're sure right about. So, how you paying?"

After Christopher held up his phone, Ryan quickly set up the transaction. The lamia smiled as he tapped his phone against the terminal, picking up his drink.

"Very nice to meet you, Ryan. I've heard a lot about you around school."

". . . Yeah, that sounds about right. But for sure, great to meet you. I'll try to remember your name until next time, Christopher with a *C*."

"I hope you do," Christopher replied, quickly turning around. He slithered back to the door, and soon made his way outside. Ryan pulled the payment terminal back over toward himself, looking at the screen. The payment earlier went through without issue, but now the screen was showing some display errors. The confirmation screen was overlaying the default logos that were there when the terminal wasn't in use.

"Dammit, not again . . ." With a click of his tongue, Ryan shook the terminal. He stopped for a few moments, and then held his hand out toward the side of the counter that was hidden by some signs. Maximus stepped out of his domain. "Just watch the place real quick. I'll be right back."

The small knight nodded his head, and Ryan quickly made his way to the back of the store. He only had to go to Runar anyway; he apparently had a replacement terminal somewhere, so Maximus was just there as a security system while Ryan was gone for a minute.

He rushed up the stairs into the flat, and made his way to Runar's office. He was about to knock on the door, but it was slightly ajar, and Runar's voice came flowing out.

". . . this Saturday? Seriously? It's way too soon, I can't just—" he started, stopping only as he was interrupted. "I've got my nephew here, man. I don't want him to get involved in this. At least give me some more time to talk to him about some things . . . Wait, are you joking right now? How do you expect me to . . . okay, fine, that does change things slightly, I guess . . . but still, don't drop things like this on me without warning anymore. I don't care that I—Okay, whatever. I'll call you back later to talk more about this, I—Yes I'm busy, I've got a fucking store to run. Okay. Bye."

As the call ended, Runar let out a deep, loud groan. Footsteps approached the door, and Ryan felt his heart skip a beat. He pushed the door open. "Yo, Runar, the terminal is acting up again."

Taken aback, Runar caught the door. "Oh, right, uhm . . . I'll grab the other one. I thought I fixed this thing . . ." With a click of his tongue, Runar grabbed the terminal from Ryan, who swiftly turned back around.

"I-I'll head back down," Ryan stuttered out, already on his way back downstairs. He was pretty sure that Runar didn't notice how he was acting, but either way, that really wasn't important. What exactly was Runar trying not to involve him in? And what exactly was going to happen on Saturday?

What the hell was Runar involved in?

CHAPTER TWENTY

Putting It Together

Modak tiredly pulled open the flat door.

"Morning," he yawned, giving Silvia a hug. "How're you doin'?"

"I'm . . . okay," the elf replied, almost meekly. A bit concerned, Modak looked at her face more closely as he let her into the flat. Her eyes were puffy and red, and she wasn't wearing any sort of makeup even though he hadn't seen Silvia leave her house without winged eyeliner since he met her.

"You sure?" Modak questioned. The two were walking to his room, and Silvia kept looking down at the ground.

"I . . . honestly, no? Like, I'm really not doing that great . . ." she explained, picking at her cuticles as she spoke. "There's some stuff going on, and it's really just messing with me a lot."

"Oh . . . I'm sorry. Do you want to talk about it?" As he offered this, Modak closed the door to his bedroom behind him, while Silvia sat down on the chair in front of his desk. She slowly shook her head.

"Not really? At some point, probably, but right now I'm just really . . . confused? I did talk a ton to my dad about it, though, so it's not like I'm dealing with this completely on my own," Silvia explained. "To be honest, I wouldn't even know where to start . . . I'd need to give you like twelve years' worth of context first."

Modak briefly touched Silvia's shoulder in encouragement as he sat down on the stool next to her. "I'm always ready to listen, but only when you're ready."

Silvia smiled lightly, feeling the support of her friend give her strength. "Thank you. Seriously."

After the moment passed, both Modak and Silvia felt like it was better to move on to what Silvia was here for in the first place. The orc quickly looked at the table. "Okay, so. I've been working on this for you, like you asked."

"Oh, awesome! How do I use it?" Silvia replied, looking closer at the cassette recorder on the table. Modak picked it up and turned it around to show her the parts she needed to know about.

"It's pretty basic, really. So, this old recorder only had an XLR port for microphones and stuff, so I took that out and replaced it with a 3.5-milimeter jack, so you just need to plug in your phone, play whatever you want, and press the record button. But since there was space, I actually added a small audio splitter, so you can plug in your headphones and hear what you're actually putting on there as well," Modak explained, pointing at the two small audio ports at the side.

Excitedly, Silvia looked at the recorder. "Cute! Do you think you can—"

"The screws are already loosened, you just need to pull the covers off," Modak interrupted, and a grin quickly formed on Silvia's face as she pulled apart the tape recorder, exposing the electronic innards. She leaned down to her bag and pulled out a few things; first, some sandpaper. Without another word, she started roughening up the smooth plastic surface.

"You need help with that?" Modak asked with a raised brow, and Silvia quickly shook her head.

"No thanks! Probably won't take too long. I just need to roughen it up so the paint will stick."

"You got an idea what you'll paint it?"

"Hmm . . . I want to give it this sort of sleek, vibey retro look, like, beige with colored lines on one side. I thought it'd be pretty cute like that! I mean, cuter than this boring dark gray."

Modak thought about it for a moment, trying to imagine it. "That does sound pretty neat . . . Do you mind if I continue working on something else?"

Silvia scoffed, "What, did you think I want you to just watch me paint this the whole time? I know you've got plenty of projects on your own."

"Yeah, kind of. I'm working on this one thing right now that's a little annoying to figure out," Modak started, pulling over a small box from the corner of his desk. "You've been asking me to help you out with a lot of this retro cassette stuff, so I've been thinking about it a lot. Do you know how cassettes work?"

Silvia thought about it for a moment, then answered a bit hesitantly, "They're like magnetic tapes, right?"

"Yes, exactly. Basically, when you record onto a tape, the sound is placed onto that side of the tape through some superlight electrical discharge to magnetize it. And then when you play that tape, the magnetic imprint is read and turned back into the electrical signals that we can then turn into sound."

"Right, right . . ."

"But these days, one of the most effective ways we store data is through crystalized transistors that work with mana instead of electricity. Like, there's still plenty of use cases and benefits to electrical transistors . . . they're a bit less prone to mistakes because mana-based memory can be damaged by too much ambient mana surprisingly easily, so right now we mostly use mana-based memory in bigger data farms or computers where we can shield it from ambient mana a bit more."

Silvia followed along with Modak's excited explanation, trying to see where he was going. "So . . . how exactly is that related to tapes?"

Modak smiled broadly, continuing, "I'm getting to that! So, mana-based memory is so effective because the flow of mana is a lot more precise, and it's a lot easier to read and write a lot of data at high speeds at a relatively low energy cost. Okay, now, back in the time of earlier computers and data carriers that worked with magnetic tapes, there were some attempts to store data on mana-based tapes. But the issue with that was that, back then, we didn't know the most effective crystalline structures to retain exact mana patterns, nor did we know how to block out ambient mana from getting to the tapes, so the cost was far too high for the benefit."

Finally, Silvia understood what Modak was trying to do. "You're going to make mana cassettes?" she asked with a curious expression, her hands having stopped roughening up the piece of plastic she was holding as she looked over at the objects laid out in front of Modak.

With an almost smug expression, the orc nodded his head. "Yup!"

"Any reason, or just for fun?"

Modak thought about it for a moment, but in the end just shrugged. "Mostly for fun, but I was talking to my magic engineering professor about it, and he suggested I write a small paper about it . . . He said if it turns out well, he could help me get it published, and that's going to look pretty damn well on applications."

"Oh shit, yeah! That sounds like an amazing opportunity! You should do that, for sure!"

Modak nodded, still smiling. "I'll try, yeah, but I need to get it to work first. So, after some massive trial and error, I found the right sort of crystal tape that I needed. It's this really specific thing that's super rarely used in like a handful of magic engineering applications, but it looks like it will work perfectly for what I need. But here comes the thing that I'm struggling with. On regular magnetic tape, the electrical current can be used directly to magnetize the tape, but here, I need to turn the electrical current into a magical one, and then when I read the data on the crystal tape, I need to turn it back into an electrical current that can actually be turned back into sound—otherwise it's not going to be usable at all."

"So what did you do to make that happen?" Silvia asked, looking at Modak's expression as he rambled on and on. He got like this sometimes, but Silvia didn't mind. Rather, the way that Modak was explaining it was actually pretty interesting, even though magic engineering wasn't a topic she was particularly interested in.

"So, yesterday, while we were at the robotics club, Richie mentioned something about an energy converter that's inside of his robot, right? And of course, converting mana to electricity and back isn't anything new, but I felt like the way that the energy converter seemed to work was pretty unique, so I looked it up online, and in one of the older models, the energy in question is turned into mana in high-frequency bursts, and is then transformed into whatever other energy is needed. In the new method, it's just a more constant stream because that's more useful for what they need, but for me, those high-frequency bursts are exactly what I need."

Nodding her head as if she really understood the exact details of what Modak was actually talking about, Silvia tried to understand. "So you're using that high-frequency mana stuff to actually put all the data onto the crystal tape?"

Modak quickly nodded. "Exactly! But it's really, really hard to fine-tune to actually make this something that's worth it. Like, if it all works, then we'll have a cassette tape that can store . . . three, maybe three and a half hours of audio? And that's using the same tape length as for a thirty-minute magnetic version. Not to mention, magnetic tapes degrade after like twenty years, but these will last a lot longer. Not necessarily indefinitely, but pretty long."

". . . Do you think, once you've got it all figured out, you could make me some?" Silvia asked curiously, and Modak immediately nodded his head.

"Obviously, why do you think I wanted to even do this? You'll have to use a new cassette player and recorder, though. Not like I'll be figuring this all out today anyway, though."

"Seriously, now I get why the professors are just all over you." Silvia smiled broadly, as Modak looked at his friend with some relief. Of course, she managed to pick herself up perfectly fine, but if he managed to help her cheer up a bit, Modak was more than relieved.

Ryan clicked the last piece into place, a steady frown glued to his brow. The armor that he was staring at was dull and boring. The form felt weird, the pieces too light, and the stupid expression on the face of the elven spearman almost ruined the whole thing.

". . . You ruined model building for me, you know?" Ryan groaned loudly, leaning back in his chair as he rubbed his eyes. He peeked out from behind his fingers at Maximus, who was seated on a small stack of books in front of Ryan's computer monitor. Right next to him was the mouse that he was using to scroll down the page where he was currently reading a comic that Ryan recommended to him.

A bit confused, the knight turned toward Ryan and tilted his head to the side.

"No, you're right, you didn't do anything. There's nothing wrong with the model either. I think I'm just still feeling weird about the whole Runar situation," he pointed out, and Maximus quickly moved his hand away from the scroll wheel to pay more attention to what Ryan was saying.

"And seriously, you don't know anything at all? You remember nothing from before I woke you up?" Ryan asked, but Maximus quickly shook his head. It had taken a pretty long time of going through dozens of "yes or no" questions, but as it turned out, Maximus knew maybe less than Ryan did about all of this.

Whether it was some kind of specific spirit amnesia or because he never knew anything to begin with, Maximus had no clue what was going on. He knew how to use his skills and had a very clear idea about what his values as a knight were, but basically nothing beyond that. Not if there were other spirits like him, nor why he was in that box with his father's stuff.

Though, it was probably wrong to say that he knew "nothing"; he did know that he had some kind of history with Gaia, but not how deep that history went. From what Ryan gathered, and he didn't ask too much about it as he didn't want to pry, they once were close friends. But since Maximus couldn't say when exactly that "once" was, that was a dead end as well. Maybe Gaia would know some more things once Ryan found her other two fragments.

At least there was a trace there. While he didn't have another moment like when he recognized there was something in the Abandoned Copper Foundry dungeon, he could guarantee one thing; Gaia's entire being was within this city.

Though he was only able to tell him that since yesterday. When Ryan had spotted him seated in the domain in contemplation, Maximus was in the middle of realizing that and let Ryan know afterward.

With a long sigh, Ryan leaned his chin onto his desk. "Like . . . and this could definitely just be me not wanting my uncle to be involved in some crime shit, but my gut tells me that it's nothing too bad. I mean, I'm freaking out about it, obviously, but I'm not freaking out as much as I should be . . . right? But at the same time . . . I just can't believe that he's involved in anything bad," he explained, as Maximus listened to him intently.

Ryan looked at the knight's expression, though it was really just the same unchanging helmet. "Am I putting too much faith into my raised intuition stat? It's not like it's a massive difference."

But to Ryan's surprise, Maximus also shook his head.

"Hm? Wait, do you also think it's nothing bad?"

Maximus nodded.

". . . Do you have some sort of secret knight's intuition that tells you that?"

After hesitating for a moment, Maximus just pressed his palm onto the center of his chest. Ryan sort of understood what he was trying to get at.

"You think he's a good person?"

Immediately, the knight nodded his head once more, but Ryan just sighed, "I really do hope you're right. I mean . . . we might figure something out soon?

I mean, during that call, he did say that he wants to talk to me about some things first. I guess I should trust in him a bit more?"

Feeling a sense of relief, Ryan looked back at the model that he had just built, smiling lightly. "Alright, let's get this shitty thing taken apart. I might as well repaint it to make it look a bit nicer," he said loudly, reinvigorated with a new sense of energy, as Maximus turned back toward his comic.

As Ryan looked at the model, he did get an idea, however. According to the booklets that Yanna gave him, the main way to train your stats was to push the limits of what you were currently capable of. Frankly, ever since he got his class, he hadn't spent too much time doing things with his hands besides building this model in front of him that he had put off, as well as building Maximus himself.

His palm was practically perfectly healed at this point too, so he didn't have to worry about hurting himself either. Ryan pulled out his phone, not wanting to disturb Maximus's reading time by pulling it up on the computer, and started up a stopwatch. After taking a deep breath to mentally prepare himself, Ryan quickly got started.

He grabbed the model and immediately started pulling it apart; not violently, of course, but with as much precision as he could. It took him a little while to get used to it, but before long, he was moving at a speed that he could barely recognize from himself. He had surprised himself when he'd worked on Maximus's new arm, but this was something completely, wholly different.

Ryan continued, and in the end, it didn't actually take him all too long to finish taking the model apart. It didn't have all that many pieces after all, at least compared to Maximus. Ryan looked at the stopwatch. Five minutes. That wasn't bad at all. But this wasn't the end yet; he still had to paint them.

After priming the pieces with their new base color, he was going to go in with some finer brushes to paint in details. That was also something that dexterity was supposed to excel at, so he still had plenty of chances. Not to mention . . . Ryan still had plenty of money saved up. He could buy dozens of models if he wanted to, which he did.

"Guess I'll be a bit busy." Ryan grinned broadly, standing up from his chair to grab his spray-on primer.

CHAPTER TWENTY-ONE

Trapped

[Your Dexterity has increased by 0.01]

The window popped up in front of Ryan as he was in the middle of pushing the head of a hippogriff onto its body. Excited to have increased his dexterity over the next threshold again, he placed the animal model onto the table.

In the past few days, by spending hours and hours every day building models, he managed to increase his dexterity by a total of 0.03. Of course, it was only a little more than the lower end of how much it could increase through a level-up, but for the amount of time he spent to get to this, it was an incredible growth as far as Ryan was concerned.

"Hell yeah." Ryan grinned as he stood up, stretching to get the stiffness out of his back and shoulders. His right shoulder was overall feeling fine, but he still felt some pain when he moved it around too much.

With a slight whistle, he picked up the finished hippogriff model and placed it onto his shelf with the others. ". . . I might need to make more space. Or put some away . . ." he muttered. The whole wall in front of him was filled with different kinds of models; historical warriors, famous mages, some animals, and even a few dungeon monsters. The one that he had most fun building was actually the grave worm. They were a pretty bothersome type of worm that was known to thrive in the middle of battlefields where numerous people had died, feeding on their corpses. These days, they were mostly a pest that could be found in graveyards. They weren't really that big of an issue, but considering they could grow to be up to half a meter long and as thick as a thumb, they were certainly not a pretty sight.

Apparently they were actually a type of maggot that either lost the necessity or ability to move on to the next stage of their life cycle. That being the case, Ryan remembered the stories about this graveyard that turned into a dungeon some twenty or so years ago, where massive grave worms were one of the more common monsters.

And that was the model that Ryan was looking at now; a grave worm wrapping around a skeletal hand, all at a 1:1 scale. It maybe wasn't the most complex model to build, but it was definitely a unique final product.

With a satisfied expression, Ryan looked down at his phone to check the time. "Come on, Maximus, we need to head out."

The small knight, sitting on top of Ryan's desk, quickly nodded his head. He stood up and walked to the edge of the desk, where Ryan was waiting to let him into the domain.

You ready for the battles later? he asked inwardly, and Maximus stood in the center of his domain, showing him a thumbs-up. He'd been picking up some weird habits from the comics he'd been reading lately. And to think he didn't even know what a fist bump was a week ago.

Ryan threw his bag over his shoulder and quickly left his room, making his way through the flat's main entrance. There were two different stairways, one leading right into the café, and another leading to the alley behind the building. When the café was busy, he preferred going out through the back. Ryan has been trying his best to avoid Runar as much as he could as well.

He stepped out of the door and pulled it shut behind him, then pushed against it briefly to make sure it was locked before making his way down the alley. But as he turned around the corner, walking away from Café Runic's main entrance, he heard someone call out to him.

"Mr. Aglecard, one moment, please!" With a voice that already made the hairs on Ryan's neck stand up, Simon Grand, the representative from Bluesky that just wouldn't leave him alone, came up to him.

Trying to act like he neither heard nor saw that stuck-up high elf, Ryan took out his headphones and pulled them over his head, picking up the pace a bit. However, it didn't seem to take a lot of effort for Simon to catch up on him.

"Mr. Aglecard," Simon said once more, with that annoyingly fake smile on his face, now having cut Ryan off.

"Fucking—Can you stop following me around already?" Ryan groaned loudly, stepping past Simon to continue on his way to the subway.

With a laugh, Simon quickly caught up to him again, simply walking next to him. "We have been struggling to contact you to show you further offers. You must understand that—"

"Okay, get it in your fucking thick ass skull already. I am not interested in selling my fucking class! I've told you like a dozen times, and I've already complained about you at the Awakened Center. What will it take to get you to finally leave me alone?" Ryan asked, at the end of his rope. This was probably the third time that Simon was waiting for him to leave the building so that he could talk about another one of his "offers," but no matter what, he just wouldn't listen.

The corners of Simon's mouth twitched slightly, though he was trying to keep up his smile. "There is no need for that kind of language. Bluesky Industries has a long history with the Aglecard family—"

"Oh my gods, I'm not a member of that stupid 'Aglecard' family! I just happen to have the same last name! I grew up in fucking Maidsbury, dude. You somehow managed to find out where I live, but you don't even know that?" Ryan barked at Simon and picked up the pace, rushing down the stairs into the subway station.

". . . You . . . just happen to share the same name?" Simon's voice clung to Ryan's ears, as though he was standing right next to him. "That certainly does make things a bit easier."

Ryan felt a tug on his arm as a hand tightened around his wrist. Ryan turned around confused, and was almost startled at Simon's sudden change in expression. As if he was angry that Ryan had been wasting his time, he suddenly lost any will to be cordial with him. Simon quickly pulled Ryan a bit closer and placed his other hand onto his right shoulder. He buried his fingers inside the not-yet-healed wound on his shoulder, and Ryan felt his whole body cramp in response.

"What the—" Ryan let out, or at least he thought so. But even though he opened his mouth, no sound left his throat. As he looked around, it seemed as though the whole world, practically everything beside himself and Simon, had been desaturated and robbed of its color. Meanwhile, despite what was happening to Ryan right now, nobody seemed to notice.

People in this city stared when you wore a slightly weird jacket; there was no way they wouldn't even glance over here when something like this was going on.

"Now listen to me. I think there have been some miscommunication. Bluesky wants the Spirit Keeper class. And it is in your best interest to sell it to us. We will compensate you greatly, and you will never have to work another day in your life." Simon's voice was eerie and sounded like someone was scratching their nails on a chalkboard. Whatever professionalism he had before was gone like it never existed in the first place. While Ryan struggled to pull himself out of Simon's grasp, the elf continued, "We will simply be able to make much, much better use of that class than you ever could. We have the resources to actually figure out the specifics of what it can do, and what the limits of its application are. Unique classes can bring society forward by years at a time. And you would really rob the people of this world of that chance for what? Some measly pride?"

Ryan didn't want to listen anymore. He ground his teeth together, angry at the words that this ridiculous guy was saying. He heard about some bad rumors about the way that class-trading was handled and about Bluesky as a whole, but he never expected it to be this bad. However, if they wanted to mess with Ryan, they should have at least brought a physical class.

And just when Simon's grip tightened, wisps of red light started flowing out from Ryan's face as Maximus jumped out of his domain. With a perfect punch to the nose, the elf flinched, loosening his grip on Ryan's wrist and shoulder, letting him break free. He immediately grabbed Simon's hand and pushed his middle finger backward, putting as much weight behind it as he could. As the taken-aback elf pulled his shoulder back to avoid his finger being broken—blood pouring down over his lips—Ryan swept away Simon's legs and violently kicked him away. Simon hit the stairs behind him and was left staggering for a while, clearly not having expected anything like this at all.

Without a moment's hesitation, Ryan turned around and ran down to the subway platform. He had heard the train arriving just now, so he had to hurry; he managed to rush into the train just as the doors were closing, and by the time Simon got up from the ground, it pulled out of the station.

Letting out a relieved sigh, Ryan clicked his tongue, pulling Maximus back into the domain. "Fucking psychos . . . he's an Arcane Trapper?" he muttered to himself while pulling out his phone. Without a moment's hesitation, Ryan called Aurora.

"Hey, hey~!" Silvia said with a slight wave as she stepped into the robotics clubroom, where the club's members were setting up for the test runs. Modak was standing near the door, just watching them. The orc turned around and quickly greeted his friend.

"Yo, how're you doing?"

"I'm alright, you?" Silvia replied, quickly glancing around the room, but Modak just sighed loudly.

"Ryan's not here yet."

"Huh? Seriously? He's usually pretty good at being on time."

"I know. I already texted him, but he hasn't replied yet. You think something happened?" With concern written on his face, Modak looked down at his phone.

But Silvia just scoffed and shook her head. "Ryan probably just got a bit lost in model building. He sent me a picture of the pile of boxes that were stacking up in his room; he used up that reward money really damn well."

Overhearing the conversation as he walked around the room while setting up, Richie looked over at the two friends. "Reward money? What reward money?"

Silvia glanced over at Modak, unsure if she should say it, but Modak just shrugged at her. "He didn't seem to care if people knew."

"I guess so," Silvia replied, and turned back toward the curious gnome walking up to her. "Ryan closed down a dungeon."

". . . What? Isn't that a really complicated process? Are you serious? How did he manage that?" Taken aback, Richie was practically stunned in confusion, but Modak quickly explained.

"He didn't fully close it himself. He found and destroyed the dungeon heart and then called the DMB right after. Because he called so quickly and showed them how to get to the core room, they were able to close it permanently, so he got a reward."

Richie thought about it for a moment, before seemingly remembering something, "Was it that factory in Copperbeach? That's the only dungeon I remember being recently."

"That's the one." Stepping through the door with some heavy breaths, Ryan responded to Richie's question.

"Well, good job, and congratulations. Helping close a dungeon so soon after awakening? Doubt that happens all too often." Richie looked at Ryan, clearly impressed. ". . . Do you mind if we mention that tomorrow? Like, tell people that the spirit our Duelists fought belongs to the one that helped close the dungeon?"

Ryan just shrugged. He was exhausted from the way here. "I don't care, man, do whatever you want. But, just to make it clear, I don't 'own' Maximus; he's an individual and my friend that chose to trust me with his safety."

"Ah, sorry . . . Yeah of course," Richie nervously responded. "I didn't mean it like . . ."

"All good." Ryan stopped Richie with a shake of his head. "Let's just get ready for the Duels, alright?"

"Of course!" Quickly, as if trying to run away from this conversation, Richie turned around to get back over to where the other club members were setting up. Ryan walked up to Silvia and Modak, who were both looking at him with concern.

"You alright?" Modak asked, noting the annoyed expression on his friend's face from the moment he walked into the room. And just a moment later, it became clear just how annoyed he really was.

With a click of his tongue, Ryan shook his head. "No, I'm not alright at all. You know that fucking asshole Bluesky dude? He tried to fucking threaten me and used some trapping skills on me."

"What?" Silvia let out, confused. "What do you mean, he used trapping skills?"

"He's a fucking Arcane Trapper, or at least he's got similar skills. I watched an interview with one last year, and it was exactly how he described it."

"Are you okay? Did he hurt you?" Modak nervously looked his friend up and down. "Should we call someone? The police?"

"The police wouldn't do shit anyway." Ryan crossed his arms, annoyed. "I have no proof at all beyond my word, but I did call the person in charge of me at the Awakened Center. She said she'd look into what she can do or whatever, but I'm just really pissed off right now. That fucker pushed his fingers into my shoulder, right into my wound, on purpose."

Silvia shuddered. "That crappy little—" she stopped herself, getting more and more worked up over the information. "Are you sure you're okay? Do you want to call today off?"

"Oh, I absolutely refuse to call this off. I actually need to let off some steam. Plus, it's probably going to help Maximus and me get some experience. The faster I'm at level 10, the faster those guys will permanently leave me alone," Ryan groaned, turning toward Richie and the other club members. "Yo, Richie, when can we get started?"

The gnome turned around and looked at the watch on his wrist. "Basically now? We're still waiting for someone, but she said she's on her way, so we're just pushing her back in the duel order."

"Right, so how's this whole thing gonna work anyway?" Ryan looked around the room at the setup. All the desks had been pushed fully against the walls to make as much as space as possible, and three square areas had been marked off on the ground with tape, each with a monitor right next to it.

"Basically, everyone fights against everyone once. We want to get as much actual duel data as possible. Three duels will happen at once, and there's a bit of time to check on the condition of the Duelist after each round and duel. Every duel is three rounds. Not like a first-to-two thing, just three blanket rounds to get the data we need," Richie explained, pointing over at one of the screens near the door that was just being set up. "That's the duel order, you can check it out if you want. There's twelve of us total, including you, so everything will take pretty long. We're trying to streamline the whole thing as much as we can."

Ryan quickly made his way over toward the screen, looking the schedule over. His first duel was one of the first three, and it was against a guy called Kit and his Duelist, Lightspeed.

CHAPTER TWENTY-TWO

Lightspeed

Ryan looked around the room, stepping up to "Arena 3," though it was really just a square sectioned off with tape. The monitor right next to it already read the names of the two Duelists; Maximus and Lightspeed.

Walking up to the person he figured to be his opponent, Ryan stretched out his hand. "You Kit? Nice to meet you, I'm Ryan."

A pair of horizontal pupils stared at him as the minogid in front of Ryan seemed to look him up and down a few times. The goat-man slowly stretched his hand out to Ryan. "Likewise. Ready?" he asked. Ryan looked to the side a bit awkwardly, glancing at the Duelist already waiting to get started. Kit didn't seem to be a massive conversationalist, so it was probably better to just start, as he suggested.

"Yeah, sure, let's do it. Whatever."

With a grumbled sigh, Ryan walked to the other side of the makeshift arena. As he was walking, red wisps flowed out of his pant legs and from under his shirt, forming Maximus's body. Over the past few days, the two of them had practiced the exact conditions for stepping in and out of the domain, so that Maximus could leave more freely. That totally saved his ass with Simon earlier.

Kit seemed to stare at Maximus for a few moments. He had some kind of podium set up in front of him with what seemed to be a keyboard and a tablet propped up on it. That was probably how he was going to control Lightspeed.

Similarly, there was one set up right in front of Ryan, with a tablet provided by Richie. There were just two buttons on the screen. One for the Knight's Attack skill, and one for the Knight's Guard skill. Since all the Duelists had their own gimmicks, Ryan and Richie decided that it would only be fair if Maximus was allowed to use skills as well, but since the strength and resistance boosts that came from this would change the point calculations, Ryan would need to press those buttons whenever either of those skills was active so that the data could continue being tracked properly.

Of course, since Maximus was currently using the Crusader arm instead of the base Knight arm, Ryan also let Richie know about the changed stats beforehand.

"Max," Ryan said, and the knight slowly turned around toward him. He nodded his head, showing that he was good to go. Seeing that the first three duels were good to go, Richie started the countdowns with a snap of his finger.

Looking at the countdown, Ryan took off his jacket and threw it over a chair, activating his Spirit Link skill. A thin thread formed between him and Maximus, and the two got ready. They'd have ten minutes, so depending on how quickly this and the next round ended, the skill would stay active for the first two rounds, but would be inactive for the third. Because of the breaks between every duel while other people were going, Ryan should be able to activate the skill in that same way at the start of every new duel.

Ryan cracked his knuckles, and Maximus did the same, though his gloved hand didn't make the same sounds, of course.

And then, the countdown hit zero, and the first round started. The moment this happened, Lightspeed closed the distance between itself and Maximus. Barely able to react, Maximus raised his arms up defensively as a punch came in. Ryan glanced over at the "health" scores on the monitor.

Lightspeed - 100 | Maximus - 97

It wasn't a strong attack, but the issue was the speed. Ryan clicked his tongue, watching as Lightspeed quickly moved around Maximus's body. Pulling back his arm to help prompt Maximus to move into the correct position, Ryan could feel something from Maximus. He was going to activate his guard skill. Ryan would have suggested this as well, so he was quite glad.

From the first seconds of the duel, it was clear how Lightspeed would fight. With many fast attacks. Most of the small robot's weight was in its legs, and its design seemed to be something of a fusion between a rabbit and a frog.

Ryan reached out to the tablet when Maximus's skill activated and pressed the button to mark it for the score calculations. Meanwhile, the knight's body was being enveloped in a thin red aura that pressed tightly against the plates of his armor.

The next attack came in; a quick jab. Ryan threw back his elbow to retaliate, but Lightspeed already moved around. The robot was jumping up and down slightly, positioning itself and moving like a boxer would. Ryan glanced over at the other side of the arena; one of Kit's hands was on the keyboard while the other was practically glued to the tablet, moving around rapidly.

It didn't take long until Lightspeed moved in again; jab after jab, while Maximus and Ryan could do nothing but block.

"Isn't he just being a sandbag right now?" Silvia whispered to Modak, trying not to distract Ryan or any of the club members. Modak slowly nodded his head in response.

"Yeah, kind of . . . But I guess they can't deal with that speed? I mean, Maximus doesn't even have the agility stat. Speed really isn't his forte."

"Then what's he supposed to do?"

"Well . . . something like that, I guess." Modak looked over at Maximus with a slight laugh. During one of the attacks, he had managed to hold on to Lightspeed. Ryan was actually a bit disappointed; Lightspeed was fast, but its movement was insanely straightforward. It almost felt like some kind of trap; but no, Maximus was able to grab onto Lightspeed's arm, and the robot wasn't able to escape.

It was fast, but not strong; during the flurry of attacks that it threw at Maximus after he activated his Knight's Guard skill, the Maximus's health only dropped by another twenty points. As he held on to Lightspeed, who was continuing to throw jabs at the knight's head and body, Ryan pulled back his arm as Maximus copied his movements.

With a swift and targeted punch, Maximus punched Lightspeed's torso. Since most of the focus seemed to have been put on speed, the robot very quickly received a lot of damage from the attacks, and had no hope of escaping. Maximus was strong; he had the strength of a grown man in that small body of his. And while these magically engineered robots were also particularly powerful, they were still weaker than Maximus.

And so, the battle ended with a couple more hits.

Lightspeed - 0 | Maximus - 59

Once Lightspeed's points reached zero, Maximus immediately let go and stepped back. He gave Lightspeed a quick nod before returning to Ryan's side.

Modak and Silvia came up to Ryan. "Congrats! That went pretty well!" the elf said excitedly, patting Ryan on the back.

"I guess," Ryan replied, frowning lightly as he looked at Kit, who was currently picking up Lightspeed to inspect the robot's body. A bit annoyed, Ryan walked toward Kit. "Is this a good way to get data for you? By underestimating us?"

The minogid turned toward Ryan and just looked up at him with a blank stare. "I did not underestimate you."

"Then why didn't you use Lightspeed's 'gimmick'?"

Kit looked up at Ryan silently, as if he was trying to think about how to best respond, but Silvia seemed confused and spoke up, "What do you mean? Isn't the gimmick its speed?"

"No way." Ryan shook his head immediately. "They're trying to show off to big tech companies; there's no way this is all it is."

Ryan's gut told him so. There was no way it was as simple as that. Just a somewhat fast Duelist? Those were a popular thing even in the old TV show, and there were ones that were faster than Lightspeed. Maybe it was just Ryan not wanting today to end up being as boring as that "fight" just now, if it could even be called that. Kit walked back over to his podium. "I don't have to tell you."

"Fine. But in the next one, use that gimmick already. You only get two more tries," Ryan turned around and walked back to the other side of the arena. Modak and Silvia were looking at him with concern the whole time.

"You sure you're okay?" Modak asked, worried about how aggressive Ryan was being.

Sure, he always had a somewhat short fuse, but today was particularly concerning. Obviously, he knew why; that encounter with Simon annoyed him, and it was understandable. Modak was also angry just having heard about it. But being angry at Simon or Bluesky in general for acting like that was one thing; directing that anger at other, completely unrelated people was another.

Ryan looked at his friend, and briefly nodded. "I'm fine."

"You don't seem like it," Silvia said bluntly, something that Modak wasn't able to get out.

Unable to hold back a groan, Ryan shrugged and slightly threw up his arms. "What do you want me to do? I can't just stop myself from feeling pissed off."

"Yeah, but that's also not the fault of anyone here."

Ryan looked back at Silvia, locking eyes with her. He knew she was right, but it was a bit embarrassing to admit now that it's been pointed out. "Yeah, yeah, I guess so . . . I'll try to calm down a bit."

"Great!" A broad grin formed on Silvia's face as she turned to Modak smugly. The orc smiled approvingly.

For now, Ryan and Maximus had to wait. They were ready to go again right away. So that the Duelists didn't end up too damaged, the value of the points each one had was actually pretty low, so it was really just a light tussle in the end. But of course, just to be safe, the robots had to actually be inspected. If any issue did pop up, it should be remedied as quickly as possible.

"What do you guys think?" Ryan looked at his friends, specifically Modak. He should have some unique insights.

After thinking about it for a moment, Modak glanced over at Lightspeed. "Honestly? I'm not sure. But I do agree that there's definitely going to be more to this. Those lines on the outside of Lightspeed's legs are crystal fibers. There's probably going to be a high mana output, but I've got no idea what that will look like. Crystal fibers are usually used defensively, so it could be some kind of barrier?"

"That's it?" Ryan replied, a little disappointed. A barrier would make it all quite straightforward, and that wasn't bad in and of itself, but Ryan was hoping for some more unique things here after the duel with Richie and Roxie. But then again,

Richie was a Technomancer. Maybe he shouldn't expect the same thing from him as from the others.

Either way, it was still a good experience for him and Maximus. The most important part right now was figuring out good ways to work together; to maximize their combined powers. Maximus was good at fighting, but Ryan still had a long way to go in really *thinking* about fighting. He had the opportunity to oversee fights in ways that Maximus couldn't, so he should make as much use of that as possible.

"Let's continue," Kit called out to Ryan, who quickly turned around. There were only a little more than three minutes on the Spirit Link skill, so this was good timing.

Ryan and Maximus stepped back up to the arena, and without another word, Kit started up the countdown. While he didn't exactly mind that he didn't make a fuss, Ryan almost felt like Kit didn't care about his presence at all.

Let's just get this over with, Ryan thought to himself. Before the round even started, Maximus entered a defensive stance while Ryan kept track of where Lightspeed was moving. Just like before, the moment the countdown hit zero, the robot closed the distance.

Since it moved in a straightforward way, Ryan kicked forward his leg, which was quickly translated over to Maximus. The knight's foot impacted on Lightspeed's body—or, it was supposed to.

But Lightspeed wasn't running with the intent to attack Maximus. Instead, it jumped right before getting too close. It reached high into the air, getting up to Ryan's eye level. Once at its highest point, it twisted around, and kicked the air. And it hit something.

Lightspeed was pushed down after kicking off some invisible force. A few more times, the robot jumped off other spots in the air and maneuvered around Maximus.

"What the hell?" Ryan muttered to himself, while Maximus started moving around the arena to get farther away from Lightspeed, but the robot simply landed nearby, seemingly not aiming for Maximus at all. That was just a test run.

Ryan stared deeply at Lightspeed, waiting for any sort of movement. And then, the robot leaned forward and once more started running at Maximus. This time, the knight ran forward as well to hopefully close the distance in case Lightspeed jumped up again.

Trying to jab at Lightspeed once it got into range, Ryan made Maximus push his arm forward, but the robot was almost pushed out of the way. As if it jumped off an invisible wall next to it, Lightspeed suddenly dodged to the right, and its body twisted around. It once more seemed to create a foothold to use the strength of its whole body to strike at Maximus. The knight's helmet was struck perfectly, as Lightspeed built up distance again.

Lightspeed - 100 | Maximus - 86

Compared to the last round, Kit and Lightspeed might as well have been fully replaced. Though he hadn't noticed it himself until now, Ryan's heart was beating strong in his chest. This was a duel to get excited about.

Ryan directed Maximus to move away, but Lightspeed was much faster. It closed the distance immediately, deploying barriers underneath its feet for just a moment to jump off from, navigating around Maximus at a speed that neither Ryan nor the knight were able to keep up with. It almost felt like losing track of a fly as it buzzed around the room. Having both the view from Maximus and his own inside his head was making things even harder for Ryan.

However, even so, Ryan was able to at least tell Maximus where to move to dodge and prevent much more damage. Lightspeed did scrape by the knight a few times, carefully whittling down at his points.

Just for a moment, Ryan glanced over at Kit. His eyes were focused on Lightspeed, but . . . he seemed bored. Bored by this fight as though he was just going through a routine that he couldn't wait to finish.

Of course, that didn't mean that he was underestimating Ryan and Maximus. Kit probably just wasn't as into the fighting aspect of Power Duels as he was about creating the actual Duelist. And it made sense; they were all working hard toward making something they could show off tomorrow when all those company reps came here. While Ryan was also trying to use this to get familiar with his abilities in a combat setting, if he didn't find this exciting and fun, he would have just found another way. They were here for completely different reasons. Ryan knew that.

But he was still annoyed.

The Spirit Link skill only had another minute or so until its effect would run out. Lightspeed jumped around Maximus, without giving either the knight or Ryan the opportunity to react. Maximus was slow; his focus was on power and defense. He wouldn't be able to catch up to Lightspeed, no matter what he did. But he didn't have to catch up. He just had to stand in Lightspeed's way.

Ryan's eyes closely followed the robot. Around its feet, small glisters of thin rainbow hues appeared and disappeared, as if soap bubbles burst the moment they came to be. Lightspeed kept jumping around, striking at Maximus as he was fleeing from the flurry of attacks.

But then, Ryan tensed his muscles for a moment, and Maximus was prompted to stop moving. For about a second, Maximus just stood there, unmoving, until Ryan raised his arm to the side.

And just then, the impact came. Lightspeed ran into Maximus's arm, its upper body forcefully halted while its lower body kept moving, flipping it around violently. It hit the ground after making half a turn. Before it could push itself up,

Maximus grabbed one of its legs, and with a swift motion that the knight mimicked from Ryan, Lightspeed was pulled into the air before Maximus slammed it back into the ground like a hammer. Of course, pulling his punches so that Lightspeed wouldn't be actually damaged. Ryan glanced at the monitor.

Lightspeed - 4 | Maximus - 43

As Ryan looked at the screen, he noticed a system window popped up in the corner of his eye, but he couldn't concentrate on that right now. He quickly struck back at the ground, and Maximus hit the middle of Lightspeed's chest, ending the battle.

Ryan looked at Kit, who just stood there, staring at Lightspeed. He hurried over to the robot and quickly picked it up, sighing a breath of relief when he saw that it was fine. Kit glanced at Ryan, and the two locked eyes before the minogid quickly averted his gaze and moved back to his podium to inspect Lightspeed more closely.

But Ryan didn't even care about Kit's reaction. He had no idea why, but Ryan just knew when exactly he had to hold his hand out there. Like some deep instinct that he couldn't hold back. And then, Ryan looked at the system message that had appeared in front of him.

[Your Intuition has increased by 0.01]

CHAPTER TWENTY-THREE

Instinct or Precision

Ryan stared at the system window. His intuition had increased. But . . . how? The established method for increasing intuition was by trying to sense mana and increase your magical sensibilities. It definitely wasn't just through some fighting. Did his intuition stat present differently to others? That kind of thing could happen. The exact ways that stats presented had slight differences across individuals and classes, and rarely, they affected the user in more unique ways.

Considering that Ryan had a unique class, maybe that was a possibility to consider. Whichever the case, Ryan really didn't mind. If he could boost his intuition just through fighting, then that was nothing but a benefit to him.

Ryan squatted down in front of Maximus, taking a closer look at the knight. There were scratches covering his armor. Nothing major, but at this rate, these scratches were going to stack up.

"Want me to fix you up a bit?" Ryan asked, and Maximus looked down at his body. He shook his head, pointing over at Kit and Lightspeed. Ryan glanced over and slowly nodded. "Right, I guess we should wait for the last round to be over . . . But are you alright? You're not hurt or anything?"

Quickly, Maximus shook his head again, and Ryan sighed a breath of relief. The connection from the Spirit Link skill didn't really tell him all too much; he could tell what it was that Maximus was seeing and hearing, and he could feel the impacts from Lightspeed's attacks earlier. But there was no pain. And Ryan didn't know if that was because of the nature of the skill, or because Maximus didn't feel any pain to begin with. He was a spirit, and the armor was his body. Since Ryan could feel the impacts in the first place, Maximus clearly could sense touch through the armor, at least.

"Are you gonna be fine fighting on your own in the last round?" Ryan asked, though he already knew the answer to that. Maximus was a great fighter; rather, he was probably a better fighter than Ryan.

When Ryan fought, he did so with tricks and instinct and without hesitation. He used whatever he could, improvising along the way. But Maximus was different. He fought with precision and a plan. Most of the time when he was in his domain, he was training his techniques on the straw dummy. Ryan never even saw him try to sleep, even though he had a bed in there.

Ryan stood back up and walked over to Modak and Silvia.

"That was over quick," Silvia pointed out. "But also, wasn't that just so cool? Lightspeed was basically flying!"

Modak slowly nodded, seemingly deep in thought. "Yeah . . . so Kit was using the crystal fibers to deploy barriers for a foothold? I didn't realize that was possible . . . I'll have to ask him about that later, that's fascinating."

"You know him?" Ryan raised his brow. He found that barrier foothold interesting as well, but he didn't care about it all too much from a technical perspective.

Modak slowly nodded. "Yeah, I know everyone here. They're all in the magic engineering course. Kit is a second-year; he's the teacher's aide for one of my math classes."

"Huh." Ryan turned around and glanced at the minogid, before whispering to Modak, "Is he always like . . . that?"

Unsure what exactly Ryan was talking about, Modak looked over at Kit as well. "Like what? I guess he was a bit more quiet than normal, but he put a lot of work into this project, so he's concentrating, right?"

Silvia looked at her friends and let out a long sigh. "Guys, he's anxious. All of them are."

Ryan thought about it for a moment. "What, he's anxious about doing well tomorrow or something?"

"What? No, he's anxious about fighting you, dumbass." Silvia let out a long sigh. "Everyone here knows about you. And rumors tend to be exaggerated. People call you the 'Knight in Scuffed-Up Armor.' You're not known to . . . hold back. They're all clearly worried about you damaging their Duelists or getting mad. I mean, you're basically shadow-boxing right behind Maximus; that's not necessarily a calming view."

Was that it? Were these guys . . . scared of Ryan? It certainly wasn't impossible. As he looked around the room, he locked eyes with one of the club members momentarily. They immediately averted their gaze, actually turning their whole body away from Ryan.

Oh gods, they're actually scared of me? Ryan's stomach sank. His attitude as he came in here earlier probably didn't help with that either. Letting out a loud, involuntary groan, Ryan rubbed his eyes.

"Should I, like, talk to them about it? Try to get them to . . . not be scared?"

"I don't think they're actually *scared* of you. Richie said that the only people you'd be 'duelling' are the ones that agreed to do that, right? And clearly they all agreed," Silvia pointed out. "They're probably just a bit on edge, you know?"

Ryan scratched the side of his neck. "I guess you're right . . . Man, this is annoying. Should I go on some kind of massive 'I'm not scary' campaign?"

"I think that could make it a little worse," Modak pointed out. "But really, the moment people actually get to know you, it's fine. We'll be spending all day with everyone here. That's a good opportunity to mingle, right?"

"Yeah . . . yeah, you're right. Sorry, today's already been a weird day," Ryan admitted, taking a long, deep breath to calm himself down a bit. Right around then, Kit seemed to be ready to continue. The Spirit Link skill had been deactivated automatically and had around half an hour of cooldown left until he could activate it again, so this whole fight was going to be handled just by Maximus. Ryan's only task was pressing the buttons on the tablet in case Maximus used either of his active skills.

Ryan walked back over to the podium, leaning onto it. Kit glanced over at him as well, and the two locked eyes before Kit quickly looked back away and activated the countdown. Ryan sighed lightly, looking over at Maximus.

"You good to go?" Ryan asked, and the knight briefly turned around and nodded, continuing to stretch before the last round against Lightspeed started.

"What are you doing?" Kit asked, as the countdown reached zero. He saw that Ryan didn't seem to have the intention to "control" Maximus anymore.

"Hm? Oh, I'm just letting Max do his thing," Ryan replied, as if it were obvious. At the same time, he was trying to sound a little more friendly than he did before, forcing himself to smile, although he wasn't really in the mood. "I was using a skill for the first two rounds that let me and Maximus sort of 'sync up' for a bit. But now he's just doing his own thing."

Kit looked at Maximus seemingly surprised. It was one of the first times that he didn't have that tense blank expression on his face. At that point, Ryan realized that none of these people had seen Maximus fight without Ryan being directly involved through a Spirit Link.

"Don't worry, this data will be useful for you guys too. Now, get started, alright? Max is looking bored," Ryan pointed out. The knight was stood on his side of the arena, patiently waiting for Kit to be ready despite the countdown already having reached zero.

And though he seemed a bit hesitant, the minogid looked back at Lightspeed to get started. And then, the robot shot forward. Maybe even faster than before. And this time around, it really wasn't holding back with those barrier jumps either. As if Kit was trying to confuse Maximus with complicated movements, it jumped up and down and left and right, moving around the knight at high speeds.

But no matter what Kit tried, this time around, Lightspeed never hit Maximus. He tried, of course, but Maximus didn't get the slightest scratch on him. With careful, precise steps and twists of his body, the knight simply stepped out of the way no matter what Kit tried. It didn't matter what; Maximus dodged it all with relative ease.

And, throughout it all, Maximus wasn't only looking at Lightspeed. Others probably couldn't tell, but Ryan did. Maximus was regularly glancing at Kit. He was listening to the sound of the keyboard keys clattering and the taps on the touch screen of the tablet. It was like he knew exactly what sound corresponded to what movement, filling in the gaps that he couldn't gather just from looking at Lightspeed alone.

Of course, it was an impressive sight in the first place. The only strikes that Maximus allowed were minimal and light, seeped with purpose behind it. He did end up losing a bit of health, though, along the way. That was, until Maximus finally activated his Knight's Attack skill. Ryan almost didn't manage to press the button on the tablet in time before Maximus threw a precise punch forward as he dodged backward, striking Lightspeed in the head.

It might have looked similar to what Ryan had done earlier. It was the same outcome, really. Both times, Lightspeed's movements had been predicted. But while Ryan did so basically on pure instinct, Maximus predicted it by simply realizing Lightspeed's movement patterns and knowing that if Kit did certain things on his keyboard, it was going to lead to specific reactions in the robot.

It was much more technical and . . . impressive.

Lightspeed fell to the ground, but quickly recovered. In that time, Maximus had closed the distance and glanced at the monitor for just a moment.

Lightspeed - 90 | Maximus - 73

Ryan noticed that the punch, despite the activation of Maximus's skill, didn't actually do that much damage. But it didn't take him long to realize why.

Maximus struck at Lightspeed once more before it could properly recover. It was a light strike, just as before, but it brought the robot down to eighty points exactly. As Kit maneuvered it around Maximus, trying to attack however it could, the knight kept on striking instead. And each time, Lightspeed's points were reduced by exactly ten points. And at the same time, Maximus never struck the same place twice. The first targeted the head, the second the shoulder. Then the hip, the chest, the back. It didn't take Ryan long to know what Maximus was doing. He was giving Kit precise "data," as if trying to make this duel worth it for the minogid.

And before long, Lightspeed's points dropped to zero.

Kit silently lifted his hands from the keyboard, staring at his robot. He walked up to it, and Ryan felt like he seemed maybe a bit dejected.

With an inward sigh, Ryan walked up to Kit. "Hey, good job! Those barrier footholds were crazy cool."

Kit glanced up at Ryan as he slowly grabbed Lightspeed. ". . . Thank you. I did not expect that we would be beaten this easily."

"I mean . . . You don't really play fighting games, do you?"

"I prefer strategy games," Kit responded carefully.

"Exactly. Maximus and I know how to fight, it's kinda our thing. But for you, you had to control Lightspeed as if you were playing a game you weren't used to. That's not a great matchup, right?"

Kit looked up at Ryan, hesitating to respond. "I appreciate that. But whichever the case, this was quite insightful. Exactly as you said, the way you and . . . Maximus, was it? Anyhow, the way you two moved and fought was different to how Duelists can. I appreciate the help."

Ryan shook his head, lightly smiling. But compared to before, it was a bit more genuine. "Nah, man, we're getting something out of this too. I awakened like . . . a week and a half ago? This is amazing practice. I should be the one thanking you."

Kit was silent for a few more moments, but soon, he held his hand forward. "Thank you for the duel, Ryan."

"Of course."

The two shook hands as Modak and Silvia came up behind them.

"Kit, just how the hell did you make that work? Don't barriers usually move with the deployment conduit? That's like . . . lifting yourself up." Modak's curiosity immediately came over him. And Kit didn't hesitate to mirror that energy.

He held Lightspeed up, running his fingers over the crystal fibers on its legs. "I use fibers to actually manifest the barrier, but the actual conduit is inside a magnetic tube inside the leg. The conduit is shot up at the moment of deployment, and since a barrier isn't physically but magically connected to the conduit, it can provide enough resistance and leverage for Lightspeed to jump off."

"Right, I see . . ." With a curious grin, Modak took a closer look at the Duelist. "How does that translate to a higher scale?"

". . . Not well, but it's theoretically possible if the barrier's formula is changed and a stronger power source is used. Neither of which I could do with the resources I have."

"Ah . . . yeah, mana output is always a weird thing. I'm working on my own small project right now, and I struggled a bit to find the right thing."

"Oh? What is it you're working on?"

As Kit and Modak continued talking about some very technical things that went far over Ryan's and Silvia's heads, the two decided to step to the side. It was time for the next two people to start their duel in this spot, so they had to move anyway.

Silvia looked down at the small knight that Ryan was carrying around. "So . . . Maximus is actually pretty strong, huh?"

"You kidding? Maximus is ridiculous. If he were our size, even with the stats he has right now, he'd dominate the lower Awakened League," Ryan scoffed smugly. Maximus averted his gaze, almost embarrassed at what Ryan had just said.

With a smile, Ryan pulled open his backpack's zipper. But he also noticed Silvia's expression, and looked at her with a raised brow. "What? Do I have something on my face?"

"No, no, you're fine," Silvia replied immediately. "I just thought that your mood improved pretty quickly."

". . . Shut up." With a click of his tongue, Ryan pulled out his father's wooden box out of his backpack.

"What did you bring that for?"

Ryan turned to Silvia with a smug grin. "Just watch."

After he quickly opened the box, a number of tools were revealed. But the one that Ryan pulled out was none other than the silken handkerchief. It had deeply intricate patterns embroidered on it, and in two of the corners, on each side, a cursive *A* was written. And then, all those patterns slowly lit up as Ryan activated his Spirit Construction skill, just as the patterns on the clippers did. As Ryan had found, everything inside that box was a tool that reacted to the Spirit Construction skill somehow; even the needles. He hadn't found the use for all of them yet, but maybe he would at some point. Whichever the case, Ryan looked at Maximus with a smile, as the spirit slowly held his arms to the side and lifted his chin up. Ryan carefully ran the handkerchief over the scratched-up metal plates on Maximus's chest, and the scratches seemed to fade. Almost as if Ryan was using an eraser to get rid of mistakes on a pencil sketch.

"Huh?" Silvia watched curiously.

"It's cool, right? It doesn't look like Maximus can repair his body on his own, so 'upkeep' seems to be one of my tasks," Ryan explained. "I ended up playing around with the skill a bit while building models the past couple days. I was wondering if it would make any difference, but it didn't, so I ended up trying some other things, and found out that this worked."

". . . And how does it work? Are you, like . . . shaping the metal? Like smoothing clay or something?" Silvia wondered, but Ryan was quickly able to deny that.

"It's nothing like that, no. So, apparently spirits are like fully made of magic, right? And that seems to be the case with Maximus as well, just that his body is a bit different from most other spirits. But it's still magic in the end. I think I'm maybe just filling in the gaps with 'new materials'? Either way, it's pretty neat, and I feel like I'm getting a better—"

In the middle of his sentence, Ryan felt a deep cramp in his shoulder and his whole body tensed up. "Oh shit, gods-fucking—" he groaned loudly, letting go of the handkerchief and stepping away from the table that had been pushed up against the wall that he and Silvia were standing at.

In a panic, Silvia looked around, unsure what to do. "A-Are you—"

"All good, don't worry, it's just . . ." Ryan held his shoulder as he carefully moved it around. "I haven't been able to move my shoulder around a lot so it's been getting super stiff. I think I overdid it a bit earlier. The doc said to stretch a bit when this happens, but it'll settle down soon, don't worry."

Ryan continued to stretch, moving his arm around. However, maybe it was because the only one really focusing on him was Silvia, or because he forgot that the shirt he was wearing was kind of old and had shrunk down in the wash before, making it a bit shorter than normal, but he didn't pay too much attention to what others were able to see.

As his shirt slightly lifted, revealing part of his belly and back, Silvia's eyes widened. She stared at her friend's lower back, not sure if she was seeing right.

Ryan turned around a moment later, looking Silvia in the eye. Almost immediately, he realized what happened, pulling down his shirt. A little awkwardly, Ryan grabbed his jacket and put it back on, even though it was a bit warm in this room. Silvia was just watching silently.

Ryan nervously looked away. "I . . . I'll tell you about it later. Just not right now, okay?"

CHAPTER TWENTY-FOUR

Roxie

Ryan was seated on the edge of one of the desks, watching everyone get ready again. They had just taken a longer break, now that half of the duels had all been fought. Just from those six duels, Ryan learned a lot of things.

All the Duelists were unique, and as Richie had said, they all had their own gimmicks. There was one that detached its limbs from its body, letting them move around independently. Another that flew with thin butterfly-like wings. By now he had either fought them himself, or got to watch them fight other duels while he and Maximus were taking a break, and Ryan couldn't wait to get his turn. It was all so impressive.

There was only one person that he hadn't seen fight yet. Rather, that person wasn't even here right now. This person called Vanda, who had already been pushed to the back of the turn order, but was still running late.

"Hey, everyone." Before the first duels post-break were to start, Richie made a short announcement. "So, Vanda is on her way—there was an emergency she had to take care of. She'll be here in around ten, maybe fifteen minutes. Because she's a bit late, it's probably going to cause some issues with the duel order, so anyone that doesn't have the time or simply doesn't want to stay later to get their turn with Vanda's Duelist is obviously free to leave at any point."

Ryan glanced down at his phone to check the time. 3 p.m. He and Silvia didn't have anything to do today, and even Modak didn't have work, so they could all stay here until the end. Though, ever since earlier, Silvia's been kind of on edge. It felt a bit uncomfortable to Ryan, but he also understood why she reacted as she did. It wasn't the kind of thing you saw every day. Maybe she wanted to leave earlier; maybe she was going to stick around. Either way, Ryan wanted her to do whatever she felt was right. Though, it did mean that he and Silvia were stuck in an awkward silence while Ryan tried not to let his mind run too far with what Silvia could possibly be thinking about.

Modak wasn't here to fill up this awkward air either; he was busy talking with the club members about their projects, and even showed off his magic cassette to them.

Before long, finally breaking the silence, Richie came up to Ryan. "Are you ready to go?"

"Hell yeah, we are," Ryan replied with a broad grin, pushing himself off the edge of the table. "I've been watching your duels the whole time—looks like you improved Roxie a bit since last time."

"Just some fine-tuning." Smugly, Richie turned around, quickly walking to the arena for this duel. "I've been watching you two as well—you've got a pretty damn good win record going."

Ryan smiled lightly, for a moment focusing on Maximus as he sat in the domain, getting ready to come out. "Yeah, I guess so," he agreed. Ryan and Maximus had won most of the fights, with only four total rounds being taken from them so far. Once they got used to the gimmick of the specific Duelist, they were able to react pretty quickly and figure out some ways to beat the Duelist.

As the duel was about to start, Maximus quickly stepped out of the domain, getting into the position on his side of the arena.

"Ready?" Richie asked, putting on those special Technomancer gloves of his. Ryan quickly nodded, activating his Spirit Link skill. It actually leveled up once today, just before that longer break earlier.

[Spirit Link]
[Level - 4] [Proficiency – 4%]
[Allows for the user to mentally link with the target Spirit,
guiding their actions. During the activation period,
the user has an extremely strong understanding of the target
Spirit's body and the effect of their skills.]
[Effect – Spirit Link for 11 Minutes]
[Cost – 10.75 MP] [Cooldown – 40 Minutes 30 Seconds]

It wasn't a massive difference, obviously. Twenty more seconds for the effect, ten more seconds for the cooldown, and a slight increase in the mana cost. There also seemed to be a bit of an improvement in the actual link between Ryan and Maximus, but he wasn't sure if that was actually because of the skill or because he had spent all day actively using it.

The magical thread formed between Ryan and the spirit standing in front of him. Ryan glanced at the countdown, waiting for it to reach zero. And the moment it did, both Maximus and Roxie started moving. However, they didn't run at each other, as was the case with a lot of other rounds and duels in general. Instead, they were both acting very cautiously. Roxie had extremely high power output and could move in ways that neither Ryan nor Maximus were really used to. Flying or jumping around midair were things that you could gain some insight into, to a degree at least. But with Roxie, its movements were almost random at times as its momentum suddenly changed. Whatever that thing that Richie was using to make this happen was, it was a ridiculous invention, and Roxie was an even more ridiculous application of it.

Similarly, Richie was cautious of the pair in front of him because they were just good at fighting; there was not much more to say about it. The skill and control they showed during all the duels so far was something that really put Richie on edge, whether it was when Ryan was the one in control, or when Maximus was acting on his own.

Maximus slowly crept forward, trying to close the distance between himself and Roxie. The problem with Roxie was that it could start moving at a moment's notice. Richie could use his magic to manipulate the flow of energies throughout Roxie's body with the help of that energy transformer inside of it. That meant that Roxie could reach sprinting speeds without a moment's hesitation.

Of course, at first it seemed a little confusing why exactly Richie was doing this; it was extremely wasteful, and you couldn't sell any new inventions or applications to others if making use of them meant you needed to use technomancy. But the moment that Ryan heard that Richie already had a job lined up for after his graduation, things started to make sense.

Different to all the other people in the club, Richie wasn't trying to advertise anything with this project. He was really just trying to have fun. He didn't have to worry too much about energy efficiency, and he also didn't need to create something marketable, and could just do whatever he wanted to.

Before long, Maximus and Roxie were close enough for a proper collision to happen any moment now. Ryan and Maximus decided to take the initiative.

Ryan threw a punch forward and Maximus copied it perfectly. Roxie immediately blocked the attack, as a sudden jolt of movement practically pushed the robot out of the way. Maximus immediately closed the gap and struck at Roxie once more, but as the two came into contact, sparks flew around and Ryan could feel an electrical heat flowing through Maximus's arm.

While Roxie lost some points, so did Maximus, even if a bit less than the robot. Clearly, this was a type of fight that Ryan and Maximus had to be particularly careful of; even if they did everything right and Maximus was never hit, he would still take damage from the specific type of defense on Roxie's body.

"So annoying," Ryan muttered, a broad grin plastered on his face. What followed was a quick-paced exchange of attacks, all of which were relatively weak. It felt like both Ryan and Richie wanted to stretch the fight out as much as possible; if either Roxie or Maximus landed a couple strong hits on the other, the round would be over, and that was something neither side wanted to come all too soon.

But what made things particularly rough for Ryan and Maximus was just the ridiculous ways that Roxie was moving. During the last fight earlier this week, that "momentum canceling" was used on Roxie's body as a whole. It would stop moving and then start moving and then stop and start; it was jarring, but it was something that still had some level of predictability because there were a limited number of things Roxie could do next. This time around, however, this seemed to have been applied to every small part of the robot's body separately.

While the robot ran around, its leg would suddenly stop moving, or its upper body would slow down while its arm sped up. These movements were erratic and almost seemed random, as if Richie was just having fun messing around. Of course, there were plenty of attacks mixed into the fray, but in the end, due to Maximus's defensive capabilities, especially with his Knight's Guard skill active, it wasn't anything all *too* troublesome just yet. It was just that Maximus and Roxie were dancing around each other, hit after hit, whittling down on each other's points, until they both ended up with less than ten.

Roxie - 8 | Maximus - 9

It was to the degree that a single perfect hit could end the whole thing. Ryan and Richie glanced at each other, locking eyes for just a moment. And as they did, Roxie was suddenly pushed forward. When close enough, its body leaned backward, as if locked in space, while its lower body rapidly sped up and a kick was quickly directed at Maximus. The knight stepped back and returned a kick on his own. Their legs hit each other with a clang and sparks flew out.

Roxie - 4 | Maximus - 3

After the legs impacted and were bounced back, Ryan pushed forward his arm to have Maximus reach out to Roxie's leg, using the momentum from his own leg being bounced away, but just before he could grab it, the leg suddenly stopped moving and seemed to change directions instantly. Ryan smirked lightly as Maximus's other arm was already in the way of the new direction, hidden in Richie's narrow blind spot right behind Roxie's body. Maximus managed to grab the leg and lock it down, but sparks immediately flew as Maximus pulled at Roxie's leg, forcing the distance to close one way or another while throwing a punch.

Simultaneously, the contenders snapped their heads toward the monitor.

Roxie - 0 | Maximus - 0

"Wait, seriously? It's a tie?" Ryan scoffed loudly, though he really wasn't mad about it. It was a fun match, all things considered. Similarly, Richie didn't seem to be upset about the outcome either.

"Well, that's some good data . . . I guess?" Richie laughed, quickly looking over at Ryan. "You ready for round two?"

"Right away? Don't you need to check on Roxie first?"

"Already have. I can passively sense every type of electronic around me, and if I concentrate, I can look a bit deeper. And when I'm directly synced with it like with Roxie, I just know everything right away," Richie explained quickly, snapping his finger to reset the points on the monitor. Roxie also moved back to its initial position, and now the only one that had to make a choice was Ryan.

He looked down at Maximus, locking eyes with him. He didn't hesitate to nod.

"Alright, sure. We're good to go right again as well," Ryan replied, and Richie immediately started the countdown. The moment it hit zero, Maximus and Roxie started inching toward each other. Different from before, they had a good feeling for the other, and had less of a need to be this hesitant.

This time around, the first strike came from Roxie. It was a simple jab that Maximus could easily dodge, but the distance was closed immediately. Roxie's momentum stopped, but in return, its fist shot forward like a bullet, scraping by Maximus's armor. However, the attacks weren't boosted through electricity.

So he's just forcing the full body's electricity into just the arm? Ryan thought to himself, trying to think about a way to react. And that was when the next jab came. Just then, Ryan threw up a punch of his own, targeted at the underside of Roxie's arm. Maximus broke the robot's balance and moved in closer, not giving Roxie the opportunity to move back. Even if Richie created momentum for the robot, that momentum wouldn't be fast enough to escape right away.

Maximus reached out and grabbed Roxie's shoulder, pushing down on it to try and stop any further movement. Though a strike from Roxie came, Maximus had the opportunity to easily target the robot's body. As he did, a large shock of electricity flowed through Maximus's body as Roxie also grabbed the knight's shoulder. It was like being tased, a massive flow of electricity shooting through his whole upper body. It didn't hurt, but it felt quite bad for another reason.

Either way, Maximus had to release and step back, but this time, Roxie closed the distance. Maximus tried to raise his arms to block, but something stopped him.

A sudden jolt of confusion flowed through him as he felt something approach from behind. A familiar energy, together with a strong pull that forced Ryan and Maximus both to turn around immediately. This seemed to come from Maximus, but Ryan felt something else as well. In her domain, Gaia's fragment was shivering.

But all that he could see was a young hobgoblin making her way into the room, sweat running down her face and heavy breaths making her chest rise and drop rapidly.

"What the—" Ryan let out confused, but just then, Maximus was struck by Roxie, and it pulled the two of them back out of that sudden sensation. Ryan looked at Richie. "Sorry, but . . . I just . . . Is she a member?"

Richie looked at Ryan confused, trying to understand why exactly he interrupted the duel for no reason. He looked past Ryan and at the door. "Yeah, that's Vanda—what about her? Come on, let's just continue. Your skill doesn't last that long, does it?"

"I mean sure, but . . ." He had been completely taken out of the situation. He knew that there was something going on, but how the hell was this random girl supposed to have a fragment?

Maximus seemed quite focused on the fragment as well, but after he and Ryan locked eyes for a moment, it seemed like he understood what Ryan wanted to do. He couldn't just walk up to Vanda and demand the spirit core. After all, he had no idea what she was doing with it, or why she even had it on her.

I mean, the last one was inside a dungeon heart . . . something sketchy is going on, so I need to be careful, Ryan thought to himself. A spirit core's fragment wasn't the sort of thing you could just find laying around on the street. Obviously he wanted to demand it from her right this second, but that seemed far too risky.

Before continuing the round, though, he looked inward. He looked at the fragment of Gaia floating in the middle of her domain. *I'm sorry . . . I'll get you fixed up soon, but I can't be rash. I hope you understand.*

With anxiety welling up in his stomach, Ryan looked back at the gnome across from him. He took a deep breath, and got ready to continue.

CHAPTER TWENTY-FIVE

The Gift

The dim violet light illuminated the otherwise dark space that was filled with smoke and the powerful scent of sweet fruit. A man leaned back against the mountain of pillows stacked up behind him. The deep black lower body of the lamia was wrapped around the table in front of him. He pulled in a deep breath of the flavored smoke, holding it in for a few moments before streams of white flowed from his nostrils.

The man kept sitting there, enjoying his time in peace, when someone else walked up and took a seat next to him.

"What do you want?" the lamia asked, hissing at the one that silently joined him. The man smiled lightly, though his swollen and red nose seemed a bit distracting.

"Now, now, don't be like that," the man replied with a laugh, glancing at the hookah stood between him and the lamia. "I've always been doing a good job, haven't I?"

"I'll ask you again, Simon. What do you want?"

The elf's smile dropped, and he leaned back into the seat before crossing his legs. "Ryan Aglecard. He's not who you told me he was, Mr. Blanchard."

Unsure what Simon was talking about, the lamia placed the hookah's mouthpiece onto his lips. "I don't know what you mean."

"He may share their name, but he's unrelated to the Aglecard Foundation. We looked into him a bit more."

"What are you saying?" Unsure what Simon was getting at, the lamia let out a long sigh, pushing out more smoke as he did so.

The elf grabbed his bag and pulled out a laptop, which he quickly flipped open. The bright light overpowered nearly everything else, and as it was turned toward the lamia, he clicked his tongue, annoyed. "You could have just told me with your words."

He leaned forward and took a closer look at the information written in the file. "So? What about it?"

"A cozy town over west, with a whole twenty thousand citizens. After the death of his father, an accountant at a small chair manufacturer, his mother raised him alone. She remarried for a short while, but her husband was soon arrested. She now works as an office manager at a company producing rubber ducks."

The lamia read through the information to double-check it, and then looked back up at Simon. "Let's assume that our information was wrong. What do you want us to do?"

". . . More information. Mere minutes after the registration had gone through, I was called and told to find a way to purchase this . . . 'Spirit Keeper' class under any circumstances, but to be careful as he was a member of the 'Aglecard' family. I need to know more about what this class is supposed to be."

With a scoff, the lamia shook his head. "And why exactly should we tell you something like that? Just do what we pay you to do."

"Because that man summoned something that could move even within one of my traps that should have made this impossible," Simon explained bluntly. "That thing just jumped at me and broke my nose. We have to know more."

With a slow shake of his head, the lamia stared back at the elf. "No. You will not get to know more. I told you to do everything you can to get that class. Whether it is through money, or violence, or hell, by making him fall in love with you!" Slowly, the lamia lifted his upper body, soon towering completely over Simon. His tail started to wrap around his body, tightening around him. "You will get us that class! But the one thing that you will *not* do is make demands of *me*. Understood?"

Simon stared up at the lamia, shivering anxiously. The lamia's eyes reflected the violet light of the nearby lamps, and his face was clearly twisted in anger. The white tattoos on his arms were practically interrupted by the furiously bulging veins all over them.

Nervous and filled with fear, Simon nodded his head. "I-I understand, but I—At the very least, we need more time, just . . ."

Simon and the lamia locked eyes for a few moments, before the elf was released. "Fine. You have as long as you need. But if we don't get that class . . . you know what's going to happen, right?"

"Of, of course, Mr. Blanchard . . ."

Simon meekly walked away, unsuccessful in his attempt at getting more information from this man that sent the specific request to Bluesky. The Blanchard family were people that Bluesky couldn't afford to disappoint, so they accepted without hesitation.

"Gods-damned . . ." Simon clicked his tongue, pulling out his phone. He dialed some number and quickly held it against his ear. He waited for a few moments, rushing out of the hookah lounge, and spoke the moment someone on the other side accepted the call. "Gather your men. At midnight tonight, come to the address I'm about to send you."

Back inside, the lamia settled back into his seat, an annoyed frown on his face. "How hard can it be to defend yourself against a damned spirit?"

He looked down at the watch on his wrist, trying to use the dim light to read its face, "But speaking of . . . I should check up on Vanda. I need to make sure my little 'gift' does its job well tomorrow."

Christopher smiled lightly, pulling out his phone. The idea of what must be going on right now was quickly lifting his mood.

Ryan squatted down with a long sigh. He hadn't been able to concentrate on the last two rounds against Richie and Roxie at all. It wasn't a total failure, but it definitely wasn't close to as satisfying for either side. Even the round where Maximus was fighting on his own, he was sluggish and clearly unable to concentrate on anything but Gaia's fragment.

"Are you okay?" Richie asked, with a concerned frown. "Is your shoulder acting up?"

". . . Something like that, yeah," Ryan replied. That was a good excuse, though it was clear that Richie knew something else was going on. He was sensible enough not to pry, though, and Ryan was quite happy about that.

"In that case, if you want to call it a day, you can—"

"No, no, it's fine! I just need to take a break, don't worry," Ryan assured him, not wanting to leave just yet. He had to stay nearby and figure out what exactly this "Vanda" was doing with the fragment.

Currently, she was setting up everything that she needed to start her first duel of the day, rushing to get ready. Ryan kept glancing over at her the whole time. Now that the Spirit Link skill wasn't active anymore, he couldn't sense the fragment on his own, but Maximus and the fragment already with Ryan definitely could.

"Dude, what's going on?" Modak knelt down in front of Ryan. "Are you alright?"

Ryan looked around to see who exactly might be able to overhear him, and slowly stood up. He asked Modak and Silvia to follow him outside the room, and the moment the door closed shut behind them, he started to explain.

"She has one of Gaia's fragments," Ryan explained immediately, and both Modak and Silvia were taken aback.

"What? Who? And how, even?" Silvia asked. Ryan had filled them in on Gaia's fragments before, but that being something that suddenly popped up here seemed just far too random.

"That Vanda girl, I don't know why or how, but she has a fragment on her. I can feel Gaia shivering in my head." Unsure how to better explain it, Ryan tried to word it that way. But it was much more than just shivering. Gaia was practically crying, wanting to be reunited with another part of herself.

Modak looked at the door, clearly unsure what to say to that. "I mean . . . can't you just talk to her about it? She's really nice, like . . . I've known her since before uni, we went to the same school. Her siblings are friends with mine, and . . . I can't imagine her having any bad intentions, you know?"

Able to tell that Ryan seemed to be assuming the worst, Silvia suggested something else, agreeing with Modak, "Right! What if she just . . . happened to pick it up somewhere?"

Ryan considered it for a moment. His gut was telling him that there was more to it than her just having randomly found it, but he couldn't say for sure that this wasn't the case either.

"So what, I should just ask her about it? 'Hey, do you happen to have a spirit core's fragment somewhere on you?' I doubt that's going to work all too well," Ryan pointed out, and Modak thought about it for a little while.

"I get why you're nervous about it, considering where you found the first fragment, but . . . can you link with Gaia's core? I mean . . . maybe you'll be able to figure out more? Like exactly where it is, and what Vanda's doing with it," he suggested. Ryan raised his brows immediately, carefully thinking about the idea.

"That . . . could work. It's worth a try at least . . . but what if she won't give the fragment to me? I can't just steal it from her . . . can I?"

"Let's not worry about that for now," Silvia replied, trying to calm Ryan down a bit. "If she doesn't want to give it to you, we can figure something out then. Let's not resort to stealing, alright?"

Ryan slowly nodded his head. "Yeah, alright. You're right. Thanks, I'm just really . . . I don't know, there's just a ton going on today that's kind of stressing me out, you know?"

His gaze slowly wandered over to Silvia, and they locked eyes for a moment. Silvia looked away, and Ryan sighed inwardly. "Alright, let's just . . . get in and wait? There's another twenty minutes until I can use the skill again anyway."

"Alright, I can try to talk to Vanda for a bit as well. She seemed a bit stressed earlier," Modak replied, and Ryan slowly nodded.

"Right, of course, do that," he responded with a nod, pulling open the door. Since Vanda and Modak knew each other already, maybe his presence could calm her down enough that even if it came to the worst-case scenario, it would help improve the situation a bit.

The three stepped back into the room, and Modak quickly walked over to the hobgoblin. "Yo, Vanda, how are you doing?"

"Oh, hi, Modak! Yeah, I'm fine, just a bit stressed . . . Sorry about the other day, by the way, I kind of pushed my way through you guys and didn't even say hello," she replied, setting up her Duelist to get it ready, while Modak just shook his head.

"All good, I could tell you were busy. Honestly, it looked like you didn't even see us properly," Modak pointed out. "You were already gone by the time I realized it was you as well."

"Yeah . . . I really should pay more attention to what's going on around me sometimes," she pointed out, carefully glancing past Modak over toward Ryan. "So your friend is the one that awakened? I saw him and his . . . summon thing during the duel earlier. I guess they're not used to things yet?"

Modak wasn't sure exactly what to reply. Clearly, Ryan and Maximus were acting off because of the fragment Vanda had on her, but that wasn't something he could just tell her. "He's had a pretty bad day, I guess. He's a great fighter, usually."

". . . Clearly not good enough to get a physical class, right?" she pointed out bluntly. Modak noticed that she seemed a lot more confident around him than she did around most of the club members, though that could probably just be attributed to the fact that they'd known each other for years now. And clearly, through some kind of miracle, Vanda didn't know about Ryan yet. So, he figured that he shouldn't mention it.

"Well, what about you? You happy with your Duelist?" Modak asked, slowly trying to move the conversation away from Ryan. The hobgoblin grinned smugly and quickly looked down at the small robot in front of her.

"Happy? I'm ecstatic. I was struggling so much to get this to work. So, I'm using both electricity and mana to get this to work, right? I'm intertwining them together, and because I need the mana to function in a specific way, I had to overcompensate with a ton of it. So I wasn't able to get the right mana source, until just earlier this week."

Modak's stomach dropped as he listened to her words. "Mana source? Like, a really good battery?"

"Hm, something like that? You know how there are types of crystals that just hold a ton of mana?"

". . . Yeah, but those are really expensive, aren't they?"

"Well, sure . . . and don't tell this to anyone, but I met this guy recently—he's really nice and we've become really close friends. When I told him about the Power Duel projects, and what exactly I was struggling with, he offered me this crystal. His family is apparently really well-off, like, old money well-off. And he just . . . gave it to me."

Modak frowned in confusion. So someone else gave her the fragment? In exchange for . . . nothing? That felt off. Really, really, off. "So are you going to be paying him back or anything?"

"Well . . . I'm going to try to? I can't right now, obviously, but depending on how tomorrow goes, I might get some good job offers. Right now, all he asked for was to . . . try Energizer out before tomorrow. It's part of why I was late, actually . . ."

Modak glanced over toward Ryan. He seemed to be trying to concentrate on calming down, but was still glancing over here every once in a while.

"So . . . this crystal, is it going to run out of mana anytime soon? You probably only have one, right?"

"Oh, no, no, Energizer doesn't use *that* much mana. The crystal should last for quite a while."

"Do you think you're still going to need it after the presentation tomorrow?" Modak asked, and Vanda raised her brow, confused.

"I might, yeah. If they like Energizer and anyone wants me to show it to them again some other day, I'll obviously need it then," she explained. "Why, do you need something like this as well?"

"Not really, I do have something I'm working on, but I managed to get it to work pretty well already. Hold on, I actually have it with me," Modak pointed out, about to head over to his bag to get the magic cassette out again, but Vanda just shook her head.

"My first duel is about to start, but I can take a look at it later. Oh, if you want, you can look at some of my notes about Energizer, though—here." Vanda pushed open her old and thick laptop that was already open to some documents and sketches.

The hobgoblin quickly stepped away and moved over toward her arena together with her Duelist. Modak was going to take a look at the notes in a second, but for now, he had to tell Ryan, though he was nervous how he was going to react.

CHAPTER TWENTY-SIX

Energizer

Modak walked up to Ryan and leaned closer toward him, cupping his hand by the side of his mouth as he whispered, "She's . . . using the fragment as a battery."

The orc could practically hear his friend's heart skip a beat as he snapped his head toward him. "What? She's doing what?" Ryan asked, in full volume, but Modak quickly pulled him to the side.

"Calm down, seriously. It looks like she doesn't know what it is, someone else gave it to her," Modak explained, as Ryan tried to slow down his rapid breaths.

"But . . . how can I just let her use Gaia like that? It's not . . ." Ryan muttered, frowning deeply as he stared at the small robot stood at the edge of the taped-off arena. His role was to protect her, and letting this happen definitely didn't feel like he was doing a very good job at that.

"Just . . . wait it out, alright? Try to link with the core, and maybe . . . see how it . . . she's doing? If she seems fine, then we can just calmly figure something out," Silvia suggested, trying to place her arm onto Ryan's back but flinching back before she could, as if worried. He didn't notice this either.

Ryan took a deep breath and nodded. "You're right . . . you're right."

He looked at the other side of the duel area, seeing Kit standing across from Vanda. Lightspeed and Kit were going to be her first opponents. It seemed like most people that weren't actively partaking in a duel were gathering to see Vanda's Duelist, Energizer, put into action. It was the only one that they hadn't seen yet. Even the ones that *were* actively taking part in duels were peering over, almost wanting to take a quick break.

One of the two club members activated the countdown, and both Kit and Vanda got ready. While Kit was using a combination of a keyboard and a tablet to control Lightspeed, Vanda seemed to be making use of a customized game controller. It had more buttons and dials placed onto it, to the point where it seemed completely over-the-top and unusable, but Vanda seemed confident.

The moment the countdown hit zero, Lightspeed shot forward to get to Energizer. Vanda's Duelist, however, was just carefully walking forward, almost casually. Kit didn't immediately have Lightspeed use the "jump pads," as he had dubbed them, but instead was just making use of its generally fast speed. It struck Energizer with a kick, and Vanda seemed to "parry" the attack with a swing of the robot's arm. It honestly just seemed like a light tap, but Lightspeed was thrown away, unable to find balance against before dropping onto the ground. Kit seemed taken aback, but quickly recovered. Just like before, he stuck to his guns and, for the first round, didn't use Lightspeed's "gimmick."

Lightspeed continued to try and attack Energizer, but it seemed almost impossible to get a good attack in. Energizer wasn't moving fast, or rather much at all, but Vanda's control over the robot was almost perfect. Parries, counterattacks—they were all timed perfectly, and Lightspeed didn't seem to claim more than just a couple of points at a time.

However, on the opposite side, every single one of Energizer's attacks, even if they just barely grazed by Lightspeed's body, did an immense amount of damage and threw Lightspeed across the improvised arena, forcing it to close the distance just to repeat the same thing again. The power running through its body was ridiculous; almost impossible for what it was showing. But then, Ryan had a small hint of understanding why exactly that was.

Energizer was not only strengthened through whatever methods Vanda had found, but also by the Garden Golem's power. As Ryan understood it after talking to Maximus about it, part of their power and stats were inside their bodies; the ones that Ryan built for them. But another part of it, the part that actually grew stronger when Maximus leveled up, was within the spirit core. So while Energizer wouldn't be able to use the full extent of that, some of Gaia's stats were clearly flowing into Energizer's body. It was like a mock version of what Ryan could do, giving Gaia a body to use. But it couldn't be more different from the way that the Spirit Keeper's method worked.

Ryan could see threads of green mana flow out from Energizer's body, though he knew nobody else could. It was Gaia's mana that was being used to strengthen the robot's body. The only reason he could see it was because he was Gaia's keeper, even if he only held the first fragment thus far. But as Ryan looked at the mana, his stomach churned. These threads were supposed to flow beautifully, like the wind over densely grown tall grass.

But these? These were tangled and cut, a mass of frayed ends. Just seeing them like this made Ryan feel like he failed.

Today was not a good day for Ryan. He was already anxious to begin with, considering that tomorrow was the day that whatever Runar was dealing with was going down. Then, the bit of excitement he had while heading out to this exact event was immediately replaced with anger after he was attacked by Simon.

Once he finally arrived here, he was met with the fact that most people in this room were scared of him. Not only that, but Silvia, one half of his best friends, saw his back and started acting distant immediately after. And now this. He couldn't go a second without feeling Gaia shivering in his mind. If she could produce them, her tears would probably have formed a puddle underneath the fragment currently in the domain.

They weren't tears of pain or anger; that was something that Ryan was sure of the more those emotions constantly filled his head. Instead, they seemed more like an immense sense of loss or fear that Gaia was experiencing, unable to handle with a fraction of her being. Honestly, all Ryan wanted to do was step into the arena and rip open that damned robot to just take the fragment; it was taking all he could to not just do that right now.

Inside his head, the cooldown of the Spirit Link skill kept counting down, and he was clinging to each second, as if trying to speed it up. But of course, he couldn't. He just had to wait. Ryan chewed on his lips nervously, tapping his foot impatiently, as if the activation of the skill would just fix everything magically.

The duel continued on. It was a fairly simple win for Vanda and Energizer, and both sides quickly went to grab their Duelists to check up on them. In particular, Kit was looking over Lightspeed with a bit of concern due to the strength of those attacks.

In the meantime, as the break between the rounds continued, Modak started making his way back to Vanda's laptop, reading through the notes that she took during her construction of Energizer. But Silvia stayed with Ryan.

"It's going to be fine, don't worry. It will all work out," she tried to reassure Ryan. Silvia knew what kind of person Ryan was. When he saw someone in trouble, he couldn't hold back. It was ingrained in his DNA. Whether it was a service worker getting yelled at by an entitled asshole, or some kid being picked on, he always intervened in some way. Though of course, not always violently, but in more extreme cases, it did come to that. Silvia couldn't imagine what exactly Ryan was experiencing right now.

He slowly nodded his head, closing his eyes. "I hope so. Thanks."

". . . I'm sorry for how I was . . . you know, acting after . . ." Silvia slowly let out, not sure how to best word it. She was good at speaking most of the time, but this situation was different.

Ryan turned his head and glanced at her. "It's fine, I get it. It's not really something you see every day. I won't go into any details, but . . . they're basically ancient, you know? They're healed, they've faded as much as they're going to, and they don't hurt or anything. I forget about them most days now, it's not like I can see them super easily. You've got nothing to be worried about."

". . . Alright. If you ever want to talk about it . . . even if not with me, I could ask my dad?"

Ryan scoffed lightly and shook his head. "I'm fine, really. I've been in therapy for it for like ten years now. I do need to find a new one here, but . . ." He looked to the side, weirdly feeling calm while being distracted from the fragment, even if the topic that was distracting him was something as big as the scars covering his entire back. But then, he saw Silvia's confused expression.

Quietly, she let it out, concern. "Ten . . . years?"

". . . It's a long story, obviously. Maybe some other time," Ryan replied, patting his friend's shoulder. At least he didn't feel any pity from her, though he couldn't blame her, even if that had been what she felt.

By the time the next round for Vanda and Kit started, there were only twelve minutes left on the cooldown of Ryan's Spirit Link skill. Sometime during the last round, he should be able to activate the skill. Though for now, the second round itself had to finish.

This time, as in every other duel until now, Lightspeed began jumping around on the barriers that it could create under its feet. It got a lot more hits in due to how unpredictable its movements had become, but even so, Energizer barely seemed to be taking much of any damage. High defense and high damage. That did certainly sound like a golem.

While the battle was more drawn out than before, it did end sooner or later; obviously. But that being the case, Vanda didn't seem like she had really broken a sweat. As if she was only just getting started.

The break between the second and third rounds was shorter than the first, as if both sides wanted to quickly return to the duel. Whether that was to save time or because they were both excited to continue was a bit unclear, though.

Ryan took a deep breath. Just five more minutes and he could connect to Gaia's fragment. Or at least, he could try.

The last round of the duel started, and Lightspeed shot forward, once more jumping around wildly. However, Energizer was acting different to before. Vanda was getting more excited about this fight, and seemed to act a bit different. Something had changed in Energizer; Ryan could see the threads of green mana change just so slightly. Larger lumps of knots but shorter distances between the cuts. And the moment Ryan seemed to recognize this, Energizer started to move. Fast. A speed that easily seemed to match Lightspeed, despite Energizer's larger size and weight.

Finally, Ryan realized why exactly the way the robot was moving had seemed familiar to him this whole time. It was a classic battle approach for Enhancers. Through their skills and ability to manipulate both aura and mana, they were able to intertwine the two energies into each other in specific patterns, boosting them in a number of ways.

Strengthening their muscles or eyesight, improving their intelligence or even the effects of magic spells in some rare cases. And what happened to Energizer just now was that its body was a classic method of switching between different "modes," as they were referred to by many Enhancers. Going from strength to defense to speed within moments. Energizer was clearly something created to imitate the way that Enhancers fought.

Frankly, it was impressive; clearly this was something that Vanda had worked very hard on. The only bad part was that she, apparently unknowingly, used Gaia's fragment to make it all work. But it really didn't matter what her intentions were. It didn't matter how impressive it was. This was clearly like some kind of ridiculous torture for Gaia herself.

Ryan was focusing back on the cooldown of the Spirit Link skill, but as he tried to, he noticed something else.

The threads of mana seeping out from the cracks of Energizer's body were starting to . . . change. Their color became muddy, as though they were soaking up the water of a dirty puddle. The more mana was used within Energizer and the more that this mana leaked out, connecting with the fragment of Gaia already with Ryan, the more that corruption seemed to spread.

"Huh?" The confused mutter came from the other side of the room, from Vanda. She was fiddling with her controller, the way that you did when it stopped working. But despite that, Energizer kept moving, only much more erratic than before, as if its limbs were being jerked around by some other force.

Its arms were being twisted around in an all too familiar way. It was the exact same thing that happened when Maximus settled into his new body. But . . . still different. It just felt completely wrong to Ryan; there was no other way to say it than that. Energizer kept moving forward toward Lightspeed. Kit was also able to tell that something was going on, and was looking at Vanda when it happened.

Energizer grabbed Lightspeed. It wrapped its right hand around the other robot's neck, and then began tearing its arm off its body.

"Vanda, what are you doing?" Kit asked, confused, trying to get Lightspeed out of Energizer's grip.

"I-I'm not doing anything—it's, it's doing that on its own!" she stuttered out a response. Vanda was trying to get the robot to respond to her input, but no matter what she did, it didn't work.

And then, Lightspeed's arm was ripped off. Wires were exposed as the robot's whole body started to spasm.

"Vanda!" Richie yelled out, snapping his finger toward the two robots to try and take control. Energizer flinched for a moment, and the corrupted mana in the robot's body seemed to all gather toward Richie. The threads began to climb through the air, toppling over each other to carry the corruption over to Richie. It happened too fast for Ryan to respond and stop it, and the corrupted mana crept up on the gnome.

Richie fell to his knees, grabbing his head in pain. "Aargh!" he screamed loudly, clear physical pain in his voice. Everyone stared at him as Energizer continued. It threw Lightspeed to the side and proceeded to pull apart the arm. The metal plating was pressed on top of Energizer's plates, while the wires wrapped around its limbs. Ryan watched the threads of mana break down the metal plates, pulling them into the rest of the body. It looked all too familiar to him; it was just like how the monsters in the Abandoned Copper Foundry looked and seemed to advance their bodies.

At this point, Ryan didn't hold back anymore; he had to do what he could, and practically jumped at the robot. Similarly, Maximus tried running at it, though hesitant due to the nature of what was happening to it. But Energizer was too fast and small, and immediately jumped out of the way of either of them.

With just a single leap, it reached the podium in front of Vanda, who was staring at her creation as it went berserk.

CHAPTER TWENTY-SEVEN

Corruption

Vanda dropped the controller onto the ground as Energizer jumped onto it. Like a wild animal, it began to tear the piece apart, pressing any small piece it could onto its body. Wires and screws and even plastic. All of it was fused into its body in one way or another. However, as it did so, Ryan was able to grab it in the midst of its attempts.

He wrapped his hands around it and tried to keep it tied down, but his palm was quickly cut up by the sharp edges of metal and plastic that were covering it now.

"Fucking—" Ryan clicked his tongue, trying to persist through the pain. But the cuts weren't all; Energizer was also strong, far stronger than anything of this size should be. Rather, the only thing that Ryan could think of that had similar strength at that size was Maximus. Gaia's fragmented core seemed to be somehow reacting to this false "body" that had been created for it.

He ended up dropping Energizer, but Maximus was already waiting down below. He caught the robot, holding on to the grooves of its body and quickly slammed it onto the ground. For a little while, Maximus was successful at restraining Energizer, but Ryan was able to see something that he really, really didn't like. The formerly bright green, now dark enough to be called black, threads of mana were wrapping around Maximus. Ryan had a bad feeling; and it was quickly confirmed.

[A corrupting force is encroaching on Maximus]

Without hesitation, Ryan forcefully pulled Maximus into his domain, scanning the spirit's mana with his gaze. Some wisps of Maximus's mana were dyed black, but when they touched Ryan's skin, it was like a layer of oil or tar was scraped off. He could feel the corruption laying on his skin, like a living scab attempting to dig into his skin. But before he could even swat it away, it fell apart and disappeared, unable to live on without something to cling onto.

Ryan had managed to save Maximus from the corruption, but at the same time, this led to Energizer being freed again. The "possessed" robot jumped up and immediately ran back around the room. None of the club members were able to catch it, no matter what they did; it was like trying to catch a mouse, but the mouse had sharp edges all over its body and the capabilities to break their hands with ease. Ryan couldn't blame any of them from running away instead of actually attempting to catch it for more than a few moments.

"Ryan, what's happening?" Modak asked with deep confusion and concern. He was squatting down next to Richie, trying to help him out as he recovered from that pain.

"I don't—Something is corrupting Gaia's fragment, and now it's going wild! It's trying to add anything it can to its body and grow stronger," Ryan warned the others.

Richie, hearing what Ryan was saying but not understanding, glanced over to him. His eyes were completely bloodshot. "What do you mean . . . ? What . . . fragment?" he forced out, and Ryan looked over toward Vanda with some hesitation.

"The 'crystal' Vanda used as a battery is the fragment of a spirit core, and now *something* is trying to corrupt the part of the spirit left inside of it," he explained, though that was really all that he *could* tell them. He had no idea why this was happening, or what was corrupting Gaia. That didn't seem like the kind of thing that could just happen from being used as a power source. There was something else that was affecting Gaia, Ryan was sure of it.

Richie stared over at Vanda, who was now hearing about this for the first time as well. "What . . . what do you mean, 'spirit core,' that's not . . . That's not what it is!"

With a deep glare directed at the girl, something that came involuntarily, Ryan barked out, "Yes it is!"

It wasn't like he was mad at Vanda directly; she was just the only one that he could be angry at right now. It wasn't like he knew who was actually behind this; and frankly, he wasn't totally convinced that Vanda was actually innocent here.

"I'll try to control it again, I just—" Richie pushed himself off the ground, reaching his hand out toward Energizer as it started ripping into the case of one of the old computers stacked up in the corner of the room.

"No! The corruption was trying to take you over too. I have no idea what that's going to do to you." Ryan stopped him, pushing the gnome's hand down again. "Even Maximus was about to be taken over. I think I know a way to stop this, but we need to somehow get to the fragment."

"Can't you do that domain thing? Pull the fragment in? I thought you just need to be close enough!" Silvia suggested, but Ryan immediately shook his head.

"No, I tried earlier, and it didn't work. I think all the mechanisms are keeping it locked in somehow—it's not responding," he pointed out, turning back to the rampaging Energizer.

By now, it had climbed inside the computer's case and was pulling apart the broken electronics, making them part of its own body. Before long, it climbed out of the case again, larger and clearly stronger than before. It was now barely recognizable as the robot that it started out as; instead, it seemed to be a mass of wires and metal and plastic in the shape of what it used to be. And from Ryan's perspective, the whole thing was kept together by threads of Gaia's corrupted mana.

Ryan looked down at his hands; they were cut up and covered in blood. None of them were particularly deep, and they should heal quickly enough, but it was painful and annoying. And more importantly, it meant that Ryan wouldn't be able to do this barehanded. He walked over to one of the nearby podiums; they were quite simple. Metal bars holding up angled wooden boards. It was really wonky. It was easy enough for Ryan to kick away the thin crossbeams that were keeping it somewhat stable.

Ryan handed Silvia the tablet that was on the podium. She saw the blood that was on it but wasn't able to stop him before Ryan picked up the podium, carefully approaching Energizer.

It was still running around, now hanging on to one of the monitors. It practically shoved its hand through the screen as if it were some thin fabric just waiting to break. The sharp shards of glass were also being fused into its body, making it even more impossible to grab it. But Ryan didn't hesitate to push the podium right against the robot. The monitor completely broke, and its stand fell over with Energizer still on it. Ryan pressed down on it, using his full weight to try and break it.

But instead of Energizer breaking, the podium's wooden top cracked apart, and the robot grabbed the podium's wooden legs. Its hand fused into the metal, starting to absorb it into itself.

With a click of his tongue, Ryan pulled away the metal bar that now had Energizer stuck to it. "Fucking idiot," he groaned, proceeding to slam the robot into the ground like a hammer. This time, pieces that it had only just connected to were flung off. One was shot up at Ryan, scratching his cheek. Just a little higher and it could have hit his eye.

Ryan kept going, until suddenly the weight of Energizer seemed to mostly disappear. It had grown to weigh a few kilos at that point, so Ryan noticed it before he saw or heard it be thrown around the room and hit the wall. It seemed like its arm had been torn off, and said arm was still attached to the end of the metal bar, in the midst of the robot trying to absorb it. Not only that, but it was still wriggling around, and Ryan could see the threads of mana wriggle like worms trying to crawl out of the detached limb. Ryan placed his hand in front of it, pulling the escaping mana into Gaia's domain. The mana was properly pulled inside, while the "corruption" stuck to his bloodied palm. And this confirmed it for Ryan.

This corruption couldn't do anything to him, at least not like this. It was like Ryan's body rejected it. He didn't know why, but that didn't matter right now. The important part was that this meant he could still save Gaia's fragment from this. He just had to get to the core, and the more he hesitated or waited, the harder that was going to get.

The room was filled with complete panic. The club members were picking up their Duelists, trying to save them before they were torn apart, like some of the others already had been. And then, they ran out of the room, not even thinking about what they were doing.

"Wait, no, stay in here!" Ryan yelled out. "Keep the fucking door closed!"

Taking the opportunity that was given to it, Energizer ran out of the room. It could clearly tell that it was going to be in danger if it didn't run away. This was different to the dungeon. Of course, in both cases, the fragment was being protected. In the dungeon, it was done by a monster, but here, it was done by the body around the fragment itself. Instead of counterattacking Ryan, which it could tell would lead to a loss, Energizer fled. Or at least, for now.

This was the engineering building; this place was chock-full of numerous computers and technologies that the robot could absorb into itself. And as it did so, it would get stronger. Without hesitation, Ryan ran outside and chased the rogue machine down the hallway, ignoring Silvia and Modak as they tried to yell after him. But he couldn't pay attention to that right now; he had to hurry. In his hand, Ryan was still holding the metal bar with Energizer's arm fused to its end.

And then, Ryan saw the robot enter a door at the end of the hallway and could feel his heart almost skip a beat. It seemed to be just a storage room . . . but a storage room in this building meant that it was filled with the exact things that Energizer needed. Ryan pulled open the door and immediately spotted the metal cabinet across the fairly small room. Its thin door was crumpling up as the metal was pulled into Energizer's body. Beyond it were a number of power tools. Ryan swung the improvised weapon in his hand down at the robot, but it barely made it budge. It released its grasp from the metal door, already having pulled off a fair chunk that was now covering half of its body like an armor.

Energizer tried to jump into the pile of laptops and computers stacked up in the corner of the room, but Ryan stabbed the metal bar forward, hitting it out of the air. He was about to once more swing down at the Energizer, but before he could, someone pulled on his arm from behind.

"Don't! You can't break it anymore!" Vanda was pulling Ryan back, tearing at his jacket and almost making him fall backward.

"What the hell are you doing? Get off me!" Ryan yelled out, as the hobgoblin flinched upon seeing his expression.

"You can't . . . if you break it, you'll ruin everything, you'll . . . I . . ." Tears welled up in Vanda's eyes as Modak quickly grabbed her and pulled her away from Ryan.

The orc looked her in the eyes, trying to explain the gravity of the situation. "No! If he doesn't do this, then that thing is going to keep rampaging!"

"B-But just . . . why can't he just *not* break it?! Just take out the core and—" she pleaded loudly, and for a moment, even Ryan was hesitating, remembering what Richie had explained to them; the event tomorrow was something that could potentially change the lives of the club members if things went well. Ryan didn't know her situation, but Vanda must have put a lot of pressure onto tomorrow. He understood it, and he could feel her pain, but he couldn't let that dictate what Ryan was going to do.

". . . I'm sorry," he responded, trying to tune out Vanda's yells and screams as Modak and Silvia were pulling her away. Ryan looked back inside the room, and was met with a horrible sight. All the electronics were covered in thin, tangled threads of dark mana. They crumpled and tore and were all pulled to a specific spot in the corner of the room.

Ryan stabbed the metal bar at that spot to try and open up a way, but it didn't work; that mass of metal and plastic and glass was too dense for him to get through. The crunch of the materials was so loud that Ryan could barely hear himself think, until it all went quiet.

Ryan backed out of the room as the large mass revealed itself. He had no idea what happened, but *something* made Gaia's mana spread so much faster than before, and now, Ryan was looking into the face of a two-meter-tall mass of electronics that had been completely torn apart. Gaia's core was deep inside that figure. More and more, the idea of safely recovering the fragment from inside the original robot seemed impossible.

The mass stepped out of the room, clearly not feeling the need to flee from Ryan anymore. It stretched out its hand toward him, pushing a mountain of sharp edges toward his face. However, it still only had one arm; it hadn't been able to rebuild its limb from scratch. All it could do was build on top of an existing base.

Trying to be as fast as he could, Ryan pulled his jacket off, then held it in front of him while carefully backing off. Luckily, it seemed that, while capable of making use of the abilities that Vanda had given its body, essentially making it a sharpened, metallic Enhancer, the way that it moved and acted was fully on instinct. It didn't think about the best tactic or try to figure out what Ryan was doing. So, before long, the robot jumped at him to try and tear him apart.

Ryan threw his jacket over its arm and tried to push against it; it didn't work, due to the sheer weight of the thing he was trying to grapple. But that was fine; Ryan grabbed the jacket's sleeves and tied its arm up as well as he could. At least this way it couldn't punch him anymore, which was a pretty good improvement from Ryan's point of view. Now, he was dodging back and forth, sometimes getting hit by the rapid attacks, but at least he didn't get cut up and would only end up with some bruises here and there.

All he was doing right now was waiting something out, and before long, that moment came to be. The Spirit Link skill's cooldown had ended.

Ryan stared at the figure in front of him, trying to focus on the mass within its very center. Like when he linked with Maximus, he tried to find some kind of spark to hang on to. Amidst the corrupted mana, there were some threads here and there that were still glistening in Gaia's original vibrant green. They were growing fewer and farther between by the moment, but right now, Gaia was still in there.

From within Ryan, threads of that original mana appeared, climbing toward Gaia's fragment and piercing through that mass of metal and plastic, as Ryan connected not only with the fragment in front of him, but the one still within the domain in his mind as well.

CHAPTER TWENTY-EIGHT

Cleansed

Ryan formed a link with Gaia's fragments; both the one within his mind and the one inside the walking mountain of metal, plastic, and glass in front of him. The moment the link fully formed, a sharp pain coursed through his mind; a splitting headache, as a connection with two fragments of a not-whole mind came to be.

It was like looking through a shattered mirror. One side, the one already with Ryan, showed an almost irreparable sorrow that made Ryan want to break down into tears himself. Meanwhile, the other side had nothing to offer but a deep malice. Pure hatred. And all of it, right at this moment, seemed directed at nobody else but Ryan.

Ryan could see the corrupted mana climb the thread of the link, all the way up to Ryan's chest. But within a few centimeters of his chest, the corruption seemed to be repelled. As if an invisible wall surrounded him. He still didn't know what was going on, but he obviously didn't mind this situation. It was coming in pretty handy for him right now.

With a jump back, Ryan tried to build some distance between him and Energizer. And though it didn't exactly copy Ryan's actions, it stopped moving, and its legs flinched, as if *trying* to jump back before interrupting itself. Clearly, he could influence the fragment to some degree, maybe even more than he could with Maximus, but the corrupting malice fought against him every step of the way.

Ryan focused as much as he could on trying to actively "control" Energizer. He didn't try to suggest anything; he tried to command. To force an action to be taken onto the fragment. As much as it hurt him, that was the only thing that he could do, and with how weak the mind within the fragment itself clearly was, it might work.

"Stay still." Ryan stared deeply at the face of the metallic abomination, taking a step forward as he reached out to the jacket wrapped around its arm. Though it was trying to move, Ryan was stopping it every step of the way. It was making his own movements somewhat clunky, but it was fine. He didn't need to move much anymore. He held his breath as he untied the jacket, letting it drop to the ground. It still didn't move.

And then, Ryan took a few more steps back, reaching out to his own chest. He grabbed his shirt, and managed to make Energizer copy the action. It crunched the metal of its chest within its grasp and then tore it away. It was a lot, but not enough. There were still some layers between Ryan and the core.

Right at that moment, Maximus climbed back out of his domain. Ryan had been trying to hold him back, because it would be too dangerous for Maximus. If he ended up being corrupted as well, Ryan would never be able to forgive himself. But Maximus wasn't a child; he was a knight. His job was protecting others and slaying monstrosities like the one in front of them right now.

"Go back to the clubroom and find pliers . . . or anything else to open up the original robot," Ryan told Maximus, who didn't hesitate for a moment to do as told. He sprinted past Energizer back toward the clubroom, while Ryan and the thing in front of him were stuck in a stalemate.

The more he was trying to dictate Energizer's actions, the more it was fighting back. Like it was learning what it had to do to stop him. At this rate, Ryan wouldn't be able to hold it back until Maximus returned. He had to think of something else. Some way to stop that thing and save Gaia's fragment.

That was when Ryan felt something move by his chest. He glanced down for just a moment. The corruption was slowly encroaching on him, creeping closer by the second. Whatever was protecting Ryan, it wasn't invincible.

Ryan tried to glance around without letting go of his focus on Energizer, trying to see if he could find anything that might be of help to him. But there was nothing; he was just in the hallway, in a standoff against something that could rip him apart if it got a proper grasp on him. His heart beat heavily, though at this moment it didn't feel like fear.

"Ryan!" Modak's voice came from behind Energizer. Ryan quickly glanced past the robot to try and see what was going on, and noticed the orc running toward him with not only a large wrench in his hand, but also Roxie, while Maximus was running right by his side. On the other end of the hallway, Ryan could see Richie, still weak from those few moments of being attacked by the corruption.

"What are you doing here? You need to—"

"Oh shut the hell up already!" Modak barked out. "I'm here to help!"

Modak slowed down when he got close enough to Energizer, glancing down at Roxie in his hand. He took a deep breath while Ryan was trying to figure out what his friend was doing. And then, something happened. The flow of mana inside the figure across from Ryan suddenly changed. It was like it was being pulled away, like water creating a vortex as it flowed down the drain. Not only that, but Energizer started shivering. Like an earthquake running through its body.

Once this started, Modak rushed around Energizer, taking a closer look at the gaping hole in its chest. "Do you have it locked down properly?"

". . . For now, but I can't . . . I can't do it much longer," Ryan responded, watching as Modak glanced around the interior for a moment before shoving the heavy wrench into a very specific spot. The corrupted mana immediately tried to pull the wrench into itself, practically gluing it into that exposed layer.

And then, without hesitation, Modak started pulling on the wrench with his whole bodyweight behind it. His large hands were wrapped around the handle; his knuckles clear and apparent as the veins in his hands bulged.

Ryan didn't even have to ask what he was doing; it was the exact thing that he himself had been planning on doing once Maximus came back with some kind of tool. Modak was trying to finish the job and tear the last layers off Energizer. But then, Ryan might not have been able to concentrate on locking Energizer down like this.

The last few layers were slowly being peeled back. This would be impossible if it were made just out of metal, but it was layered with plastic and wires and foils; things that made it ultimately weaker to what Modak was doing. As the layer was removed, Ryan could see nothing but an ocean of black threads, slithering around each other like worms or maggots, climbing onto one another as if fighting for dominance. There was nothing left of the calming sensation of Gaia's mana.

"Alright, keep it locked down. I got this—" Modak started, but Ryan immediately tried to stop him.

"Wait! Don't do that! The . . . the corruption attacks mana. It tried to latch onto Richie earlier and Maximus as well. I don't know if it can do that if the mana's not directly exposed, but—"

"It latches onto mana? That makes this easier, then," the orc responded as he shoved his hand inside that writhing mass that he himself couldn't see. The only reason Ryan could was because it was originally Gaia's mana, and he was already Gaia's keeper. Modak might not understand the gravity of the situation, or at least that's what Ryan thought.

Modak wrapped his fingers around Energizer's original body, and Ryan could feel the sensation on himself, as if needles stabbed into every part of his skin, over and over again. He could feel the skin on his arms tear and pain flow through his muscles as if it was the only thing he ever knew. His face went deathly pale as he tried to resist, soon watching the original Energizer's torso be torn out from the mass.

Ryan's arms felt numb as he stared at the writhing mass of blackness that Modak was fiddling with. But he didn't feel like he could let go of the link yet; there was something he still had to do. Meanwhile, the figure that had been built around Energizer was now just standing there in the middle of the hallway. A one-armed statue with a gaping hole in its chest, made from both old and new electronics. Ryan was finally able to properly see it, as all the mana was falling away now that it was disconnected from the fragment.

And the same thing happened just a moment later, as Modak managed to finally pull the fragment from Energizer's torso. That black mass fell away from the small robotic body and all that could be seen was a small glass tube with a mostly black crystal within it. But around the edges, Ryan could still see a green hue. It seemed like the mana was no longer being pulled out of it now.

"Thanks, man, this . . . thank you," Ryan said, carefully taking the corrupted fragment from Modak, but the orc pulled back when he saw Ryan's hands.

"Are you okay? Your hands are clearly . . ." he pointed out, and Ryan looked down at his palms. They were still bleeding, but they didn't particularly hurt anymore. Stinging and burning, sure, but nothing else. He should get them cleaned up properly, though, but that could wait right now. Modak gave the fragment to him, and Ryan pulled open the glass tube, letting the fragment fall onto his palm. The link was still up, and the corruption from within the core was still trying to attack Ryan.

"That's fine . . . come here," Ryan whispered, rubbing his fingers over the fragment. He tried to speak to the part of Gaia within it, now overcome with nothing but hatred and fear. Without the link, he doubted he would be able to even get through to it at all.

Slowly, the fragment fell apart into threads of mana that climbed along the link, directly into Ryan's chest. Parts of the corruption were stripped off at the point of that wall that it couldn't pass earlier, but it soon broke through and touched Ryan's skin. Just like what happened with Maximus before, most of the corruption was then stopped by his own skin, but even that wasn't enough.

Part of it bore into Ryan, into his flesh. He could feel the tendrils of the corrupting force spread over his chest, as if someone had poured molten metal over him. But the pain soon settled down, and he only felt some numbness as a number of system windows appeared in front of him.

[You have found another Fragment of Gaia (2/3)]

[The Fragment of Gaia has been purged of Corruption]

[The -Spirit Domain- Skill has leveled up]

[You have leveled up!]

Ryan took in a deep breath, placing his palm onto his chest. He could feel that something was off, but that could wait. He looked inward at Gaia's domain.

The second fragment had properly settled and joined the first. Currently, they were floating beside each other, moving in a slow dance as if happy to be reunited.

At the same time, he noticed that the two domains had grown a little larger again, giving both Maximus and Gaia more space, though the latter obviously had no use for it just yet. Now that he checked on Gaia, he had to focus on Modak again.

"Are you okay? You just stuck your hand in that—did you not feel anything?" Ryan asked nervously, looking at his friend's hand, but Modak just slowly shrugged.

"Well . . . no, I didn't. You said it latches onto mana, right? I mean, I . . . don't have any mana."

A bit confused, Ryan looked up at his friend. "What do you mean?"

". . . Mana rejection disorder. My body physically cannot hold any amount of mana. Not even healing magic works properly on me," Modak laughed awkwardly, clearly hoping to move the conversation away. He turned to the "statue" now stood beside him. "So . . . we probably have to report this, right?"

"Yeah, we definitely have to, yeah. Let's head back to see how the others are doing, first," Ryan sighed loudly, reaching down to pick up his jacket. The inside was completely torn up, as he had feared. But better the jacket than himself. His shoulder was more than enough in that regard already.

Ryan also reached out to Maximus. "Want to get back into the domain?"

The knight shook his head, looking deep into Ryan's eyes. Looking at the spirit, he could tell that Maximus was probably not too happy about how little help he ended up being just now, and wanted to stick by Ryan out here just in case.

As he walked past the figure of metal, Ryan looked at its back. Roxie was fused into it, barely recognizable.

"Richie altered it so that it would immediately turn as much mana as it could into kinetic energy," Modak explained, and Ryan scoffed lightly.

"And he did that without hesitation? I've got to thank him for that. I could feel it resisting my influence less when its mana went out of whack."

The three made their way back to the clubroom, which had emptied out a fair bit. There were still some people in here, but even most of those were in the middle of heading out after all of this. Besides Silvia, the only club members that remained were the three whose Duelists were destroyed: Kit, Richie, and of course Vanda.

Kit was in the midst of trying to salvage what was left of Lightspeed. Luckily, only its arm was really torn off, so it might be possible to repair it. As for Richie, he had sat down and was still recovering from the corrupted mana. It must have been a real shock to him. Once again, Ryan felt grateful for whatever it was that protected him, though that protection was clearly used up by now.

And meanwhile, Vanda was seated in the corner, her face in her hands, sobbing. Silvia was next to her, trying to comfort the girl somehow. Ryan immediately beelined toward them.

"Vanda," Ryan called out, and with a flinch, the hobgoblin looked up. She could see the blood dripping from his fingertips.

"I-I didn't . . . I didn't know that was going to happen, I-I just—"

"I know, don't worry." Trying to be sympathetic, Ryan squatted down in front of her. "It would be stupid for you to do that kind of thing. But either way, I need you to tell me where you got that fragment from. Who gave it to you?"

Vanda hesitated for a few moments, glancing past Ryan at Modak, who slowly nodded his head. She tried to calm herself down, closing her eyes while wiping the tears away from the fur on her cheeks. She opened her mouth . . . and not a single sound came out. Vanda looked up at Ryan and Modak, confused. "I said it was ——! Why can't I . . . It was ——, ——!"

Whenever Vanda tried to say the name, she simply was not able to. Something had forbidden her from doing so.

CHAPTER TWENTY-NINE

Confrontation

Yes, sir, of course! I'm sorry about the delays, I will have the reports on your desk on Monday morning! Yes, of course, I'm making sure that Mr. Blanchard's request is well taken care of." Simon Grand sat in his car, a fake broad smile on his face as he spoke to his superior on the phone. This upbeat demeanor was something that he had practiced for more than a decade now. A broken, swollen nose wasn't enough to make that façade crumble. "I apologize that you had to worry about this at this time of day! Please rest well!"

Before long, however, the call ended, but Simon's white-knuckle grip on his phone continued. He ground his teeth together in absolute anger, looking at himself in the rear mirror. Simon fixed the slightly tilted plaster on his nose, which continued to infuse the swollen, broken nose with high-class healing properties. By Monday, it shouldn't be visible anymore, at least not right off the bat.

"That fucking brat." Simon leaned back in his seat as he pulled out a packet of cigarettes from his inner jacket pocket. He pulled one out and placed it onto his lips, providing himself a flame through his polished, almost-shining metal lighter. Simon stared down the street at the pale green sign. CAFÉ RUNIC.

His instincts as a trapper told him one thing; that he had to be careful of that place. But at the same time, he had no choice but to do this. If he didn't, then Christopher Blanchard wouldn't just let that be. If not this "Ryan," then it was Simon's life that was going to be ruined. He was already walking a dangerous line here.

Obviously, the company didn't openly approve of these kinds of methods. It was more a case of them looking away when it was done by request of an important client or business partner. But even then, it was only if the actions of executives like Simon didn't become publicly known. If he messed this up in any way, he would either be thrown to the wolves by the company he dedicated his whole adult life to, or he would end up in the tight grasp of maniacs like the Blanchards.

Even Simon didn't like doing this kind of thing. His original awakened class was Archivist; he much preferred a quiet desk job where he could file paperwork all day, but things didn't work out. He had been in need of money at some point, made the wrong kinds of contacts, and ended up in a position where he had to run around, licking the boots of newly awakened brats all day long.

Maybe it wasn't quite fair to treat this one kid so harshly. The only thing he did wrong was share a last name with the most influential family in the city. No, the whole country, really. Awakening with a unique class wasn't his fault either, obviously. It just so happened that everything came together perfectly to make Simon snap earlier today.

Not that any of it would matter anymore after tonight. Simon called some of the scum that he knew wouldn't mind getting their hands dirty in exchange for some petty cash. After making a bit of a mess of the café and Ryan himself, things should settle down quickly.

Simon took a deep pull of the cigarette, then pushed it out of the car's window. He looked at the clock, groaning loudly at how long he still had to wait.

The subway came to a screeching halt, and Ryan tiredly stepped out into the station. He turned around, seeing Silvia and Modak following behind.

"You guys don't actually have to drop me off at home, you know?" he pointed out, but his friends clearly thought differently.

Modak shook his head as he stepped up to Ryan's right side, while Silvia took his left. "We're not going to leave you alone with that Bluesky guy running around."

The elf immediately agreed, glancing down at Ryan's hands. "Especially not while you're hurt."

"It's not that bad, it's just some surface-level stuff. Seriously. I still have that healing salve, my hands will be fine by . . . Sunday, I guess." Though he was trying not to worry his friends too much, he did have to admit to himself that his palms were in a ton of pain right now. Though, that might also be the overly tight bandages that had been wrapped around his hands earlier.

They had called the university's security and filled them in, and they had of course called an ambulance for Richie. The EMTs ended up taking Richie to the hospital, and quickly cleaned and wrapped up Ryan's hands while they were at it, though they were clearly in a hurry to help Richie. The presentations tomorrow had obviously been pushed back, but that wasn't even the worst part. Vanda had been taken in by the police afterward.

Of course, since it was her robot that had caused all the damage. However, Ryan was able to fill them in on some things, assuring them that it wasn't her fault. He even went so far as to explain that it was a spirit core that was corrupted, though when he told them that the core "disappeared," he didn't go into enough detail to tell them that it disappeared into Ryan's domain.

In the end, Ryan hoped that Vanda would turn out all right. With things like this, they would probably involve some spells or Awakened that could sense lies, so it should be easy enough for her to prove her innocence. At least, that's what Ryan was hoping; he knew the reality always looked a bit different.

The three stepped out into the streets, already dark, though the sky was still showing a few hints of the summer sunlight. Ryan glanced around, trying to see if Simon was lurking around somewhere.

"Don't worry, we got you," Modak reassured Ryan, who couldn't help but feel embarrassed.

"I'm just checking, alright? I'm not scared of that guy, I just don't want to be jumped again."

Silva patted Ryan's arm. "There's nothing wrong with being scared, you know?"

With a long breath, Ryan nodded. "I know, I know . . ."

However, the three managed to make their way to Café Runic without any sort of incident. Ryan unlocked the door and led his friends up to the flat.

"You guys want something to drink?" Ryan asked as he slipped his bag from his shoulders.

"Do you mean, like, water? Or beer?"

When he considered Silvia's suggestion for a little while, Ryan's brows curved upward. "I mean, we *do* have some in the fridge. And I could use some after today."

While the others were still putting down their bags and hanging up their jackets, Ryan made his way into the kitchen first. He pulled open the fridge, immediately seeing another half-eaten takeout container, added to the collection.

"Godsdamn—Runar, just finish your old food before you order more . . ." he sighed, grabbing three bottles of beer from the top row in the fridge. Ryan placed them on the table and grabbed more bottles from the crate in the corner of the kitchen, replacing the ones that he just took out of the fridge.

Ryan dropped onto the nearest chair as Silvia and Modak followed in kind. "Your uncle's not home?" the elf inquired.

"I honestly have no idea," Ryan replied. "He's probably either out doing some shady bullshit, or in his basement doing gods-know-what."

". . . And you still don't know what's going on?" Modak wondered. "You said Runar mentioned something about filling you in on that phone call, right?"

"Right, but that hasn't happened yet . . . To be honest, I've just been avoiding him all week. Not that it was hard; whenever he wasn't working, he was in the basement or something. He tried to bring something up a few times, but I managed to get away with some pretty basic excuses every time," Ryan replied as he opened up the three bottles.

Silvia seemed surprised by this. "You didn't want to know what's going on? I mean, what's going to happen tomorrow?"

Leaning back in his chair, Ryan contemplated that question for a moment. Of course, he wanted to know—how couldn't he? It might answer a lot of his questions. But maybe that was exactly why he *didn't* want to hear Runar out. "What if . . . it's horrible? What if Runar does turn out to be a vile person? What if my father was caught up in things that I don't really want to know about? And . . . what if my class is a bad omen?"

"If that's the case, then you'll have to face that sooner or later anyway. And honestly? I'd say better sooner than later," Silvia pointed out, looking around the table. She looked at her friends, feeling her heartbeat speed up. "I . . . my birth mother is not a good person, and it took me a long time to really accept that. But in the end, the sooner I learned about all the choices she made, all the things that she did to me that I hadn't realized at the time . . . the sooner I was able to move on. Now I barely think about her anymore, and I was able to become a full part of my actual family. The people that love me and care for me."

Ryan and Modak looked at the elf, who was clearly trying not to lock eyes with either of them. Instead, she was just staring down at the label of the beer, fiddling with it nervously.

"Thanks for sharing that." Modak softly smiled at her, briefly holding his friend's hand to comfort her.

As Ryan looked at Silvia, his stomach churned. She was right; facing the truth and a past that he didn't know would help him. He couldn't run away from it. And there was something else that he didn't want to keep hidden anymore; something he was sick of hiding whenever his back was even slightly exposed. They had only known each other for half a year, but Ryan already trusted Silvia and Modak more than he ever trusted anyone else in his life.

". . . I think I should tell you guys about something that I've been meaning to show you for a while now. Silvia saw it earlier, and I'm sure you, Modak, glanced at it a couple of times before too. I just want to tell you guys about it so that I don't need to hide it anymore." Ryan stood up, dropping his torn-up jacket from his shoulders. He turned his back toward them and pulled up his shirt. His stomach was turning upside down as silence filled the room.

Ryan's back was covered in faded scars, as if someone were trying to fit as many of them onto the empty space as they could. Some were long and thin, others were short with ragged edges. Others were small round dots scattered across. Some of the scars seemed to form patterns or letters, as if someone had cut up his back for fun, or out of boredom. Like scratching your name into a desk at school.

Nervously, Ryan started to explain after pulling his shirt back down. "My mother remarried a couple of years after my dad died. You know, to give me a 'normal' life, whatever that means. He was . . . not a good person, either. Uhm . . . I . . . I know that Runar isn't *this* kind of bad person, but I don't know what I'm supposed to do if I can't trust him anymore after all of this."

He sat back down, refusing to look at his friends in case they were looking at him with pity. It was one expression he didn't want to see them make right now. Even disgust might be better than that.

"You guys, I'm so sorry that you both had to deal with those kinds of things. Neither of you deserved to go through that," Modak said, trying to reassure his friends that everything was fine. "And, Ryan, I know this is scary, but you have to talk to Runar. You can't run away from this. It's going to just keep eating you up from the inside. At the end of the day, it's your choice, but we all know that you can't just ignore this."

As if Modak's words had summoned him, the flat's door opened and shut with a loud slam. Ryan's heart skipped a beat as he stood back up. "You're right. I'll have to talk to him."

Heavy footsteps rushed through the hallway, and Runar rushed past the open kitchen door for a moment, before stepping back and peering inside. Seeing Ryan, his eyes immediately widened, and he rushed in, carrying what seemed to be a birdcage with some dark fabric covering it.

"Runar, we need to—" Ryan started, but he was quickly interrupted as Runar placed the birdcage onto the ground and rushed up to his nephew. He didn't even glance at Silvia and Modak as he stepped up to Ryan, grabbing his head with both his hands to stare deep into his eyes.

"Are you okay? Are you hurt anywhere?" In a complete panic, Runar started to "inspect" Ryan. His eyes let off a soft, pale-green glow that made Ryan flinch and move back in confusion, but his uncle didn't let go of him at all.

Ryan was about to ask Maximus for help, but the knight was seated in his cabin, simply observing the situation. It all overwhelmed Ryan a bit too much, but before he really needed to do anything, Modak had already jumped up and was pulling Runar away.

"Keep it easy!" the orc exclaimed, as Runar turned around toward him with a startled expression.

"Wait, you—Why are you guys here?" Runar pushed away Modak, who unknowingly stepped onto the edge of the fabric that was tossed over the birdcage, making it slip off ever so slightly. The others didn't seem to notice, but Silvia saw something move inside the cage, and it didn't seem to be a bird.

"We all came back here together after everything that happened today." Ryan pulled away, and Runar stared at him nervously.

"Wait, what happened today?"

"What—You don't even know and you're acting this insane? Dude, what is going on with you? I literally texted you that I was jumped by that Bluesky guy, you don't respond to me, and then you come home, act like a maniac, and then say you don't even know what's going on?" With an almost furious glare, Ryan stared into his uncle's eyes. "And are you seriously using a skill right now? You're a fucking Awakened?!"

When Runar realized what he just heard, his eyes widened. "You were jumped?! Did that guy hurt you anywhere? Was he the one that tried to infect you with the corruption?"

The words coming from Runar's mouth confused Ryan even more. He had no idea what was going on right now. How did Runar know about the corruption? Rather, if he didn't know that Ryan was jumped, how did he know that something happened to him in the first place?

But what ended up really making Ryan's mind short-circuit was when Silvia lifted the birdcage, pulling the covering off it. And what was inside of it was not a bird. At least, not a bird that Ryan had ever heard of.

It was a creature from storybooks. The fairy tales that parents read to their kids. Inside the cage was a small pixie.

CHAPTER THIRTY

Under the Basement

Ryan stared at the sleeping pixie within the cage, and Runar's neck snapped around in a panic. "Okay, I know this looks really weird, but I can explain everything, alright?"

"Oh, can you? Are you going to explain to me why you have a . . . a thing that I didn't even know was real in a cage? Why you know about the corruption? And will you finally tell me the truth about what you know about what the fuck a Spirit Keeper is?!" Ryan wasn't able to keep his voice down anymore. It was all just boiling over, and he couldn't stop himself. Runar looked at his nephew, and then let out a careful, slow sigh.

". . . Fine. I . . . I promised your dad I wouldn't get you involved in this, but . . . honestly, I think it's a bit too late for that now," Runar sighed loudly, before turning around toward Silvia. "Also, please put the cage down. I barely got her to fall asleep on the way, she's a very anxious young girl. Alright?"

Silvia looked back at Runar, glancing past him over at Ryan. He nodded his head, though hesitantly. After Silvia put the cage down, Runar turned back to Ryan. "Do you want them to be here for this?"

Ryan didn't even need to think about it. "Of course, I trust them both implicitly."

"It's your choice, just don't regret it," Runar replied. "But first. Before I tell you anything at all, you have to tell me what happened with the corruption. Did it attack you, did it latch onto you?"

Slowly, Ryan placed his hand onto his chest. He could feel the traces of whatever that was still writhing on his chest. He looked at it earlier, and it definitely didn't look pretty. With a sigh, Ryan pulled off his shirt. While he didn't know what was going on, he *wanted* to trust his uncle. He wanted to believe that Runar was the good guy.

On his chest, black tendrils had embedded themselves, bulging like thick veins that were ready to burst. Runar's face went pale as he looked at his nephew. "How are you even standing like that? It's got to hurt, right?"

Ryan shrugged. "I mean, kinda, but not really. It's just kind of numb, to be honest."

With a long sigh, Runar leaned forward to take a closer look. "Alright . . . it looks like it latched onto your skin, but . . . not your mana? Wait, is . . ." Slowly realizing what happened, Runar let out a loud laugh. "Your mana poisoning is protecting you."

". . . What?"

"Yeah, you were exposed to a massive amount of mana, and a bit of it is still inside of you. It basically acts as a shield to the corruption. Dungeon mana is almost impossible to corrupt. It's trying, which is why it's still latched onto you, but it can't actually do it," Runar explained, sighing with some relief. "You're lucky as hell, you know that?"

Ryan looked down at his chest. "Was that why the corruption was repelled like that?"

"That . . . was for a different reason. I placed some protective runes on you that held back the corruption, but since it's already latched onto you, I can't remove it just like that, but we have a bit of time until it gets worse anyway," Runar pointed out, sighing a breath of relief as he straightened his back, noticing Ryan's deep stare.

"You're . . . a Rune Mage?" Ryan asked, with a slightly confused smile on his face.

Runar raised a brow. "Yeah, you got a problem with that?"

"No, it's just . . ." Ryan didn't know how to say it, but Silvia luckily didn't mind saying what they were all thinking.

"Your name is 'Runar,' you own a place called 'Café Runic,' and you're a Rune Mage? Isn't that kind of playing into the theme a bit too much?"

"Okay, firstly, rude. Secondly, I didn't name myself, and my brother came up with the name for the café. Alright?" Runar turned around and picked up the bird-cage, stepping into the hallway. "Now follow me. Oh, and by the way, even if Ryan trusts you two, I should make something clear. If you two say even a word about what you'll find out, you should be prepared for the consequences that come with that."

On an ominous note that didn't bode well for Silvia and Modak, he left the kitchen. Ryan put his shirt back on, and looked at his friends, "If you guys don't want to know, you can—"

"Shut up, you kidding? Obviously we're going to come along," Modak scoffed. "That's a pixie in there! A real pixie!" The orc's eyes were filled with curiosity and excitement, and Ryan couldn't blame him. His heart was beating strong in his chest, and not just out of anxiety.

"Silvia, what about you? Really, you don't have to," Ryan pointed out, but Silvia seemed to be of the same opinion as Modak. She had pushed for Ryan to figure out the "mystery" behind his class and father in the first place.

"I will not let you two get involved in some secret underworld without me." With a scoff, Silvia stepped out of the kitchen as well, and Ryan and Modak followed behind.

Inside his domain, Maximus was seated on his bed, without the intention to come out anytime soon. He was still just watching, barely even reacting when Ryan tried to talk to him. Whether he finally ended up remembering something, or whether he himself was just anxious, something was going on, and it was putting Ryan on edge.

The three followed behind Runar. They walked out of the main flat and made their way down the stairs to the basement. The door itself seemed very ordinary. Old and wooden, fitting what you would expect from a building like this. Runar pulled a key out of his pocket and unlocked the door, pushing it open with a creak. And what they walked into . . . was a regular basement.

There was a workbench in the corner, some tools hanging on a pegboard on the wall. Boxes stacked up in the corner and lots of clutter everywhere. Really, nothing out of the ordinary. It was kind of disappointing, really.

". . . This is the big secret?" Ryan asked with a sigh, but Silvia playfully hit his side, clearly enjoying the situation.

"Don't you watch any movies at all? There's clearly some hidden passageway somewhere," the elf pointed out, looking over at Runar excitedly. "So, where is it? Behind that old bookshelf?"

Runar turned toward her and sighed, shaking his head, "No, it's not there. But honestly, you're taking all the fun out of the reveal, you know?"

He stepped into the center of the room and squatted down, pressing his palm onto some runes that had been carved into it. The wooden boards creaked loudly and shifted aside in a familiar way, revealing some stairs spiraling downward. Ryan looked at Runar, locking eyes with him as he looked up. "What?" Runar asked, and Ryan scoffed lightly.

"A 'friend' installed the adaptive door, huh?"

". . . I mean, I couldn't tell you *I* did it," Runar pointed out. "Though I guess it's just another lie on top of everything else, so . . . sorry about that."

"No, honestly, I should've known. No way you'd have friends," Ryan said quite bluntly, stepping down into the dark stone stairway.

While waiting for Silvia and Modak to go down as well, Runar started complaining, "Man, I know that tension between us is high right now, but that one was *really* uncalled for."

Once everyone was in the stairway, the wooden boards shifted back over them, for a moment encasing them in perfect darkness. But it didn't take long until that changed; along the walls and on the stairs, like safety lights, long lines started to glow. Runes were written within the lines at regular intervals.

The group continued climbing down the stairs, down and down, much farther than Ryan would have ever imagined. The stairway was narrow and spiraling, to the point where it was starting to make Ryan dizzy. However, that didn't last long, as before long, the group reached a chamber at the bottom of the stairs, with a large stone door on the other side of the room.

"Another layer of defense?" Ryan asked, growing more and more nervous. This situation was already ridiculous in the first place, but somehow, seeing something like that gave him even more anxiety. What kind of things was Runar involved in that he had hidden this space to this extent?

Runar stepped up to the door. "You can never be too careful. There are a lot of things to protect behind this."

He placed his palm onto the door, once more activating some runes that covered it all over. The heavy door scraped open, and Ryan's heart skipped a few beats. What was behind there? Treasure? A drug den? A secret murder hole?

Was it a bad idea to come down here with Runar after all? Ryan turned around toward his friends. They seemed similarly anxious, though he could see a bit more curiosity on their faces than Ryan imagined on his own. But really, he had no idea what his face looked like right now.

But what he saw instead was something he really didn't expect. Plants. Thick leaves and vines right in front of the door that it tore through while opening up. Runar rolled his eyes and shook his head as if disappointed. He quickly stepped through the door, pushing the leaves and branches out of the way. "Every single time . . ."

Confused, Ryan, Modak, and Silvia followed behind him, unsure what to say. They took a few steps forward and the door quickly closed behind them. As they continued on and the plants seemed to become less dense, Ryan was able to see something as he peered up through the thicket.

He could see stars. Which didn't make any sense, obviously. They had gone down so far, so how could there possibly be stars here? And then, Runar pushed aside the last wall of plants, making way for Ryan, Silvia, and Modak to step through.

"This is the Sanctuary of the Hidden," Runar explained with a certain proud smile on his face, though Ryan could tell that there was some bitterness in his voice and face. But really, he couldn't focus on that right now. Instead, he focused on what was in front of him.

A trampled dirt road, some houses, and even street lights. They were all made of old stone, like some of those really old structures left behind from Old Riverside. It was basically a small village surrounded by trees and vines that seemed to climb up on the sky itself.

"What the actual fu—" Ryan yelled out, but Runar immediately pressed his hand onto his mouth to stop him.

"Be quiet—there's people sleeping down here," his uncle warned him, but that just confused Ryan more.

Silvia took a few steps forward, looking around curiously. "There's people down here? And what do you mean with 'hidden'? Whose sanctuary is it?"

Letting out a loud sigh, Runar turned back around and started walking again. "I'll explain it to you in a second. But really, just keep it down a bit. And . . . no matter what you see, don't make too much noise, alright?"

They continued walking forward, and Runar seemed to be looking for something. And, as though he found it, he pointed his hand forward, speaking in a clear, but not loud, voice, his foot impatiently tapping on the ground. "You, come here."

"Hm?" Ryan let out, looking into the direction that Runar was pointing at. But he was just pointing at some plants. Though, those plants soon started walking. It was a mass of ivy, as if a statue was overgrown.

With its head hung low, the moving plant approached Runar, who slowly looked past them. "You two as well," he added, and from the thicket, two more came out. One was a lot shorter, seeming more like a child made of moss, and the other didn't look like a person at all. Instead, it just looked like a decently large dog made of thorny vines and some roses blossoming on its back and head.

"What did I tell you about blocking the doors?" Runar asked, clearly waiting for an answer. The person made of ivy started to . . . shift, as if the leaves of its body were trying to respond to the question.

Runar sighed, "You say that every single time, but I assure you, nobody besides me can come through there anyway."

Slowly, the three sentient masses of plants looked at Ryan, Silvia, and Modak, who were watching this scene unfold in a mixture of shock and confusion. Shaking his head, Runar assured those plant people. "Don't worry, this is my nephew and his friends. They're fine, they're with me. You can trust them," he explained, before turning back to Ryan, finally starting to explain. "These three are dryads. There's around two dozen of them down here, and as you can see, they're intelligent and sapient plants."

"Uhm . . . hi? Nice to meet you, I'm Ryan," he nervously said, looking at the three dryads, instinctively trying to reach out to shake their hands. However, they all backed away, scurrying off back into the thicket.

Runar patted him on the shoulder with a smile. "Don't worry, they're just not great with strangers. I'm sure with time, they—"

"What the actual fuck is going on here?" Ryan immediately asked, pulling away from Runar with a deep stare, not sure exactly why he acted so casual about sapient plant people just now.

Runar looked away, continuing to walk down the road. "Our family has been protecting those who can't protect themselves for . . . a thousand years now?"

"And what's that supposed to mean? Protecting whom? From what? And 'our family'? Does that mean my dad was involved in this as well?"

"It means exactly what I said. We protect people and animals that can't do it on their own, and we mainly protect them from society itself. 'Our family' means the 'Aglecards.' And yes, obviously, that includes your father."

"So . . . you're the good guys?" Ryan asked hesitantly, hoping that he was understanding things correctly. Runar stopped walking and turned around, staring at his nephew.

"Hold on, did you actually think I was a criminal or something?"

"Well, yeah, what did you expect? I overheard that phone call earlier this week about something that's supposed to happen tomorrow."

". . . Right, I was afraid that was the case. That situation is a bit more complicated still; we're doing something like a test run tomorrow," Runar explained with a long sigh. He started walking up the stairs leading into one of the buildings. Ryan quickly followed behind, more focused on Runar. But Silvia and Modak were just stunned as they looked around excitedly.

"So this is a secret society thing?" Silvia asked excitedly, practically jumping up the steps. Runar simply nodded.

"It sounds a bit silly, doesn't it? But yes, that's basically what it is," Runar explained, pushing open the door in front of him. The space inside the building was fairly simple; a single large space with some couches in the corner and a desk on one side of the room. There were bookshelves and some metal filing cabinets set up as well, but the thing that stuck out the most was the small ball made of sticks, leaves, and flowers set up on a small pedestal right next to said desk.

While Ryan, Silvia, and Modak were still looking around, unsure what to expect, Runar made his way to the desk and put down the birdcage, then opened it up a moment later.

Carefully, Runar scooped up the sleeping pixie to place it inside the spherical "nest" next to the desk. Once that was done, Runar sat down on the chair on the other side of the desk, and looked at Ryan, locking eyes with him.

"Alright, sorry that I've been still a bit dodgy until now. But let me really fill you in now. My name is Runar Aglecard. I awakened as a Rune Mage at the age of thirteen. Five years later, I was officially named the head of the Aglecard family."

CHAPTER THIRTY-ONE

The Family Business

You're the head of a motherfucking secret society?" Ryan let out almost involuntarily after he heard his uncle's words, and Runar slowly nodded his head.

"Yes, I am. Your father was supposed to inherit that position, but before that could happen, he cut contact and moved away to Maidsbury. He became an accountant, met your mom, and . . . got sick," Runar explained. "He never wanted you to be a part of this whole thing. It was his biggest fear, to be honest. But he asked me to take care of you should you be forced to get involved."

Ryan stared back, a bit confused. "What do you mean, 'forced to get involved'? This is about my class, isn't it?"

"Obviously it is. It . . . your class is a—" Runar started, but the conversation was quickly interrupted as someone, or something, stepped through the door. It was a small, stout, one-meter-tall figure. Its body was round, and its arms and legs were short and stumpy. It was also completely made of stone, except for the large hole in its head that revealed a complete crystal interior.

Ryan immediately stepped between it and his friends, but Runar jumped up a moment later. "Wait, wait, wait!" He tried to stop Ryan, running over to the side of the small stone figure.

"This isn't like a monster or anything, they're called geodes. They're made of stone and crystals, and they're also very much alive and one of the people that we protect," Runar explained. "Nothing down here is inherently dangerous, alright? So . . . don't beat anyone up."

The geode in question slowly looked at Runar. The crystals revealed through the hole in its face glowed and then dimmed again, in rhythmic patterns, while at the same time a soft whistle like wind chimes sounded out. Runar seemed to be listening and watching intently, slowly nodded his head.

"Hm, okay, thanks for letting me know," Runar sighed lightly, rubbing the bridge of his nose annoyed. "I'll go to talk to him in a bit, alright?"

Happy with that answer, the geode turned back around and walked away, without paying attention to Ryan and the others at all.

Modak curiously peered after them as they waddled away. "I've never heard of a 'geode' before . . . was that it talking just now?"

Runar looked at the orc with a raised brow. "First of all, 'they,' not 'it.' Geodes aren't objects, they're people. I know they might not look it, but let's treat them like it, alright? But second, yes, that was them talking. They communicate with light and those small vibrations that make that ringing sound. Took me years to learn how to understand them properly. And then all the different languages . . . that was a pain, really. But worth it. It's much better than having them all write down messages for me."

"I don't . . . I don't get it," Ryan slowly let out. "So this place is a 'sanctuary' for people like them? People that don't . . . look like us?"

"It's not about how they look," Runar replied. "We take care of some people that look just like anyone else, and visually wouldn't stick out. But . . . they can't coexist that easily with others for other reasons."

Ryan frowned lightly, "What other reasons?"

Trying to find the right words, Runar ran his hands through his hair. "So . . . let's take pixies as an example. They're smart, they have sapience, and they hit all the official marks for a 'person' that's been established by the World Rights Organization. But they can't speak. They don't have vocal cords, and they're legally deaf as well. However, they can innately sense mana, and manipulate the mana in their bodies to talk to each other. But because they weren't able to communicate with other species, they are officially classified as . . . animals."

"Wait, really? Weren't there any other ways to check that?" Silvia asked, looking at the spherical nest with a sad frown. "Like having them write, or . . . or, I don't know, just anything other than assume they're animals?"

"Of course they could have, but why would they? People just assumed pixies weren't intelligent and didn't care to check." Runar walked over to the couches, then sat down on one. He motioned toward the couch across from the small coffee table to have Ryan, Silvia, and Modak sit down as he seemed to prepare himself to continue. "And then, they found out that pixie . . . pixie blood, flesh, and bone have healing properties. Back in the day, many high-quality potions or elixirs were made with them as a prime ingredient. It was better for people to *not* think about the 'what-if.' But at this point, pixies are an endangered species. We're not entirely sure, but we think that we're currently protecting about 90 percent of all the pixies left."

Ryan's face went pale as his stomach turned upside down at the thought of a person being turned into medicine. "So what, this is what you do every time the store is closed? You go and try to save people in danger?"

"I mean, I don't go out and do it myself, usually. We . . . have a lot of people working with us. I end up having to do a lot of administrative work. People come and go; my entrance isn't the only one. We have a couple others nearby that might be a bit safer depending on the circumstance. But I had to go this time because of the situation that the pixie girl was in," Runar explained, as something that Ryan had never seen from his uncle before appeared on his face. "She was about to be auctioned off as a pet . . . I managed to bust the auction. We work with the police to some degree, as necessary. They know we're doing *something*, but they stay out of it as much as possible."

A thought crossed Modak's mind. He felt horrible about asking this the moment after Runar spoke about illegal auctions, but since he had ties to the police, he just had to come out with it. "Do you think you can help my friend? She . . . she's clearly going to get in trouble because of everything that happened today . . ."

Runar looked at Modak with a slightly confused frown. "I mean, I try not to get involved with legalities for unrelated matters, you know? I'm sorry about your friend, but . . ."

"It . . . is related," Ryan replied, glancing over at Modak before turning back to his uncle. He started filling him in on the events of the day. Runar listened intently but nervously, finally understanding the source of the "corruption" that had latched itself onto Ryan's chest.

He leaned back in his seat and sighed. "So that's what happened," he muttered, turning to Modak while pulling out his phone. "I'll tell my people and have them take care of this Vanda girl, alright? You don't need to worry, she'll be fine."

"You have reception down here?" Silvia asked, pulling out her phone to check, but Runar shook his head, pulling off his phone's case. On its inside, arrays of runes were revealed.

"You guys won't, but I'm transmitting the signal from my phone to a point upstairs," he explained, starting to write up a text while glancing back up at Ryan. "Now, you have the second fragment? That's good, that makes things a lot easier. Even those guys can't hide the last one if we have more than half."

Ryan frowned, leaning forward. Clearly, Runar knew more about the spirit cores than he wanted to admit. But now, he wasn't in a situation where he could hide that anymore. "Alright, you have some stuff to explain to me. What is my class?"

Runar, still typing the message to his "people," started to explain. Though, he seemed to be using it as an excuse not to look at Ryan directly. "The 'Spirit Keeper' has always held a special position within our family. The first 'Aglecard,' the one who founded our family, was a Spirit Keeper. Since then, it's been passed down, but only after the death of the last Spirit Keeper. There's only one at a time. Though, it wasn't always the family head. Actually, the Spirit Keeper hasn't been the family head for . . . five hundred years? Your father would have been the first one in a while."

Taken aback, Ryan looked at his uncle. "Wait, but . . . my class has never been registered before. If my dad was one, then how . . . ?"

"Well . . . The identity of the current Spirit Keeper has always been kept a secret, until you. It's always been safer that way. Again, the Spirit Keeper class is a bit special. Or rather, it holds a special meaning for those in our circles," Runar explained. "Like a symbol; a beacon for those that need help."

Ryan slowly averted his gaze. He looked inwardly at Maximus, once more trying to pull him out. This time, he didn't resist. The knight appeared on the table between the two couches. Looking at him, Ryan asked him something that he had already asked him a few times. He just hoped that he would be able to remember this time. "So? Do you have anything to tell me now? You knew about all of this too, right?"

Maximus stood there, clearly not sure how to respond. But Runar quickly responded for the spirit. "I . . . I actually don't think so," he pointed out, and Ryan glanced at his uncle again.

"What do you mean?"

"I knew Maximus before. He was one of the spirits that Hayden protected, and was at the forefront of any battles. Of course, I only saw him a couple of times; I was just a kid, after all," Runar explained, "But . . . when your father . . . when he cut off his connection to the system, that stopped. He was the keeper of many spirits, but their cores were completely scattered. Most of them were injured in some way, whether it was by fragmenting or even irreversibly shattering. We haven't been able to wake up the few that we managed to find, but we've always assumed that the process led to irreversible mental damages. Honestly? Amnesia seems to be a light consequence. His personality is still the same, it seems."

Ryan was trying to follow along. He felt bad for doubting Maximus, especially since he was clearly a victim here.

"My father cut his connection to the system? What . . . what's that supposed to mean?" he asked, though Ryan already knew. He clenched his fist, his knuckles turning white as his fingernails dug into his palm.

Modak and Silvia had been trying their best to stay silent while this conversation was going on, not wanting to interrupt something as heavy as what was being revealed right now. But that didn't mean that they weren't there to support Ryan. Modak patted his friend's back, while Silvia placed her hand onto Ryan's clenched fist, trying to get him to relax.

Ryan closed his eyes and took a deep breath. Seeing that, Runar carefully responded.

"It means that he reversed his awakening." Runar looked down at Maximus, with a bitter, regretful expression. "And in the process, he hurt a lot of spirits that only deserved to be protected."

"And how's that even possible?" While Ryan heard and understood what Runar was saying, the idea of someone "un-awakening" just didn't make sense. In the first place, the way the system really worked and the reasons behind its existence still weren't known even more than a millennium after it first came to be. Reversing an awakening was a ridiculous idea.

And even Runar seemed to agree. "It's insane, I know, but it's what happened. He did it all on his own. I've been trying to look into it since I became the head, but . . . nothing."

Ryan looked at Maximus. He was abandoned by Ryan's father, clearly without the latter contemplating the consequences of his actions. But there was something that made Ryan even more mad, specifically in regard to the knight. "So my father . . . doomed a ton of spirits, and then kept Maximus around as a souvenir? Are you fucking with me?"

Runar leaned back in his seat, slowly nodding. "Yeah, that's basically it. Maybe he kept Maximus around for the next Spirit Keeper. But until you awakened, we thought that Hayden got rid of the class altogether, so I really don't know. Clearly, though, it was the right time for the keeper to come back."

Ryan was a bit confused. "What do you mean? 'It was the right time'?"

"Well . . . the Spirit Keeper isn't usually handed down from parent to child, and you becoming the keeper isn't because you're Hayden's son either. The Spirit Keeper is chosen by . . . 'fate'? Frankly, most of the time, they weren't directly related to our family, and we found them and took them in after they awakened. It was always people chosen because they deserved the title and the weight behind it, and because they would cherish the spirits."

Ryan scoffed, not particularly happy with the idea, "So . . . what? 'Fate' brought Maximus to me?"

"Is . . . fate even real?" Modak asked, deeply skeptical at the idea.

And before Runar could respond, Silvia looked at the orc. "Of course it is! Fate is all around us, constantly! Guiding us, helping us, leading us to where we're supposed to be."

"Yes! Yes, that is true, but . . ." Runar quickly took over, looking at Modak who still wasn't entirely sure, ". . . fate isn't forcing you to do anything. It's this complex amalgamation of mood and timing and all these little coincidences that might bring you to the right point in time. It's still your journey, you are the one in control. For example, if Ryan weren't a good person, and didn't actively make the choice to protect and help others when he can, no matter *how* he does it, he wouldn't have awakened as a Spirit Keeper. Fate isn't some omniscient force either; we've learned that in the past, other people that were candidates to become Spirit Keepers were given the opportunity to awaken by fate, but due to their actions and personality, it didn't happen."

I guess that's a pro? Ryan thought to himself. The idea of "fate" being the only reason he awakened, something beyond him that he couldn't control, felt almost demeaning. But if the reason for his awakening was that the choices that he made in his life were bringing him onto the right path, and that it meant that he could be trusted with the safety of others, despite the mistakes that he has made in the past, that felt . . . good. Just good.

"This is all . . . a lot," Ryan pointed out with an awkwardly nervous smile on his face. "So what does that mean? Do I have to fulfill some kind of role now?"

Runar shrugged. "Not if you don't want to. I mean, the family elders might complain a bit, but my word goes above theirs. If you want to help out somehow, we can find a way for you to do that. If you want to not get involved in any of this, I can keep you blacklisted."

". . . Blacklisted?"

"Basically, it just means that no member of the family or adjacent groups we work with is allowed to contact you directly. It's usually used more for like . . . an exile thing? But it's useful here as well," Runar explained. "I can't justify keeping it up if you get too involved, and once it's removed, I don't think I will be able to reverse it."

"Can I think about that for a bit? I think I need to sort of . . . digest it all, you know?" Ryan asked, his mind racing with far too many thoughts for him to make such a decision right now. His gut was telling him to just agree, and to see what the hell this new world he didn't know about had to offer him. But at the same time, making such an important decision without considering the consequences? That would be insane. There was clearly something bigger going on, something darker than was obvious right here. Ryan had to consider if that was something he wanted to deal with.

But there was still something else that Ryan needed to know. "So, what's going to happen tomorrow?"

Runar's face immediately dropped as he leaned forward, almost startled. "A-About that . . . So, there's a species we're currently working on integrating into society. But we can't just *do* that, you know? So . . . we're doing a test run. It's this ten-year-old kid. He'll go to school, he'll make friends, and hopefully act as a great example that they *can* live well in society with the tools we're providing."

Surprised, Ryan raised his brows. "Oh . . . I thought it was going to be a bit . . . more than that. What's the trouble with that, then? Why were you freaking out so much?"

"Well . . ." Runar sighed loudly, not sure how to say it. In the end, he chose to just come out with it. "He's going to be living with us."

CHAPTER THIRTY-TWO

The Vampire Kid

Could you repeat that?" Really not sure if he heard right, Ryan stared at his uncle with a perplexed expression.

Runar sighed loudly, "Listen, it's part of the job, alright? I end up housing a lot of people upstairs, especially individuals that struggle because of curses or mutations or things like that. This is just the first time that it's going to be a long-term thing."

"Where's he even supposed to stay? I'm not sharing my room with a kid, you know?" Ryan pointed out, but Runar quickly calmed him down.

"Of course not, don't worry. I guess you didn't check it yet, but I cleared out my office. We're having some people come tomorrow to properly set the room up for a kid his age. A bed, a proper desk, windows that we're darkening, and a bunch of school stuff for when he starts."

Ryan frowned lightly, glancing at his friends to see if they noticed it as well.

"You're darkening the windows? Why?"

"Oh, the kid's a vampire. They have awful sun allergies so we need to block it in his bedroom, obviously. We have this really potent sunblock for when he goes outside, though, but his bedroom should be even safer."

Considering that there was a sapient mass of rocks talking to Runar with lights and vibrations earlier, and a pixie was sleeping just a couple steps away, Ryan knew he shouldn't be surprised by the fact that vampires were still around. Though Silvia seemed like she just had to make doubly sure.

"Vampires are still around? Seriously? I thought they all died out centuries ago . . ." she asked, both taken back and curious. Runar let out a long sigh and nodded his head.

"Yes, they're still around. And so are ghouls, and succubi, and titans, and—you know what? I'll give you guys a list later; that might make this a bit easier. A lot of species thought to be either extinct or fictitious are real and hidden from society's eye," he replied, slowly pushing himself off his seat. "But yes, again, vampires still exist. Yes, they're allergic to sunlight; no, they don't mind garlic, and they're also not vulnerable to holy magic or depictions."

". . . So, why are you struggling to integrate them into society?" Ryan asked, waiting for the other shoe to drop. Runar sighed loudly. This was the part that he was worried about revealing the most, obviously.

"Because they have to live off blood. Or rather, the mana dissolved in all of our blood. They can survive off animal blood for a while, but most animal blood doesn't have the right quantity or quality of mana, and it can lead to plenty of health issues. Something like . . . extreme, extreme scurvy, basically," he started to explain. "But most species of people have a higher quality of mana, so that's where they would need to go for their blood. And you can imagine why that would cause . . . friction. It's the reason why the vampires of the past were slaughtered like monsters in the first place."

Ryan held his hand to his neck carefully. Everyone that had heard stories of vampires knew about the classic bite mark on the neck. Runar was immediately able to tell what he was thinking, and quickly shut his thought process down.

"Oh, no, that's not how that really works these days. I mean, there's always vampires that go rogue, but that's really just comparable to other criminals, you know? We have been buying up excess blood from blood banks for a while and providing it to any vampires that have made contact with us. So there's no direct physical contact. But we have actually been working on something that just left its last clinical trial phase, hence why we're doing a proper test run now. We've been working on artificial blood." Runar stood up from his seat and walked over to his desk, looking for some documents that were scattered around.

Ryan turned around, looking at his uncle with some disbelief. "You guys invented artificial blood just so that vampires don't have to feed off people anymore?"

"Well, not *just*. It's going to take a little longer to adapt it to every species and blood type, but once we do, it's going to go into trials to be used in the medical sector, but that's still a bit away."

Finally finding what he was looking for, Runar picked up a piece of paper and brought it over to Ryan, Silvia, and Modak, handing it to them. It seemed to be the results of the trials that they had run: "In our long-term tests, a full 98.7 percent of vampires were able to fully replace their blood intake with our artificial blood. For the remaining 1.3 percent, who were only unable to do so because of things like indigestion and mild intolerances that came with the artificial blood, we believe we can adjust the formula as we would into different blood types to make this possible. Oh, and of the ones that *were* able to replace their intake, 95 percent had an improvement of health over the course of the next three months, and none had a decrease."

"So . . . what? You can distribute this to all vampires? And then you'll hold a big press conference, announcing the existence of vampires?" Ryan asked, unsure exactly how this was all supposed to go. He was happy that he wouldn't have to worry about being randomly bitten by the kid that was going to live with them starting tomorrow, but this was still a bit confusing.

"Well, we're going to be adjusting the formula and using it as a base for something like those meal-replacement drinks, so that vampires can also start enjoying their meals a bit, and then we'll try to sell them in stores across the country and then expand internationally. And otherwise? We'll just have vampires slowly reveal themselves. They already live in society; people just don't know that they're vampires. They look near identical to humans, just with slightly more pointed ears, so people probably assume they have some elf blood in them. Well, a press conference isn't a bad idea, though. Just to make it clear that vampires aren't dangerous."

"Wait . . ." Ryan placed the piece of paper down on the table, looking back at his uncle. "So if they're already living alongside us, just 'hidden' . . . the test run means that the kid is going to live with us, and we're going to publicly tell everyone he's a vampire?"

"Yep. Legally there's already no issue with vampires coexisting with us as long as they don't harm other people, and since we've practically solved that problem now. It should all go relatively well. Frankly, these days, people *are* very open. The last species that we properly integrated a few decades ago were the arachnids, and that was a challenge itself, but we got through that, so vampires should be alright."

Modak raised his brows surprised. "Wait, you did that with arachnids?"

"Oh, yeah. Non-humanoid species are always a bit rough to integrate, but it all worked out. You know Aranea, the head librarian at your university? She's actually the great-granddaughter of the arachnid representative from when our family helped them integrate." Runar smiled lightly. "I've met her a couple of times, since we still work with arachnids to ensure that they're treated well and their rights are kept up. Actually, I—"

In the middle of Runar's sentence, his eyes widened, confused. "Who the hell—" he let out, jumping onto his feet, groaning loudly. "Godsdammit . . . sorry, there's something I need to take care of."

As Ryan looked at his uncle, whose irises had started glowing in a soft green light, he saw an expression he had seen plenty of times before. Usually, when there was an annoying customer in the café that Runar was dreading dealing with, he would make that exact face. Usually Ryan would end up taking care of it, but this time, it was different.

"You guys go ahead and stay down here. It won't take long, and running up and down the stairs multiple times just gets annoying sometimes. There's still a lot that you guys should know about." Runar walked over to his desk and grabbed something that was laying on it. A black engraved fountain pen with golden inlays and small metallic feathers on its end. The engravings looked similar to the ones that were on his father's model-building tools. "I guess it's a good chance for you to just digest everything, and maybe talk out what your plan is after this. Oh, and Ryan, if someone comes here and is confused about who you are and why you're here, just tell them your name, and you should be fine."

"Uh . . . Sure, I guess. Do you need any help?"

Runar looked at his nephew, as if contemplating it for a moment, but he just shook his head in the end. "Nah, I got this. Alright, I'll be right back!" He rushed out the door, shutting it behind him. His footsteps quickly faded away, and Ryan leaned forward, burying his face in his hands. Silvia and Modak were similarly silent, until the dense air was cut apart.

"Holy crap, Ryan!" Silvia let out loudly, looking at her friend as she jumped up from the couch. "A secret society? A secret! Society?!"

"Don't look at me like that, I had no fucking clue! Honestly, I *still* feel like this is some weird, elaborate prank!" Ryan admitted, throwing up his arms. "Like . . . how is this kind of shit even real? This isn't some kind of book . . . is it? Are we in a book? Is this whole thing a stupid fucking book?"

"Calm down, guys. This is crazy, but it's clearly real." Modak slowly stood up with a long sigh, but both Silvia and Ryan were just staring at him.

"Don't act so big, you're obviously freaking out right now," Ryan retorted.

"No I'm not."

"Yeah you are."

"What makes you say that?"

"Your eye is doing that thing again."

Modak held his hand to his cheek, feeling his eye twitch nervously. With a click of his tongue, the orc replied, "Okay, fine! This is insane! How could I not be freaking out right now?"

Seeing how his friends were reacting, Ryan slowly stood up and looked at them both. "I . . . if this is too much for you guys, I can tell Runar and you guys don't have to get involved in any of this."

Though they both wanted to reply immediately, neither of them was able to. This was much too complicated for them to come out with an immediate response. There was so much weight on all of this, and they barely had any time to process any of it.

Finally, Modak asked, "What about you? Will you . . . stick around? Will you become a part of this whole . . . thing?"

Ryan thought about it for a moment. He turned toward Maximus and looked inwardly at Gaia, her two fragments floating in her domain. "Yeah. Yeah, I'll stick around. I can't back away from this anymore. There's no way I can go back to living a normal life, always wondering why my father would . . . doom so many spirits. And come on, this is the perfect place for me. I can actually help people. I can . . . I can . . ."

"If you're sticking around, so am I," Silvia said bluntly. "I mean, I know that it's probably different for us, and our decision in this has less weight, but still. I'm not going to leave you alone here."

After the elf's immediate response, Ryan was overcome with relief. Not having to do this alone was going to make this all so much easier. But Modak still had some concerns.

"What if this is dangerous?" he wondered, clearly worried about some things. "I mean, Runar literally placed a protective ward on you. That's not something you do if there's no threat of something horrible happening. Not to mention, that 'corruption' thing? Are we sure that's a level of danger that any of us want to be exposed to?"

Ryan once more didn't have to think about the answer too much. "Dangerous or not, this is something I have to do. I can't not do this."

". . . Alright. In that case, I'm staying as well," Modak replied, though the answer seemed to be coming with quite a bit of concern. Nonetheless, Ryan knew that Modak was just as curious about all of this as Silvia was, even if he showed it less than the elf.

"Thank you, guys. I cannot tell you how much it means to have you guys here with me," Ryan smiled lightly. "This shit is so weird and tough to wrap my head around, and not having to do it alone means a lot. And Maximus, you—"

He turned around and looked at the small knight, just to be quite taken aback by what he saw. Tiny figures just barely reaching a little above Maximus's knees. There were seven of them, roughly humanoid and completely ink black. Their bodies were practically a "blank slate"; no eyes, ears, or mouth. Their heads were perfectly round and their limbs round and straight.

These things were all standing in front of Maximus and staring up; even the knight himself didn't seem to have noticed yet, as he was focused on Ryan. But realizing that something seemed to be wrong, Maximus glanced down, finally spotting the figures.

Startled, he took a step back, where another one of them was standing. As Maximus's leg hit that figure, it fell apart into a black smoke that unnaturally moved around the knight's body, gathering in front of him and turning back into that figure.

"What are those?" Silvia took a step forward and squatted down in front of the table. "They're kind of cute!"

"I think those are . . . sprites?" Modak suggested, also squatting down next to the table to take a closer look. "Yeah, yeah for sure! I still have a children's book with these in it that my mom would always read to me; they helped the main character with something . . . Finding some jewel in the forest or something?"

"Are you talking about *The Hundred Tales of Shazir*?" Ryan asked, a bit surprised to hear it brought up. It was a story that he loved as a kid; rather, the one memory that he had of his father was being read this story by him. "Right, they helped Shazir find that gem . . . that massive ruby; Tiar, or something, right?"

Modak quickly nodded his head. "Yeah, that's them, right?"

"I think so?" Ryan responded, glancing down at the small figures.

Runar jumped up a few steps at a time, sighing with an annoyed expression on his face. He already had plenty of things to deal with, so why were those meddlesome bugs here to waste his time?

Once he got out of the stairway and the floor closed back up behind him, Runar quickly stepped out of the basement. He didn't even bother locking the door behind him; this wasn't going to take him long.

Runar held the fountain pen in his hand forward, drawing something in the air. It was a series of runes floating in front of him in a soft green; the color of Runar's mana. Droplets of magic were detaching off the writing, and he let out a long sigh. "Man, I should really get some more sleep. My mana control's completely out of whack."

As if triggered by it, an exhausted yawn left his mouth as he pulled back the pen from the runes in the air. The mana began to glow for a short moment before dissipating in a flood of individual droplets, spreading all throughout the building. And before he knew it, Runar could see the outlines of everything beyond the walls of the break room he was in. The counter, the tables, and the chairs pushed up against them; the shards of broken glass on the ground; and of course the seven men that were standing inside the café.

"Two Awakened . . ." he muttered to himself as he spotted the large quantities of mana in two individuals, one of them being a twisted purple he recognized. "Those damn sparrows really don't hold back, do they?"

CHAPTER THIRTY-THREE

The Patriarch

Oi, quiet it down, will you?" Simon barked with an annoyed glare, watching the grunts walk through the café.

"Don't tell them what to do," responded the man next to him, speaking for everyone in the room. Simon glared at the man's feline face and the graying fur around the tips of his muzzle. "It's already bad enough you called us here so short notice."

"You're being paid well enough, aren't you? And for the record, I didn't pay you to smash a fucking window."

"What does it matter? We're trashing the place anyway, right?"

"Yes, but a broken window can be seen from the outside. If anyone calls the police, then it will make things a lot more troublesome." Simon clicked his tongue, but the other man shook his head.

"Not like this is going to take long. The only guys that live here are some random middle-aged weirdo and a freshly awakened kid. This many people's already total overkill."

"Don't underestimate that 'freshly awakened kid.'" Simon touched the plaster still on his nose. The swelling had gone down quite a bit, but you could still see that his broken bone was healing.

"Exactly, you can't underestimate him. Plus, thirty-nine is *not* middle-aged. I'm technically still in my thirties, you know?" Runar added, throwing his arms around the two men from behind, as if he were casually joining two friends.

He noticed Simon flinch as the felisad's fur stood on its end. They both wanted to move, but their bodies were completely paralyzed.

"Who—Wait, you're that kid's uncle, how the—"

"Shut it," Runar interrupted Simon, who had alerted the grunts to the situation. "You're paying for the window, by the way."

With a casual stride, Runar took a few more steps forward while the grunts were looking at him, confused. From their point of view, it was just another guy that had joined in, and seeing neither their boss nor the guy that was paying them do anything made them hesitant about what they should do. However, the felisad quickly changed that.

Baring his sharp teeth—his fangs covered in a thin layer of gold—he hissed a command at his men, "Get this guy already, you absolute imbeciles!"

Seeing their boss's expression and hearing his command, the grunts—a group made up of more felisads and the doglike canirs—quickly came rushing at Runar. However, Runar simply stretched out his hand and wrote a single rune into the air. The moment he closed his eyes, that ancient symbol lit up in a bright light that fully illuminated the room in a flash for just a moment, as if he had summoned the sun to him.

As they were recovering, Runar closed in on one of the canirs, grabbing his arm and twisting it around with a clean motion. Together with the clean snap of some bones, a whimpered yelp sounded out.

"Seriously? You're gonna try to break into someone's place despite being this weak?" Runar sighed as he pushed the canir back, making them fall onto their back. As this was happening, one of the felisads got to Runar, swinging a baseball at his back. But Runar just stood there, unamused, not even flinching at the impact. He grabbed the bat, closing his grasp around it. The aluminum was crushed easily, and the cat-man let go of the bat nervously.

"What the fuck?" he let out, backing away. The other grunts also seemed very hesitant at attacking Runar; he was an Awakened, and a powerful one at that. Figuring that he should just finish this, Runar held his pen forward and drew patterns into the air. The green writing fell apart into droplets that quickly flowed toward each of the five grunts, forming metal bands that wrapped itself around all of their ankles. As this was happening and the grunts anxiously tried to get rid of them, Runar wrote something else into the air.

"S-Stop him, you morons!" their boss yelled out, but before they were able to do anything at all, Runar was finished. One of them tried swinging at Runar, but he fell forward as the metal bands were locked into their position. They weren't heavy; it was just impossible to move them now.

Now that this was taken care of, Runar turned back toward the two men that he already locked down with another method. From Runar's own point of view, they were both enveloped in a thin layer of his green mana. Simon was clearly trying to do something to free himself, but the quality and density of Runar's mana wasn't something a guy like him would be able to go up against.

"So, what was the plan supposed to be here? Trash the place, threaten Ryan, and get him to give up his class?" Runar asked, staring into the elf's face, who was overcome with nothing but confusion.

"Y-You're not supposed to be an Awakened. You're not registered, you—"

"And you're not supposed to break into other people's places or fucking jump a kid, you little piece of—" Runar stopped himself and tried to calm down. The protective ward he secretly placed on Ryan already broke down today, so the idea of something else happening to him was more than just infuriating. "Who told you to do this?"

". . . I acted on my own. Getting our company a unique class? That kind of thing's worth a hell of a bonus," Simon said with a nervous grin. Runar knew that he was lying. There was no way that even Bluesky would go this far without being pressured by someone, and considering what Ryan's class was, that was even more obvious.

Runar looked toward the felisad next to Simon. "Did he tell you anything?"

Instead of saying anything, the man just spat at Runar. He dodged it, of course, but it still annoyed him.

Runar rubbed the bridge of his nose. "I'm going to go insane over this . . . Alright, so. You've got a couple of choices. First, you tell me everything you know, swear to never let me lay eyes on you ever again, and then get out of here with nothing more than a few bruises or broken bones. Second, I call the cops on you and let the legal system handle this. Or third, you refuse either of those options, and I make you regret ever crossing the Aglecards."

Simon flinched. ". . . What? But . . . that kid's not . . . he said he wasn't related to *those* Aglecards, so I checked the registry and every record I could find . . . there's no connection between that brat, his father, and the Aglecard Foundation!"

Runar sighed, annoyed, "You really think records can't be changed? Who do you take us for?" He clicked his tongue. "I'm just saying this once, as the current patriarch of the Aglecards, that my nephew is under my personal protection."

The elf's face went pale. "Patriarch?"

"I could explain, but why would I even bother? You know what, you've annoyed me too much, we're going with choice number three." Runar snapped his finger, and the startled yelps of five grunts could be heard as the metal bands wrapped around their legs forced them to approach Runar.

He wrapped his fingers around the first grunt's throat, pulling his hand up until he was fully in control of the position and movement of that felisad's head. Even though he tried to do everything he could to pull Runar's hand away, the Rune Mage didn't let that happen. Instead, he started writing something into the air right in front of the cat-man's face. It was a complex collection of runes that came together into an intricate pattern. Once Runar activated it, the felisad's eyes rolled back until only the whites could be seen. His hands fell to the sides of his body. It was like he was unconscious, yet still standing.

Runar repeated this same thing with the other grunts, and then looked over at their boss. "Let me guess, he only hired you for this?"

The two locked eyes, and the felisad hesitated to respond. His instincts were telling him one thing; run. Usually his fight-or-flight response leaned toward the fight side, but that wasn't even an option here. That attempted spit earlier was a rebellion against his instincts, but what followed was nothing but a deep, biological fear.

"I-I . . . I'm just doing my job, I . . ." the felisad nervously whimpered, and Runar sighed, starting to write that same pattern into the air in front of him.

"Fine. I can get all my answers from this stuck-up sparrow, then."

"W-Wait, I-I'm sorry, just please don't—"

The man's eyes rolled into the back of his head as his shoulders slumped, unconscious like his subordinates. Runar snapped his fingers, making the metal bands disappear from the grunts' legs while getting rid of the hold that he had on their boss. "You will all go back to your hideout, or homes, or wherever else you were gonna go after this. You will believe that when you came here, this elf guy . . . Simon, was it? He told you that the plan changed and sent you off. You will cut all ties with him for wasting your time. You will forget ever seeing me or speaking with me, or even that I exist. Oh, and the reason that guy's arm is broken is that he got into a fight with the guy with the bat or something, and the bat broke in the process. Now, leave and never come back here."

The moment Runar finished talking, the hired brutes made their way out of the café, jumping out through the broken window. They walked down the alley and disappeared without another word.

Runar walked up to the window, grumbling to himself. He thought for a moment and then started writing a few more runes into the air. After the activation, each shard of glass was surrounded in what seemed to be a thin film of magic while Runar's eyes were glowing with a similar magic. He squatted down and started picking up the pieces, then put them back together. The shards of glass practically fused back into one piece, but Runar was able to pick out the right parts as if he had the instructions right in front of him. "Should've made those guys do it before leaving."

While he was repairing the window, Simon was still locked down, unable to move for the most part. However, even though he was surprised and wasn't able to do anything right away, it didn't mean that he was weak. He knew how to use magic quite well, and had been pushing the tendrils of his mana through the magic surrounding his body so that he could try and cast a spell.

"I wouldn't do that if I were you," Runar pointed out, glancing over at the elf.

"I'm just trying to do my job here, alright? It's not my fault that the bra— That the kid awakened a unique class. They're always popular with powerful people, you know?" Simon pointed out. Though it seemed like he was changing tactics into talking himself out of the situation, Runar could still feel the subtle movements of magic as Simon uselessly tried to break out of the spell.

"But does that mean you have to stalk him and then try to jump him when you find out he can't retaliate?" Runar asked, locking eyes with Simon for a moment.

". . . As I said, I'm just doing my job here."

"Excuse me? I know Bluesky is a scummy, corrupt organization, but I didn't expect them to openly teach people to act like delinquents," Runar laughed.

". . . While I admit that some sides of our business should rather stay hidden from the public, I don't believe that is a correct characterization of Bluesky Industries."

"Then you don't know who you're working for. Bluesky's the scummiest of scum. The bottom of the barrel. The dragon's litter."

A frown formed on Simon's face. Obviously he did believe in Bluesky, but there was no reason for him to completely defend the company even in the face of someone that was so overwhelmingly more powerful than he was. Especially not considering the fact he was unable to move and utterly defenseless. But there was something bothering Simon. "You sound like you've dealt with Bluesky before."

"Hm? Oh, yeah, plenty of times. Actually, I just went to this auction earlier; it was an underground thing where they sold drugs, weapons, magic beasts, and even people as pets. Though I guess you might not consider them people just yet. Anyway, it's almost exclusively funded by Bluesky. Well, legally there's no connection, and they hid the paper trail far, far too well to do anything officially, but everyone kind of knows who's the big shot over there," Runar explained. Simon wanted to protest; a group as prestigious as Bluesky Industries would never stoop to running some sort of illegal auction like that. But at the same time, the fact that he was being told this so openly made the elf anxious.

". . . Why are you saying all this? Are you going to . . ." Simon asked, though he wasn't even able to finish the question. With a loud laugh, Runar looked over toward him and shook his head.

"At least you've got a sense of humor, huh? No, I'm not going to kill you; we don't do that kind of thing. Though, you *are* going to forget everything that happened tonight, just like those guys earlier."

". . . What?"

Runar chuckled to himself, "Well, tonight, plus the past . . . hmm, what sounds good . . . the past seven weeks? Yeah, seven sounds pretty good."

". . . Alright," Simon let out, closing his eyes for a moment. Frankly, losing memories of the past seven weeks was much preferable to dying, so if he had to choose, it was obvious. Though, it looked like neither was going to happen. The tendrils of Simon's mana had escaped the restraining shell around him, and he was able to start casting a spell. It was a very simple one too, one of the Arcane Trapper's staples. It was quite destructive, but one of Simon's class traits allowed him to completely ignore the magic damage from his own traps. Though, it would take a bit to set it up, and some conditions needed to be fulfilled by Runar.

"I figured you'd complain about it a bit more. Losing your memories isn't a fun thing, you know? It's not the kind you usually hear about either; this type is permanent."

Simon couldn't help himself but laugh. "Permanent mental interference? Please, that's just a myth."

Runar shrugged. "So are pixies, and I have one in my basement."

The elf's heart skipped a beat. Runar was serious. He was so clearly serious about what he was saying. Simon was going to forget the past seven weeks without chance of recovery? That was . . . insane. Still better than dying, but insane.

"Anyway, before that . . ." Runar started, taking a seat on the table behind him while looking at Simon, "let's get started with you telling me exactly who told you to 'acquire' the Spirit Keeper class."

"No, I don't think so," Simon replied, a grin forming on his face. Runar was close enough to activate the trap.

With a large, violent explosion, bright yellow flames filled the entirety of the café's interior. They swallowed the chairs and tables, and even Runar was completely enveloped. Simon couldn't help but grin broadly as the shell holding him down shattered. With a loud laugh, Simon pushed the hair out of his face. A thin cloud of mist formed in front of his mouth as he spoke, "This is what happens when you . . . when you . . ."

The realization came a bit delayed. Why was there mist when he was breathing and talking? Why was it so . . . cold? Of course, the flames shouldn't hurt him, but he should still be feeling the heat. The flames faded away. Nothing was scorched; there wasn't even the slightest hint of soot or damage, no matter where Simon looked. And Runar was still sitting on top of the table.

"You done?" Runar looked back at him with a yawn, clearly bored by what was happening. "Gods, you're acting like a toddler right now."

Simon stared back at the man in front of him. That was his most destructive and powerful spell. And it didn't even touch a single hair on Runar's head. No, it was even worse than that. Runar had somehow made Simon's flames *cold*.

"What . . . what are you?"

Runar sighed, pushing himself back off the table, "I said it before, right? I'm the patriarch of the Aglecard family."

CHAPTER THIRTY-FOUR

Aides

With an exhausted drag, Runar climbed up the stone stairs in front of his office, then pushed open the door with a yawn. He stepped inside, seeing Ryan, Silvia, and Modak huddled up around the coffee table.

"Hm? What're you guys doing?" he asked, curiously taking a step closer. And what he saw did surprise him. It was Maximus. In double. Of course, there was the original Maximus, his silver armor with red highlight plates, just as he had looked before Runar left. But right in front of him, mirroring Maximus perfectly both in form and motion, stood an ink black counterpart.

"Back already?" Ryan asked, surprised. He looked down at his phone, checking the time. "That was barely thirty minutes . . . it took us like ten to get down here."

"As I said, there was just something small to take care of," Runar explained, squatting down next to the table. "So, exactly why are the sprites copying Maximus?"

Modak immediately snapped his head toward him. "So they really *are* sprites?!"

"Mhm. They're made completely from mana. Like magic that has come to life." Runar smiled lightly, looking at the small black figure. "They're actually pretty unique in some other ways. They both do and don't have an individual, sapient experience. When sprites are physically close, they synchronize with each other, sharing their minds and experiences with each other. But each one undeniably is an individual."

Ryan glanced back at the sprites. They had all fallen apart into that black mist and formed a single larger body that looked exactly like Maximus. "Hmm . . . so are they one of the people that you're trying to help integrate?"

Runar shrugged. "We're working on it. Though in their case, similar to elementals, we're less trying to help them be protected on a societal and legal level. Basically, we want them to be given the same rights and protections as spirits."

". . . How would I come into all of this? How would I . . . help?" Ryan asked, looking up at Runar. He thought about it for a moment, but didn't seem to have an answer ready.

"Honestly? However you want to, I guess. I mean, your main task will always be centered around spirits who don't have the ability to form their own bodies, but beyond that, you can try and become part of any area of the Aglecard family," Runar explained, and Ryan seemed to take a moment to think about it. But that moment of silence was perfect for Silvia to ask something.

"Right, about that," she started, her curiosity practically oozing out from every pore as her ears twitched to her heartbeat. "How come some spirits can't form their own bodies? Plus, why does Maximus have a 'class'? I mean, spirits can awaken and all, I know that, but that's different from this, isn't it?"

Runar looked at the elf, sighing lightly. He knew this question was coming, but he knew that it wasn't what they wanted to hear. "We don't know. We have some guesses, but no proof."

Silvia's expression immediately drooped. "Seriously?"

"Yeah, sorry about that," Runar chuckled, looking over at Maximus. "We have two main theories, though. One, all of those spirits without their own bodies are conceptual spirits, but their concept is system-adjacent. So, Maximus wouldn't be a 'Spirit of Knighthood,' but rather—"

"A 'Spirit of the Knight Class'?" Ryan finished the sentence, and Runar quickly nodded his head.

"Exactly. There's a lot of evidence to support it, but not totally. For example, what does the Knight class have to do with 'roots' or 'plants'?"

Immediately, everyone looked at Maximus's body, even the sprites that had come together turned to look at him. Maximus himself glanced at his arm. He was overgrown with roots, and rather, his core was actively held in place by those roots. That was totally unrelated to the concept of "Knights."

Modak turned back to his friend's uncle. "So then what's the other theory?"

Runar hesitated for a moment, though he figured there was no need to hide this. "That there are spirits that simply don't have the ability to form bodies on their own. The Spirit Keeper class was created as a reaction to that phenomenon, and when a spirit links with the keeper, they're awakened into a class adjacent to their concept."

"Excuse me?" Ryan let out in disbelief. "You think that the Spirit Keeper class can force others to awaken?"

Runar sighed, shaking his head, "No, it's just a theory. And it's not 'others'; it's just spirits."

"Does it happen to other spirits? Ones that already have a body?"

"No idea. A spirit that has a body already never joined the keeper. I don't know if it's impossible or something, but . . . it hasn't happened yet, in a thousand years, so I wouldn't count on it happening anytime soon," Runar explained, before letting out a loud groan. "Listen, I can keep telling you all this stuff, but . . ."

Ryan looked at his uncle. He knew what Runar was saying. "I need to decide first?"

"Yeah. Listen, I know it's—"

"I'm joining. I'm a part of this now," Ryan immediately said, and Runar pulled back, startled.

He looked at his nephew hesitantly. "Are you sure? You don't need more time to decide?"

"I could push this decision back a year, but my choice will end up being the same."

Runar let out a long sigh, closing his eyes in contemplation. "Fine." He stood back up, his hands on his hips. "In that case . . . I'm going to need a bit of time. You two sticking around as well?"

Silvia and Modak didn't hesitate to nod their heads. "Of course! If Ryan's doing this, then so are we!"

With a click of his tongue, Runar walked over to his desk. "Well, easier said than done. You two will just have to be considered Ryan's aides for the time being; the Spirit Keeper always has a couple of those."

"Aides? Like . . . assistants?" Ryan asked.

"Uhh . . . basically, I guess. But it's just an official thing to get the elders off my back about this," Runar explained, pulling open drawers on his desk to look for something. Finally, he grabbed what looked like two large coins with a thumb's diameter. He used his fountain pen to write some runes on each of them, glancing at both Silvia and Modak every once in a while, and then threw each of them one of the coins.

"So . . . what is this?" Modak asked, raising his brow curiously as he held the coin up to take a closer look. Runar placed his pen onto the table and walked toward the door, motioning for the three to follow him while he reached out to the sprites that were still in the shape of Maximus. Seeing that they were prompted at, they quickly popped apart and back into their original forms, quickly climbing up Runar's arm until they reached his head. They quickly hid between the strands of his messy hair.

"We use them as a sort of ID. Just a symbol for those that belong to *this* side of the Aglecards, so if anyone here tries to cause trouble for you, show it to them. I put some extra protections onto them as well, so keep the coin close, preferably even while you're sleeping." Runar closed the door behind everyone and led them back to the exit.

Silvia looked around a bit confused. "Wait, are we leaving? I thought you're going to fill us in."

"Tonight?" Runar sighed, "Do you know how late it is? Go home, rest, make sure your parents know you're alright, and come back tomorrow around 3 p.m."

"Awe, man . . . does that mean we'll have to climb up all the stairs again?" Silvia asked as they all walked along the road of these ancient ruins hidden below the city.

"Get used to it. You'll have to come into ruins like this plenty from now on," Runar laughed, walking up to a nearby building. He scooped up the sprites from his head and held them toward the wall. They all quickly looked over at Silvia, Ryan, Modak, and Maximus, who was being carried by Ryan, and waved at them a few times before jumping right into a hole in the wall.

And with that, the small group made their way back upstairs, leaving the underground village behind for now. Runar locked the basement door with that old key, bringing Silvia and Modak outside.

Ryan quickly hugged them. "Thanks for everything, guys. Seriously."

"Don't mention it, man." Modak smiled, looking toward the café's door. "I mean, you're letting us be a part of a secret society . . . that's kinda neat, right?"

"Just 'kinda'? Are you kidding me?" Silvia replied immediately. "This is so freaking awesome!"

Ryan smiled at his friends, about to send them off when Runar stopped them.

"What are you guys doing?" he asked, his brow raised. Modak looked at him, confused.

"We're heading home? As you told us?"

"Yeah, but you're not going by train, not after everything that happened today," Runar pointed at the expensive black car that was parked right in front of the building. "They're going to drive you home tonight."

Startled, the orc looked at the car, not sure what to think. "Wait, seriously?"

Runar nodded, walking up to the passenger side window. It rolled down slightly, though just a slit. "You have the addresses, right?"

Though there didn't seem to be an answer, Runar quickly looked at Silvia and Modak.

"Get into the back. Oh, and don't bother trying to talk to them; they're not very talkative," he explained. Even if they were a bit curious now that Runar had said this, they were also very excited. They got into the back of the car, waving at Ryan as they did so, and the car quickly pulled out into the road and disappeared a moment later, leaving the uncle-nephew pair alone.

They silently stood on the sidewalk. Ryan turned around, walking back to the door to make his way into the café again. As he dropped onto one of the nearby chairs, he looked up at his uncle who had followed him back inside.

"Would you have ever told me about this if I hadn't awakened?" Ryan asked, and Runar slowly opened his mouth, but Ryan wasn't finished yet. "You know, actually, scratch that. Even after I awakened, after I showed Maximus to you, after I found Gaia's first shard . . . you weren't planning on telling me. Even with some fucking weird miasma or whatever stuck to my chest, you were hesitating to tell me."

Runar pulled up a chair and slowly sat down on it. He was moving so slow that Ryan was wondering if he was trying to buy time to come up with an answer.

"Listen, I . . . I promised your father not to get you involved in this."

"Excuse me? My father, who apparently caused the death of, and crippled even more, spirits that all trusted in him? Why the hell would you do that? Why did you even get involved with him again?" Ryan asked, unsure what he was supposed to think about this whole situation. Knowing his father did something like that made him sick to the stomach. He didn't know why Runar would want to welcome someone like that back into his life.

"It's . . . complicated."

"Dude, I don't care how complicated it is. If that's really what happened, that's inexcusable. Or are you still hiding something? Something that makes what he did suddenly 'okay'?"

Runar looked down at the ground, as if he was embarrassed to face his nephew. "No. There's nothing that would ever make what Hayden did okay. And I did hate him after he left for what he did, but . . . he was still my brother. I asked him so many times why he chose to cut off the connection to the system, but he wouldn't tell me. And . . . and he was sick, alright? How could I . . ."

Even though he wasn't sure exactly what to feel, Ryan looked at his uncle and his expression. At the white knuckles of his fist. He had no idea what the situation was like from Runar's point of view.

"Sorry, it's just very . . . weird, you know? Suddenly being told all of this, I mean," Ryan explained, letting his chin drop to his chest. No matter what the two spoke about now, it would be impossible for Ryan to collect his thoughts well enough to have a fully coherent conversation about everything. So instead, he moved on to something else.

"So . . . you guys have other spirit cores?" he asked, and Runar looked at his nephew with raised brows.

"Right, of course, we do! We have one that's responsive and awake, though we obviously haven't been able to communicate properly. Then there's one that seems awake, but doesn't respond no matter what we do. And then we have small fragments of two more cores," Runar explained, trying to recall the exact number. "We don't know which they are, though."

"Then . . . do you think I could meet them?"

"Obviously! It's going to take a little while to get them here, though. I'll keep you updated." A smile formed on Runar's face, as if he was excited to get this done and give those spirits a proper home.

"Right, thanks. Uhm . . . I do have one more question, though," Ryan started, and Runar's smile immediately dropped. ". . . Why exactly am I building spirits like they're plastic models?"

Relieved that it was just that, Runar let out a laugh. "Oh, that. Well, that part of the Spirit Keeper's abilities presents differently for everyone. Every keeper has a knack for building things, obviously, but it sort of focuses on what they're used to. One of them was a sculptor, who would carve their bodies out of wood or stone. Another a blacksmith who had to forge their bodies. Your father was really into model building, and that's how it presented for him. Guess it was lucky that your dad kept his tools and that you had the same interests."

"Huh," Ryan let out, a bit surprised, "so how would the blacksmith have made, like, Maximus's roots?"

"Oh, all the spirits that were with him were just fully made of metal; it just looked a bit more like wood, I guess. I mean, the one that Hayden, and now you, built were made of plastic and fabric, so—"

"No, Maximus is made of metal. Like, real metal. And the roots are made of wood, and his gloves are made of leather," Ryan interrupted, and Runar seemed to freeze up for a moment.

". . . What?"

"Yeah, like . . . he's made of metal, not plastic. Didn't I tell you about that?"

"I don't believe you did. That . . . I'll look into our records to double-check things about the past Spirit Keepers, but that shouldn't be the case." Runar placed his hand in front of his mouth in contemplation. "I mean, it's good . . . but a bit weird, that's all. Maybe when Hayden cut his connection to the system and forcefully removed his class, some changes were made to it."

Ryan looked over at Maximus, but he really just seemed to be curious about his own body after Runar mentioned this. But, his uncle just mentioned something that interested him. "You took records of the class? Do you have like a skill catalogue?"

"Of course. I can get it to you. We store all our data physically, since it's easier to safeguard it. But it should be easy enough to get a copy here together with the cores." Runar pushed himself off his seat, patting his nephew on the shoulder. "But for now, go upstairs and rest. Dealing with the corruption in your body must be exhausting."

". . . By the way, we're getting rid of that, right?" Ryan asked, pointing at his chest, and Runar laughed and nodded without hesitation.

"Of course we are. I'll be working out a way to do it safely, but we've got a little bit of time for now. So again, just rest."

Ryan nodded his head, standing up as well. He let out a slight sigh while pulling Maximus back into his domain. Without much else to say, he made his way upstairs. He awkwardly pushed off his trousers and dropped into his bed, throwing his arm over his eyes.

"What the actual fuck, man."

CHAPTER THIRTY-FIVE

Liam

Finding himself submerged, Ryan swam through the water sluggishly. Tree-sized plants were shooting up beside him, and rocks the size of buildings blocked his way. On the ground were a number of small pieces of stone and wood, arranged in the form of a person. Not any particular person, just something roughly in the shape of one.

As Ryan continued to swim, he soon found his way blocked by a wall. By glass. He was swimming in a tank. It didn't feel all that jarring to him, though; he had been here for quite a while, after all. Though he did miss the pond that he used to live in quite a—

"Open your eyes, servant!" a voice yelled out right next to Ryan's head. Startled, he jumped up and threw his legs over the side of the bed as his dream faded from his mind before his feet even touched the ground.

"What the—" he yelled out, staring at the face of the person that the voice came from. It was a kid, with short, pure-white hair that practically melted into his just-as-pale skin. It all just made his glowing blue eyes stick out even more. The kid was standing there, fists on his hips, and showing off the prominent fangs in his mouth.

"Perfect! Now swear your eternal loyalty to me, offering me your neck to seal the contract!"

Ryan stared at the boy as the memories from last night caught back up to him. "You're the vampire kid, right? The one that'll be staying with us?"

Smugly, the boy smirked and nodded his head. "I see that my legend has spread far and wide already! Now, show me your—"

Ryan rolled his eyes and got up from his bed. He walked out of the open door into the hallway, then quickly made his way to what used to be Runar's office up here. Though, it was clear that it was just for show, now that Ryan had seen the one below the café. The boy was startled and followed him.

"Did you not hear me, servant?! Show me your—"

"Yo, Runar, what the hell is happening?" Ryan asked, stepping into the room. His uncle stood there, sorting in some books from a cardboard box into the shelf. He turned around, surprised.

"Hm?" he let out, as his eyes moved from Ryan over to the boy standing next to him. "Oh, you already met? You could have slept a bit longer, it's still pretty early."

"I would have, if this kid hadn't yelled into my ear." Ryan glared down at the boy, though he felt a bit silly for it. He was just a kid. Kids were assholes. Everyone knew that.

Runar let out a long sigh. "Right, I should have warned you. Liam is a bit . . . loud."

"I simply have a voice befitting a king! One that can be heard across the battlefield!" Liam proudly exclaimed, letting out a loud laugh immediately after.

"It's 1354. I don't think you want to get involved in the battlefields we've got going on these days," Ryan pointed out, but Liam simply let out a long sigh, shaking his head disappointedly.

"And this is why you're a mere servant, you simply don't understand the art of war."

". . . Runar, why is he talking like this? He's creeping me out."

"He was raised by one of the elders, who just happens to be a total historical fiction nut," Runar admitted, finishing placing the last book from the box onto the shelf before walking up to Liam, speaking to him directly. "We spoke about this, right?"

Liam smugly nodded his head. "Yes, you told me not to make the children at school my servants! You did not say anything about the peasant wasting away in the other chambers!"

Awkwardly, Runar looked over at Ryan, who was just showing a bit of an expression of defeat. "Sorry, he's . . . just kind of like this."

"I can see that," Ryan responded. "Definitely the best choice to show others that vampires are normal people. Also, tell him to stop asking me to show him my neck."

Runar immediately snapped his head toward Liam. "Excuse me?"

The boy pulled back slightly. "I . . . well, that's what the vampires in my books always did, and . . ."

Rubbing the bridge of his nose, Runar sighed loudly, "Yes, and it's not only very dangerous but also really inefficient. No sane vampire feeds like that anymore. Do you not like the blood we've been giving you?"

". . . The artificial blood tastes so bland. No flavor," Liam pointed out, glancing toward Ryan. "But it's not about food anyway! It's about him showing his loyalty and servitude to me!"

"Ryan is not your servant. Nobody is your servant. Stop doing that, or the other kids will think you're weird."

"Hmph!" Liam huffed, pushing out his chest. "You may call it 'weird,' but I call it the aura of a noble!"

Ryan smirked lightly, patting the kid on the top of his head as he turned back around. "Oh you're going to be bullied so bad."

While Liam was trying to protest, Runar peeked out the doorway. "Put on some pants while you're walking around the flat."

"Calm down, I'm wearing boxers. It's only us anyway, right?" Ryan yawned as he tiredly turned into the kitchen, scratching his belly with closed eyes. As he opened them again, he saw two people he didn't know. A dwarf with a finely braided beard that had jewelry woven into it, standing in front of the counter to make himself a sandwich. And seated right at the table was a young demon woman with intricately carved horns and black tattoos creeping up on her neck on her bloodred skin.

Ryan looked at the two people, who awkwardly stared at him as he stood there only wearing a loose, old shirt and boxer shorts. He was trying to process the information for a few moments, but then just gave up and walked up to the fridge, then pulled it open to grab the milk carton. He turned to the dwarf.

"Don't use up all the gouda, please. Wanted to use some for lunch," Ryan requested, pulling the package of granola off the top of the fridge.

"A-Aye, of course!" the dwarf stuttered out, unsure what else to say, as Ryan grabbed himself a bowl and spoon. He poured some of the granola into a bowl and poured milk over it, and after returning both to where he grabbed them from, he sat down at the kitchen table to eat with his phone pulled out.

After quickly turning around the corner to see what was going on, Runar let out a long sigh. "Ryan, what are you doing?"

"Eating breakfast?"

"You could also introduce yourself."

"Bro, I'm tired as shit, just found out that we're part of a secret society, and had a vampire try to yell me into subservience," Ryan replied. "Let me be antisocial for a bit."

Runar sighed loudly, starting to sign toward the demon. "Fine, whatever. Anders, Yamada, that's Ryan. I told you about him. Ryan, these are Anders and Yamada, my 'aides.' Well, they're like assistants, really."

Nervously, only just now realizing he hadn't introduced himself, the dwarf stepped up to Ryan and stretched out his hand. Trying not to groan, Ryan grabbed the man's hand and forced out a smile.

"Anders Steinberg, pleasure to work with ya!"

"Ryan Aglecard. Likewise," he replied, before having another hand stretched out to him. The demon shook Ryan's hand silently so he glanced over at Runar.

"Do you know any sign language?" Runar asked, and Ryan shook his head.

"Not really . . . should I learn?"

"Wouldn't hurt. You'll probably need to learn a few other languages too. Which second languages did you take in school again?"

Letting out a loud groan, Ryan remembered that annoying past. "Just Gardian, my school didn't offer anything else."

"Better than nothing, I guess." Runar rubbed the back of his head. "Well, sociability should help with that."

Ryan raised his brows. "Sociability makes it easier to learn languages?"

"To some degree. It definitely increases your language-processing ability, and learning languages is a decent training method for the sociability stat," his uncle responded, continuing to sign so that Yamada could follow along properly. "But whatever, that's not important right now. Luckily Yamada does know how to read lips to a degree."

"Got it," Ryan replied, looking up at Runar. "So, what's the plan for today?"

Runar looked over at Anders, who quickly took out a notepad from his pocket and flipped it open. "We'll be grabbin' some more things for the lad, then we're droppin' by our men in Eastbanks ta get some pixie grub, and then in the evenin' we've got an appointment at the symbiote nest fer Ryan."

When Ryan heard something that he didn't expect, his spoon stopped mid-air right before his mouth. He slowly lowered it and stared at Runar. "The 'what' nest?"

"I'll explain it to you later. It's nothing bad, don't worry," Runar replied, before turning back to Anders. "Did you hear back from the legal department about that Vanda girl?"

Anders immediately nodded his head. "Aye, just earlier today we got the university to drop the charges against 'er. We're roundin' up the ones that witnessed it and havin' them sign an NDA as well, so by the start of the week things should be settled."

Ryan glanced at his phone. It was barely 9 a.m. How did they already get everything figured out?

". . . The power of money is terrifying," Ryan muttered to himself, suppressing a shudder.

Modak pulled open the door, stepping into the robotics clubroom. There weren't many people here; just Kit, Richie, Vanda, and some man in a black suit with slicked-back hair. The man turned around as Modak stepped into the room.

"Excuse me, we're having a private conversation. Would you mind waiting outside for the time being? It will just take another minute," the man asked, and Modak looked over at Richie, confused. Vanda was seated on a stool, her face buried in her hands.

Richie looked at the man and quickly explained, "He was here yesterday as well, he knows what happened anyway. Actually, he helped take the thing down," the gnome replied, and the man raised his brows, glancing at Modak from behind his thick glasses.

He took out a small notepad from his pocket. "What's your name?"

Hesitantly, Modak stepped farther into the room. Unsure what was going on, he looked at the others for help, and Richie just nodded toward him before the orc responded, "Modak Stonebreaker."

The man frowned immediately. "I see. In that case, before we continue, I need you to sign something before we continue."

Even more confused, Modak shook his head. "I'm not signing anything."

"Don't worry, it's just a simple nondisclosure agreement. What happened yesterday was an accident that should not have happened. An experimental power source was recently illegally acquired and made its way here, causing some small interference with electronics," the man explained, taking out a folded-up contract from his chest pocket and placing it onto a nearby table. Modak stared at him, glancing at the small pin that he had on his chest. It was a cursive *A*, one that Modak had already seen before. He sighed lightly and pushed his hand into his pocket, pulling out the coin he was given last night. Modak tried to hold it in a way where the man could see it but Richie, Vanda, and Kit couldn't, and the man's eyes widened for a quick moment before a broad smile appeared on his face.

"Ah, actually, I remember your name being amongst the ones that already signing the contract, correct? In that case, there is nothing to worry about," the man quickly said, before turning back to the three students behind him. "Well, as I said, please contact us if you have any inquiries about damages to personal property. We are ready to fairly compensate you for any issues our out-of-control power source caused."

Without further ado, the man then walked past Modak, giving him a quick nod, before walking out of the clubroom.

". . . What was that just now?" Richie asked with a confused frown. "He just left like that?"

"Was he bothering you?" Modak glanced back at the door, but Richie shook his head.

"Not really bothering us. He was just being pretty pushy about everything that happened yesterday," he explained, glancing over at Vanda.

Modak looked at the three nervously. "So you're all okay?"

"'Okay' may not be the right word," Kit pointed out, clopping his hooves on the ground, clearly annoyed. Vanda sank into herself even more.

"I . . . I'm sorry. I didn't know that was going to happen, I just . . ." Vanda started, but she couldn't finish her sentence, unable to find the right words to explain everything. And Modak knew exactly why; she had no idea *how* to explain things. She just knew that her robot rampaged.

"Where did you get that thing anyway? They called it an 'experimental power source,' but Ryan mentioned something about some kind of core? Does he know what that was?" Richie wondered, looking directly at Modak as he spoke. The orc hesitated. He obviously wasn't able to just tell them what was going on, now that he knew what he knew, but he also couldn't just leave them completely in the dark.

"It looks like it has something to do with Ryan's class? You'll have to ask him; I only know a few surface-level things." Modak tried to excuse himself from that sort of conversation. Acting like he didn't know anything was the best for the time being. "But more importantly, what about the showcase thing? It's been canceled, right?"

Richie nodded. "Yeah, we had to push it back a few weeks. That's why the three of us are here right now, talking about what to do next, since our Duelists are the ones that broke. But Vanda, she . . ."

"I'm not participating anymore." The hobgoblin shook her head immediately. "I ruined everything! Because of me, both of your Duelists are broken, and I—"

"Lightspeed is not completely broken," Kit interrupted, and Vanda slowly glanced at him. The minogid quickly explained, "Its arm was torn off, and it short-circuited in response, but it should be something repairable over the next few weeks."

"And I was just doing it for fun anyway." Richie shrugged. "It's kind of a shame that Roxie broke, but as long as nobody got seriously hurt, it's alright."

"But . . . but you got hurt, and Ryan did as well, so I—"

Richie quickly interrupted her, "It was just a bit of a shock to my magic circuitry. It's happened plenty of time while I was trying to learn new spells."

"And Ryan's alright too," Modak added. "His hand got a bit scratched up, but by the time we were at his place, he didn't seem to really care anymore."

Vanda slowly looked up at the others around her. "I ruined everything—why are you being so . . . nice?"

"Because that clearly was an accident," Richie laughed a bit, rubbing his bulbous nose as he leaned against the table behind him. "I mean, you're definitely to blame for how you acted while things were going on . . . Energizer was rampaging and you were begging Ryan not to destroy it, but I also get why you did that. But at the end of the day, this all started because of an accident. If you could purposefully make something like that, you'd be a genius amongst geniuses. And you're smart, but you're not *that* smart. No offense."

Vanda scoffed lightly, in disbelief over what she was hearing. She rubbed her tears out of her eye. "Even so, the others don't think the same, right?"

Richie rubbed the back of his head. It was true that the other club members were furious about what happened, even though they were able to get away pretty quickly without any of their private property being damaged. And while the gnome personally didn't believe that it was Vanda's fault, it was also hard to blame others for being upset and not wanting Vanda to be a member of the club anymore. It was a "weird" situation, to say the least. Even Modak wasn't totally sure about it for a bit, but by the time he realized that Vanda wasn't even able to speak about who gave her the fragment, it was clear she was just used by someone with a bigger goal in mind.

"I'm sure we can figure something out, alright?" Richie suggested, and Vanda slowly nodded her head. Kit also seemed ready to forgive her, especially after hearing her side of things.

The minogid slowly stroked his goatee in thought. "Do you think it would be possible for you to create a new prototype Duelist until the new showcase?"

Vanda shook her head without hesitation. "Are you kidding? It took me months to build the old one. And I don't have the money either. Plus, even if I did have everything, I'd just run into the same old problems as before."

"About that . . ." Modak started, looking at Vanda while pulling something out of his bag. He had texted her earlier, and she said she was here, so he figured coming to this place on his way to Ryan's place would save him some time. The orc soon held forward his mana tape and customized tape recorder. "That's actually what I'm here for. Your issue was that you weren't able to create high-frequency mana patterns, right? I think I've got a solution for that."

CHAPTER THIRTY-SIX

Emotion

Silvia stretched as she climbed out of bed, a broad smile on her face. She glanced at her phone, seeing a message from Fae, and her smile grew even bigger as she took her phone to respond.

Almost *too* energetically considering she just woke up, Silvia practically skipped out of her room and made her way downstairs into the bathroom to get ready. As she was brushing her teeth, Yanna walked past the open door, glancing inside.

"Wait, you were here?" she asked, surprised. "You were out pretty late. I thought you'd be staying over somewhere," Yanna pointed out, grinning as she said so. But Silvia just shook her head, not minding the slight tease.

"Nope, but I *am* hanging out with Fae tomorrow. I was just with Modak and Ryan last night," the young elf explained, and Yanna seemed a bit confused at that.

She leaned against the door frame curiously. "So what's got you this giddy all of a sudden?"

"Alright, so, yesterday, we—" Silvia was almost about to just spill it all. She had never kept any sort of secret from her sister before. But at the same time, this wasn't her secret to tell. ". . . Actually, I don't think I can tell you . . . sorry. It's a Ryan thing; if anyone, he has to tell you. But don't be mad if he doesn't, it's . . . complicated."

"Now you've got me *really* curious." Yanna slightly leaned forward. "But well, if he wants to tell me, he'll tell me."

Just before the minotaur was about to turn back around, the doorbell was rung. Yanna smiled lightly. "I've got it."

"Thanks~!" Silvia replied, continuing with her morning routine as Yanna made her way one more floor downstairs to get to the door. Silvia could hear the door open and her sister's strong voice spoke.

And then, there was another woman's voice. It was muffled by the time it got all the way up here, but Silvia still shuddered. Silvia's grip on her toothbrush tightened, and her heart beat heavy in her chest as her breathing sped up. Her sight turned hazy as a flood of thoughts forced itself into her head, all moving together into a massive wall that blocked any coherent idea, or any action that she could do. Close the door, drop her toothbrush. Even dropping onto the ground was something she wasn't able to do.

Her knees locked up, and her body froze, petrified like she had been just a statue all along. She didn't even hear the door close a moment later, her thoughts drowning out everything else that was going on around her. Even when Yanna came back to her, she didn't notice until her sister touched her shoulder.

All the tension disappeared in an instant, like a pressed-down spring that was finally released. Silvia pulled back, staring at Yanna, startled and shaking.

"Wh-Who w-w-was—" Silvia let out, but she wasn't able to even finish her thought before Yanna wrapped her arms around her younger sister.

"It's alright, don't worry. I told her to leave, okay? She's gone." Yanna held Silvia tightly, feeling her anxious shakes vibrating throughout the elf's whole body. "I'll call Dad, okay?"

Silvia forced out a slow nod as she tightened her grip on the back of Yanna's shirt, and the minotaur ground her teeth in pure fury.

"Ouch, dude, come on!" Ryan flinched, pulling away his hand from Runar, who just stared back at his nephew and rolled his eyes.

"Stop complaining, I'm just swapping out your bandages. If you stopped acting like you're not hurt and were a bit more careful with your hand, this probably wouldn't hurt as much," Runar pointed out as he started wrapping up Ryan's hand with clean bandages. The cuts on his palm that he got from grabbing Energizer right after it went berserk had closed well enough, and due to the healing salve, there wasn't all too much swelling either. But that probably just made it easier for Ryan to use his hand for things while ignoring the fact that he was clearly injured.

"The burns only just healed, what the hell are you doing? Wear some gloves, will you?"

"I was wearing gloves in the dungeon, they didn't help either," Ryan defended himself. "And it's not like I could've predicted what happened yesterday."

". . . Still. Take better care of your hands, alright? You can't help the spirits if your hands are completely messed up."

Ryan looked at his uncle and inwardly sighed, trying to ignore just how rough Runar was being as he wrapped up his hand. He slowly glanced over at the boy sitting on the living room couch, distractedly flipping through channels on the TV. They were on the other side of the room, and he tried to speak in a low voice, "So . . . you said he was raised by one of the elders?"

Runar glanced up at Ryan and turned his head to Liam for a moment. "Officially, at least. In reality, I imagine it was more like he was raised in one of that elder's hidden facilities. I'm sure you can count the amount of conversations they've held on both hands."

". . . And that was enough for Liam to start acting like he's a king in some grand story?"

"He's an Awakened above level 70, Ryan," Runar explained. "There's no sane high-level Awakened. All the facilities that guy runs are basically LARP camps."

Taken aback, Ryan stared at his uncle. "Level 70? Seriously?"

"We have a lot of powerful people in our family."

Runar stood up after finishing the bandage, and a question that Ryan has been curious about almost since the beginning popped into his head. "So . . . what level are you?"

The Rune Mage slowly turned around, a slight grin forming on his lips. "That's a secret."

"Oh come on, seriously?"

"There's literally no person besides me that knows my level, so yes, seriously. There's a reason why I'm not registered; you have to get your level measured regularly," Runar pointed out. "Now come on, it's almost three. Silvia and Modak said they're on their way, right?"

"Yeah, they should get here any minute now," Ryan responded. "So what are we even doing today?"

"Nothing much. Just meeting people, introducing yourself to everyone downstairs, learning a bit about the things that we have to do. I also called over an acquaintance from the Magic Tower to help us track down Gaia's last fragment."

"Wait, seriously? You know someone from the Magic Tower?"

"Yes, I know someone from the Magic Tower. I . . . briefly worked there after I awakened." Runar hid his face as though he were embarrassed about it, and Ryan couldn't help himself but let out a short laugh of disbelief.

"Are you serious? You worked at the Magic Tower?"

"It wasn't really 'working.' I was like thirteen, it was more like an internship."

"You awakened at thirteen? As a mage?!"

Ryan's disbelief had turned into shock as Runar looked at his nephew with an annoyed look on his face. "I get that it's not normal, but I feel like you're being a bit insulting . . . The Aglecard bloodline is predisposed to magic users, and I happened to be a little talented. That's all."

"No, but like . . ." Ryan looked away as he tried to gather his thoughts. "How the hell do you always keep forgetting the pin to your phone? It's like four digits. I was legitimately worried about you at some point, but you're the type of genius that can awaken at thirteen and start working in the Magic Tower?"

Runar just shrugged, as though he had already accepted it. "I'm bad with tech, that's all."

"That—That has nothing to do with being bad with tech; your pin is your birthday!"

"Hmm . . . Nah, I think it's just the tech," Runar pointed out, but Ryan still wasn't convinced.

"Didn't you say you linked up your phone so you can use it from downstairs or something? That doesn't sound like you're bad with tech to me."

"Well, that wasn't about tech. I just adapted the Message spell into a semiper-manent link between two points."

Ryan narrowed his eyes, glaring at his uncle. "I have no reference point for how insane that is, but it sounds insane."

"Oh, shut up already." Runar walked up behind the couch, knocking on the young vampire's head. "Liam, you too, come on."

"Huh? Why would I do something like that?" the boy huffed, clearly not feel-ing like joining, but Runar already prepared the perfect answer and replied smugly.

"Don't you want to meet all your potential subjects downstairs?"

Liam immediately perked up curiously, "That . . . does sound like the duty of a king, I assume. Very well! I shall accompany you two!"

Clearly excited now, Liam jumped up from the couch and ran into the hall-way to put his shoes on, a broad smile plastered on his face. Rolling his eyes, Ryan picked up the remote and turned off the TV. "Dude, do you *want* him to get bul-lied at school or something?"

Runar shook his head with a slight yawn. "Oh, calm down, it's not that bad. He's got a big personality, people gravitate toward people like that. And it's not like he's a bad kid; there's a reason why we picked him out for the test run."

". . . Alright, that's fair. Just make sure he doesn't yell at me to show him my neck again."

Runar laughed quietly and nodded his head. "I'll try my best."

"Excuse me? What do you mean, it's not happening?" Christopher stared at the man in front of him, who pulled back nervously. The lizardman was scratching his neck nervously, making his scales almost pop off. Being faced with the fury of a boa lamia was more than just nerve-racking.

"The . . . the event of New Riverside University's robotics club showing off their latest project has been pushed back. There was an incident yesterday where one of the . . . where one of the robots went out of control and broke a bunch of private and university property," the man slowly explained as Christopher's unblinking glare only got more intense.

"No, it was supposed to go out of control today, during the showcase, not yes-terday. I specifically made sure that it wouldn't go off during the last tests yesterday." The lamia ground his teeth together, pushing down at the desk in front of him. Moving around erratically, his tail was bumping into nearby furniture. "What happened to Vanda?"

". . . The girl was questioned by the police and the university immediately chose to press charges," the man started, hesitating to finish what he was saying. "How—However, early this morning, the university has dropped those charges."

"Hah? Why would they do that? Vanda's got no contacts, no power, nothing. That's why I picked her for this."

". . . Looking at the records, the university has just received a large donation from the Honeydew Fund, one of the Aglecard Foundation's—"

"I know what the bloody Honeydew Fund is!" With an almost deranged hiss, Christopher hit the desk. A nearby couch was pushed across the room into a bookshelf from the force of the lamia's tail violently swinging around. The lizardman flinched as books from the shelf dropped onto the ground and the couch. "Fine, whatever. You recovered the fragment, though, right? We can just try again with something else."

The lizardman's heart skipped a beat. He couldn't answer that question. There was no way he could. Christopher would have his head, and it wasn't even his fault! However, with the lamia's deep glare laying on his scales, he had no other choice but to finally respond, "We . . . we sent someone in to retrieve the fragment, but we were unable to find it."

The lamia's fingers dug into the surface of the desk. "Excuse me? You're telling me that we not only lost a prime opportunity, but we lost both the fragment and a seed of corruption?"

"There . . . there's more to it," the lizardman explained. Christopher would find out sooner or later anyway, and it was better to just say it here now instead of being punished for hiding it later. ". . . They called an ambulance as someone was injured during yesterday's events. According to the reports, they treated a student named 'Ryan Aglecard' due to the injuries he received while subduing the rampant robot."

Christopher stared at the lizardman. "Excuse me? Why was he there? Why was he at the robotics club, of all places?!"

"I . . . It looks like they were trying to have test duels between the robots and the spirit that he cont—"

"Get out." Christopher turned his head away, placing his hand in front of his eyes. The lizardman wasn't sure if he had heard right, and was about to ask for confirmation, when Christopher turned back around and swung his arms across the desk. The monitor, keyboard, notes, and small trinkets were all thrown onto the ground. "I told you to get out!"

Once the man was out of the room, Christopher ground his teeth together, pulling out his phone. He dialed a number. It rang a few times, but nobody responded. "This little . . ."

So, instead, Christopher dialed another number, and someone picked up before the first ring even finished, "Mr. Blanchard! What a pleasure to hear from you! How can I help?"

"Put me through to Simon Grand immediately."

The man on the other side of the phone was silent for a few moments, before responding with a tone of voice that showed that bad news were about to follow. ". . . Simon Grand is currently being treated at a hospital. He will be unable to work for the time being. We were actually about to call you and introduce you to a new employee that could take over his—"

"Was he injured? I thought you have world-class healers at your company for situations like this."

A nervous laugh came from the other side of the phone, "Mr. Blanchard, while I have no idea what 'situations' you are speaking of, Simon's issues do not seem to be injury-based."

Christopher frowned, "Then what's the issue? I need to talk to him, I have to ask him some questions about my request."

". . . That is exactly the issue, Mr. Blanchard. Simon has no memories of the past two months, believing us to be in the month of Notis instead of Konter. He will be unable to continue to work with you on this request. I truly apologize for this inconvenience, but we promise to make it up to you as well as we can. We . . ."

Even though the man on the other side of the phone was hurriedly trying to explain the future plan of actions, Christopher wasn't paying attention. His tail was moving around him, tightening around the legs of a chair, crushing it under the pressure of a boa lamia's muscles. Staring at the shadow that he was casting onto the ground due to the sunlight pouring into the room behind him, Christopher almost shivered in anger.

"So the Aglecards are involved, and have the fragment now. And Ryan has probably been pulled into the main family now. That's fine. I still have a few more tricks up my sleeve."

CHAPTER THIRTY-SEVEN

Factions

Alright, guys, this is Liam. He's the vampire kid that'll be staying with Runar and me from now on." Ryan stood next to the boy and introduced him to his friends.

Modak smiled as though he were looking at his siblings. Zigg and Mogh were a bit younger than him, but they were around the same height as Liam. He figured that maybe these three could become friends. "Nice to meet you, Liam. I'm—"

"A sturdy orc and a beautiful elf, I see. They will do." Liam nodded his head approvingly, before getting a light slap to the back of the head. It was really just enough to get his attention and not hurt him, though.

"Don't be rude. And don't call people older than you 'beautiful'—that's just weird," Ryan scoffed lightly. Rather than finding Liam annoying, he was starting to understand the humor in the boy's actions. The fact he was being so serious about it all just made it funnier. Obviously that was only the case as long as he didn't start actively insulting others.

"Ow! Don't hit me, I'm just speaking the truth!" Liam complained, clearly overacting how much that light tap hurt. Ryan rolled his eyes and looked at his friends.

"That's Modak and Silvia, they're my best friends. Treat them well, please, and don't treat them like servants. That's not what they are."

"I mean . . . technically we're your 'aides' now, right?" Silvia pointed out with a slight laugh. She was looking pretty rough despite trying to act as she usually did. Modak seemed to have noticed it earlier as well, but right now wasn't the time to talk about it. Not in front of everyone else. And she said she would be fine, so Ryan and Modak had to trust that.

Ryan shrugged lightly. "Just officially, though. Anyway, Liam, don't be a dick to my friends."

"Don't call him a dick. He's ten," Runar yelled out from across the café, holding a wooden crate in his hands that he brought from upstairs.

"Yeah, but he's also being a dick." Ryan shrugged, and Runar simply sighed loudly.

"Whatever, just come, we're heading downstairs."

Runar shifted the crate's weight onto just one of his hands as he unlocked the basement door. The wooden boards cried out under every one of Runar's steps, as though he had suddenly tripled in weight. The boards were old, but even the towering Modak was able to walk over them with only some minor squeaking.

"What's in the box?" the orc curiously asked. The top was slightly open so he was trying to take a peek, but there was nothing but darkness in there.

Runar turned back with a slight grin, clearly excited to show it off. But even so, he was trying to stay patient. "You'll see. It's pretty cool, don't worry."

"Hm . . . alright," Modak muttered. "Oh, and by the way, I met with Vanda earlier. You really took care of everything overnight, huh?"

"Yeah, I guess. Thanks the gods for all the nocturnal species in this city, huh? This kind of thing takes so much longer in other parts of the country," Runar explained, pressing his palm onto the runic patterns on the floor. He turned back around as the ground opened up, revealing the stairway down below. "I was a bit surprised that we managed to get it all done on the weekend, though, but I guess we got a bit lucky."

Lucky? As if, Ryan thought to himself. There was no way that *luck* solved all of this. He stayed up pretty late, just scrolling through article after article describing Aglecard Foundation's work. It was a massively influential organization.

While they were largely a philanthropic group, they had their hands in many industries to some degree. Construction, agriculture, journalism, clean energy; all the companies that were directly supported by the foundation were leading actors in their specific industries.

The Aglecard family was not only extremely wealthy, but vastly powerful and influential. It was almost to a scary degree; the more Ryan dug around, the larger and more shrouded the scale of this all seemed to become. There was no "luck" involved in the fact that Vanda's situation could be figured out overnight while they were headed into a weekend; it just showed the ridiculous and vast power of the Aglecard family.

"So you were checking up on Vanda?" Silvia asked as the group started walking down the stairway, and Modak slowly nodded his head.

"Yeah, I wanted to talk to her about something. Her Energizer imitated the powers of an Enhancer, right? But the way those powers work is by alternating, high-frequency energy patterns, and she was struggling to figure out a way to do it at the low-power output that she needed, so she had to use some weird tricks," Modak explained, turning back toward the elf walking behind him. "I showed you the mana tapes a bit ago, right? I figured maybe the mana-inscribing method that I used would work to solve Vanda's problem."

Ryan looked at his friend with raised brows. "Oh damn, so what does that mean? She can rebuild Energizer without having to use a spirit core?"

"Hopefully. And really, she didn't know. She was given the fragment by someone else, right?" Modak pointed out, and Ryan let out a slight sigh.

"I know, I know . . . I just . . . feel really weird about the whole thing. Like, what was the plan there? *Why* did some rich kid give her one of Gaia's fragments?" Ryan pointed out, inwardly glancing at the two fragments in his mind. "Runar, do you know anything about that?"

"Sadly not," he replied, "I've got some guesses, but none of them are substantiated enough to really be worth adding onto your pile just yet. You've got plenty of other things to learn and know. And whichever the plan was supposed to be, you foiled that."

"I . . . guess?" Ryan let out, unsatisfied, but he figured it was a good point. However, he looked back at Modak with some curiosity. "Also, what's this about mana tapes?"

"I can show you in a second. You know how Silvia and I have been customizing some older retro tech together? Like cassettes, flip phones, those box TVs, and monitors."

"Ugh . . ." Runar groaned loudly. "That stuff is 'older retro tech' now? That was practically sci-fi for me when I was growing up . . ."

"Wow, how old *are* you?" Liam asked bluntly, and Runar flinched lightly.

"Hearing that from a kid that grew up while cosplaying the Middle Ages really doesn't feel great . . ."

Modak laughed awkwardly, "Uhm . . . either way, I was working on some stuff that Silvia asked for, and more recently, a lot of newer tech is integrating mana more directly, so I figured, why not give it a try and see if I can adapt some older stuff with mana-based tech? So instead of giving the actual tapes a magnetic charge to store data, I figured out how to do the same thing with mana," the orc explained with clear excitement in his voice. "I mean, it's useless in a practical sense, because even if the mana cassettes can store more data than regular cassettes, even a small USB stick completely shatters the amount of data that can be stored in comparison. It's just a neat little thing I had fun playing around with."

"That does sound kinda cool, though. Doesn't need to be 'useful,'" Ryan pointed out. Though he didn't really understand much about this kind of thing, he did know enough to realize that it was something pretty damn impressive.

While they were talking and Modak explained a bit more about how it all worked, Ryan noticed that his uncle was paying pretty close attention to the whole thing. And not just that, it looked like he was thinking about something, and Ryan doubted that it was just him trying to understand what the orc was saying.

Before long, the five made it all the way down the stairs, walking through the hallway to that large stone door. Runar pushed it open with his back, as he was still carrying that small crate in his hands. This time around, there weren't any plants growing in the way, and the overgrown path had been trimmed down for the most part. And then, once they got to the other side, Ryan was able to see these ruins properly for the first time.

It was a large cave that had clearly been cut out to accommodate this space; in parts of the walls, more ancient structures were sticking out above the tree line, some being used by the people living and working here, and others being taken over by some kind of bird's nest. As he was looking around, it took surprisingly long for a very simple fact to dawn on him; it was incredibly bright in here, to the point where it was almost disorienting.

But Ryan soon understood that this was due to the large crystals embedded in the ceiling. He remembered how this place looked last night; those crystals were also the cause of the "stars" that he had noticed here last night. However, the thing that he really did notice most of all was just how busy this place was now that it was daytime.

Hiding between the thicket and the bushes and trees were dryads of many different types and forms. Some looked like people, others like animals. Along the roads, there were many geodes walking around, and though they were quite small, sprites were hopping around the walls and on top of boxes. There were also plenty of other people here, most of whom looked like any other person aboveground. In regard to their appearance, there was clearly no difference between them and other people, so Ryan wondered what exactly the thing holding them back from joining up with mainstream society really was.

"Whoa!" Liam let out, looking around excitedly, for once showing some proper childlike excitement. "Now *this* is what I call a castle!"

"You could call it that, I guess." Runar smiled lightly, walking along the path as the others followed behind. The people in this small, hidden underground town were throwing glances at the group as they walked, muttering to each other curiously about these people that they had never seen before.

"Alright, Liam," Runar started once they got to the building that seemed to be his office, "Anders is waiting for you inside here. He's going to show you around and introduce you to the couple other vampires we have here specifically."

Liam raised his brow, surprised. "There are other vampires here?"

"There's four others living here. None that are your age, but it would be nice if you got to know them, alright?"

Liam carefully walked up the stairs, looking around as if trying to see if he could spot the other vampires from here. His demeanor completely changed the moment Runar mentioned other vampires, something that definitely didn't get past Ryan.

"Is he alright? I thought he'd be a bit more excited and say something like 'Finally, some noble compatriots' or crap like that," Ryan pointed out once Liam closed the door behind him, but Runar slowly shook his head as he continued guiding the three others down the road.

"I don't think there were other vampires where he grew up. About 90 percent of the vampires in Riveria are here in New Riverside. There are plenty of jobs that allow them to live nocturnally to avoid the sun, and with how many people there are here, it's hard to notice if someone is being 'weird.'"

"So he's just nervous?" Ryan asked, and Runar quickly nodded.

"I guess so. Anyway, let's worry about you for the time being," he replied. "It's going to take a while until you can really figure out what you want to do as part of our family, and since we do a lot of different things, you're going to have to test out a few things. I think this is also going to help all three of you figure out if you actually want to do this."

Silvia picked up her pace, walking up next to Runar, a bit confused. "Didn't we already join? You gave us those coins, right?"

"Those coins just mean you're affiliated with me directly. It doesn't mean you've joined us, just that you're someone that's important to the head of the family," Runar quickly explained. "Frankly, I'm going to be dragging out any official announcements for as long as I possibly can. Luckily everyone here is in my faction, so they'll stay quiet about it."

"Did you just say 'faction'? As in, there's more than one of those in our family?" Ryan asked with a concerned frown.

". . . Yeah, it . . . I was a bit worried that I played up the good side of our family a bit too much yesterday. The way things work, the thing I'm directly involved in . . . those are the ideals laid out by our founder that I fully support." Runar turned around the corner, walking down a sloped road to a lower part of this large cave. "But not everybody in our family is convinced of those ideals . . . There's a reason why I could understand that your father wanted to leave, though I obviously couldn't support the way he achieved that. Our family has a lot of ugly sides to it, and depending on what you choose to do, you will face them more than you're already forced to."

Ryan turned back toward Silvia and Modak. The fact he was worried was written boldly on his face. It was one thing to get himself caught up in something potentially dangerous, but dragging his friends into it was a whole other matter.

"So . . . what will be the first thing we're dealing with?" Ryan nervously asked, as Runar finally slowed down a bit. They were on the outskirts of that small, half-ruined "town" and standing in front of an old building that didn't seem to be particularly in use. If it weren't for the glowing coals in the forge at its side, it would certainly look like a completely abandoned structure.

Runar finally put the crate down onto the ground. "Something that I feel would be a good introduction to some of the 'weirdness' we deal with on a day-to-day basis. So, I mentioned it briefly, but we don't only deal with 'people.' We deal with animals as well. Usually, these are magic beasts who are treated horribly due to certain magical qualities they have. Other times they're regular animals that have mutated to attain some magical quality. Frankly, almost all the beings that we deal with, whether person, animal, or otherwise, are in danger because they're, in one way or another, 'magical' in some form."

Silvia's eyes slightly widened in nervousness. "Wait, wouldn't that also include changelings?"

Runar thought about it for a moment, but in the end just shrugged. "Kind of. Changelings came to be because they evolved in an isolated valley that was practically flooded with chaotic magic. The way their bodies adapted to that was by allowing them some level of shapeshifting. And then, when the valley broke open for some reason or another, they came out into the world and met other people. They developed their abilities specifically to let them become part of the already developing civilization. So our help really wasn't needed there."

"I see . . ." Silvia replied, thinking of Fae and the idea that she and her family and other people like her could have been in the exact same situation as all these other people walking around here if things had just developed a bit differently.

"So . . ." Modak curiously looked around, trying to figure out why they were here. "What do animals have to do with a blacksmith?"

Runar smiled lightly, pointing at the crate that he had just put down on the ground. "Ryan, go and grab a piece."

Obviously curious, Ryan walked up to the crate, then pulled the top off. And what was inside was nothing but finger-sized rods of metal. He picked one of them up, and slowly turned toward his uncle in complete disbelief. This much had to weigh literally a ton. But could those old wooden boards even hold that much weight? This was definitely genuine metal. "You carried all this down here? Dude, seriously, what level are you?"

Runar laughed and stepped up next to the lit forge. "Not telling. Anyway, hold your hand out with that piece of metal on your palm. Like in a petting zoo."

Nervously, Ryan did as told, taking a step forward. He had no idea what was about to happen. Runar carefully ran his hand over the bricks making up the top of the forge. "Come on, wake up. It's time for lunch."

With loud creaks and the sound of shifting stone, the forge at the side of the building started to move. As if unfolding, a form started to appear. Strong hind legs and large clawed wings, all made of stone, while its yawning maw held all the red-hot coals.

The old forge that had just taken on the form of a dragon curiously tilted its head to the side as its eyes landed on the piece of steel on Ryan's hand.

CHAPTER THIRTY-EIGHT

The Living Forge

The stone dragon stood in front of Ryan, curiously looking at the piece of metal on his palm. Though, *looking* was probably the wrong word; it didn't have eyes, after all. But even so, Ryan could tell that it was focused on the small metal rod on his hand. It slowly took a step forward, its winged forelegs moving hesitantly, as though this hulking mass of rock that would tower over even a troll or cyclops was the one that was scared.

Ryan's body was completely tense and frozen. He knew that this creature wasn't dangerous, otherwise Runar wouldn't be standing there so casually, but it was still taking Ryan quite a lot to not turn heel and run away.

As the stone beast approached, Ryan could feel the heat pouring out of its mouth. Beyond the jagged rocks that acted as its fangs, the glow of hot coals emanated outward. But somehow, even though the heat was growing horribly intense as that mouth came closer to Ryan's hand, it wasn't painful in any way, just uncomfortable. Ryan held his breath as the dragon's teeth carefully bit into the piece of metal, quickly pulling it away. The heat that he felt then was somewhat like when you stuck your hand into an oven; incredibly hot, and if it lasted for a while, it would most certainly start to hurt, but because of how fast the living forge had pulled away, he was only left with a slightly warm hand.

"This . . . What is this?" Ryan asked, watching as the dragon held the piece of metal up in the air, letting it slide into its mouth as if it were eating a fish. Ryan had seen this exact kind of thing before. Wyverns were rare, but he had seen one in a zoo in a large city before when he and his mom went on a trip for his birthday. This was the exact kind of thing that he saw then.

Runar slowly ran his hand over the creature's back. "It's an elemental. As magic gathers in an object or natural force, it might attain some sort of intelligence. A gust of wind, a particularly dense cloud, or a stream of water. It's very rare, but it can happen if a lot of things coincide. And similarly, when an old object gathers a lot of mana with in, it may turn into an elemental. This one is the 'Forge.'"

"That's so cool . . ." Silvia let out, staring at the elemental wyvern with a broad smile on her face. "So why does it look like that? And what's its name?"

Runar shrugged, responding to both questions. "We still don't really know why elementals take on the forms they do, and she hasn't accepted an official name yet."

"Wait, what do you mean 'accepted an official name'?" Ryan asked, glancing at the living forge, and Runar looked back awkwardly.

"So . . . do you know how dungeons will have official names? Like the . . . 'Abandoned Copper Foundry' you went to. Since elementals are kind of similar to dungeons in some ways, they can also have official names. But this girl hasn't accepted any names according to our appraiser," Runar explained, "So, that being the case, she just goes by 'Forge' for now until we find a name that truly suits her."

"I don't . . . I don't even know where to start with that, so I'll just ignore the fact that you said they're like dungeons." Ryan closed his eyes and took a deep breath. "So, what is it that we'll be doing for now?"

"You're going to help take care of the animals today, that's all," Runar responded. "It's not easy work, but I feel like it's a good way to get used to things and meet the people you need to meet."

"Awe, man . . . couldn't you have told us beforehand? I'm totally not wearing clothes for that kind of thing . . ." Silvia looked down at her outfit; a skirt, black boots, and an expensive-looking blouse definitely weren't the best fit to take care of animals all day. Runar glanced over at her and quickly replied.

"We've got outfits for you all to change into. They're just simple overalls and rubber boots, though."

". . . Hm . . . What color are the overalls?"

"I don't know, black, gray, blue . . . we've got a couple different ones, I think," Runar replied, a bit confused about why Silvia cared about something as trivial as the color of the overalls.

"Alright . . . I can make that work," Silvia replied as she got lost deep in thought. "Do you mind if I take some . . . creative liberties with them?"

Runar let out a long, quiet groan. "I really could not care less. Do whatever you want."

"Yay~!" A broad grin formed on Silvia's face, and both Modak and Ryan seemed to calm down a bit. Her mood was clearly being lifted as she became more distracted from whatever had her so down before.

Runar continued. "Well, we'll bring you guys to a spot you can change in a second, but first, you should meet our head animal caretaker," he said, pointing to a figure that was slowly approaching. Forget overalls; what they were wearing was practically a complete hazmat suit covering them from head to toe. They walked up to Runar and quickly greeted him with a salute, keeping their distance.

"Good day, Mr. Aglecard," the woman's high-pitched voice flowed out from behind the thick, darkened helmet.

Ryan nervously looked at his uncle. "Do . . . do we need one of those as well?"

"No, she's just more comfortable wearing that around other people," Runar replied before turning back to the fully covered woman. "Rose, this is my nephew Ryan and his friends Silvia and Modak. They'll be helping you out for a few hours, so take care of them well, alright?"

With a quick, exaggerated nod, Rose replied, "Yes, sir!"

"Okay, perfect. I actually have some other stuff to prepare. I'll just be in my office, so come over if you need anything," Runar explained, letting out a long yawn as he turned around, muttering to himself, "So much shit to do. I just want to keep the café open . . ."

And so, Ryan, Silvia, and Modak were left with the forge elemental and Rose. The girl's muffled voice quickly spoke out as she nervously flailed her arms around.

"It, it's nice to meet you! I'm Rose!" she introduced herself properly again, and Ryan took a step forward, holding out his hand to shake hers.

"Ryan, nice to meet you," he said, but Rose quickly pulled away and built some distance between them.

"Yes! Likewise!" she replied, clearly not comfortable shaking Ryan's hand.

Figuring that there was no need to force it, Ryan pulled his hand away, turning to the living forge next to him. She was looking at Ryan curiously, her mouth slightly opened and letting out a soft glow from behind her teeth.

"So . . . Are there more elementals? Or what are we doing today?" Ryan asked, as Rose carefully walked up to the crate on the ground that had all the pieces of metal in it.

"We do have a few elementals, but not only. Mr. Aglecard only asked me to have you accompany me on my lunch route, so I can show you all my babies today!" she explained, throwing a few of the metal bars from the crate into the air. The forge quickly reacted, catching them in her mouth with some smooth motions. Rose placed her hand onto the side of her snout, rubbing it carefully. "You know, this girl started out as just a little flame!"

"Huh?" Modak let out, clearly confused by what he heard. He was already baffled by the revelation that elementals were similar to dungeons, but this was a whole other thing. "What do you mean? I've heard about elementals, but . . . they change?"

"Modak, right? Mr. Aglecard told me you're interested in these sorts of magical things already." Rose carefully started picking up a few more metal rods to keep feeding the forge. "So, you know how dungeons have multiple stages? Stage

0 being that the seed of a dungeon settles into a space, a cumulation of tons of mana that interact in seemingly random ways. Stage 1 is when that seed sprouts and pours mana into the space that it inhabited. And then, Stage 2 is when you have a proper dungeon."

Ryan glanced at the forge. "So they have similar stages as well? Elementals grow over time?"

"Exactly!" Rose said immediately, pointing at Ryan as if he got the right answer in some quiz. "We can compare the initial birth of an elemental to a dungeon's second stage, and they keep growing and affecting things around them to a degree, growing slowly but surely into something . . . more."

"Isn't that kind of dangerous, then?"

Rose laughed slightly, something that spread through her whole body. For someone that hid herself with a hazmat suit, she was extremely expressive. "Have you ever met a completely harmless animal, or even person at that? Of course, if disturbed, they might be dangerous, depending on how old and powerful they are. But elementals are also so rare that most of the time, when one pops up, they are the ones that need protection. Plus, elementals never affect the world around them; they simply add to their bodies! Our cute little forge here used to be flames of a forge, not the forge itself. But over time, as she grew older and more mana accumulated, she got the body she has now. We're keeping her here and trying to fix up the smithy in case she feels the need to grow more in the future."

". . . Well, alright. So . . . what first?" Ryan asked, glancing over at his friends who seemed quite excited to see all the different animals that were being protected down here.

"First, you get changed!" Rose quickly turned around, starting to lead the three down the road. As they were walking, keeping their distance from Rose as that was clearly what she wanted, Modak carefully leaned over to Ryan.

"I did not expect that we would do *this* of all things today . . ." Modak pointed out, and Ryan looked at him nervously.

"You don't *have* to if you don't want to. Runar said this is just a way for us to figure out what we'd like to do and to learn about different sides of the family, but if you can already tell that you'd rather not, then . . ."

"Oh, no, that's not it. It's not that I don't *want* to, it's just . . . I'm not very good with animals." Almost embarrassed to admit it, Modak scratched his cheek. "I think it's a mana thing. Animals are more sensitive to it in general, and since I don't have any . . ."

"Wait, what?" Silvia asked, looking at the orc confused. "What do you mean you don't have any?"

"I . . . have mana rejection disorder. My body can't hold any mana."

"It kind of saved my ass with Energizer, though," Ryan added. "So it's not all bad, right?"

Modak sighed lightly, "You don't need to be like that. It's annoying, but I've dealt with it my whole life. I'm fine."

Silvia slightly patted Modak's back. Both she and Ryan understood how much he loved magic at this point, so not having mana must be a massive blow. Even without awakening, it was possible to use magic if you were dedicated enough to learning how to. And having something like mana rejection disorder holding you back from even trying must be crushing.

But with magic engineering, Modak seemed to have found a good middle ground between what he could and couldn't do, since it let him deal with magic somehow.

"At least you don't have to worry about Liam trying to bite your neck," Ryan scoffed lightly. "He stood in my room and yelled at me to offer him my blood this morning. That was how I met him."

Modak laughed lightly, "Hey, I mean, that does sound like what a kid would do. Zigg and Mogh had this Hero phase, and they'd come into my room to slay the 'Slumbering Titan.'"

"Yeah . . . I just hope that he doesn't act like a total ass at whatever school he'll go to," Ryan sighed. Modak and Silvia shared a look for a moment, and then turned back to their friend.

"You're already that worried about him?" Silvia asked, though it was more like she was pointing it out. Ryan shrugged.

"I guess. I was a bit of a weird kid too, so I get what it's like," Ryan replied, as the group walked into a nearby building.

"I'm sure all three of us were pretty weird kids, right?" Silvia pointed out. Modak thought about it for a moment, and just ended up shrugging.

"I guess I was kind of weird," he replied. "I hid in my elementary school's library after closing hours once so I could just read all weekend."

"How long did it take them to find you?" Ryan wondered, and Modak thought about it for a few moments.

"Hm . . . I think my dad dragged me out at some point that night. But it's been a while, I was in first grade."

"Aww, little baby Modak." With a slight giggle, Silvia looked around the room as the orc awkwardly hid his embarrassed blush. But before they could continue talking, Rose was waving them over.

She stepped to the side as the three got closer, letting them see into what seemed to be a supply closet. "We keep some spare work clothes here. Just pick whatever fits you, and then come back outside! I'll be waiting! We've got some changing rooms right over there."

Silvia stepped into the supply closet first, curiously looking at the different options. And before either Modak or Ryan could even pick something out, she pushed some options into their hands. "These would look good on you!"

The orc looked at the dark blue overalls and sighed, "It looks exactly the same as the one I wear when I help my dad at the garage."

"Yeah, and the color suits you!" Silvia immediately pointed out, as Ryan unfolded his red overalls. He couldn't complain, it would probably fit him pretty well. It wasn't a bad color either.

And Silvia herself quickly picked out a pitch-black one for herself, but she also grabbed something from her backpack. A small sewing kit. She took out a small pair of scissors and cut into the fabric without hesitation.

"Wait, you're actually going to alter it? Now?" Ryan asked with a bit of disbelief in his voice, and Silvia grinned up at him.

"Nothing big, but yeah! Why not~? Don't worry, it won't take long, it's just a small change!"

"Sure, if you say so." With a laugh, Ryan and Modak made their way into the changing rooms. They were all single-person spaces, so each of them took their own small cabins.

Ryan took off his jacket and trousers, then placed them onto the small shelf. It was deep summer, and it was so incredibly hot upstairs. Down here, underground, it was quite pleasant, but upstairs he was almost dying every day. He glanced down at his legs, seeing the scars that covered them. They were more sparse than the ones on his back, but still enough for Ryan to feel self-conscious about them. But maybe he should try to just not give a shit about it anymore. Why would he care what strangers thought about him, if his best friends supported him to the point they joined a secret society with him?

Ryan let out a slight sigh as he put on the overalls. He didn't pull it over his upper body, instead just tying the sleeves around his waist like a belt. The shirt Ryan was wearing was kind of old anyway, so he didn't care if it got dirty. And so, Ryan stepped out of the changing room, ready to get to work.

CHAPTER THIRTY-NINE

Cockatrices

Carrying a large plastic box, Ryan trotted down the well-used dirt road toward the large coop that Rose had pointed out to him. Modak was following while carrying a hay bale, and Silvia was already waiting with two large water buckets by the coop's entrance.

"Alright, now, you guys wear *these*," Rose said, quickly walking up to each of them with sunglasses in her hands.

Ryan put down the plastic box confused. "Eh . . . Why do we need these? What are we doing here?"

"Why does it matter? They're cute," Silvia pointed out smugly, placing the sunglasses onto her face and peering over them with a grin. Ryan glanced at her with a slight laugh. Ryan didn't expect her to be able to do much in the short time she had to alter the outfit, but it was surprisingly effective. She cut off the sleeves and added a belt, which she carried with her for some reason, onto her waist. She then cut a strip out of one of the sleeves and used it to tie up her hair into a bun. It wasn't a lot, but she definitely looked a lot more fashionable than Ryan and Modak did.

"How they look really doesn't matter—please just keep wearing them properly and never look out from beyond the glasses directly. Periphery is . . . fine, but should also be avoided if possible," Rose explained, carefully stepping up to the fenced gate. There were thick blackout sheets surrounding the whole thing, as if they were trying to hide what was in here.

"Oh, and they're a bit rowdy, but they're not dangerous or anything. As long as you keep the sunglasses on. Seriously, do not . . . please do not take them off," Rose reiterated, as she slowly opened the gate, then stepped through and waited for Ryan, Silvia, and Modak to do the same. In front of them was another gate to make sure that the ones in here couldn't get out as easily, and once more, there were blackout curtains to ensure that nobody caught a glance of them as the gates were opened and closed.

Ryan swallowed nervously as Rose closed the first gate and then opened the second. They all stepped through, and Ryan's eyes widened. The fenced-in coop was completely filled with what at first looked to be just overly large chickens. They had white or brown or black feathers on their backs, but their belly and throat were covered in scales instead. Similar to those of a wyvern, something still freshly in Ryan's mind after seeing the forge elemental earlier, they had clawed wings and large, sharp talons. They had long tails that were carefully slithering around on the ground behind them, ending in a few small feathers.

"Wait, these are just . . . cockatrices?" Ryan let out, confused.

Rose quickly shook her head, holding her arms in front of her body to form an *X*. "They are not *just* cockatrices! These are *the* cockatrices!"

". . . What?" Ryan asked, turning around toward his friends who seemed just as confused as him.

"The ones that you see out in zoos or at farms are a specific breed of domesticated cockatrices; they're basically blind because they've been bred to weaken their eyesight. These here are wild cockatrices. Their habitat was being encroached on so we rescued, and we're trying to find a good place to relocate them to right now," Rose explained, and Modak shivered. His realization was boldly written on his face even with those thick sunglasses.

"Wait, so . . . that's real? Can cockatrices petrify people?"

Rose hesitated for a few moments, but finally nodded her head. "Yes, they can. Though it's not 'petrification'; it's a very powerful paralysis, and it's strong enough to usually lead to cardiac arrest in most animals and people," she explained, squatting down. One of the cockatrices came up to her, rubbing its head against her leg. "But it needs eye contact to activate. Sunglasses seem to block it somehow. And it's not something they can really control either. They're very calm and affectionate otherwise."

Silvia was the first to squat down to get closer to the cockatrices, holding out her hand carefully to let herself be approached. They carefully approached her, though keeping their distance in general. Rose stood back up, her focus lingering on Silvia for a little while longer, before she spoke up.

"Okay, we've got a ton of other places to go, so let's get started! We've got to replace some of the hay on the ground, feed them, and give them some fresh water," Rose explained, walking up to the side of the coop's hut where the cockatrices' nests seemed to be. At its side was a small door that she opened up, then pulled out two pitchforks, held one herself, and gave another to Modak after he placed down the hay bale.

"Ryan, you fill everything from the box into the trough, and Silvia, you fill up the water bowl. Modak and I will start shoveling the hay while the cockatrices are eating."

And so, they quickly did as told. Ryan brought the box over to the side of the fodder trough and opened up the lid. Some of the cockatrices were already closing in, knowing what was about to happen. Inside the box was a mixture of mealworms and chunks of meat, all mixed together with some sort of pellets. Ryan placed the box onto the side of the trough and carefully filled it up. The moment he was done and pulled the box away, the cockatrices came rushing over and immediately started to eat.

Ryan took a step back, inwardly looking at Maximus. He had decided to stay inside the domain and train himself. Since last night, he seemed to be deep in thought, and training looked like the best way for Maximus to clear his thoughts. Ryan was a bit worried, and he did ask Maximus if he wanted to join earlier, but Maximus wanted to focus on his training for the time being.

"H-Hey, stay back!" Modak's anxious voice sounded out from across the coop. It seemed like not all the cockatrices had decided to eat right away, and one of them was standing right in front of Modak. The cockatrice was building itself up in front of him, pushing forward its chest while hissing.

Rose carefully walked up toward him. "Calm down. Sometimes they can be a little tense, but as long as you don't back down, they won't do anything. Just stand strong, and show her you're not scared of her."

"But I *am* scared of her!"

"Then try to act like you're not! It's all about confidence," Rose reassured him. "They're really not dangerous, so you—"

Just as she was saying so, the cockatrice lunged at Modak. Startled, he took a step back, the pitchfork in his hand digging into the ground behind him. He tripped over it, twisting his body to catch himself. But as he did, the sunglasses fell off his face. Rose immediately rushed over to him, trying to pull the cockatrice away, but once more she was too late.

Ryan's heart skipped a beat as he ran forward to Modak as the cockatrice stared into his eyes. However, instead of being paralyzed, Modak jumped up from the ground, then pressed himself against the fence behind him while keeping his eyes shut. "Shit, shit, shit—I—What am I supposed to do, I—"

Ryan slowed down as he noticed Rose standing there in clear disbelief, dropping her arms, confused. "You didn't . . . You weren't paralyzed?"

And even more than that, the cockatrice that had just jumped at him in an attempted attack, was now tightly rubbing its body against his leg, almost affectionately.

"Wh-What's happening?" Modak asked as he pressed his hand onto his chest, scared of the cardiac arrest that Rose mentioned earlier.

"Did you . . . you locked eyes with her, right?" Rose asked, stepping up closer to Modak, who slowly nodded his head.

"Y-Yeah . . . I definitely did . . . When is this supposed to happen?"

"Instantly . . . it's usually instant. It's their way to hunt; if animals could keep moving after locking eyes with them, that would be really dangerous . . . you should be affected, what's going on? I don't even know why it attacked, you, I'm . . . I'm so sorry!" Rose apologized, carefully trying to pull the cockatrice away from Modak's leg. However, it seemed like she didn't want to leave him alone anymore, and was instead hissing at Rose for trying to pull her away.

"I think . . . Modak, is it because of your MRD?" Ryan asked, and Modak turned toward him, his eyes still closed.

"What do you mean?"

"It's like a . . . magic thing, right? Like, the paralyzing 'curse' or whatever it is. That kind of thing uses mana as a conduit, and you don't have any. So it wouldn't work," Ryan suggested, and Rose looked back and forth between Ryan and Modak.

"Is that what you were talking about earlier? You have *no* mana at all? None?"

". . . Yeah . . . not an ounce. Usually people with MRD have a tiny, tiny bit, but I was a special case because I have *none*," Modak explained, and Rose took a step closer toward him. She seemed to, for just a moment, lift her helmet up ever so slightly, and closed it down just a moment later, just to let out a long sigh of relief.

"Oh, thanks the gods . . . yeah, you have none at all, you're fine! You're totally fine! You can open your eyes!" Rose replied, and Modak carefully opened just one of his eyes.

"Are you sure?"

"Yes, definitely! Trust me, I know more about these babies than anyone else in the world!"

Nervously, Modak opened both of his eyes, glancing down at the cockatrice below him. They once more locked eyes, but Modak felt nothing at all. As if happy, the cockatrice started loudly purring.

"That also explains why she likes you so much all of a sudden!" Rose added. "She thinks you're a giant cockatrice rooster!"

Modak immediately stared at Rose. "Excuse me?"

"Yeah! The only ones that don't get petrified by cockatrices are other cockatrices, and since these hens love a large rooster, that must be what's going on here!"

Ryan scoffed involuntarily, "So . . . the cockatrice wants to give his cock-a-try?"

As Silvia laughed in the background, Modak intensely stared at his friend. "I . . . I hate you with a passion."

"No, you don't." Ryan grinned broadly. "But hey, at least you're popular with *some* animals now."

". . . Whatever," Modak grumbled lightly, carefully squatting down. He was still hesitant; his whole life, animals had either avoided him or been aggressive toward him. Cats would hiss and scratch at him; dogs would bark when he walked past. The reason his family wasn't able to have any pets was because they were all scared of Modak, and he was scared of them in turn.

He carefully held his hand out to the affectionate cockatrice, who pressed her head against his palm. "Well . . . I guess it's not all bad."

Rose pulled at Modak's arm to get him to stand up again, excitement flowing through her whole body. "If you don't have any mana at all, there is another beast that I would like you to meet! I wasn't going to introduce you all to him just yet, but we've been having quite a lot of trouble with him . . . Do you mind?"

Unsure what to say, Modak looked over at Ryan and Silvia. "What do you guys think? Should we?"

"I don't see why not, we're here to learn about this place anyway, right?" Ryan pointed out, and Modak carefully nodded his head.

"Alright . . . as long as it's safe."

"Yes! It should be totally safe for you!" Rose exclaimed, still holding on to Modak's arm. He slowly pulled away to pick up the pitchfork that he'd dropped.

"Sure . . . And I think maybe you should invest in sunglasses that *can't* fall off . . . Like those swimming goggles or something . . ."

Rose immediately nodded her head. "Yes, yes, of course! I will look into it and order some!"

And with that, they continued to clean up the coop to replace the old hay. Ryan ended up taking over for Modak as he was being surrounded by all the other cockatrice hens once they realized that they weren't able to paralyze him.

Since Rose seemed even more motivated than before, the four of them were able to finish this task pretty quickly. After that, they continued on to finish all the other tasks, which mostly consisted of feeding all the different animals and cleaning them up a bit.

Common animals that had been cursed or simply had some sort of disease with magical origins, a couple elementals beside the forge elemental, and they even met a few of the other people living down here on the way. Everyone seemed happy to meet them. They were kind, laughing, smiling . . . but Ryan still felt that something was off.

Everyone that lived down here had the same air surrounding them. An air that Ryan knew well. He felt similar in his hometown, though obviously for different reasons than all of these people. They felt stuck in this small place. They wanted to leave and live their lives, not be stuck in a place, hiding themselves from the world.

But they were trying their best to figure out how to make this work for them. Some of them seemed like they were only down here temporarily, and would either leave to someplace where it was easier for them to live, or try to hide themselves in New Riverside. But there were also plenty of people that had no other choice but to stay here. The geodes or dryads? They would never be able to hide, and walking around amongst other people without the ability to properly communicate with others wasn't going to just work either.

It wasn't just people that had to hide because their species was staying hidden either, though. Some of them, similar to the animals, were here because they were suffering from certain types of curses or magical diseases. Regular hospitals were only equipped to handle the most basic curses at the level of regular illnesses, and not the kind of thing they were dealing with here.

Forced, painful mutations of limbs, out of control magic, and even things like lycanthropy. This whole organization was doing their best to help all of these people, and Ryan wanted to do whatever he could to help that. Maybe taking care of animals wasn't the way for him to do that, and he most certainly didn't have the organizational and political skills needed to help whole species of people integrate. But helping out individuals was something he could do. Something he had to do.

And so, before long, Ryan, Silvia, and most importantly Modak, followed Rose to the place where that "troubled child" stayed. They made their way to the edge of the cave, walking up some stairs that climbed up to one of the buildings carved into the walls. Before they reached the top, Rose turned around and looked at the three behind her.

"Okay, you've got to stay calm now. He's not dangerous; he has never attacked anyone . . . we just can't get close to him. But still, we should try not to scare him."

Modak nervously clenched his fist. He had no idea what he was about to see, but if he was the only one that could really help, then he had to do this. Rose pushed open the wooden door on the balcony at the end of the steps. And as they walked inside, what the group saw was not a wounded animal that wouldn't let others get close, which was what this sounded like all along.

No, the only thing in this room was a single wardrobe.

CHAPTER FORTY

Pep Talk

In this dark, cold, and quiet room, there was nothing but a single old wardrobe. Its wood was worn-out and half rotten, but you could tell that it was once an expensive and high-quality piece.

Ryan slowly turned to Rose. "What's going on? What is this?"

"That's 'Kindly.' He has a curse that infects others by latching onto their mana," she explained calmly, staring right at the wardrobe.

"Got it . . . and that's why he's hiding in there?" Ryan asked, but Rose just laughed and shook her head.

"No, he's not hiding at all," she explained, and started clapping her hands together a few times, "Come on, Kindly. Wake up!"

With loud creaks and the sound of wood cracking and bending, the wardrobe started to shake ever so slightly. Unsure what was about to happen, Ryan looked to his friends, both of whom were just fully focused on what was happening in front of them. As Ryan turned back, the wardrobe had already changed into something . . . else.

The wood of the wardrobe cracked, and dozens of red and yellow eyes were peering out from the darkness. Its door was pushed ajar, and wart-covered, fleshy black tentacles were slithering out from beyond it, latching onto the wood and ground. Ryan's heart almost skipped a beat as he stared at the thing inside the wardrobe. No, as he stared at the thing that *was* the wardrobe.

"He's a mimic," Rose explained. "They're like hermit crabs turning objects like this into their homes. But instead of just living inside of them, those objects turn into a part of their bodies. But Kindly's current body is breaking down because he's slowly outgrowing it, but we can't coax him out of it, no matter what we do."

Modak stared at the mimic, another creature that he had only read about in fairy tales. But different from the others that he had seen here so far, mimics were always monsters. Things that hid in small nooks and inconspicuous places, ambushing them to get something to eat between their teeth.

"How can I . . . how can I help? Am I supposed to pull him out of there?" The orc couldn't move his eyes away from the thin, clearly sick tendrils of the creature in front of him. But Rose quickly explained what he had to do.

"No, that's not it at all! Definitely don't! He's just . . . he's hurt. We're already trying to figure out how to deal with his curse, but that's going to take a while to resolve. But he has these really nasty cuts and gashes and wounds, and he won't let anyone get close to him."

Modak slowly understood. "So . . . I should treat him? I don't know anything about veterinary medicine . . ."

Rose shook her head. "You don't have to, I can walk you through it. It's nothing too complicated, but we don't have anyone that can do it . . ."

"I . . . Can I think about this for a second?"

"Of course! Take your time!" Rose immediately replied, some panic in her voice. Modak turned around and stepped out of the room back onto the balcony, rushing down the stairs.

Silvia and Ryan looked at each other, and the elf hesitantly opened her mouth. But before she could, Ryan spoke up, "I'll go after him, you can stay here."

She slowly nodded her head, and Ryan left the room. Silvia was also dealing with some things right now. Though Ryan still didn't know what it was, he was sure Silvia wasn't in a state of mind to give a pep talk to someone else right now.

Modak was already at the bottom of the carved stone steps, pacing around in circles on the trampled patch of grass. From here, Ryan could see some dryads curiously peeking out from the dense artificial forest spreading around the edges of the whole cave, trying to see what was going on.

"Hey, man, you alright?" Ryan slowed down as he got to the bottom of the stairs, and Modak immediately and violently shook his head.

"No, I'm not alright! What the hell is going on?" he let out, heavy breaths pouring out of his mouth. "This morning, I've never so much as petted an animal without being hissed or barked at, and now I'm the king of cockatrices and the only one that can treat a fucking mimic? How the hell does that makes sense?"

"Yeah, and yesterday I was still the son of an accountant and a bookkeeper, and now I'm the direct descendant of millennium-old secret society. Things change very quickly these days," Ryan scoffed, sitting down on the steps with a laugh. Modak turned to him and sighed loudly.

"It's just . . . so much. It's not that I don't want to help, but I . . . I don't even really like animals all that much. I don't *hate* them, obviously, but until now they were just kind of a topic I stayed away from. I don't know if I can do this." Modak let out a laugh of disbelief, continuing to pace around. "I don't know the slightest thing about how to handle animals whatsoever. I don't even know how to handle *people.* If you and Silvia weren't the way you are, my university experience would be very, very different."

Ryan narrowed his eyes, staring at his friend. He wasn't sure if he was understanding him correctly. "What are you even saying? You were friends with everyone in the robotics club. You walk up to your professors and talk to them about topics I've never even heard of."

". . . That . . . that's not the same thing."

"How is it not? Why do you keep underestimating yourself? You're a literal fucking genius. Who cares if you don't know much about animals? You can do this. Especially with the help of someone that awakened as a Zoologist."

Modak slowed down and just stood there for a few moments, his back turned to Ryan. "Can you just . . . tell me what I should do?"

"Are you shitting me?" Ryan asked, almost angry about being asked this. He stood up from the steps and walked around the orc to look straight into his face. "I'm not going to tell you what to do; that's not how this all works. You're not my aide. You're my best friend. But genuinely . . . I fully believe that you can do this. I just can't tell you if you should."

Modak and Ryan locked eyes for a moment. And then, with a loud groan, Modak threw his head into his neck. "Okay, fine. I'm doing it."

"You sure?" Ryan asked, a slight smile on his face. "Nobody's forcing you to."

"Oh, shut up, you want me to do it, right?" Modak sighed.

"I don't *not* want you to do it." Ryan held forward his fist toward the orc. "Come on, man. You got this."

A smile formed on Modak's face as he bumped his friend's fist. "Yeah . . . I got this."

Runar sat in his office, peering through a magnifying glass at the thin metal plate in front of him. He was using an extremely fine brush to carefully paint patterns onto it as his eyes let off a soft green glow.

"Still doing that kind of busywork?" a woman asked as she walked up to the desk. Without even looking at her, Runar calmly replied to her.

"I'm definitely not letting anyone else set up a permanent magic array here, so I'm the only one that *can* make these," he pointed out, slowly pulling the brush away from the metal plate to glance at the elf now standing in front of him. "Also, I'd appreciate it if you could knock before coming into my office."

"Oh, don't be like that! You're the one that invited me here," she responded with a slight laugh, sitting down on a chair across from Runar. Rolling his eyes, the Rune Mage continued his work.

"Yes, but I don't remember sending anyone up to let you in, so that means you broke in."

"That's a strong word, don't you think?"

"No, actually. I don't think so." Runar stayed calm despite the watchful gaze of the woman in front of him. She shook her head and sighed a few times as Runar was working, until he had enough of it.

"Alicia, what are you doing?" he asked, trying to hold back a groan. Alicia just shrugged and leaned back in her seat.

"I didn't do anything."

With a slight laugh, Runar raised his brow. "Alicia. Tell me. What is it?"

". . . A four-pointed array for the third circle would be much more effective than a five-pointed array. You're just wasting mana like that."

"That would be the case if I were working with a standard mathematical model, but I'm using a combined runic model. Because of the Syt rune right here, I need the additional stability that a five-pointed array provides."

"Well, that *would* be the case if you weren't already using Bak right at the connection between the second and third circles."

"Bak? What do you—this is Het!"

". . . Didn't I tell you to fix your handwriting?"

"My handwriting is fine. How about you start wearing your fuckin' glasses for once?" With a click of his tongue, Runar leaned forward and continued drawing these complex patterns onto the metal plate. Alicia crossed her legs and shook her head as she replied.

"Glasses don't suit the shape of my face," she pointed out, placing her palm onto her cheek with a slight grin.

". . . Mhm."

For a few minutes longer, until Runar was done, Alicia just silently observed. And then he finally pulled back and placed the plate next to the other two that he had already finished. He stood up and stretched, finally properly looking at the woman in front of him with a smile on his face.

"Thanks for coming on such short notice," he said, walking around the table to give the elf a hug. She returned it happily and shook her head.

"Anything for my favorite student."

"Oh please, I was horrible."

"You were also half the age of the second-youngest person at the tower, so you're getting some bonus points," Alicia laughed. "So, you have three new arrivals, I see?"

Runar looked at the metal plates. The paint that he just applied to them still had to dry for a little while longer. "It's a bit complicated, but yes. It's . . . Ryan, and his two closest friends."

"Ryan? That was . . . that was your nephew, correct?" Runar slowly nodded, and Alicia placed her hand onto her chin in remembrance. "I thought you said you were trying not to get him involved."

"That's what I promised Hayden, so yeah. But then he became the Spirit Keeper, so that changed very quickly."

Alicia's eyes widened in surprise. "The Spirit Keeper? That is quite the coincidence . . . and his friends are trustworthy as well?"

Runar hesitated for a few moments. "I think so. I actually did some background checks on them a while ago, and they came out clean. Well, one of them has some mana deficiency thing, but that's more troublesome for *him*, and the other has quite a complicated family history, but . . . there are no connections to any other factions in the family, nor to the Shadows or anything of the sort. And Ryan has a pretty good eye for people these, and an even greater moral compass. If he trusts them . . . so do I. Worst case, I make them forget about this whole thing, but let's hope I won't need to."

"You still meddle with memories so easily?"

". . . I don't *easily*. I just don't hesitate to do it when I need to. Not anymore," Runar pointed out, quickly trying to move on from the conversation. "Anyway, you brought everything you need for your clairvoyance, right?"

"Of course." Alicia petted the ceramic bottle hanging by her hip. "Though, you still didn't tell me what you want me to find."

"Oh calm down, you already know, right?"

"I have a guess. I would just like to hear it from you directly."

"Ryan has found two-thirds of a spirit core," Runar explained, glancing down at the watch on his wrist as he walked up to a nearby shelf, then grabbed a box from on top of it. "So, we need your help finding the last third."

Alicia smiled lightly, narrowing her eyes. "Has he now? He just 'found' them?"

"Can you stop acting like you don't know about all of this already? You already knew that Ryan awakened as the Spirit Keeper, and you also already know that the Shadows are involved."

Alicia looked up contemplatively, slowly shrugging. "I am very good at guessing."

Runar rolled his eyes as he opened up the top of the box, pulling a small larva out of it. It was around half the size of a pinkie, and was still slightly moving. He stepped up to the spherical nest, carefully placing the larva into its entrance. Hesitantly, small hands covered in dull feathers grabbed it, pulling it deeper inside.

"A pixie?" Alicia asked curiously. This time, it was real curiosity. The difference was pretty obvious to Runar; she hadn't known about the pixie girl.

"We rescued her from an auction yesterday. She's still too scared to let us properly check on her, but I think she's warming up to me."

Alicia smiled lightly, squatting down in front of the nest. The pixie, currently trying to eat the larva, was startled as she looked at Alicia. She pulled the larva closer to her body, as if trying to hide it. The elf carefully held out her finger as Alicia's eyes took on a soft, mellow pink. Runar couldn't see her mana directly, but he could feel some of the most refined mana he had ever seen flow from the elf's fingertip.

Just a moment later, the pixie's demeanor changed completely. While she had been scared and hiding, she now wore an excited expression, jumping onto her feet. Her injured wings fluttered quietly as her innate mana started pulsating and flowing around her, responding to Alicia.

The elf chuckled slightly, looking up at Runar, "You should really freshen up on your pixie-speak. She called you dull."

"It's my pixie-speak. I just don't have your ridiculous level of mana control. But I've been working on an array to make it a bit easier for me; I've just been a bit busy since last night," Runar pointed out. "Plus, I wanted to let her take it easy for now. She went through a lot."

"Right, right, you dull little boy," Alicia laughed, watching the quite reinvigorated pixie continue with her meal. "Alright, let's go meet this Ryan now. He's the one with the dungeon mana stuck in him, right?"

"Hm?" Runar saw Alicia's gaze move into a specific direction of the cave, as if she was looking at something beyond the walls of this building. And he immediately realized where she was looking. "Wait, why are they . . . But yeah, that's him. Sorry, can you see what they're doing?"

"The three of them seem to be taking care of a cursed animal. That's par for the course here, isn't it?"

Runar raised his brow, confused. "The three of them? Sorry, does one of them have red, kind of spiky mana?"

"Mhm, and quite a lot of it too. There's one with a little bit, but not enough to be of substance, really."

With a confused frown, Runar picked up his pen from the table, then wrote a series of runes into the air. His eyes took on a green glow as he started seeing the mana of the people in question. There was something weird there. He wrote a rune in front of his right eye, then closed his left as he activated it. His sight was quickly magnified. Just like Alicia, he could see three people. Ryan with that thick dungeon mana stuck inside of him, Rose's ridiculous amount of innate mana, and someone with clean but unrefined mana. And then there was of course Kindly, whose cursed mana was like a splotch of ink accidentally thrown onto a canvas, sticking out. But right in front of Kindly, there was an outline.

A spot where there was no mana at all. A complete absence.

"Is that . . . Modak?"

CHAPTER FORTY-ONE

Kindly the Mimic

Runar rushed up the steps at the cave's walls, then ripped open the door once he got to the top. And what he was seeing was exactly what he thought. To his left, startled by his uncle's sudden appearance was Ryan, who stuck out like a sore thumb because of the dungeon mana in him. The corruption was still wriggling on his chest, trying to dig its way through.

Next to him was Silvia, whose mana was fine, but not anything special. And then, Runar turned toward Kindly the cursed mimic, and the sight of his mana practically assaulted Runar's sight, fully distracting him from Rose's dense mana. But the only thing that he could focus on was that "hole." More than just a complete lack of mana, it was like the space taken up by Modak fully rejecting the very existence of mana.

It even took Runar a while to realize what was actually happening here; Modak was treating Kindly.

"What's going on, what are you doing?" Runar asked, still not sure what he was looking at. Rose immediately shook her head and waved her hands around.

"It's not what it looks like! He doesn't have any mana, so he's unaffected by Kindly's curse!" The animal caretaker tried to make sure that Runar knew Modak was safe in what he was doing. "He wasn't even affected by the cockatrice's paralysis!"

Runar stared at Rose, taken aback. "He locked eyes with a cockatrice? How the hell did that happen?!"

Rose was startled at Runar's raised voice. "I-I'm sorry, it was an accident! He fell and—"

"Rose, I entrusted them to you, you should be the one to prevent those exact accidents!"

"Dude"—Ryan stepped up to his uncle, stepping between him and Rose—"I get what you're saying, but it really wasn't her fault. Animals get weird around

Modak because he doesn't have mana, and a cockatrice tried to jump at him. He fell down, his sunglasses fell off, and that was that."

Runar looked at Ryan for a few moments, sighing loudly, "Fine . . . as long as he's alright, that's all that matters. But still, why is he treating Kindly? Even if the curse won't affect him, treating a mimic can be very dangerous."

Rose quickly shook her head. "No, with other mimics, maybe, but Kindly isn't the same as other mimics; he's much, much smarter. He's less aggressive, and he understands things at a wholly different level!"

Runar rubbed the bridge of his nose. "That doesn't mean that he can't be dangerous, Rose. Especially an injured mimic can be dangerous. Even more so if it's an *awakened* mimic."

Ryan's head snapped toward the wardrobe, deeply staring at it. "Excuse me?"

"Hm? What?" Runar asked with a deep frown, massaging his forehead to get it to relax.

"No, just . . . I thought you just said that the mimic . . . that Kindly awakened."

"Yeah, that's what I said."

"But isn't Kindly a mimic?"

"I don't understand the problem." Runar looked at his nephew with a confused expression, and Rose quickly explained.

"Ah, about that . . . I believe that it's not particularly well-known that animals can awaken," she explained, but Runar let out a scoff.

"Seriously? I guess it's a lot rarer than for people, but I figured Ryan would know," he pointed out, quickly turning to his nephew. "Aren't you kind of an awakening nerd?"

Ryan stared into space for a few moments, trying to really process that information. He had read through every single known class on the Awakened forum, but there was no info about any classes that belonged to animals. But then again, it wasn't like there was anything that said animals *couldn't* awaken.

"Whatever, that's not really important right now. Modak, are you okay? Are you hurt anywhere? Any scratches, bumps, or other injuries?" Runar asked, looking the orc up and down, but Modak quickly shook his head.

"No, I'm fine . . ." he replied, slowly looking back at Kindly. "And I'm just treating some wounds on him. That's fine, right?"

Runar hesitated to answer. Obviously there wasn't anything wrong with him taking care of the mimic, but this was just too risky. If Modak did something wrong and hurt Kindly even a little, Kindly could lash out and do a lot of damage to an unawakened person. That being the case, though, Runar knows how important it is to get Kindly fixed up quickly. It wasn't even possible to use healing magic on him because the curse would break down any spell it came in contact with.

"Fine." Runar let out a long, deep sigh. "But let me do something first."

Runar waved Modak over, and the orc carefully walked up to him. He was trying to keep his hands behind his back since he was wearing rubber gloves and didn't want to get them dirty. With some swift motions, Runar used his pen to write something right in front of Modak's chest. He activated the runes, and for just a brief moment, Modak was surrounded in a thin light.

With a click of his tongue, Runar put the pen away. "I've put a mark for a physical protection spell on you, so that should do it in case something goes wrong."

"I thought Kindly's curse infects all mana; wouldn't that happen with that too?" Silvia wondered, but Runar shook his head.

"That's why it's just a mark. If something happens, I'll activate the spell from here. Kindly's curse can't infect anything right off the bat, so it should work. I can't keep it active for much longer than a moment anyway because the spell probably won't take proper hold on Modak and will break down pretty quickly," Runar explained quickly, taking a step back to where he could properly watch Kindly and Modak. The orc slowly returned to the mimic, continuing to properly clean and treat his wounds.

Using salves that were specifically created with the minimum amount of mana possible, as well as some medicine that was fed to Kindly directly, Modak was able to finish the treatment properly as Rose carefully guided him through the whole process.

Ryan stood on the other side of the room. His heart was beating strong as he watched Kindly twitch at the slightest touch. Squeezing his eyes shut, trying to persist through the discomfort. Those thin, wart-covered tentacles curled up, wrapping themselves around the legs of the wardrobe. Through it all, no matter how strange Kindly appeared, no matter how monstrous his form would look to others, Ryan couldn't help himself but think of a child at the doctor's office.

The fear and pain of being treated, of knowing and understanding that this is what had to happen, but having this unending anxiety in your chest.

". . . His curse, what kind is it?" Ryan asked in a whisper, leaning toward Runar, who slightly raised his brow, glancing at his nephew before going back to watching Modak and Kindly.

"It's a type of corruption, one bred to spread, specifically," he replied, and Ryan's stomach sank.

The corruption that was latched onto his chest barely affected him; it burned and was uncomfortable, but the dungeon mana protected him. Richie reacted how he did after just being scraped by it. Ryan couldn't imagine what it was like to be fully infected like that.

". . . Can it be cured?"

"Regular types of curses can, but corruption is different. It's like a living thing, latching itself onto others to feed off them. We're trying to find something to counteract it, but . . ."

"Then what's the plan supposed to be for me?" Ryan asked, glancing down at his own chest. Would he end up having that thing in there forever?

Runar scratched his throat, trying to find the right words. "We're going to try and . . . force the curse out of your body, I guess? In your case, it just infected your physical body, and not your mana. We could technically just cut it all out, but that's obviously not preferable. So, if everything works out tonight and we're a bit lucky, then . . . you'll be rid of the corruption in a couple of days."

"Hm . . . alright . . . So there's no way to help Kindly right now?"

"Not any more than what's happening right now. Honestly, this is already close to a miracle . . . Most people or animals that are affected by some kind of corruption don't die because of the corruption itself. But rather, because it drives them wild and they end up injuring themselves to a point where they will die without treatment. And because of Kindly's corruption specifically, we can't even treat him," Runar explained. "The fact that Kindly was able to persist through the mental effects and recover his sanity, and that we have someone that can treat him on top of that . . . He's quite lucky."

Ryan looked over at Modak and the mimic. Now he understood why Runar was so on edge. But it seemed like Modak was finishing things up for the time being, applying the last of the bandages on one of Kindly's limbs.

Rose loudly clapped her hands together, with pure excitement apparent in her whole body. "Alright! And that's done! We should let Kindly rest now. I'm sure the medicine has made him a bit tired. Once he feels a bit better, maybe we can finally get him into his new shell!" she said gleefully, as Modak carefully stood up, an exhausted smile on his own face.

"I'm glad I could help," the orc replied, stepping away from Kindly. However, the mimic had wrapped one of his tentacles around his leg, unwilling to let go. Before Modak could really process this, more of Kindly's limbs stretched out toward him, wrapping themselves around the orc's body. Seeing this, Runar flinched and tried to stretch out his hand, but Ryan immediately slapped it back down.

"Dude, calm down. It's just a hug."

Runar stared at his nephew, then slowly turned back to the wardrobe. As Ryan has said, nothing happened. Kindly pulled Modak in for a few moments, tightly holding him, and then let go just a moment later.

"For someone that said he's bad with animals, you're sure popular with them, huh?" Silvia laughed, looking at Modak's wet, slime-covered body. With a sigh, the orc stepped away.

"Shut up," he groaned, trying to walk to his friends, but Runar immediately stopped him.

"Nope, stop. With all of that on you, you need to get cleaned up first, so stay a few steps away from everyone," Runar said, stepping away from the door to let Modak step through first. Modak groaned and nodded his head, making his way outside. Before he left through the door, though, he glanced back at Kindly one more time.

Keeping some distance from the orc, the others quickly followed behind, though Runar stopped Rose from stepping outside. Waiting until the others were out of earshot, he looked at the woman in front of him. "Okay, first of all. Before you let someone that didn't even know mimics existed until an hour ago treat a cursed mimic, run it by me first," he started, his foot tapping on the ground as he stared through the hazmat suit's darkened glass front as Rose took a nervous step back. "And second. I get that meeting someone that won't be affected by you is exciting, but he's barely eighteen. Keep it professional and respectful, okay?"

"I-I wasn't, I—" Rose stuttered out nervously, trying to turn her head away so that Runar couldn't look at her face. But she quickly realized that hiding from Runar wasn't possible. ". . . I understand. I'm sorry . . ."

"No, it's fine. You didn't do anything. I get that your situation is rough, I definitely do. I mean, come on, you're wearing a fucking hazmat suit all day, every day. Just . . . don't be weird about it to him." Runar turned around and stepped out the door, quickly making his way down the steps. He looked around a little nervously, trying to find someone, muttering to himself, "And where the hell is she?"

"So . . . what now? If it's so dangerous, Modak can't just walk through the streets like this, right? And especially not that dense forest," Ryan pointed out, and Runar slowly nodded his head. He kept looking around.

"Yeah, yeah, we'll get him some water in a second, don't worry," Runar replied, and just as he did, a cloud formed above Modak. It was almost cartoonish, with the size and shape appearing like someone just plucked a perfectly fluffy and white cloud from a child's drawing.

"I can help with that," Alicia's voice pointed out, and Runar snapped his head toward the source of that sound, staring at her almost pleadingly. She had appeared out of nowhere with that annoying grin on her face. The elf held forward her hand, pointing at the cloud, locking eyes with Runar. He let out a long groan and rubbed the bridge of his nose.

"Modak, do you have your phone on you? Or anything else that can't get wet?"

"Uh . . . no, I kept it in the changing room with my other stuff . . . what's happening, exactly?" the orc asked nervously, but Runar didn't fill him in.

"Just hold your breath."

Before Modak could ask why, Alicia snapped her fingers. A massive flood of water poured out of the cloud. It wasn't even just to the extent of heavy rain, but as if someone was emptying out a bathtub over his head. In just a few moments, all the slime that was stuck to Modak was completely washed off. But weirdest of all, neither he nor the floor around him was wet whatsoever. Like the water just completely disappeared.

"There we go~!" Smiling broadly, Alicia took a step closer to Modak, looking him up and down. "So, you're the one without mana, huh?"

Modak slowly nodded his head, staring at the woman in front of him in stunned disbelief. However, Alicia quickly turned to Ryan. "And you're the nephew, the Spirit Keeper, huh?"

"Yep, and who are you?" Ryan responded, raising his brow as he looked back at the woman in front of him.

"Straightforward. I like it," Alicia replied, looking at the young man in front of her with a curious smile. "I'm Alicia. Runar called me over to help you find the last fragment of that spirit core you have."

"Oh! Yeah, that's great!" Ryan replied, his heart almost skipping a beat. He inwardly looked at Gaia's two fragments floating in her domain. She was still asleep now, as she had been since the two fragments were brought back together. Realizing that he might be able to wake her up soon, Ryan looked over at Runar. "Are we doing this now?"

Runar looked over at Alicia. "Are we? Are you ready to go?"

"I don't see why not," she responded. "Let's get going back to Runar's office. That should be a better place for me to work than here."

Without further ado, Alicia turned around and started walking down the dirt path, quickly followed by Runar. Ryan and Silvia were about to follow as well, but Modak grabbed both of their arms, pulling them back for a moment.

"Guys . . . that . . ." Modak started, staring at Alicia with wide, open eyes, "do you know who that is?"

"I don't know; someone from the Magic Tower that Runar knows. That's what he said at least," Ryan replied, and Silvia looked over at her curiously.

"Why, do you know her? Is she famous?"

"Famous? That's not just 'someone from the Magic Tower'—that's Alicia Ethel Boreard, the Mistress of the Magic Tower. She's probably the most powerful and influential mage in the world right now!"

CHAPTER FORTY-TWO

Light of Guidance

Runar placed dark curtains over the windows of his office, completely shutting out the light from the cave outside. Instead, the room was only lit by seven candles that had been placed on the ground. Alicia was drawing a pattern on the ground, where each of the candles acted as what seemed to be an important component tying it all together.

Once she was done drawing the pattern, Alicia placed the ceramic bottle she was carrying on her hip into its center, pulling its cork with a slight *pop*.

"Alright, so . . . what now? How does this work?" Ryan asked, staring at the bottle. He was both excited and anxious, worrying whether or not this was really going to work. If this woman really was the most powerful living mage, and even *she* couldn't find the last fragment, then nobody would be able to, right?

Alicia slowly stood up, petting the dust off her long skirt. "It's very simple. Spirits are special beings. They are beings made of mana, and we have found that mana can cause mana with the same wavelength to resonate over long distances. Actually, from our tests, there doesn't seem to be a real decline in the resonance when comparing medium distances to extremely long distances. Even across planar dimensions, it seems like mana of the same wavelength can resonate with itself."

Ryan tried to follow along with what she was saying. "So basically . . . because spirits are made of mana, you can make Gaia's fragments resonate with the last piece?"

"Yes, exactly." With a slight hum, Alicia nodded. "That being the case, in a practical, non-experiment setting, things get a bit more complicated. Since we don't already know the location and are trying to find it, we need to set up a beacon, and this beacon needs to consist of a large amount of mana. In this case, it means we need more than half of the spirit core, which you have!"

Alicia held forward her hand, as if waiting for something. She looked at him with a smile for a while, but Ryan didn't know exactly what she wanted.

"Ryan, I think she needs you to give Gaia's fragments to her." Silvia nudged his side, and he quickly reacted.

"Oh, right, sorry, uhm . . . just let me . . ." Slowly, Ryan looked inwardly at Gaia's domain. The two fragments were still peacefully floating, and Ryan tried to carefully pull them both out, as he would with Maximus. Before long, threads of green mana flowed down Ryan's arms, gathering together to form the two crystal fragments on his palm. And at the same moment, red wisps of mana flowed down Ryan's legs as Maximus appeared beside him.

The knight had been inside of his domain since last night, but clearly wanted to be out here to watch what was about to happen. Curious, and unsure what to focus on directly, Alicia's eyes moved back and forth between the fragments and the actual spirit standing next to Ryan.

"Oh! Look at how wonderful they both look!" Alicia pointed out, "Their mana is just so beautiful!"

Slowly, Ryan placed the two fragments onto Alicia's hand. He was a bit nervous to let them go, but if Runar knew her personally, she wouldn't do anything wrong with them . . . right?

Maximus's sight was following the fragments the whole time, and Ryan looked down at him. Ryan squatted down. "Are you alright?"

Maximus turned toward Ryan, nodded his head just once, but then quickly looked back at Alicia with the fragments. Ryan didn't know what was going through the knight's head, but hearing all those things from Runar last night must have not been easy for him either. Hearing what exactly caused these problems, and there were many more spirits out there that had suffered similarly, could not have felt great to him.

"We'll find them all, don't worry," Ryan promised, and Maximus hesitated briefly, but then once more nodded. Though Ryan said that, he wasn't even sure himself if that was possible. Sure, it was what he wanted, but you couldn't get everything you want in this world. But if what Alicia was about to do worked, then that was a first step in achieving that.

"Don't worry." Runar walked up next to Ryan, placing his hand onto his shoulder for a moment. "Clairvoyance is one of Alicia's strong suits."

"One of many~!" Alicia agreed, as she placed the two fragments into a small circle within the drawn pattern.

"H-How . . . how did you end up meeting Miss Boreard anyway?" Modak wondered, curiously looking at Runar, who couldn't help himself but scoff.

"Miss Boreard? Seriously?"

Alicia glared at Runar. "Leave him be, the boy's got manners. You could learn a thing or two from him, you know?"

"Yeah, yeah, whatever. I awakened pretty young, and Rune Mage is a pretty rare class. We didn't have anyone directly in the family that could teach me, so I went to the Magic Tower for training. And Alicia is the one that taught me." With crossed arms, Runar looked over at the elf, who was nodding her head proudly.

"And look at how well he turned out for it. He learned from the best," she pointed out, and Modak was almost stunned, barely able to get his words out.

"Y-You were her student? That . . . really?" he let out in disbelief, and Runar slightly narrowed his eyes.

"I'm not sure why you're in such disbelief there. I'm a very capable man."

Ryan scoffed, "Yeah, sure."

"What's that supposed to mean?"

"You know exactly what that's supposed to mean," Ryan smirked.

"Well, sure . . . I can be a little forgetful sometimes, but I've got a lot of things on my plate. And, I'm capable enough to make you guys these!" Runar quickly walked over to his desk, trying to find the three metal plates he prepared earlier. He had to search for a while because he had a hard time seeing things with just the dim candlelight, but he found them soon enough. Runar walked over to the three newcomers, handing each of them one of the plates.

"Put this into your phone case, with the array pointing to your phone, and you should get a signal down here," he explained, turning to his nephew with a smug grin. "I feel like that's pretty capable, don'tcha think?"

"Well . . . it's a good start," Ryan joked lightly, pulling out his phone. He peeled the case off and placed the thin plate inside. As he turned the screen on, almost being blinded by the bright light, he soon saw a few bars appear in the corner of the screen. He was even getting a Wi-Fi signal from upstairs now. A few messages came in that he had missed while down here.

One from his mom, sending him a recipe for lemon bars that she found. Some from Yanna, talking about a workout plan that she and Ryan had been trying to figure out. And then, in the flood of random notifications from apps of phone games he meant to uninstall for weeks already, there was an email from the Awakened Center. An invitation to something that Yanna had already mentioned. A get-together for newly awakened individuals. He mentally noted it to take a look later, but for now he put his phone back into his pocket. That kind of thing wasn't important right now.

"You kids ready to do this?" Alicia asked, just waiting for everyone to get ready. "Please don't use any spells or skills that use mana right now."

Ryan watched as Alicia pressed her palms together, as though she were praying. She let out a long breath at such fervor that it seemed almost impossible for her to hold it for as long as she did. Almost instantly, she stopped, and carefully pulled her hands away from each other. With a soft pink glow, a staff appeared between her hands. It was made of wood curling around itself, holding on to a round pink bulb at its end. Alicia held that end right over the ceramic bottle in the center of that pattern on the ground.

With a whispering, almost fading voice, the elf started to recite a chant. It was rhythmic and musical, enthralling to the point where Ryan's eyes were almost stuck to her lips as she spoke. He turned to the side, and he noticed he wasn't the only one; the others were staring right at Alicia, as if they were watching the most engaging movie ever.

By the time Ryan looked back toward Alicia, some liquid was carefully flowing out of the top of the ceramic bottle. It was fully translucent, but it seemed too thick to be water. It was just a step before gelatinous. Once out of the bottle, the liquid split up into eight parts, each forming a small bubble.

Seven of these bubbles moved to the candles, trapping their flames. But instead of extinguishing them, the liquid just made it all brighter. The walls were quickly covered in fractured light, which swerved back and forth. It was like what happened when light reflected off a body of water. The last of the bubbles moved toward the two fragments of Gaia, carefully scooping them up before carrying them to the center of the pattern, floating just between the ceramic bottle and the tip of Alicia's staff.

The whole time as this happened, Alicia hadn't stopped her chanting for even a moment, not even to breathe. Her eyes were deeply focused on the bubble containing the fragments. Carefully, she tapped the top of the bubble with her staff, pulling the liquid up into a thin strand. Ryan's heart almost skipped a beat as he watched the reflections on the walls peel off the surfaces. They floated through the air and were pulled toward the pattern on the ground, like a dome of light that was slowly shrinking, leaving nothing but darkness behind. Before long, Ryan and the others were taken in by this darkness as well. He couldn't even see his own hands anymore. By the time he looked back in front of himself, that "dome" had reached the magic circle on the ground, but it didn't stop there. These reflections continued on farther, even beyond the candles that created them in the first place. A few moments later, the only thing that was visible in this room was the bubble containing the two fragments.

It was an almost uncomfortable darkness, one that Ryan had never seen before. It was even darker than just closing his eyes usually was. Right now, he would have had no idea if they were open or not, if it weren't for that single ball of light dancing right in front of him. Soon, the light pulled up the thin strand that Alicia had created earlier. Her voice, so serene and quiet as it had been, was now so deafening that it seemed like she was screaming, though in reality it was still nothing but a steady whisper.

The light soon gathered at the tip of the strand, forming a small, marble-sized ball. Ryan's eyes were deeply focused on them, as he finally started to see something else beside the light. Alicia's hands were slowly closing in around it, her pale skin illuminated by the magical lights. As if they were physical, Alicia grabbed it in her right hand. Her whispered chanting ongoing, she held it toward Ryan. He didn't even have to be told and carefully took a step forward, taking the marble of light from her.

Out of everything that was happening, the part that truly surprised Ryan the most was that it was cold to the touch. He looked away from it, watching Alicia guide her fingers to her lips. The light of the marble was reflected in her eyes, and she was staring right at Ryan. He didn't know why, but it was like his body was acting on its own. He mimicked Alicia and placed the marble to his own lips. And then, he took a piece of light into his mouth, swallowing it.

As the whispers cut out immediately, the light of the candles slowly returned and the room was filled with that soft yellow glow. A system message appeared in front of Ryan.

[You have taken in the -Light of Guidance-]

"What . . . what's the Light of Guidance?" Ryan let out, and as he spoke, he realized that he had been holding his breath up until now. At the same time, he could see the liquid move back into the bottle after placing down the two fragments. Alicia smiled at Ryan.

"It's how we can find Gaia's fragment. It's going to guide you there," she explained, tapping her head. "Just try to concentrate on it."

Ryan nodded his head, closing his eyes for a moment, trying to search for the Light of Guidance. However, he didn't have to look for it for long. Inside of Gaia's domain, a small orb of light was floating. As Ryan focused on it, he could feel it practically pull him in a direction. It was perfectly to the right. To test it out, Ryan slightly turned his head. The pull of the light was still aimed in that same direction.

"Have you found it?" Alicia asked. "Now, this part might be a bit tricky, especially since you haven't awakened that long ago. You need to let go and let it pull you to where it wants you to go. It's going to feel almost like . . ."

"Like a very strong 'want' to go somewhere? Yeah, I think I got it?" Ryan replied, and Alicia blinked a few times in surprise.

"Wait, you already got it?"

"I think so? It's trying to pull me right over there." He pointed in the direction where the light wanted him to go. It was slightly to the right of the door.

". . . Didn't you just awaken a few weeks ago?" Alicia tried to confirm, not sure if Runar maybe lied to her.

"On the fourteenth, yeah. I feel like I'm pretty good at handling mana, I guess. Plus, the fragment is just inside of Gaia's domain right now, so it was easy to find," Ryan explained, and Alicia clicked her tongue as she turned her head away.

With crossed arms, the elf glared at Runar. "Like uncle, like nephew, huh? Your family is just so annoyingly talented at using magic."

Muttering to herself, Alicia walked over to a bag placed on one of the couches. She pulled a scroll out of it; a full-on proper scroll that looked like it came straight out of a movie.

"What's up with her?" Silvia asked curiously, and Runar couldn't help himself but grin as he responded.

"When she started teaching me, she would always get super annoyed at how quickly I learned the basics. She wanted to explain and teach it to me more, but I'd skip whole lessons."

Alicia narrowed her eyes and stared at Runar. "Your bloodline is cheating."

"Oh get off it," Runar scoffed. "Just open the map already."

Alicia sighed, unrolling the scroll she was holding. On it was an old, hand-painted map of what seemed to be New Riverside. It wasn't particularly detailed, but apparently quite accurate. The elven mage looked away from the map and at Ryan. "Now, place your palm on there, and act like you're pulling out the light. As you did with the fragments earlier."

"Right, just hold on," Ryan replied, quickly walking over to the magic circle that had been drawn on the ground. Gaia's two fragments were still laying there, and Ryan quickly picked them up. He pulled them back into Gaia's domain where they would be safe. They were floating just below that orb of light.

And then, Ryan came back to Alicia who patiently waited, and he placed his palm onto the map. It was rough and clearly pretty old. Ryan took a deep breath and concentrated on the light in the domain, pulling it out through his hand. He could feel the same chill that he felt when he touched the light earlier; it was like cold water was flowing down his arm onto the paper.

Alicia prompted him to put away his hand, and as he did, a small circle appeared on the map, drawn around part of the Channel's island.

CHAPTER FORTY-THREE

Shadows

I t's in the Channel?" Ryan asked with a light frown, and Runar loudly clicked his tongue.

"Of course it is. Fuckin' Shadows . . ." he muttered quietly. Even so, Ryan still heard him.

"What do you mean, 'Shadows'?"

Though hesitant, Runar knew that this was an important aspect of this situation that Ryan had to be filled in on. He couldn't *not* tell him. ". . . Alright, so . . . we're not the only group acting at this 'level.' One of the main groups that's being a bit of a bother is, well . . . they're called the 'White Shadow Society.'"

"Seriously?" Silvia scoffed, hearing that name. "That's kind of . . . weirdly cliché, right?"

"Well, when they got their name, it was very innovative," Runar pointed out. "But their name isn't important. They're also in the business of dealing with the mystical, and those that are 'hidden' for one reason or another. But . . . instead of trying to help the 'hidden' not be 'hidden' . . . they're trying to get rid of them altogether."

When Ryan heard his uncle's words, the hairs on his neck stood up. "What? What do you mean?"

"I mean exactly what it sounds like." With a loud groan, Runar walked over to the windows to pull the curtains to the side and let some light in again. "They're honestly the main force we're fighting against. With every step we take to help the hidden, they take a step against them. They basically hunt all that they deem 'dangerous' for one reason or another. They're also the ones pulling the strings behind the auction, and they have massive influence over so, so many companies. Bluesky is one of their major fronts."

"Blue—what? Seriously?" Ryan let out in disbelief.

Similarly, Modak and Silvia didn't know what to think about what Runar just said. The orc quickly shook his head. "No, but Bluesky is a massive corporation, they . . . why would they . . . ?"

"Because they were made specifically for this. Awakened people are a massive force. They can get almost impossibly powerful. And Bluesky is the biggest player in every Awakened-related industry that exists," Runar explained. "Why do you think they were going after Ryan that hard? It's not just because he's got a unique class."

"So that Simon guy was one of the 'Shadows' you're talking about?" Silvia wondered, but Runar quickly denied that.

"He's just a goon, I guess. Some random asshole working at the company who doesn't even know who he's really working for. Honestly? I doubt there's more than four or five people at the whole company that actually know everything."

"So . . . they stole one of Gaia's fragments?" Ryan asked, and Runar hesitated as he once more shook his head.

"First of all, they didn't 'steal' it. After your father, you know . . . The fragments were ready for the taking. And frankly, I believe they might have simply found the full core, probably damaged, and fragmented it themselves."

Ryan ground his teeth together. "So . . . they're the ones that gave Vanda the fragment? And what, they somehow placed the fragment in a dungeon?"

The word *hesitation* was practically written on Runar's face at this point. There were a lot of things that he had to tell Ryan, but he didn't know if this was the right moment. However, Runar promised to fill him in, so he did. "The formation of dungeons can be . . . helped along, so to say. The 'seed' was probably already there, and then they pushed it a step further with the help of Gaia's fragment. You said her title was 'Garden Golem,' right? That fits the monsters in the dungeon quite well, right?"

"Are you serious?" Ryan asked, confused. "Why the fuck would they do that? How does creating dungeons even help those guys? If their goal is total genocide of everyone they don't like, what do dungeons have to do with that?"

Before Runar could reply, Alicia spoke up with her own guess, "To get rid of spirits."

Runar snapped his head toward the elf. "We don't know that! That's not—"

"Get rid of spirits? What do you mean? Runar, what does she mean?"

Not just Ryan, but Maximus as well; they were both getting worked up. The spirit was staring deeply up at Runar, and Ryan followed suit. The Rune Mage tried to think how to best word it.

"We don't know for sure, but . . . We believe that they are trying to make spirits seem dangerous," Runar explained. "The dungeon was not particularly strong. Like, come on, a level 1, newly awakened kid was able to find the core room in a couple of hours. If it had been anyone else . . . they would have found the core room, the dungeon would have been closed, and the only thing left behind would have been a spirit core. That would have reported, and . . ."

Ryan was stunned, unsure what he was supposed to think. In these moments of silence, Modak slowly spoke, "So . . . they're trying to make it seem like spirits cause dungeons?"

Runar slowly nodded. "That's the only reason I can think of, yes. It would be great if it's some kind of misunderstanding, but . . . after what happened yesterday, with that robot? That just supports the idea further."

"Wait, how so? Even if Ryan hadn't been there, that clearly wasn't the fault of Gaia's fragment, but because of how it was used! Plus, the university wouldn't want to spread too much about it either, right?" Silvia asked, not really understanding the purpose behind that, or what Runar was insinuating. But Modak quickly filled in the gaps.

"It wasn't supposed to happen yesterday." Modak rubbed the bridge of his nose, finally understanding everything. "When I met with Vanda earlier, she wasn't able to tell me anything about who gave the fragment to her, but she *did* mention that he was very interested in the showcase that was supposed to happen today. Even said he might show up himself, to watch. What if Energizer was supposed to go berserk today, and not yesterday? In front of dozens of important people from big tech companies and news people ready to jump on any little incident."

"Wouldn't that be a pretty big oversight?" Ryan frowned. "They must have known about the test runs yesterday, right?"

"Sure, but they probably didn't know you would be there." Modak suggested, "And if the fragment that was already with you reacted to the one in Energizer, who's to say it didn't happen the other way around? You just being there could have made things speed up."

"Are you serious? So it was my fault . . . ?"

"No, it's not like that," Runar immediately replied. "If anything, you being there was the best outcome. Nobody got seriously hurt, and we were able to deal with everything quietly."

". . . So . . . So what now? What else are they gonna try?" Ryan asked, trying to calm himself down instead of getting angry right away. Getting angry didn't help him. It never did. It was just so hard to stop it from happening sometimes, especially in situations like this. What was he supposed to do? Just act like everything was fine?

But Runar just shrugged. "Honestly? No clue."

"S-Seriously? Aren't you the head of the family? Just use the head's . . . brain, or something, I don't know, just fucking . . . come on!" Ryan's frustration was obvious, and he really wasn't able to hold it back.

"Listen, we're trying, okay? But first, we need to figure out *where* it is. That should help. The map is linked to the core's location now. It's not super accurate, but as long as we search the area in the circle, we should be able to use the Light of Guidance to find the exact spot," Runar explained. "I'll arrange what we need to, and then tomorrow we're heading out to search for it."

"Tomorrow? Seriously? Let's just go right now!" Ryan protested, staring at his uncle, unwilling to just leave Gaia's last fragment with people that want to use her for such ridiculous things.

"And do what? Just barge into whatever building they're keeping it in? On our own? No, that's ridiculous. We have people that can retrieve it after we find where it is, maybe without the Shadows even knowing. But I can't just call on them in a couple of hours. Plus, we need to take care of your corruption first. I'm sorry, but that's more important to me right now."

"But . . . we have the world's most powerful mage, and I'm perfectly fine. The corruption thing can wait!"

"We have what, now?" Alicia asked with a laugh. She was sitting in Runar's chair at his desk. "I'm sorry, but . . . the guidance spell was one thing, but I'm not getting involved in this any further. The Magic Tower strives to stay completely neutral."

"What do you mean, neutral? You're Runar's teacher!" Ryan pointed out, and Alicia looked back at him, her smile slowly disappearing. Runar's expression also turned a bit more complicated.

Alicia crossed her legs, leaning back in the chair. "And I was also the teacher of the former leader of the White Shadow Society. Granted, I didn't know his association to them at the time, but it really wouldn't have changed anything. The Magic Tower doesn't get involved in these things. We're an institution of knowledge. Not politics."

"Preventing genocides isn't politics! It's common sense, what are you even— How could you be like this?"

"I'm sorry, but it's the oath that I, and all my predecessors, have upheld for a thousand years. It's one thing to do a personal favor for a friend, and another to take sides in a war like this," Alicia replied, though she clearly understood what Ryan was saying. "Listen, even if I wanted to, it's not something I can do. There's too much at stake here. Obviously we don't want anything to happen to spirits either, and seeing innocent people get murdered day after day? I'm sorry, but that's not . . . When I say 'oath,' I don't mean it metaphorically, or the kind of promise that kids make when they say not to eat snacks before supper. I cannot help you. I'm sorry."

The elf slowly stood up, then passed by Runar. She gave him a short hug as the student spoke to his teacher. "Thanks for the help, anyway."

Ryan's eyes were closed. He concentrated on his breathing, trying to count backward from ten to calm himself down. Though he hadn't done this in years, it used to work pretty well, so he figured he might as well give it another shot instead of letting out a massive shout here.

"Oh, and . . ." Alicia's crystal clear voice cut through Ryan's counting, but before he could open his eyes to see what she wanted, he felt her finger tap his chest. It was nothing but a light touch, that much was clear not just from the outside, but to Ryan as well. But it was right in the middle of the part of Ryan's chest where the corruption had taken hold. All the air immediately escaped Ryan's lungs as his body tensed up. His legs went weak as he dropped to his knees, trying to clutch his chest but holding back in case touching it would make this even worse.

As Ryan felt Modak and Silvia come to his side, and Maximus stepped in front of him with both of his active skills turned on without hesitation, ready to defend him, Alicia continued to speak, ". . . You're absolutely not fine. Go get yourself fixed up before you think about helping others. Like this, you're just going to make things worse for everyone involved."

The elf stepped up to the door, ready to leave. She fully expected to just be able to go without another word from anyone, but Ryan had something else in mind. His foot slammed on the ground as he forced himself to get back up. "And . . . and how would you know?" he asked, grinding his teeth as he stared at the back of the woman in front of him. "You're too much of a coward to get involved in the first place."

Alicia turned back around, locking eyes with Ryan. She couldn't help herself but smile, slowly turning to Runar. "And you're sure you two are related?"

". . . I doubt it myself sometimes," Runar laughed lightly, in disbelief over the sheer fervor that his nephew was showing. "But . . . it's probably better if you go. I don't think I need to show you out, do I?"

"I wasn't shown in, so, yeah, I think I can find my way out on my own." Alicia stepped out the door, and the moment it shut behind her, Ryan dropped back down onto one knee.

"Fuck . . . Godsdammit . . . why . . . why the fuck does it hurt so much?!" Ryan forced his eyes shut while struggling to keep himself calm.

"Is he okay? Is the corruption spreading . . . ?" Modak asked anxiously, trying to help keep Ryan upright, but Runar just shook his head in response while approaching his nephew, the pen in his hand.

"It's nothing like that. The corruption is basically . . . an open wound? It attached itself to Ryan's flesh, and just the slightest impact can feel like absolute hell. I said it before, but it's basically alive, and trying everything it can to stop it from being forcefully pulled out. And the best way to do that is to make it hurt like hell to even touch it." Runar pulled up Ryan's shirt, exposing his back. Though he had already shown it to Modak and Silvia, being exposed like this all of a sudden would still usually feel horrible to him, but Ryan really wasn't in the state of mind to think about that. The pain was keeping him paralyzed against his will. He could barely even feel the nib of Runar's pen touch his skin. And then, he couldn't feel anything at all, as the pain faded almost instantly.

"That . . . huh?" Ryan let out, "What's going on?"

"I numbed your sense of pain. I'd usually prefer not to do that, 'cause not having a sense of pain at all is dangerous in itself, but it's better than what's happening right now," Runar pointed out. "Though to be honest, I'm pretty sure anyone else would have passed out by now. Get up."

Still unsteady on his legs, Ryan stood up with Modak and Silvia's help. Runar motioned for Ryan to pull up his shirt, and he awkwardly did as told.

"What the—" In disbelief over what he was seeing, Runar stared at Ryan's chest. "How are you even standing right now?"

"It's not that bad . . . is it?" Ryan asked, slowly looking down at his chest. But what he saw definitely wasn't what his chest looked like earlier. The black tendrils of the corruption had spread all over his chest, and the skin around each part of that horrible darkness was deep purple and blue.

"This . . . that's definitely not from Alicia tapping you just now. We really need to get that shit out of you quickly." Runar started nervously tapping his foot on the ground as he pulled out his phone. As the dial tone sounded out through the speaker, Runar quickly stepped in front of the door. "Anders? Yeah, come here immediately, we need to . . ."

The door closed, and Runar's voice faded away as Ryan, Silvia, Modak, and Maximus were briefly left alone. Neither the elf nor the orc knew what to say. Even the Knight Spirit was even more speechless than usual.

However, the silence was soon broken by Ryan. At least that shock of pain after Alicia left let him calm down pretty quickly.

"Uh . . . yeah, so that's . . . not good."

CHAPTER FORTY-FOUR

Ruby Symbiote

Ryan stepped into the car, with Modak and Silvia following behind pretty quickly. Yamada, Runar's demon assistant, was the one driving, while Runar himself was sitting in the passenger seat.

"Eh . . . is it fine to just leave Liam here?" Ryan asked, unsure if that was a good idea. It was Liam's first day here, so leaving him alone felt sort of bad.

Runar quickly replied, "Yeah, Anders is staying with him. He's pretty good with kids. I mean, he's got a couple on his own, so he better be."

"Huh, well, I guess it's fine, then?"

Curiously, Silvia leaned forward. "He's got kids? How old are they?"

"Uh . . . good question, I keep forgetting," Runar said, looking over at Yamada. He leaned forward and signed to her so she could read his hands without having to look away from the road. She held up her left hand and quickly replied, signing the numbers in sequence.

"Ahh, right, right. They're twenty-seven, twenty-four, and twenty," Runar translated, and Ryan slightly narrowed his eyes.

". . . Anders looked like thirty, what the hell?"

"Well, dwarves look thirty from when they're twelve, and stay like that until they're eighty, so. Yeah," Runar joked. "But yeah, he's . . . fifty-seven? Yeah, fifty-seven."

Ryan raised his brow. Something about that felt weird, but he also really didn't care too much. He barely exchanged two sentences with Anders, so it didn't really matter. That being the case, he was also a lot more focused on trying not to let the seat belt press onto his chest. Even if he couldn't feel it right now—since Runar completely blocked his ability to feel any sort of pain, or even the slightest touch— if the corruption tried to fight back and continued injuring Ryan's body, that wasn't going to turn out all too well for him.

"So, where are we going right now? You said something about a 'symbiote nest'?" Ryan asked, and Runar quickly explained.

"Yes, so, it's exactly that. It's the place where we keep symbiotes. They're a species that require a 'bond,' because they can't really survive on their own for too long. Once they're bonded to someone else, they practically fuse into their body. They improve one's general health, their immune system, their ability to heal wounds, and all sorts of good stuff. In some cases, they even extend their bond's lifespan a good bit."

"Oh, that . . . what the hell?" Ryan asked, unsure why he keeps getting surprised. "And let me guess, you're protecting them because rich assholes will try to exploit them?"

"Yup, basically. But the thing is that symbiotes are living, thinking individuals. They're hard to classify exactly, but if we had to, we would put them more into the category of 'people' rather than 'animals,' but they're probably a bit too unique to be put into categories like that. Anyway, they choose their bond. If they don't like someone, they will refuse to bond with them. If someone then tries to force that to happen, shit goes *really* wrong, and both parties sides usually die or get crippled permanently."

"So . . ." Modak started, trying to collect his thoughts about this a bit, ". . . you're hoping that one of these symbiotes will like Ryan enough to want to form a bond with him?"

"Mhm, exactly." Runar turned around, smiling at the orc. "The issue is that there really aren't many symbiotes, and they would rather die than form a bond with someone they dislike. So . . . only about a tenth of all symbiotes form a bond before passing. And there's only about a dozen under our protection."

Silvia nervously looked over at Ryan. "So, there's only a 10 percent chance that Ryan can bond with a symbiote and get rid of the corruption?"

Runar scoffed, unable to hold back a laugh. "No, not even close. It's a 10 percent chance that an individual symbiote will like any of the candidates we present to them over their lifetime. And we present *many* to them, trust me. The chance of a symbiote finding any individual adequate enough to bond with them is probably less likely than awakening."

"Then what if it doesn't work?"

"Then we'll have to try something else," Runar replied, turning to the elf. "But honestly, there's one weirdo amongst the symbiotes that I think will like Ryan quite a bit. And come on, do you know how lucky Ryan's been since he awakened? Even when he's unlucky, like with the mana poisoning, it all works out because the dungeon mana let him avoid being infected by the corruption."

"What, do you think that's another 'fate' thing?" Ryan asked. He still didn't like the idea of things being controlled by some external force he couldn't even understand, but if it helped him, then he couldn't really complain all too much. Runar seemed to think about it for a moment, but in the end just shrugged.

"Maybe, maybe not. Either way, you're fucking lucky as hell. And I'm confident in betting on that," Runar grinned, turning back around to look away from the back seats.

"So . . . do I have to do this symbiote thing? It sounds kind of weird," Ryan pointed out. "I mean, it's one thing to take care of, like, spirits and keep them basically in my body, and it's a whole other thing to let something called 'symbiote' directly fuse with my body."

Runar immediately turned back around, rapidly shaking his head. "Oh, no, no, you don't *have* to, definitely not. I wanted to explain it a bit more before we head out, but the corruption is a bit worse than I expected, so we have to hurry and figure out a solution. I'll explain it all a bit more now, but seriously, you don't have to if you're not totally comfortable with it. I mean, you can't really undo it, so you do need to be sure."

". . . Okay, that doesn't really make me feel much better, to be honest. So it's either permanently accepting something into my body, or getting a large chunk of my chest cut out?"

"Yes? Technically?" Unable to deny that, the Rune Mage looked back at him. "But the thing is, symbiotes are a . . . two-way road. That's kind of their whole thing. It's not really a 'choice' thing. It's like a wavelength. Like when you meet someone and immediately get along. A sort of . . . connection at first sight. Unless that happens, the bond will not freely form. Even if the symbiote takes a liking to you, if you somehow don't feel truly comfortable accepting them, the bond will not form. It's as simple as that."

"That one *does* make me feel better, I guess." Sighing a breath of relief, Ryan leaned into the seat, still holding the seat belt away from his chest. "So, what's the one you mentioned like? The one you're thinking of."

Runar smirked, "Well, to be blunt . . . you kind of share a hobby."

They floated through the water, their bodies melding into the cool liquid around it. There were pretty lights blinking all around that were quite nice to look at, but otherwise, this place was pretty boring. Compared to this, even that dirty lake they grew up in was better.

The insects, the fish, the . . . everything. It was beautiful, much better than here. Sure, it had been dangerous, and they got injured and sick a lot, so they had little reason to really complain. But still, something was missing from here. Something that they couldn't quite put their finger on.

Hm? What was a *finger*? It was that thing that those people outside the water had at the ends of those dangly limbs. The people had mentioned that word a few times, and that phrase in particular sounded pretty funny, so it quickly became one of their favorites.

That was the part of their day that they enjoyed the most. Some people or animals would come, and they, as well as their siblings, were brought out for a quick introduction. Once or twice before, one of their siblings chose to form a "bond," but that barely ever happened. They never really liked any of the people, and the animals were too stupid to seem interesting at all. But there was one thing that they started to like! Using the pebbles and plants at the bottom of the tank, they started to try and make more of those people. Those were the most interesting, so they figured if they could be reproduced, they could have fun all the time!

But the ones that they made never really looked right, and their siblings would always come and break them. Their siblings were all bigger, and just because they were the only one that stuck out in the water, they were always being picked on. They really didn't like that at all. They really wanted to go back to the lake.

Oh, the people were opening that small door at the bottom of the tank. That meant they were supposed to come out to meet someone new. It was kind of annoying. They weren't going to like that person anyway.

"Whoa, look at that one!" Silvia gleefully exclaimed, pointing at one of the fish swimming through the reinforced glass tube above the group. It was a species of fish that none of the three had ever seen before, similar to how there were tons of animals and people that they hadn't seen before in the hideout under the café.

This place wasn't specifically a repurposed ruin, though, and was instead a place that seemed to have been constructed for this in the river-lake right next to Lakeview. Plenty of aquatic people lived not only above water, but here in the submerged district of New Riverside. And this place was built in an underwater cave right at the edge of that submerged district where the lake met the central river island that most of New Riverside was built on.

The one that was currently guiding them through this space was a piscette; specifically, a goldfish piscette, whose bright orange scales stuck out very strongly even in here. And even though piscettes were supposed to be somewhat sluggish out of water, this one's steps were so fast that it was kind of annoying to try and keep up with him.

"And here we go!" he exclaimed, as they all finally reached their destination. Though, it really just looked like some kind of empty tank. It connected through a tube to a slightly larger one that actually had some plants, but there still didn't seem to be anything swimming in there.

"Uh . . . so . . . this is where the symbiotes are supposed to be?" Ryan asked, looking at his uncle, who quickly leaned onto the edge of the tank.

"They're not 'supposed to be' here. They are here, look." Runar pointed at the water. Taking a closer look, Ryan narrowed his eyes. And that was when he saw it; there was something wriggling at the surface of the water. He squatted down, trying to look at the water level, and that was where he saw them. Almost perfectly translucent blobs, like a bunch of near-invisible jellyfish.

Modak and Silvia also soon noticed them, and the orc looked up at Runar, almost disappointed. "These are symbiotes? They look kind of . . . disappointing."

The piscette that had been guiding them let out an awkward laugh. "Please do not say things like that right in front of them. They can understand Riverian perfectly fine."

"O-Oh, that . . . I'm sorry . . . I didn't mean it like that! I'm called disappointing a lot too!" Modak tried to make up for accidentally insulting the symbiotes, but it only resulted in a laugh from Ryan.

"Dude, come on. Seriously?"

"I didn't mean to insult them!" Modak whispered nervously, but Runar quickly calmed him down.

"It's fine, they usually don't really care about that kind of thing. They're probably thinking much worse about all of us, anyway," he pointed out, searching through the tank with his gaze. "I can't find the red one. Did something happen to them?"

The piscette glanced around the tank. "No, they should be okay. I just saw them this morning! They're usually one of the first ones out . . . Oh! There they are!"

Just as the piscette said this, Ryan spotted something come out from the tube that connected to the other, larger tank. It seemed to be the symbiote that Runar mentioned; the only red symbiote. While the others were fully translucent, this one had a deep red color that looked like someone had mixed blood and water together. This symbiote looked almost shy, the way they were moving along at the bottom of the tank. Also, though he couldn't see the size of the other symbiotes perfectly, the red one seemed to be a lot smaller than the others too, almost half the size.

"That's weird. I've never seen them act like that . . ." the piscette pointed out, and Ryan carefully glanced over at Runar, who had a massive grin on his face.

Ryan looked into the water. For some reason, he felt like that small blob of red was familiar. Rather, it was like this whole place, tank and all, was familiar. He couldn't quite put his finger on it, though; it was like an extreme sense of déjà vu.

Nervous, Ryan did as his uncle had said earlier. He placed his hand into the water. It was a bit weird, though. Since he still couldn't feel anything, the disconnect from seeing the water swallow his hand and not being able to feel it happen was quite jarring. But either way, Ryan just held his hand in the water for a while. The other symbiotes seemed to quickly move out of the way, but the red one was the only one that didn't react too much. Instead, they were moving a bit closer, though very slowly. But it wasn't just the symbiote either. Ryan weirdly hated admitting that his uncle was right, something he might have to try and evaluate sooner or later, but he weirdly did feel a kind of connection with that red symbiote, even if they didn't form a bond yet.

It wasn't the exact same, of course, but it was kind of similar to how when he first met Modak and Silvia. That immediate sensation of closeness that was hard to truly define. Slowly, the symbiote touched Ryan's finger. Even though his body was still supposed to be numbed, Ryan actually felt it.

Carefully, the red symbiote climbed up his finger and onto the back of his hand. That living mass of goo wriggled once out of the water, as if trying to shake the wetness away as a dog would.

Once they calmed down, the symbiote pressed themselves flat onto his skin. They slowly shrank down, being absorbed into Ryan's skin. But they never seemed to fully disappear, as a red swirl was left on the back of Ryan's hand. That swirl continued to move, flowing over Ryan's skin. He could feel the symbiote move up his arm, and soon reached his chest.

Ryan could tell what was about to happen, but he was quickly distracted by the system message that appeared before him.

[You have formed a bond with a -Ruby Symbiote-]

[The Ruby Symbiote is expelling the Corruption from your body]

All at once, a wave of shock flowed through Ryan's body. As if all the pain that he was supposed to feel over the past one and a half hours returned to hit him all at once with some bonus interest. Ryan's eyes rolled into his head as he fell over backward, but he was able to catch himself in the last moment, forcing himself to stay upright. Grinding his teeth, Ryan grabbed his shirt. He wanted to just take it off normally, but he couldn't really control himself well enough for that. So, instead, as his fingers dug into the fabric, Ryan completely tore his shirt off his upper body. As he did, he could see the black mass latched onto his chest pulsating to Ryan's heartbeat.

Bit by bit, with every beat, it seemed to protrude more and more. The tendrils digging into his skin were starting to loosen. There were marks left behind, but Ryan didn't really care too much about that. He just wanted this thing out of there. He tried to grab at the corruption, but Runar held back his nephew's arm.

"No, don't! Just let the symbiote do their thing!" Runar's voice somehow managed to pierce through Ryan's current state of mind, and he slowly nodded. But of course, it was easier said than done. Despite what his uncle was saying, he couldn't help himself but want to tear it away, like some kind of instinct. However, Runar simply grabbed both of Ryan's wrists, holding them in place without struggling whatsoever. It was like Ryan was locked to a brick wall, though it was probably easier to resist that wall compared to Runar at this point.

And then, after what seemed like far too long, the black corrupted mass fell off Ryan's chest. A burning sensation was left behind in its stead, but that paralyzing pain was gone, all at once. The last thing that Ryan could see before everything went dark was that thing crumbling away into dust.

CHAPTER FORTY-FIVE

:D

With his chest aching painfully, Ryan couldn't stop himself from groaning and flinching as he sat up. He was lying in a hospital bed, but from the large aquarium right in front of him, and all those weird fish swimming through it, he figured he was still inside of that hidden base in Lakeview.

Glancing down at himself, Ryan was only wearing his trousers. For a moment, he was confused, but then he remembered what happened before he fell unconscious. He had completely ripped apart his shirt by himself. At least it was already pretty old, so he didn't care too much.

However, as he looked down, there were two things that caught his eye more than the fact he was shirtless. First, there was the large, ugly scar covering his chest. As Ryan touched it, it still felt sore, so it would probably fade a lot, but he doubted it would go away completely. One more scar wouldn't really make a difference at this point anyway.

But then, there was something else that was bordering the scar. The edge of the left side of his chest, as well as his whole left shoulder and arm, was covered in bloodred patterns intricately flowing over his skin. At first glance they looked like a complex sleeve tattoo, but of course that wasn't the case. This was the symbiote that Ryan had bonded with. As if they realized that Ryan was looking at them, the symbiote's patterns reacted to him, slightly shaking. When he looked down at the back of his hand, a small, familiar symbol appeared.

:D Ryan scoffed in surprise, unable to stop himself from laughing, "Really? That's what you're going with?"

Quickly, the symbol was replaced: :)

"You can't write other things? Do you have a name?"

:(

"I'm guessing that's a 'no.' Do you want me to help you come up with one?"

Immediately, two symbols started rapidly replacing each other on the back of Ryan's hand. *:D ! :D ! :D ! :D !*

With a laugh, Ryan threw his legs over the edge of the bed. "And I'm guessing that's a 'yes.'"

As he said so, Ryan carefully stood up, when the door opened up and Silvia's voice was quickly heard. "Hm, no, that one tastes kind of gross."

"Really? I kind of like it," Modak replied, clearly chewing on something. He looked into the room, seeing that Ryan was up. "Oh, perfect! Ryan, have you tried those orange-flavored droplet candies?"

"I think so? Are those the sour ones?"

"Mhm, exactly," Silvia replied as she threw one over to him. Ryan quickly caught the small package and groaned.

"Ew, individually wrapped candy . . ."

"That's what I said!" Modak threw up his hands. "But it's vending-machine stuff, so you can't really be picky, I guess."

As Ryan fiddled with the edge of the small candy wrapper, Runar stood in the doorway, staring at the three in disbelief. "Are you . . . are you seriously talking about candy when Ryan *just* woke up?"

The three looked at each other for a moment, and then turned back to Runar, as Silvia spoke for them all. "Honestly? Getting worked up about stuff is starting to be kind of exhausting."

"Yeah, plus you *did* warn us beforehand that this might happen," Modak added, and Runar shook his head in disbelief.

"Kids these days," Runar sighed as he walked up to Ryan. "Come on, let me take a look."

Ryan quickly turned his shoulder toward his uncle, holding his arm forward. "They're a 'ruby symbiote,' by the way. According to the system, at least."

"Ah, alright, I figured they were a subspecies. But ruby symbiote, huh? Haven't heard that one before." Runar curiously looked at Ryan's arm as Modak and Silvia also took a closer look.

"Is there a difference?" Silvia wondered, and Runar seemed hesitant to answer with certainty.

"Well . . . yes? There's pretty strong individual differences between symbiotes anyway. You know, every person is different, and every symbiote is different as well, so their specific bond will be very different. Like in any other type of relationship. Just because they're a subspecies doesn't mean they have any special qualities, but it also doesn't mean they *don't*. It's kind of a case-by-case thing, so we'll just have to wait and see what happens."

Runar's eyes slowly wandered down to the back of Ryan's hand, where the ruby symbiote's smile was being proudly displayed: *:D*

"That is . . . interesting. I'm not sure if that counts as a 'special quality,' but I don't remember emoticons being usual patterns."

? :(?, The three symbols flashed on Ryan's hand, and Runar's eyes widened.

"And that is *definitely* not usual. Can you say anything else?"

:(

Quickly, Ryan translated, "That one means 'no.'"

"Thanks. Couldn't have figured that one out withoutcha." Runar rolled his eyes, before looking away from Ryan's arm and to his chest instead. "That one looks pretty nasty . . . are you okay with that?"

Ryan shrugged, though that motion itself kind of hurt. "I mean, I can't really change it anymore, now can I?"

"I mean, we could hire a really good healer to prevent as much of a scar as possible," Runar suggested.

Ryan thought about it for a moment, but in the end just shook his head. "It's fine. To be honest, I'm just glad I'm rid of that thing. It's fully gone, right? I don't have any of it on me anymore?"

"No, no, you're fine. I triple-checked," Runar assured him, and then quickly handed Ryan what he had been holding this whole time. "Here, a new shirt."

"Oh, thanks. Getting kinda breezy," Ryan awkwardly pointed out as he unfolded it. He quickly pulled it over his head, and only then noticed that it had something written on the front. The shirt showed a small translucent blob, with text underneath that read: I BONDED WITH A SYMBIOTE AND ALL I GOT WAS THIS T-SHIRT.

"I . . . can I . . . can I wear this outside? Why do these exist?"

Rubbing the bridge of his nose, Runar shook his head. "Don't ask me, Ryan, I have no idea. I think it was some inside joke between the people that work here, and someone had a couple of them made at some point. But . . . yeah, honestly, who cares? Most people don't know about symbiotes anyway, so it doesn't matter."

"I guess so . . ." Ryan still wasn't convinced, but he figured it was better than running around shirtless. He looked at the back of his hand. "What do you think?"

!!! :D ! :D !!

"You like it, huh? Fair enough," Ryan responded with a chuckle. "So . . . can we leave now? I am so exhausted."

"Yeah, sure, let's go. It is getting a little late," Runar agreed. "Yamada is waiting by the car. We'll drop you two off at your places on the way back, but let's grab something to eat first."

"Oh thank the gods, I could really eat something right now . . ." Modak grumbled. "Something more than candy, I mean."

"Perfect, then let's go."

Exhausted, Ryan stepped into his room. He dropped forward onto his bed, groaning loudly because he forgot that his chest was still in immense pain. "Ouch . . ."

He pulled his face away from the pillow, glancing at his hand.

:(

"Don't worry, I'll be fine. I don't think I thanked you for getting that thing out of me yet, by the way. So . . . thank you."

:D

"Though . . . I guess I should properly introduce you to someone. Uh . . . can you see just through my palm? Or can you see what I can see?"

:(! :(

"So . . . no to both?"

:)

Ryan thought about it for a moment, trying to figure out what seemed to make the most sense. Thinking back, to begin with, the symbiotes didn't have any eyes or any other sensory organs. So maybe they just sensed things differently in the first place. "Do you just sort of see everything around you? Even if I don't?"

:D

"That makes things easier," Ryan yawned, though he realized something else very quickly. "Oh, but you're probably also going to be sleeping while I am, right?"

The symbiote quickly changed the pattern on the back of Ryan's hand. :)

With a tired sigh, Ryan propped himself up, using the pillows to support his back. Maximus was already good to go, so the spirit simply appeared on the blanket in front of Ryan, who quickly faced the back of his hand toward the small knight.

"Maximus, this is . . . my bonded symbiote, and for-now-nameless-symbiote, this is Maximus. He's a spirit, and you two will be seeing each other a lot."

Maximus bowed forward to greet the symbiote, and Ryan noticed the sensation of their pattern changing very rapidly on the back of his hand. It was like a slight tickle. Taking a closer look, he soon saw a flurry of symbols that showed clear excitement.

:D ! :) C: !!! :D :O ! :D

"You okay?" Ryan asked with a slight smile, and the symbiote seemed to hesitate for a moment, as their last symbol very slowly and deliberately turned into a new one that Ryan hadn't seen from them yet.

->

Ryan raised his brow, slowly moving his hand around. The arrow shifted, always pointing in a specific direction; the shelf on the other side of the room. Slowly, Ryan stood up and walked over toward it, picking Maximus up as he did.

"Are you interested in the models?" Ryan asked, smiling lightly. "Runar told me you'd try and make small models of the people and animals you meet from what you found in the tank, right?"

:D :O !!! :D

"I can show them to you tomorrow, if you want. Today I'm a bit tired, alright?"

:D !

With a yawn, Ryan walked back over to his bed, glancing at his desk as he did so. "Oh, and Maximus. Do you want to go back to the domain, or stay up and read? I can turn the computer on for you, if you'd like."

Maximus looked up at Ryan, thinking about it for a moment. From Ryan's perspective, Maximus's mood had improved vastly once he realized that they now basically had an arrow pointing right at Gaia's last fragment. Plus, he could enter and exit his domain whenever he wanted, whether or not Ryan was awake, so he could rest and let the spirit do his own thing.

Carefully, Maximus pointed at the computer monitor, and Ryan quickly nodded. He turned on his computer, propping up the books for the spirit the way he liked it. When the computer turned on, he navigated to the site that Maximus was reading comics on last time, and quickly left the spirit to do his own thing. "Don't stay up too late. I know you don't really need sleep, but reading all night can still be pretty exhausting."

Ryan quickly turned off the lights, letting the room be illuminated only by the monitor, though it didn't matter much for Ryan. He was too tired to care, anyway.

"Goodnight, you two," Ryan said quietly, then he slowly dozed off into sleep.

Modak turned the key around in the lock, pushing the door open in front of him. As he stepped inside, the smell of cigarette smoke practically assaulted him. "Urgh, Dad, come on . . . Why are you smoking inside?"

After he stepped into the adjacent living room, Modak's father let out a slight grumble. "Pah! I can smoke whenever I want!"

The young orc sighed, walking across the room to open the window. "I didn't say you can't, but I thought Mom told you not to smoke inside."

"Your mother's not here, so who cares?"

Modak raised his brow, confused. "What do you mean, she's not here?"

With the cigarette in his mouth, the ash dropping onto his dirty shirt and getting caught in his beard, Modak's father continued grumbling, "With that friend of hers . . . Mala was her name, was it?"

"I think so," Modak replied, walking over to the kitchen. He pulled open the fridge and freezer, and let out a quiet sigh of relief. There wasn't any prepped food, so that meant his mom would be coming home tonight. But at the same time, that meant Modak would have to get his dad to stop smoking, or else this would start a fight when his mom got home.

Though, frankly, it wasn't particularly hard. Modak walked up to his father, standing between him and the TV. "Dad?"

". . . What?"

Without saying another word, Modak simply stared at his father for a few moments. Growing nervous, Brog groaned and reached over, pressing the half-smoked cigarette into the ashtray. "Happy?"

"Yup," Modak replied, grabbing the ashtray to empty it out in the trash.

Looking at his son's back, Brog seemed to get curious. "So, what did you do today? Ya had work?"

Modak quickly shook his head. "No, I was at Ryan's place."

"Hm . . . are you sure you're not—"

"Yes, Dad, I am positive that Ryan and I are not dating."

"I wouldn't mind if you were, you know?" Brog pointed out, staring at his son. With a slight laugh, Modak shook his head.

"Again, we're not. I *am* kind of talking to someone, though. I might bring her over sometime."

"Is it that Silvia?"

"No, it's not Silvia either, Dad. Her name is Yanna, and she's very, very nice."

Brog turned back to the television. "Can't blame me for thinkin' you've got somethin' going on with one of those two. You spend all your time with them!"

Though the young orc wanted to deny that, Modak quickly stopped himself. That part was true; the three did spend a ton of time together. But even so, "I promise you, I am not dating either Ryan or Silvia. Technically I'm also not dating Yanna yet, but . . . we're getting somewhere, I guess."

"Good! I wanna meet my grandkids someday! The gods know your older brother ain't givin' us any!" Brog laughed loudly, and Modak's smile quickly dropped.

"Sister, Dad. Older sister. Not brother," he explained, once again, and Brog nervously sat up straight.

"Oh, I'm . . . I'm sorry, son . . . I try, you know?"

Modak sighed lightly, trying to force his smile back up, "I know. Just . . . keep trying, alright? Anyway, I'm pretty tired, so I'll head to bed now. Goodnight, Dad. And please, don't start smoking again. And close the window before you go to bed."

"Yes, yes, I'm not a child!" Brog laughed, and Modak smiled as he made his way into the hallway.

"Night, Dad."

"Good night, son!"

A bit annoyed at his father for taking everything as lightly as he *always* did, Modak shut his bedroom door behind him. And he really did not want to see his father's face when he realized that Yanna was a minotaur, so even if they wanted to, the two would never be able to have kids together. Not that it mattered to

Modak much anyway, but his father always kept going on and on about grand-kids for some reason.

Modak let out a long groan as he dropped his bag on the ground, then quickly got undressed. He already lay down in bed, when he realized he hadn't brushed his teeth yet. After contemplating whether it was worth it to get up again now that he was already in bed, Modak groaned and forced himself up. He wouldn't be able to fall asleep otherwise anyway.

CHAPTER FORTY-SIX

Hot

The early morning's sunlight shone through the cracks in the window blinds, while the rhythmic beeps of the phone's alarm went off over and over again. Trying to force his eyes open, Ryan patted the bed where his phone usually was. Annoyed to find that it wasn't where he usually put it, he let out a loud groan and sat up.

Ryan eventually found his phone under his pillow, but not without spotting Maximus, still seated in front of the computer. With a raised brow, trying to keep his tired eyes open, Ryan looked at the time. 9:01 a.m.

"Did you pull an all-nighter?" With a slight groan, Ryan pulled his legs over the edge of the bed. His whole body was aching all over, as if he had worked out every single muscle yesterday. The knight turned around, confused, and quickly glanced at the time in the bottom right of the monitor.

As if in a panic, Maximus waved his arms around, but Ryan just waved him off with a long yawn. "You're good, man. It happens. As long as you're alright, it doesn't really matter."

A bit awkwardly, as if he were standing on new legs, Ryan got up from his bed. The moment he did, his stomach growled, so loud that it could probably be heard from the hallway. Ryan had never been more hungry than he was now. And though he didn't know for sure, he had a pretty good guess as to why.

On the back of his hand, he could see a spiral slowly shaking on his skin. The spiral extended outward onto his arm, branching out into more complex patterns, though compared to last night, they were definitely a lot simpler.

It seemed like the symbiote that Ryan had formed a bond with last night was still asleep, so he figured he shouldn't wake them up. But right when he thought so, the spiral started furling away and opening a ring on the back of his hand, before three simple symbols appeared.

Zzz The symbols were still waving around, not being as bold and clear as the ones from yesterday.

Ryan scoffed lightly, "So, you can use letters for this, but not to write?"

The symbiote's symbols slowly became more solid as they woke up. *:,c*

"Don't worry, maybe you can learn how to someday. Though this works right now too, right? I can understand you, at least."

:D

Ryan smiled lightly and looked down at his chest. The large scar from yesterday was still very blatant, though it was a bit less red. Though maybe that was also because now, he had the symbiote's large red pattern encroaching on the left side of his chest. The way that the pattern was wriggling was slightly unnerving, like it was alive, but it wasn't an uncomfortable thing. Ryan just wasn't used to it yet.

But thinking about it, it was a kind of weird feeling. He had the corruption stuck to him, something that infested his body, threatening to take over. And the way that he solved that was by letting something else directly infest and spread through his body. Logically, it was swapping one bad thing for something slightly less bad, but when Ryan actually looked down at the symbiote, it just *felt right*.

This was probably exactly what Runar was talking about yesterday; the "bond" was a special thing, something that extended beyond just the physical. Even before the two connected directly, after Ryan saw the symbiote, he felt like something he just had to do. And now that they bonded, it felt like something he didn't even know was missing had come back to him. It was a weird realization, but this whole thing was surprisingly easy to get used to.

Though, that only was the case on an emotional level; his body was killing him. He was insanely sweaty after waking up and was feeling ridiculously hot; he was so hungry he could eat a dragon; and his whole body hurt with every step he took. Not to mention, he was so, so thirsty all of a sudden.

"Maximus, just feel free to keep reading. I'll be in the kitchen," he said, not even waiting for a reaction before rushing out of the door. Practically running, Ryan made his way into the kitchen. He grabbed a glass from the cupboard and filled it up with water, then poured it down his throat. After doing this a couple of times, Ryan pulled open the fridge. All those leftovers from Runar were still in there, and Ryan quickly grabbed one of the boxes.

After smelling it to see if it was still good, Ryan grabbed a fork and started shoveling the fried noodles into his mouth. He didn't even notice that Runar was standing in the doorway. "Hey, I was actually going to eat that."

Ryan looked past the edges of the box, locking eyes with his uncle. With a full mouth, he tried to get out the right words to point out that there was no way he was going to eat this, as he never did, but it was just inaudible blabbering.

"Finish chewing first," Runar sighed as he walked farther into the kitchen, putting the paper bag he was carrying onto the table. Ryan curiously watched as

Runar pulled out the items inside; protein bars, packaged meat, blocks of cheese, and tons of dry pasta.

After swallowing the food in his mouth, Ryan looked back at his uncle. "What's all that?"

"Some stuff for you to eat," Runar replied. "It usually takes about a week for the symbiote to properly settle in a body. In that time, your body will use up tons of calories, you will be experiencing the worst muscle pains ever, and you might end up severely dehydrated if you're not careful. I also bought these hydration powder things, so keep them with you when you go out."

Ryan continued eating, looking at his uncle with a slight stare. "Don't you think a warning would have been kind of nice?"

"Don't you think wearing a shirt and trousers would have been nice?"

". . . Stop fashion policing me."

Runar sighed lightly, "I figured it was better to not stress you out with even more stuff. Not like this is going to be particularly bad anyway. The muscle pain is the worst part, but you would've had to deal with that on your way to opening your strength stat anyway."

"Right." Ryan raised his brow, remembering something that Runar had said to him last night. "You mentioned that symbiotes improve strength, right? Does that translate into stats somehow? Like a specific point increase?"

"No, no, it's not like that." Runar quickly shook his head. "Symbiotes will basically adjust the hormones and proteins in your body to the perfect degrees that are needed for muscle growth and recovery. They don't directly increase your strength, but they make it easier for you to gain muscle. Basically . . . your physical stats are getting a growth boost from now on. And a pretty big one too."

"Hm . . . are you bonded with a symbiote too?"

Runar scoffed, "Nah, I wish. When I was younger, I'd try to meet every new symbiote that came in because I wanted to quickly get stronger, but it wasn't really meant to be. And at this point, I'm strong enough to not have to worry about that."

With narrowed eyes, Ryan chose to ask something that he had been curious about, though he didn't get an answer last time. "How high are your stats anyway? And which ones do you have?"

"I already said so, but I'm not telling you that."

"Oh come on, why not? I can tell you my stats," Ryan offered, but Runar just scoffed and shook his head.

"Yeah, sorry, but we're in very different situations here. There's a reason why I can't tell you. Just trust me."

"Can you at least tell me why you can't tell me?"

"Obviously not." Runar started putting away the things that he bought for Ryan. "More importantly, when you feel hungry, just don't hesitate and eat whatever you want. I have no idea if ruby symbiotes act differently, so just listen to your body and your cravings."

Ryan nodded as he finished the box of leftovers, then quickly threw the box into the bin, when a certain young vampire stepped into the kitchen. With a narrowed gaze, Liam let out a disappointed sigh. "Cover yourself, harlot!"

"Oh, calm down," Ryan scoffed, "I'm far too hot for that."

"Humble yourself." Liam shook his head, and Ryan stared back at him.

"I meant that I am physically really warm. It's like I'm in an oven or something." With a loud groan, Ryan walked out of the kitchen. "If it'll be like this for a week, then we're picking up buckets' worth of ice cream later. I'm going to take a shower now."

"Don't take too long, we're heading out to try and find the fragment in an hour," Runar yelled after him, and Ryan quickly turned around and peeked into the kitchen.

"In an hour?"

"Yeah, does that not work?"

Ryan immediately shook his head. "No, no, it works! It totally works! We can go sooner, even, I—"

"Ryan, calm down. Take a shower, get dressed, and then we can head out. Alright?"

". . . Alright. Thanks."

Without further ado, Ryan made his way to the bathroom. He stripped out of his underwear and jumped into the shower without hesitation. The cold water just felt heavenly. With a long sigh, watching the water flow down his body, Ryan noticed something that he hadn't up until just now. He had been way too busy stuffing his face. But he could swear that he got leaner, as if the symbiote had sucked up all the fat on Ryan's body. No wonder he was so hungry; all his reserves had been used up.

Sure, he looked good like this, but he didn't necessarily care all too much for it. Plus, he only ever heard about how miserable looking like this actually was; you were always hungry and cold, and that wasn't something that Ryan wanted to deal with. He hoped that after this week, his body would return to some sort of normal.

For a while longer, Ryan just stood there, watching the cold water flow down his arms and chest. Cold showers were usually his worst enemy, but right now, it was truly the best thing he could have ever asked for. But after a while, Ryan knew he had to get out. After scrubbing himself down, Ryan hesitantly turned off the water, stepping back out of the shower. He stepped up to the mirror and looked at himself properly. He definitely got leaner. And right as he looked at himself in the mirror, his stomach started to grumble again.

"Oh, come on . . ." he groaned, looking at the back of his hand. "You hungry little bastard . . ."

;P, the symbiote replied, as Ryan quickly started drying himself. With a towel wrapped around his lower body, Ryan quickly stepped out of the bathroom, then stopped by the kitchen one more time before heading to his room.

He tore open one of the large packages of protein bars, quickly grabbing a handful. While tearing away at the plastic wrappers with his teeth, he locked eyes with Liam, who was sitting at the table, drinking what looked to be a chilled bottle of that artificial blood.

"What?" Ryan asked as he shoved the protein bar into his mouth, and Liam shrugged.

"Is everyone here in the city like you?"

A bit confused about what Liam meant, Ryan raised his brow. "I'm not from here, so I'd say not really. But it depends on what you're talking about. There's definitely not as many humans as you might be used to."

Liam quickly shook his head. "No, but . . . you don't even care that I'm a vampire."

"Should I? I'm not going to treat you like the king you want to be, if that's what you're saying."

"First and foremost, I'm just behaving like the king I'm *meant* to be. But . . . others are scared of me a lot. It's annoying," Liam pointed out, looking at the bottle in his hand awkwardly. Seeing his expression, Ryan could tell exactly how Liam was feeling.

Ryan swallowed the bite of the protein bar in his mouth and then smiled at the young vampire. "I don't think you need to worry about it that much here in this city. There's so, so many different people here, I don't think vampires will really stick out too much," he suggested. Of course, Ryan knew that it wasn't really as easy as that, but he didn't want Liam to be too scared to go to his first day of school tomorrow. Plus, it was never bad to be a bit optimistic.

"Do you really think so?"

"I do. You'll be fine, alright?" Ryan said, walking past the table. He ruffled up Liam's hair, and the boy looked up, swatting away Ryan's hand with an annoyed glare.

"What are you—"

"That's more like it. Don't let anyone push you around tomorrow and act like you always do. Alright?"

". . . Hmph . . ." Liam tightened his grip on the bottle in his hand, quickly taking another sip. "You're right! It's not befitting of a leader to act like a kicked dog!"

Ryan smiled lightly as he left the kitchen, stuffing more of the protein bar into his mouth. He made his way into his bedroom and pushed the door shut. Holding one of the bars in his mouth, Ryan dropped the rest onto his desk and walked over to his wardrobe. For a moment, he hesitated, thinking back on Kindly yesterday. But since that was ridiculous, he just pulled it open and quickly picked out an outfit.

Any of them looked way too warm for him right now . . . he definitely couldn't walk around how he usually did. But almost all of his clothes were thick and heavy, and none of his trousers were shorter than his shins.

That was, except for a single outfit. It was perfectly tucked in the back, and could probably use a wash just for having been in there for so long, but he had to make do. Silvia had gifted these to him for his birthday a couple of months ago, and she made them herself. If they let her, half of Ryan's and Modak's wardrobes would be filled with clothes she made for them at this point. But he couldn't turn down a birthday present.

Ryan looked at a pair of running shorts and a sleeveless top. She had seen Ryan work out and almost overheat with his sweatshirt jacket and long joggers on a particularly warm spring day. Ryan hadn't worn them yet, beyond trying them on in his room after he got home that day.

With a sigh, Ryan dropped the towel and got dressed. It wasn't like he would really meet anyone he knew today anyway, and he would probably die if he wore what he usually did.

He awkwardly looked at himself in his mirror and let out a slight sigh. The scars on his shoulders and legs were perfectly on display. He hated it. Though, at the very least, he could show off the symbiote a bit. When they stayed still like this, they really just looked like a red-ink tattoo.

"Maximus," Ryan said, slowly looking away from the mirror toward the small knight seated in front of the computer monitor, "let's go, we're heading out to find Gaia."

CHAPTER FORTY-SEVEN

Yamada Hiero

From the middle of the back seat, Ryan pointed to the right in front of his face. Yamada quickly turned at the next intersection.

"We're getting closer . . ." Ryan explained, and Runar quickly turned to him from the passenger seat.

"Start pointing exactly where it's pulling you to."

Ryan quickly nodded, closing his eyes. He focused on that force inside his mind, the Light of Guidance, pointing into the direction that it showed him. Slowly but surely, the direction was changing, and Runar carefully looked down at the old map in his hands.

". . . Alright, I think I know where we need to go," Runar muttered, pushing himself forward to let Yamada see him properly. "Take a right, a left, take the left of the fork after that, and then follow the road until the underpass."

The demon quickly nodded her head, speeding up a bit now that she didn't need to focus on Ryan's instructions directly. She drove quickly and without hesitation, weaving through the cars and pushing through the traffic lights at the last second. Usually you would call this sort of driving "erratic," but the control that Yamada had over the car was ridiculous. Ryan thought you could only see this kind of thing in movies.

"She drives the carriage rather skillfully," Liam pointed out from right next to Ryan, squeezed into the seat behind Yamada's. Ryan turned to him with a frown.

"Did you just call this a carriage? I get the whole king thing, but at least call a car a car."

". . . Carriage sounds cooler," the young vampire complained, looking out the window with a clearly bored gaze.

Not only that, but as Yamada drove farther down the route that Runar had described, the faster the direction the Light of Guidance pointed to changed.

They were getting close; really, really close. It didn't take long until they reached the underpass that Runar had pointed out, and Yamada came to a stop here.

"Is this it?" Runar asked, and Ryan slowly nodded his head. The "needle" of the light was pointing right at the building that was hidden under the underpass. Ryan didn't expect to see this kind of place anywhere in the Channel. It was old and run-down; the windows were barred up like it was abandoned.

"I . . . guess so?" Hesitantly, Ryan looked at the building. At this point, just moving his head around was noticeably changing the direction he was pointed to. His eyes moved around slightly, pulling Ryan's sight right into the windows on the third floor of the building. "It's up there, I think?"

"Alright. Yamada, drive us to a safe spot nearby," Runar signed, and just then, Ryan's stomach started rumbling loudly. ". . . Somewhere with a restaurant, please."

Ryan looked around outside. This area was quite familiar; it was pretty close to the Awakened Center. "I actually know a place nearby that's pretty good . . . this noodle spot, the owner is an awakened Chef. It's in the upper area here; if we get up there, I can find it again."

"Oh? That does sound pretty good. Drop us off around the corner, I remember there being a stairway up," Runar explained, and Yamada drove off with a quick nod. And just as Runar said, there seemed to be one of those massive escalators running up to the upper level of the Channel. Ryan, his uncle, and Liam quickly got out of the car, and Runar leaned into the window, quickly signing something to the demon. There were people around, so he didn't say it out loud, though.

Yamada nodded and quickly drove off again.

"Is she finding a parking spot?" Ryan asked, but Runar quickly shook his head.

"No, she's accompanying the people for the thing," Runar explained, trying to be vague, and Ryan looked at him with a slight frown.

"Seriously? But . . ."

"What, you think a deaf girl can't carry her own weight? She's strong enough to be my aide, Yamada can handle herself." Runar quickly stepped into the building in front of him, followed by an awkward Ryan. He didn't directly mean it that way, but if he was totally honest, it wasn't totally wrong either.

"So . . . you're sure they don't need me to find the fragment?"

Runar quickly shook his head. "They'll be fine. If it's in that building, they will find it. And just because you got through a newborn dungeon doesn't mean you can play in the big leagues just yet, alright?"

". . . Fine. And I guess we can't leave *him* alone," Ryan pointed out, watching as Liam looked around excitedly. Ryan had at least been to larger cities a few times before, but he doubted that was the case for this boy. And even Ryan felt incredibly intimidated, so that feeling must be even greater in Liam. It was the same when they were traveling up the escalators to the upper level; Liam was gleefully looking over the edge of the moving stairway, excited to see what was at the top.

Before long, they did, and Ryan's stomach quickly guided the rest of the way. His hunger quickly made him forget what he was wearing, and that some of his scars were on full display. He just really needed to eat something.

Ryan looked around and tried to find the spot, and then, there it was; the dingy, small, hole-in-the-wall noodle restaurant that didn't seem to fit into this area whatsoever.

". . . This is it?" Liam asked, almost disappointed to see their destination. "It doesn't look like the food will be any good."

"Oh, how would you know?" Ryan scoffed, quickly pushing open the door. Like before, it was fairly empty, and the seats at the counter right in front of the chef were empty. Once the four-armed man saw Ryan, he raised his brows, surprised.

"Spirit kid! Ryan, was it?"

"Yup, that's me! Chantora, right?"

The chef quickly nodded his head with a smile. "What can I do for ya?"

"Alright, take the biggest bowl you can, get me the thickest noodles, a bunch of meat, and the oiliest broth you have," Ryan immediately said, and Chantora laughed.

"Hungry, eh?"

"You can say that again. He eats like a wyrm," Runar pointed out, grinning at Ryan, knowing that he couldn't deny it right now.

Runar waited for Liam to sit down next to Ryan, and then sat down next to Liam, before Chantora raised his brow while glancing toward the man in front of him. "You his pops?"

With a scoff, Runar shook his head. "No, I'm his uncle. I mean, I'm *his*, though," he added, ruffling Liam's hair. The vampire looked up disgruntledly. This was the situation as far as the public was concerned; Liam had been adopted by Runar.

This was done so that he could be the boy's guardian under any circumstance without any sort of outside interference. Of course, in the system, Liam's species was marked as "unknown" for now until vampires were added to the current International Intelligent Species Registry. It was easy enough for the Aglecard family to make that sort of thing happen, apparently. It still seemed insane to Ryan, but that's what it was.

"What do ya two wanna eat?" Chantora asked, and Runar quickly replied.

"Your recommendation for me. But Liam doesn't eat."

The aktorione frowned, "Excuse me?"

Runar's eyes widened as he shook his head quickly. "Oh, no, no, it's not like that. He's a vampire, he doesn't eat."

Ryan immediately froze up, slowly turning his head toward his uncle. Liam seemed similarly confused, and the same could be said ten times over for Chantora. The chef quickly repeated himself, ". . . Excuse me?"

"As I said, he's a vampire. They can't really digest most things," Runar explained, pushing his hand into the bag that he carried with him, pulling out one of the small opaque bottles filled with artificial blood. "I've got something for him here, though, so it's not like he'll go hungry."

"I don't think that's a funny joke . . . vampires ain't jokin' matter, ya know?"

"Well, yeah, of course they're not. But we decided that it's better for Liam not to hide himself anymore. There's this company that we got in contact with; they're working on this artificial blood that vampires can live off."

Chantora looked at Ryan, confused. "Are you . . . is he serious?"

Ryan sighed loudly, nodding his head. He definitely didn't expect Runar to just come out with it like that, but it made sense. This was the whole reason for Liam to even be here in the first place. He would go to school as a vampire. He would make friends as a vampire. Liam would live his life openly. As a vampire. This young kid was the pilot flame for the light that would guide all vampires into the open. It was a lot of pressure to put on a kid, but Ryan knew that the family thought about this well. Or rather, he hoped so. He looked back at Chantora, slowly nodding his head.

"Yeah, he's serious. Liam's a vampire," Ryan confirmed, feeling a bit nervous about just saying it like that. He knew that some of the other customers could hear as well.

". . . Well, lookit that," Chantora let out. It was clearly something hard to believe. Rather, the idea that vampires actually existed was somewhat shady in the first place. You heard about incidents like that every once in a while, where a corpse's blood was drained, so people quickly started talking about that being because of vampires. But you never knew if that was actually a vampire or just some other kind of maniac serial killer.

Ryan actually wasn't sure exactly how Runar was planning on convincing others that Liam was a vampire without a shadow of a doubt. Usually you would expect that to be something a kid Liam's age came up with for fun, especially considering that he already did that whole "king" role-play thing. But he figured there was a plan for that in place already.

All the while this short conversation was going on, even through that almost deafening silence that had spread through the shop, Chantora had never stopped moving his arms to cook. So, soon, both Ryan and Runar had their bowls of noodles in front of them, as Runar gave a bottle of artificial blood to Liam.

"So . . ." Chantora finally said, looking back at Ryan, "did ya end up goin' to that dungeon?"

With a smug grin, Ryan quickly nodded. "Yup, even managed to level up a bit."

"Oh, did ya?" Chantora raised his brow curiously.

"Yup. Though now, I guess I should focus a bit more on training," Ryan pointed out as he held a spoonful of broth to his mouth to give it a try, his empty stomach almost reaching out to pull the whole bowl into him right away. After giving the broth a try, he held himself back for just a moment from fully digging in. "That reminds me . . . a chef's most important stat is dexterity, right?"

"Dexterity 'n' perception." Chantora nodded.

"Do you have any tips on training dexterity more effectively?"

The door's lock was picked carefully. Despite being an outwardly abandoned building, the lock was in far too good a condition; it had recently been replaced. Once the door was opened, the five cloaked figures in front of Yamada got moving. Stepping into the darkness of the space, their bodies basically melted away. Once she couldn't see any part of them anymore, Yamada herself stepped into the building.

She walked down the central hallway of what seemed to be an old block of flats. One after another, the doors beside her opened up, revealing one of the cloaked figures. Each of them was giving Yamada an "okay" sign, so they moved on. She climbed up the stairs to the next floor. Usually, the stairs should continue up more, but they were demolished. Maybe there was another set of stairs on the other end of the hallway. As Yamada walked through the hallway, the hair on the back of her neck stood up.

She stopped walking, pulling back just so slightly as a hail of bullets shot through the old wooden door. She glanced at where exactly the bullets hit the wall on the other side of the door, and then reached into the inner pocket of her jacket. What Yamada pulled out was a black handgun. However, before she even held it out properly, yellow runic patterns appeared on the metal, letting off arching crackles of electricity. Her eyes gave off a similar glow as Yamada aimed the gun at the wall. Or rather, she aimed at what was beyond the wall as a small magic circle appeared in front of the barrel.

And then, she pulled the trigger. As Yamada felt the recoil traveling through her arm, she watched the remnants of her yellow magic on the untouched wall disappear. The next moment, the vibrations of someone falling to the ground told Yamada it was time to get started. She stepped in front of the hole-covered door. Looking through it, she could see three people in Bluesky-brand assault gear, carrying automatic weapons created by the company as well.

One of those three was already on the ground after Yamada's bullet passed clean through their head. Seeing their comrade fall down without them even being able to see the shooter, the other two were taken aback and distracted for long enough to let Yamada shoot their heads as well.

They also immediately fell to the ground, without a single mark being left on their helmets. The five cloaked people immediately appeared, two of them standing by Yamada's side as the other three pulled away the bodies of the gun-men, tying them up and gagging them so they couldn't make any noise when they woke up later. However, these three weren't the only people to be wary of in here. The two cloaked figures by Yamada's side quickly informed her of the sound of people coming down the hallway, so she quickly nodded her head.

She reached into her jacket's other inner pocket, pulling out a practically iden-tical handgun to the one she used just now. Magic circles appeared in front of the guns' barrels, and Yamada pulled the trigger on the left gun first, then pulled the one in her right gun just a second later. The first bullet shot through the air through the now open flat door, seeming to slow to a crawl in the middle of the hallway. The bullet was frozen midair, as if held in place by that yellow mana.

And then, the bullet from the second gun hit it at a slight angle, making it ricochet off the first. And the third, fourth, and fifth bullets did the same, as did all the others that were shot until Yamada was satisfied. She looked at the figure next to her, and they quickly gave her another "okay" sign. With a light smile, Yamada stepped back out into the hallway, catching the stationary bullet as it fell to the ground. Turning to her right, she saw six more gunmen unconscious on the ground. One of them was even carrying a bulletproof riot shield, but that didn't really help against Yamada's bullets.

She carefully stepped over them as the cloaked figures got to work, tying the rest of the gunmen up to make sure they couldn't cause any trouble if they woke up before everything was over. And it was just as Yamada had thought; there was another set of stairs here at the end of the hallway, though it clearly hadn't been here originally. It was just added to make it harder for people to get up the floors.

Now on the second floor above ground level, Yamada looked around. Her intu-ition was telling her that there were more people in each of these old flats. With a smile on her face, Yamada took a few more steps forward. Just because she had work to do didn't mean she couldn't enjoy herself.

CHAPTER FORTY-EIGHT

Berserker

Dozens of bullets shot through the air, and Yamada counted each of them as they rapidly approached her. She pulled the trigger of her gun, slightly flicking her wrist as she did. As the bullet passed through the magic circle in front of the barrel, a dozen more magic circles appeared in the air in front of the gun, each one of them releasing a copy of the bullet flickering with yellow light. The bullets continued to travel through the air at angles, curving as they intercepted the bullets that had been fired at her.

The ricocheted projectiles then intercepted others, which reflected off and did the same with even more. As the enemies' solid bullets were deflected into the walls, some of the bullets made of Yamada's mana were shot at the four men that were trying to shoot at her. Each one of them was hit in the head, and they quickly collapsed. Rolling her eyes, Yamada stepped over the unconscious gunmen that now littered the hallway. One of the cloaked people accompanying her quickly signed to her.

"All the enemies beside those on the third floor have been fully taken out. We have restrained those that have been taken down. As you asked, we have kept our own attacks to nonlethal levels. However, most defensive power seems to be focused on floor three, and I would not underestimate their power," they explained, and Yamada slowly nodded her head, moving her eyes away from the cloaked figure's hands.

She signed at them all to follow her, and then made her way to the stairs at the end of the hall. As soon as she made her way to the top of the stairs, her eyes landed on something. It was a small object; a thick tube with a small trigger at its end. Yamada shut her eyes and pulled her hand in front of them, but the light of the flash-bang reached her before she was able to fully block it. She was stunned for just a moment as she tried to recover her sight, but Yamada's senses were too strong to just push past this.

However, no matter how brief, an opponent that was able to time that flash-bang so perfectly wouldn't hesitate. Yamada felt the air brushing past her arms and face, and the scent of too much aftershave entered her nose. She pulled back and made her knees buckle as the sensation of a blade narrowly evading her nose tickled past her. As her body fell backward, she also jumped up and pressed her hands onto the ground while wrapping her legs around the arm of the person that had attacked her.

It was almost too thick for her to properly wrap around fully, so she just tried to hold on as well as she could. Yamada tried to peek at the attacker, but was only able to see a blurry outline. It was enough to tell her that she was dealing with a giant; a massive individual standing at four meters in height. She had barely reached past their elbow, and probably seemed more pesky than anything.

The giant was about to try and attack Yamada as she latched onto their arm, so she quickly pressed the barrels of her guns against their elbow, pulling the trigger without hesitation. Different from the pacifying bullets that she shot at the gunmen from downstairs at, these were the opposite. They were bullets made to cause pain. And as this pain coursed through the giant's body, stunning them momentarily, Yamada was able to pull herself up and climb onto their shoulders.

With quick, fluid movements, she sat on the giant's shoulders and tightened her legs around their neck, placing the barrels of her gun against the sides of their head. After the pacifying bullets passed through their head, Yamada could feel them buckle and fall to the ground. As they did, she held up their body a bit to hide behind it as she recovered her sight. There were probably others here, and she couldn't risk being shot at while not being able to see.

However, Yamada could soon feel the scent of smoke brush past her; the cloaked figures were moving past her and taking care of what they could while Yamada was unable to do so. Just as they had cleared out most of the flats as well as the floors above this one, they should be able to deal with most, if not all remaining, opponents.

Slowly but surely, Yamada's sight properly returned to her, and she managed to get a proper look at the man in front of her. He was different to the other grunts that she had faced before. For one, he wasn't wearing the assault gear. Instead, he was wearing a well-fitted, tailored suit. He clearly stood above the others.

Yamada got up from behind the unconscious man, looking down the hallway to get a grasp of the situation. This space was a bit different from the other floors; it was a large open room for the most part, as all the flats had clearly been torn out. Besides the pillars keeping the building up, there was only a single room here, in the dead center of the space, while numerous grunts were spread out through the space surrounding that walled-off room.

Four of the five cloaked figures were keeping those grunts busy, quickly taking them down one after another, while another was standing by next to Yamada to keep watch while they recovered. However, seeing that she was fine, the last of the figures quickly got moving as well, joining the fray.

Now that she was fine, and all of those grunts were distracted, this was a pretty good moment for Yamada. She looked around the room, marking each of the individuals that she would need to hit, holding her handguns forward. As the demon held her breath to steady her aim, she started rapidly pulling the triggers of her guns, skillfully shooting through the heads of all the grunts that she had noticed from here. And without exception, no matter how heavily armored, and no matter how actively dangerous, they all fell to the ground unconscious. The cloaked figures quickly started tying them up, and Yamada stood up satisfied.

She swiftly made her way to the door of that single room on this floor. Though it was unclear exactly what kind, there seemed to be a barrier placed onto the entrance, so they wouldn't be able to just force their way in all that easily. But that wasn't really an issue; Yamada knew the weakness of those sorts of barriers.

She walked a few steps to the side, aiming straight at the wall. The magic circle in front of her gun's barrel increased in size, and as the gunwoman pulled the trigger and the bullet passed through the magic circle, an explosion shot forward that ripped apart the wall itself.

The weakness of those barriers was simple; they usually only protected the door. The walls were neglected.

With a smile on her face, Yamada stepped through the newly created entrance. Without even looking at them, she shot through the heads of the two guards stationed inside the room itself, and then quickly walked up to the person on the other side of the room. It was an older woman, using some kind of enchanting skill on a green, uneven gemstone. From the description Yamada was given, this was the last of Gaia's fragments.

Not hesitating, Yamada reached out to grab the fragment, but the woman in front of her anxiously pressed her hands onto it. It looked like she was saying something, but she had a fabric mask covering her mouth and nose, so Yamada wasn't able to lip-read. So, instead of resorting to some kind of charades, Yamada held her gun into the face of the woman, hoping that this would be enough to convince her to pull her hands away.

But . . . to Yamada's surprise, that wasn't the case at all. With pure panic in her eyes, the woman kept the fragment covered. She was scared; absolutely terrified. But not of Yamada. She was scared of what would happen if the fragment was taken from her. And while Yamada was empathetic of that, she was here for a simple reason; to recover the fragment.

And so, with a simple pull of the trigger, the older woman was painlessly pacified. Yamada even caught her before she hit the ground, so that she wouldn't injure herself because of the fall, carefully placing her down in a safe position.

Yamada grabbed the fragment; someone had drawn enchantments onto its surface, seemingly trying to harvest the energy properly. With a slight frown, Yamada looked at the nearest of the five that accompanied her here, quickly signing over to them.

"*Take a scan of the whole—*" Before she was able to finish, Yamada's intuition told her to get back, but before she was able to physically react, something came flying through the hole that she created in the wall. It was one of the cloaked figures, unconscious and almost disfigured. Their arms were twisted around, and their bones were broken; blood was gushing out from under the black mask they were wearing. Yamada stared out from beyond the hole, watching as the giant from earlier stepped through. An ugly energy was enveloping him, and the veins on his neck, face, and hands were bulging as though they were about to pop.

The expression on his face was telling Yamada one thing; this guy had a berserker-type class, and was in the middle of a "rage." Whether it was automatically triggered by being thrown unconscious, or whether it was activated manually after he woke up earlier than expected, didn't really matter. Fact was that he was dangerous, and clearly too much for the cloaked figures to handle. They were skilled, but they were better at infiltration than direct combat. That's what Yamada was here for.

The giant was yelling something, but the way he spoke and the way his jaw was clenched made it impossible for Yamada to read his lips. Nor did she really think he had anything productive to say in the first place.

As the giant came running at Yamada, she jumped up into the air, very easily dodging over the massive figure. Her feet pressed onto the ceiling, and she kicked herself down. On her way back to the ground, Yamada caught the back of the giant's collar, using her momentum and sheer physical strength to drag him backward. If he had continued that way, he would have crushed that enchanter lady.

This wasn't enough to topple the giant over, of course, but it was enough to stop him in his tracks and ensure that he would follow her back out of the room where collateral damage was more . . . acceptable. There were still a lot of things in that room that they needed to take a look at to figure out what the actual plan was here.

Clutching the fragment tightly in her hand, Yamada aimed the handgun at the giant berserker.

Chantora looked at the young man in front of him, raising his brow. "So you want to increase your dexterity? Ain'tcha a summoner?"

"Yeah, but one of my base stats is dexterity because of how some of my skills work. I've been able to increase my dexterity by 0.03 already, but I was wondering if you had any tips," Ryan explained, and the chef looked at him surprised.

"0.03 in yer first couple weeks? That ain't bad at all, why'd you need my help?"

"Because 0.03 isn't good enough." The reply was blunt, but it was the truth. Apparently, with the symbiote's help, Ryan's physical stats would increase at a faster rate anyway, but he still had to do whatever he could to improve faster. If there were guys running around that were actively in the process of exploiting spirits and making people hate and fear them, then that wasn't something Ryan would let happen.

But no matter what was going on, Runar probably wouldn't let him take on an important role in all this unless he could pull his own weight, just like today. Ryan wanted to be there to rescue Gaia's last fragment, but all he could do was sit here and wait while stuffing his mouth with noodle soup.

"What're you in such a hurry for? Just take it easy. I didn't do much to help increase my dexterity, just everyday cookin' work. I was a chef at a large restaurant when I awakened, and just by doing what I did every day, my dexterity started ta go up," Chantora explained simply. That was how most expertise classes treated things like stat increases. For the most part, they already spent most of their day doing whatever they awakened for, so they didn't really have a lot of time to spend specifically on training. They would just start operating at a higher level while working the same amount of hours. They just got more done at a higher quality.

As he was thinking about how to respond, Ryan noticed his uncle's gaze. His expression was stinging painfully, and a nervous lump formed in Ryan's throat. Trying to clear it out, Ryan took the bowl, which only had broth left in it now, and held it to his lips, quickly drinking the rest of the soup left inside.

Ryan pulled the large bowl away from his mouth, letting out a loud, satisfied breath. As he wiped his mouth with the napkin next to him, he looked at the chef. "I just need to increase my dexterity somehow. My hobby is model building, and I can't afford to keep buying dozens of new ones, no matter how much I want to."

Hesitantly, Chantora cupped his chin with one of his hands. "My dexterity always improved the most when I've had the chance to do somethin' new."

"Something new, huh . . . ?" Ryan muttered, before an idea popped into his mind. "Do you need a part-timer here?"

Chantora scoffed, shaking his head immediately. "No, thanks. Nothin' against you, but I do very well on my own," he replied, and Ryan let out a slight sigh, before the aktorione suggested something else, "But what I *could* do is give ya some recipes to try out. Might not hurt anyway if yer as big an eater as ya seem to be."

". . . I guess that would probably work. What do you think?" Ryan asked, looking over at his uncle.

Runar thought about it for a second. "It's not a bad idea, at least. There's plenty of stuff you can do to increase your dexterity. Cooking should be a pretty good one for you right now."

While Runar was saying so, Chantora was sorting through a few things under the counter, looking for something. He quickly made his way to the small room in the back, and a moment later came back out holding a small booklet, holding it over to Ryan with a smile. "Here ya go, I've got some of my favorites in here. Some should be above your skill level, but just do what ya think you might be able to. See it as a thanks for that big tip last time."

"Are you sure? Don't you need that?" Runar asked, a bit concerned about Ryan taking away something that sounded as precious as a recipe book written by this man himself. But Chantora quickly shook his head.

"I ain't been in need of physical recipes in a decade."

"Oh! Do you have the Cookbook skill?" Ryan asked curiously, and Chantora looked back surprised.

"That's the one . . . ya know your stuff, huh?"

"I guess so." Feeling a bit awkward to have it pointed out, Ryan started flipping through the handwritten recipes in the book. "So why do you have this, then? If you don't need physical recipes?"

"Hm? Oh, I made that for a friend, but he didn't end up needing it," Chantora briefly replied, clearly wanting to move on from that topic. He took Ryan's bowl from him, though Runar was still in the middle of eating. Ryan had eaten pretty fast. "If ye're struggling, come by and feel free ta ask for some tips. Though . . . I've been thinkin' about movin' somewhere else. This part of town ain't really sitting right with me."

"Really? How so?" Runar asked curiously.

"Well, you can see how my restaurant looks in this place. I got a good deal on it when I bought it, but it's too much stress dealin' with pompous, stuck-up people all day, every day. All they come here for is to 'experience the food of the lower class,' and it pisses me off," Chantora explained bluntly, and Runar couldn't help himself but laugh a bit.

"Yeah, I can see how that'd happen here," Runar said, grabbing his wallet. He pulled out a business card for Café Runic, then handed it to him. "I own a café in Oldtown. I can introduce you to some people if you want to settle over there."

Chantora smiled as he grabbed the business card. "Thanks. I'll give ya a holler after I think it through a bit. But for now—"

The chef's sentence was soon interrupted by the deafening sound of what seemed to be some kind of explosion. When they looked outside, a large cloud of dust poured out into the street. With a bad feeling creeping up on them, Runar and Ryan rushed outside. They looked out of the alley that the restaurant was in, noticing a massive shadow cast on the buildings. Though they clearly hoped it to be something unrelated, before they knew it, the figure of Yamada was thrown through the air, shooting at the source of that shadow.

CHAPTER FORTY-NINE

Berserker (2)

As the dust settled and the initial shock was gone, the sound of the battle was drowned out by the panic of the people around. People flooded away as fast as they could, and it didn't take long before the emergency sirens went off either.

"Warning! Warning! A rampaging Villain has been spotted in the vicinity! Evacuate Immediately!" The sound blasted into Ryan's ears, only adding onto the already noisy environment. He didn't know what was going on, but that was Yamada just now, right? What was happening?

However, Ryan didn't have to wait long to have that questioned answered. From around the corner, a living mountain pushed itself forward, digging its hands into the corners of the nearby buildings for support.

Whatever that was, there was no way it was a person . . . right? But it definitely felt like one, despite how it looked. Stone covered its whole body, and the only thing hinting at a person was half the face that was still uncovered. Bulging veins that looked like metal pipes climbing up a building covered the dozen-meter-tall being. This felt far too familiar, and Ryan's suspicion was quickly supported by the thin green strands that floated off that thing's body, like spider threads on a windy day.

But while that was the case . . . the Light of Guidance wasn't pointing Ryan at that rampaging titan, but rather at Yamada, who was recovering in the middle of the road. "Yamada got the fragment, so I—"

Runar interrupted his nephew instantly, "No! Leave, now! Take Liam and get as far away as you can!"

"But I—"

"Ryan."

As the two locked eyes for a moment, frustration flooded into Ryan's body. All these people running away, scared for their lives. He never wanted to get into Heroics, but he couldn't just stand here and do nothing, right? But . . . how the hell was Ryan supposed to fight something like that? He didn't even awaken a physical class, or one actually meant for combat at all. Sure, Maximus was with him, but that didn't mean anything either. Maximus wasn't strong enough to take something like . . . something like *that*.

"Go, and take Liam. I'll try to send the fragment to you, but just get out of here for now. Yamada and I can take care of this," Runar assured. As the Rune Mage turned and ran toward the commotion, Ryan turned back to the restaurant that had already been mostly abandoned, his teeth grinding against each other. There were only two people left in there. Liam, who was hiding under the counter, his head between his legs, and Chantora, who was trying to get him out so they could all get to safety.

The bottle of artificial blood was spilled on the ground next to Liam, seeping into his clothes. Ryan squatted down next to him, grabbing the boy's arm. "Get up! We need to go!"

Liam was shaking. He was just trying to keep his hands pressed against his ears. "I-I can't, I . . . don't make me go . . . Please, please don't . . ."

The knot in Ryan's throat returned, but he had to push through it. "If we don't go, we can get hurt. Really, really hurt."

Liam glanced up at Ryan, his eyes filled with tears. He wanted to talk, but couldn't get any words out. With a slight sigh, Ryan pushed his hands under the boy's legs and tightly held on to his shoulders. "You're a king, aren't you? Then act like it, and listen to this knight of yours!"

Ryan jumped up, surprised at just how light Liam was. Sure, he was just a kid, but this was ridiculous. He was just so . . . thin. "Hold on to me, we don't have the leisure of comfort right now. Chantora, are you—"

"Just get movin' and don't worry about me! I can handle myself, just get out of here!" the chef exclaimed, practically pushing Ryan and Liam out of the restaurant. Without a moment's hesitation, Ryan did as told and rushed outside. Most people were gone from the streets by now. Ryan had to get down to the street level somehow; being up here wasn't safe at all. If that titan and Yamada were up here, they probably left quite a lot of destruction in their path. So the stairway they took earlier was out of question.

Ryan pushed himself forward as Liam's thin arms wrapped around his neck to support himself. He turned around the corner, running into a nearby alley. He remembered there being another stairway in this direction. But right as he entered the alley, the foot of the titan pressed down on the other side; the ground shook like this was an earthquake.

"R-Ryan, I—"

"It's fine, I got you," Ryan reassured Liam, smiling down at him. His legs felt like giving out right now too, but he couldn't let that happen. He turned around and continued running. "Just close your eyes and don't focus on what's happening."

Liam nervously closed his eyes, pressing his head against Ryan's chest. "I . . . I'm scared . . ."

"That's fine. It's normal to be scared in a situation like this." Ryan turned around the corner. "Just listen to my voice, we're almost out of here."

There were people running into a building, so that was either the way down or some kind of shelter. But while those people were running in, there were others running out; people carrying guns wearing assault gear.

Were those people called here to fight against that rampaging titan? Or . . . were they on that titan's side? Ryan knew that Bluesky practically had a private army, and they each carried weapons enhanced through skills, and many of them were awakened gunmen in the first place. But that didn't matter right now. He had to trust that Runar and Yamada could handle themselves.

"Are you excited for school tomorrow?" Ryan asked, trying to keep his breathing calm as he continued running. Liam almost flinched at the question, clearly not expecting it.

"Wha, what? School?"

"Yeah, are you excited? You remember Modak, right? I'm pretty sure his brothers go to the same school," he explained, and Liam quietly answered.

"That was the . . . the orc, right?" he asked.

"That's the one. His brothers are a bit of a handful, but they're good kids. I'm sure you'll get along with them." As Ryan explained, he ran up to a bench and climbed on top of it, using it to jump over the barricade between the footpaths and the road. Even up here, there were cars sometimes, but they seemed to mostly be small delivery vehicles. Just like the one that was currently being thrown through the air, right into the direction of the building Ryan was running to. He stopped and pulled back, turning around to cover Liam from any debris that might be flung around.

The young boy buried his fingers in Ryan's shirt. "And . . . and what if they don't like me?"

Surprised by the question, Ryan didn't immediately know what to say. Sure, he figured that Liam was a bit insecure behind all that "king" stuff he protected himself with, but revealing how he felt *now* of all times wasn't really what he thought would happen.

Slowly, Ryan stood back up. "Then they don't like you. That's fine. There's plenty of people that don't like me either. But I've got a couple of really amazing friends to make up for that. You'll find people like that too, alright?"

Liam carefully nodded as they got closer to the building. They weren't that far away, when the ground in front of the two cracked open. Ryan could barely pull away as a large chunk of the floor, directly between himself and the entrance to the building, fell toward the ground, soon landing on the rooftop of a small building below the overhanging platform.

Even then, there wasn't much time for Ryan to even process what was happening; he was only able to pull Liam closer to his body in case they fell, when a small blob of green appeared in the corner of his eye.

Runar jumped up into the air, clearing the punch from the oversized giant that was attacking them. He glanced over to Yamada.

"Giant berserker plus fragment experiment," she quickly filled Runar in, briefly holding one of her guns with her teeth so that she could sign. One of her eyes was shut because of blood that was flowing from her forehead, so she was already in a rough situation. Runar quickly nodded his head, flicking his wrist with his pen in his hand. He drew something into the air, and then continued running. As he did, Runar quickly wrote something on his underarm as another strike from the giant came at him.

Runar stopped moving, waiting for the right moment. The mellow green droplets spread over the skin of his arm as he swung it to the side. A pillar of rock shot up diagonally, pushing away the giant's arm rapidly. The sudden jolt against the weighed-down arm made the giant topple over, dropping onto his knees. Runar twisted his arm around, making another pillar of stone shoot right into the giant's face, throwing him backward quite a bit.

As Yamada came over to him, Runar drew another rune into the air, leaving it there for the time being. When the demon reached him, Runar quickly wiped the blood away from above her eye, writing a few runes onto her skin to stop the bleeding for a while.

After pulling back, Runar signed to her, *"Do you have the fragment?"*

Yamada quickly nodded, pulling it out of her pocket before pressing the small green stone into the man's hand.

"Keep him busy, I'll send this to Ryan so we can concentrate on taking him—" Runar started, but he didn't even need to finish before Yamada ran off toward the giant. She began to shoot at him without hesitation. Each shot seemed to take a brief moment to "charge up," but once the bullet hit, and they did without fail, large chunks of rock were torn off from the giant's body.

Meanwhile, Runar looked at the fragment, unable to stop himself from clicking his tongue. "Shabby workmanship," he grumbled, trying to erase the enchantments on the surface of the gemstone as he placed it down on the ground. After wiping some of the debris away, Runar quickly drew a magic circle around the fragment, as he turned to the side. During the battle between Yamada and the giant, one of those small delivery cars driving up around here was kicked toward Runar.

Rolling his eyes, Runar held his hand outward, blocking the empty car. Though, part of the metal was so dented that it was flung off, hitting the magic circle that Runar had been drawing. "Fucking—"

Annoyed, Runar got up. He held the pen between his lips, pushing his fingers into the metal of the car. With a loud groan, he heaved it above his head, returning it to the giant. Grabbing the pen again, Runar muttered to himself, "Berserkers . . . always messing up my work."

As he squatted back down to continue, Runar noticed from the corner of his eye that the giant had deflected the car, and it was being thrown over some of the smaller nearby buildings. Figuring, or rather, hoping, that it wouldn't hit anyone, Runar quickly continued drawing the magic circle. Before long, it was finished and Runar activated it; the droplets of Runar's mana gathered around Gaia's fragment, before taking on the form of a small fish. With the fragment floating in its center, that fish speedily swam away right toward Ryan.

Now that he could concentrate on the battle itself, Runar pulled up his pant legs, drawing a few runes onto his skin, but as he got back up, the giant had its arms raised up above its body. At first Runar wondered if he was trying to surrender, but from that completely maddened look in his eyes, that wasn't the case. The giant slammed his arms down onto the ground. Though extremely thick and built using the surrounding buildings as support, most of this area was an elevated platform above the busy streets of the Channel.

And as the giant slammed his hands into the ground, massive cracks formed that immediately spread far beyond this street. Panic set in as Runar watched parts of the platform sink down. This part in particular was above one of the Channel's main roads. Without hesitation, Runar leapt to the closest platform that was in danger of sinking down, drawing a simple pattern onto it. Luckily this spell didn't require a ton of complicated runes, since it had been fine-tuned specifically for situations like this. The moment the pattern was activated, the platform stopped sinking down, levitating in place. But this wasn't the only part of the platforms that was in danger of falling. He wouldn't be able to do anything about small debris, but it looks like the people below had been warned to evacuate as well, so hopefully nothing too bad should happen.

Having already sunken below the platform, Runar activated the spell he just placed onto his legs, jumping forward. The moment he pressed his foot onto the underside of the platform, he began to stick to it and was able to run upside down to get closer to the other large pieces falling down. After dodging past the platform's support beams, Runar kicked off and jumped to the next piece. He drew the same pattern as before, activated it, and jumped to the next. Like this, Runar jumped from piece to piece, trying to stop as many of them as he could that could potentially injure someone. In the end, he was able to stop most of the ones that seemed like they were in imminent danger of dropping near where people were running away, though the last of them stopped just a few meters above the street.

The pieces of the platform would now start slowly sinking down to the street level, and once in a solid position, the spell would deactivate. But until then, Runar could use them to get back up. He kicked off the piece that he was on right now, jumping back up to the next and then the next. When they were too far away from each other, Runar ran on the side of the closest building for a while, before finally making his way back up.

Before long, Runar made his way back up to the fractured platforms, where Yamada was still whittling down at the giant. It seemed like her pacifying bullets weren't able to take him down, so Runar had to take over. He glanced around; the runes that he had drawn into the air were still levitating in space. Perfect.

Since Yamada seemed like she was able to keep the giant busy, Runar kept jumping around, drawing different runes into the air, using them to draw a circle around the large giant. Once he was done, Runar and Yamada locked eyes for a moment, and she quickly nodded. Runar grabbed a piece of debris on the ground and threw it at Yamada, who was jumping through the air trying to avoid the holes now all over of the platform. She kicked off the piece of debris, pushing herself out of the confines of the large circles of runes. Once only the giant was left within, Runar held his hand forward.

He started to speak in a slow, clean, and deliberate manner. The words were clear, but to anyone else would sound like gibberish, as the runes whose sounds had been lost over the centuries were vocalized. As he did, not only his eyes were letting off the characteristic glow of mana usage, but his mouth was filled with that similar green light. Runes that were engraved onto his tongue, but were hidden most of the time, were glowing as he spoke, strengthening his spell.

The runes that Runar placed into the air were glowing as well, as green droplets started spreading out from them, placing themselves into a regular pattern in a dome around the giant, with the runes as the perimeter. Once they were all in place, the runes thinned out into sheets, connecting to each other and forming a barrier around the giant.

Carefully, Runar took a step forward, and as if the barrier was fleeing from him, it grew smaller and smaller. The giant didn't even know what was happening until the barrier touched his head, slowly but surely pressing him down. Completely enraged, the giant tried to strike at the barrier closing in on him, but no matter what he did, it would only grow closer, until he wasn't even able to stand anymore.

Before long, he was forced onto his knees, when the barrier began to contort to his silhouette, practically trapping him in the position he was currently in.

Runar scoffed, finally looking into the fury-filled eyes of the stone-covered, enlarged man. "See? You know how to stay still after all."

CHAPTER FIFTY

Spirit Armament

The ground shook as Ryan carried the terrified Liam. A massive crack had formed between them and the closest exit, and it didn't seem to be the only one. All over the place, cracks were spreading out, and large chunks of the ground were falling down to the roads or buildings below.

The part that Ryan was standing on specifically didn't seem all too unstable, but he also didn't have a lot of time to figure the situation out all too much before something entered his peripheral vision. It was a koi fish made of soft green light with droplets floating around it, swimming through the air directly toward Ryan. The Light of Guidance in his mind was pulling him straight toward it, and the pull grew stronger and stronger.

Before long, the fish stopped in front of Ryan, slowly dissolving. The only part it left behind was the small gemstone in its center. And he didn't have to hesitate at all either; before the last of Gaia's fragments could drop down whatsoever, Ryan instinctively pulled it into the spirit's domain, and some system messages appeared in front of his eyes.

[You have found the last Fragment of Gaia]

[The Light of Guidance has found its target and disappeared]

Ryan's heart almost skipped a beat as the last of the three fragments appeared in Gaia's domain. The three pieces were excitedly floating around each other, though they still weren't combining. He would have to try and figure that out later, but for now, he was just happy to have found all of her.

But that didn't solve the situation that he found himself in right now either. Rather, it caused a whole other problem. Ryan glanced at the direction that the koi fish had come from, and a number of those armed men were standing there, clearly looking into his direction.

"Fuck . . ." he muttered quietly. Of course, a glowing magical fish just swam toward Ryan, and considering the situation, that was incredibly suspicious. So if they were just here to deal with the villain, they might move on after seeing that Ryan was just a guy carrying a scared kid to safety. Though, that hope quickly disappeared from Ryan as he saw the ones in the front aim their guns at him.

The hairs on the back of Ryan's neck stood up as his instincts were absolutely screaming at him to get away. And he didn't hesitate to do so for even a moment. Ryan turned around and started to run away, when he heard a loud sound echoing around the buildings. He felt a sharp pain in his leg, and didn't even have to look down to see what was going on. The pain coursed through his body as blood filled his shoe.

Liam flinched in Ryan's arms, feeling him recoil from the pain, but Ryan just smiled down at him and laughed a bit, "What, a bit of noise is enough to scare you? You won't like living with Runar then . . . he tends to sing in the shower."

Confused about what Ryan was saying, Liam glanced back up at him. "H-Huh?"

"Yeah, and he's probably the worst singer I've ever heard. Can't even hit a single note properly," he pointed out, shaking his head disappointedly as he continued to run, even if he was limping. Ryan tried to hide it as much as he could, but that only went so far. Before he knew it, Maximus had jumped out of his domain, and a second gunshot sounded through the air. But instead of feeling a sharp pain, Ryan heard the sound of the bullet hitting metal, and a message appeared in front of Ryan.

**[Knight Spirit Maximus's -Right Arm- has been damaged
and cannot be used until repaired]**

Ryan widened his eyes as he felt the shattered, broken pieces enter his domain again. The arm was fully torn apart due to the impact of the bullet. These parts were in the same space that Maximus's second arm was; right now, he was using the complete Guardian model, and the Crusader model's arm was stored at the edge of the domain where Ryan could pull it out whenever he needed to. That was where these broken pieces also went, barely holding the shape of an arm. "Maximus! What the hell are you—"

Ryan could feel something pull at his mind. He knew what that meant, and Ryan activated the connection between himself and the knight. As the Spirit Link formed, Ryan's arm almost went numb, but it was just the feeling of a "missing arm" overlapping with his "existing arm." But there was no pain or anything of the sort. The only thing that flowed into Ryan's mind was a very vague feeling of confidence.

". . . Fine, I'll trust you. Just . . . don't die . . ." Ryan told him, and could quickly see Maximus glancing over at the car. It was on this side of the crack, and should be able to act as decent enough cover. Ryan quickly ran over toward it. More gunshots sounded out, and for a moment, an uncomfortable sensation coursed through Ryan's leg. It wasn't painful, but he could still feel what was happening. As if a cannonball tore through his leg.

[Knight Spirit Maximus's -Left Leg- has been damaged and cannot be used until repaired]

As the leg appeared within Maximus's domain as well, he could feel Maximus simply start to hop after deflecting a second bullet. Despite now only having one leg to work with, he still moved in an agile way, keeping up with Ryan's slowed movements. Ryan soon reached the car and squatted down behind it, carefully placing Liam down.

"Close your eyes," Ryan said immediately, but Liam shook his head.

"No! I can—"

"Liam, please, just close your eyes." Trying not to let the pain make him raise his voice, Ryan looked at the boy and pleaded. Clearly frustrated, Liam nodded his head, pressing his eyes shut as more gunshots sounded out. Of course, Ryan was still an extra barrier between Liam and the shooters in addition to the car. The kid's safety came first.

Ryan looked down at his leg, seeing most of his shin and calf covered in a thick, deep red. The bullet seemed to have gone clean through his leg at least, but he was bleeding a lot. With a groan, Ryan pulled off his shirt and tied it around the wound as tightly as he could, trying to at least slow down the bleeding. He would have to apologize to Silvia later for ruining the shirt she made him.

As he tied it around his leg, Ryan noticed the symbiote freaking out on the back of his hand.

% & ! ! ? ;;

The random symbols, which seemed to come from some kind of fear or pain that they were experiencing together with Ryan, already made his stomach drop. Holding the hand to his mouth, Ryan whispered, "Sorry . . . you've been with me for a day, and we're already going through this."

. . . :)

Ryan laughed lightly. The gunshots had stopped, but instead footsteps were approaching closer and closer. They would reach this place soon. With another whisper, Ryan spoke to the symbiote again, "If things go sour, we should at least get you a name, right . . . ?"

The symbols on the back of Ryan's hand seemed to change hesitantly into three simple dots. Ryan tried to think of something good, though for some reason, something came to his mind. It was a story that was pretty fresh in his mind. After Modak brought it up the other day, he had looked the story up again; *The Hundred Tales of Shazir.*

Shazir traveled the world in search of treasures and ruins, meeting new people and battling powerful monsters. And during one of his journeys, he met a number of fantastical beings, including sprites, which guided him toward his destination. A small red jewel imbued with powerful magics. And the name of that gemstone rang through Ryan's head. The name of the jewel of creation.

"Tiar . . . How does that sound?"

After a few moments of what seemed like hesitation, a symbol appeared on the back of Ryan's hand.

:D

[The Ruby Symbiote has accepted the name -Tiar-]

**[Tiar's synchronization with the system is growing.
A connection is being formed]**

[Connection - 0%]

[Connection - 3%]

[Connection - 7%]

Ryan was confused as he saw the messages, but that didn't really matter right now. Tiar, who seemed excited just a few moments earlier, immediately fell into a slumber. Like when they were asleep, a spiral had appeared on the back of Ryan's hand instead, and the tattoo-like red patterns on Ryan's arm were waving back and forth along with his heartbeat.

Ryan pulled Liam closer as the footsteps closed in. There were about half a dozen guys with full assault gear and guns; Ryan was lucky that only one of them shot at him. Maybe they didn't really want to kill him, and just wanted to slow him down somehow. Or maybe they were just playing with Ryan before taking him down to take the fragments back. But who knew what would happen when they actually stood over Ryan, staring down at him? He certainly didn't want to figure it out.

The footsteps grew louder and closer. Ryan closed his eyes, covering Liam's head with his hands, as Maximus got ready to attack the men as they closed in. Somehow, Ryan felt surprisingly calm right now.

As Ryan's eye peeked open, he swore he could already see the tip of a rifle's barrel, but it quickly moved away as another sound filled the area. A loud voice coming from between two of the buildings.

"Oi, ya fuckers! The hell d'ya think ye're doing?!" The voice of the kind chef that Ryan had only heard a few minutes earlier was now filled with absolute rage. "Get away from those kids!"

[Connection - 56%]

Ryan heard Chantora yell at the gunmen, and fear immediately flowed through him. Especially as he heard the men speak to each other.

"What do we do?" one of them seemingly asked this group's leader, who said some words that Ryan really didn't want to hear.

"If we were to encounter him, we were told to keep the Spirit Keeper alive. If necessary, dispatch everyone that gets in the way."

[Connection - 71%]

Liam flinched in Ryan's arms, also having heard the men speak. They heard the gunmen ready their weapons before the leader spoke.

"Immediately evacuate the area!" he yelled out to Chantora, but the chef immediately denied.

"I saw ya lot shoot at them! You fuckin' maniacs!"

The leader seemed to be annoyed. The others beside him readied their guns, clearly not hesitating to shoot at Chantora in the slightest. Ryan didn't know what was going on, but he couldn't let that happen. He couldn't let anyone die, he couldn't—

[Connection - 99%]

[Connection - 100%]

[Tiar has completely synchronized with the -Spirit Keeper- Class]

[A special combination skill has been unlocked]

[You have learned the -Spirit Armament- Skill]

Ryan's eyes widened as a new sensation entered his mind. His arm moved almost on its own and pressed onto the metal of the car he was hiding behind.

The red lines that appeared on Ryan's arm after he bonded with Tiar expanded onto the metal, tearing it apart and pulling it directly onto his right arm's skin. Piece by piece, bit by bit, the car's old and almost rusted metal took on a familiar shape. Not too long ago, he had put this together himself.

It was bulky and heavy, but completely enveloped Ryan's hand. Even the gloves and the roots wrapping around it all were made from the car's metal. Ryan's arm was covered in Maximus's armor; the Crusader model that had been intact within the domain. Now it wasn't there anymore; Ryan was wearing it. Even Maximus seemed confused by what was happening, as he clearly hadn't seen this kind of thing before.

However, Ryan didn't feel any stronger, so he didn't receive the stats the same way that Maximus did. But that was fine, he didn't need to. His arm was covered in a massive gauntlet. Solid and sharp metal covered his hands, moving like a proper glove would. It wasn't uncomfortable, as if this piece of armor was made for him to begin with. Ryan carefully let go of Liam as the adrenaline took over. For a little while, he couldn't even feel the pain of the bullet wound on his leg. Ryan jumped up from behind the car, swinging his massive metal-covered arm at the closest gunman, who was aiming at Chantora, ready to shoot.

An attack that usually would have only injured Ryan's hand was enough to throw the gunman into the others besides him. Despite the weight of the armor that Ryan was now wearing, he could swing around like it was just his normal arm. The gunmen were startled, but Ryan wouldn't just give them the opportunity to react.

He glared at the leader of the group and pushed his arm toward him. A simple strike shattered the visor of the helmet the leader was wearing, and Ryan quickly closed the distance and threw a second punch, putting all his weight behind it. The helmet was thrown off the man's face, and Ryan immediately wrapped the metal hand around his neck.

The other gunmen had realized what was going on by now and aimed their guns at Ryan.

"Don't you *fucking* dare. Throw those away, or I tear out his throat!"

Ryan glanced over his shoulder at the gunmen, and while he could see them hesitate, they still continued aiming at him.

"We know you won't, the Aglecards have always acted with nonlethal methods," one of them replied. "Stop bluffing and put him down!"

With a loud laugh, Ryan just tightened his grip. "Are you guys fucking blind? Do I *look* like I'd give a shit about what the Aglecards have always acted like?!"

Ryan's back tensed up as he could practically feel the gazes of the gunmen stare at him. His shirt was wrapped around his leg, so his upper body was completely exposed now. The myriad of scars of indiscernible sources certainly painted a different picture. Of course, these didn't come from any rough battles or really showed how dangerous Ryan was. But who would expect that they were scars he got from his disgusting, abusive stepfather who had nothing better to do than torture a little kid for fun?

One of the gunmen slowly raised his hand toward the others. ". . . Stand down. Do what he says."

The second-in-command seemed to have a decent head on his shoulders, at least. Though in the first place, they weren't supposed to kill Ryan. If that weren't the case, maybe they wouldn't be quite as cooperative.

Ryan barked at them, "Throw the guns away! Onto the other side of the gap!"

Seeing them hesitate again, Ryan slightly tightened his grip. If he kept going, he really would end up killing this guy. He seemed to already struggle to breathe as blood poured down his throat due to the sharp edges of metal Ryan was pressing against his skin.

Slowly, the gunmen did as told. The four of them tossed their weapons onto the other side of the gap after securing them. The last of them, the second-in-command, was about to do the same, when he slightly turned his head.

"So? Get to it!" Ryan yelled. Once all their guns were gone, he should be able to deal with them somehow, even with his leg in the state it was. None of them seemed to be awakened, so they couldn't be *that* strong. "I told you to fucking—"

Ryan's sentence was interrupted by a gunshot. The second-in-command had raised up his gun and shot through the back of the former leader's head. As the bullet passed clean through it and flew by the side of Ryan's head, his face was covered in splatters of blood and brains while shards of bone cut narrowly into his cheek.

The man's body went limp as Ryan instinctively let go of the man, feeling himself grow ill as the smell of blood became overwhelming. His hand was shaking as he looked back up, staring right into the barrel of the rifle.

"Wh-Why did you—"

The second-in-command, now the new leader of the group, tightened his grip on the gun. "You must have heard what he said earlier. We're supposed to dispatch everyone that gets in the way."

CHAPTER FIFTY-ONE

The Visit

Ryan stared into the barrel of the gun as his body froze up. Blood was flowing down his cheek and bits of brain stuck to his chest.

"Lie down on the ground, and deactivate that skill," the man in front of Ryan said, his finger teasing the trigger. But somehow, despite all of this, Ryan couldn't do anything but laugh.

"Seriously? So you all are the *bad* guys." Ryan wiped his face with his left hand as he turned around. "How about you go fu—"

Unwilling to play around, the gunman pulled the trigger for just a quick moment, shooting a bullet through Ryan's torso. It came back out just by his hip. Ryan didn't know if anything important was hit with that, but it definitely hurt like hell. Ryan looked across the large cracks all over the ground, looking at Chantora. The two locked eyes for a moment, or at least Ryan thought so. It was hard to tell from here.

The chef was staring anxiously at Ryan, who used the blood gushing from the bullet wound to write an *R* onto his belly, and then pointed into the direction where the fight with that titan had to be going on. It seemed that Chantora understood, standing up and sprinting away into the direction that Ryan pointed, as Ryan himself quickly covered the letter up with a bit more blood.

Tiar's patterns wriggled nervously on his arm, and the gunman groaned, "I told you to get on the ground."

"Or . . . or what? You're gonna kill me?" Ryan asked, trying to laugh through the pain. He felt like vomiting, but he could manage somehow. He walked over to one of the cracks that had formed nearby. Looking down from here, it went all the way to street level, though at least there weren't any cars down there. It was just some kind of alley. Ryan carefully crept toward the edge, trying to push down on the bullet wound that was gushing blood.

Once he got there, Ryan turned around with his heels already over the edge. "If you had to get rid of someone just because he made catching me a bit harder for you, I wonder what's going to happen when I'm dead."

Ryan could feel it through the link with Maximus. The knight was panicking, trying to come up with any way to stop what was happening here. But he had lost an arm and a leg, and could barely stay upright anymore. Not to mention, he had promised to protect Liam with the little power that he could still use.

"You're not done bluffing yet? Get away from the edge and do what we tell you, and you might get out of this whole ordeal with at least your body somewhat intact," the gunman said, and once again, Ryan couldn't help himself but laugh.

"Yeah, sure, whatever. Right now, just answer my questions, and then I might think about going with you," he lied, but it didn't really matter whether it was an obvious lie or not. Right now, the gunman couldn't do anything. Frankly, the gunman must have thought that the bullet just now would have been enough to bring Ryan to his knees so they could capture him. But he couldn't risk it again now. If he shot Ryan, he would end up falling down into that crack, and from this height, he would most certainly die. Not to mention, the wound on Ryan's leg and the incessant bleeding coming from two bullet wounds was already making him unsteady on his legs.

"We aren't here to play games. Just come with us," the gunman sighed, as the other men, who didn't have their weapons anymore, pulled up Liam from behind the car. "If you do, we'll leave the kid alone."

Ryan ground his teeth, staring at those guys violently holding on to a kid's arms and shoulders. "Are you fucking psychos? You want to kill a kid just to get me to come with you?"

The gunman glanced over at Liam and then back at Ryan. "We certainly don't *want* to do it."

"Could you be any more cliché than this? Fuck, I thought you'd at least have a bit more nuance to you," Ryan scoffed, though his voice sounded more like a rough bark than a laugh. His whole body was tensing up at the complete anger that he was feeling. Even the pain that he should be feeling was nothing compared to the rage running through his veins.

The gunman held the barrel of his rifle toward Liam, but Ryan immediately yelled out, "Stop! Stop it, you absolute—Fine, just . . . Just leave him alone."

"Giving up pretty quick despite all that big talk, huh?" The gunman stared at the chunks of metal stuck to Ryan's arm. "Deactivate the skill."

Ryan slowly nodded, taking a step away from the ledge. Some chunks of metal slowly fell from his hand, and the gunman started to approach closer, keeping his rifle aimed at Ryan the whole time. And then, without warning, the sound of a gun being shot sounded out. From the corner of his eye, Ryan could see a yellow streak for just an instant, then the person holding Liam fell to the ground. Just another moment later, the other three unarmed men fell to the ground, and the gunman glanced away confused. That was the perfect moment.

Ryan took the opportunity and jumped forward, pushing his right hand out to the rifle. Until then, only the hand had become uncovered from the armor, but now, the metal making up the rifle's body was being torn apart and bent into shape to wrap around Ryan's fingers.

The gunman let go of the weapon, seemingly trying to grab the knife at his hip, but Ryan was faster. He swung his metal-covered fist into the gunman's stomach. Due to the assault gear, it probably didn't do massive damage, but it was enough to keep him stunned for a moment. It was enough for Ryan to get in another strike, and another. The gunman's visor was thrown off, and Ryan glared into the eyes of the man with half his face covered in thick burn scars.

"Just leave me the fuck alone." Ryan placed a single punch right into the center of the man's face. Of course, using his left hand, not his right. Striking him with a fist made completely of metal could lead to a bit more damage than Ryan was willing to do.

At that point, Yamada and Runar had also properly caught up. It really only took them a few seconds to cross the whole space, jumping over those gaps as if they were nothing.

"Ryan, are you . . . are you okay? What's with your arm? You—" Runar held on to his nephew's shoulders, seeing him covered in blood from head to toe. Glancing down, he saw the dead body of a man who had just been shot a few minutes earlier. With complete fury in his eyes, Runar squatted down. He wiped away some blood from Ryan's belly and wrote a rune onto his skin, and the bleeding quickly stopped in the front. He did the same on his back, and then on his leg.

"This is just first aid . . . we're going to see a skilled healer later that should be able to take care of all this," Runar said, trying to somehow calm himself down.

"Don't worry, I'm fine for now . . . did everything go well with whatever that thing was earlier?" Ryan asked, groaning lightly as the pieces of metal really fell from his arm this time as the skill deactivated.

"We managed to pacify him," Runar replied, looking over at Yamada, silently signing to her. "*Take care of the situation here and take full credit for taking down the berserker. We'll deal with the aftermath later.*"

Yamada nodded her head, squatting down to properly tie up the gunmen so they couldn't do anything when they woke up. Ryan carefully walked up to Maximus, then pulled the knight into his domain. His limbs were broken right now, but he should be able to figure out how to repair them . . . that had to be part of this, right?

When Maximus was recovered, Ryan looked over at Liam, who had nothing but tears streaming down his cheeks. He stood there silently, just staring at what had unfolded in front of him. Ryan held out his hand toward him, trying to force a smile onto his face. "Come on, let's go."

Liam quietly grabbed Ryan's hand, and they walked away from this scene. Runar was trying his best to support them, but he had already pulled up his phone and was talking to some people. It was something about the media, or whatever. Ryan didn't really pay attention; he had other more important stuff to worry about.

With music blasting in his ears, Modak was typing something on his computer. He would briefly look away, taking some notes on a piece of paper right next to him. The orc placed the pencil into his mouth, biting down on the wood. "Hm . . . so if I do that I could speed up the frequency's wavelength while still keeping the quality . . . ?"

While talking to himself, Modak noticed his phone lighting up. He glanced at the screen and saw some messages from Silvia. Stretching with a light groan, figuring it was time to take a break anyway, Modak pulled off his headphones and swiped to look at the messages.

"Modak! There's someone at the door for you!" his younger brother yelled out to him from the hallway, but Modak just turned his head, wanting to at least read the messages first.

"Just a second!" he replied, managing to read the first line at least.

Silvia
Something's going on in the Channel right now, do you know what . . .

"It sounds important!"

With a groan, Modak looked away from the screen, figuring that he could just reply after checking who it was at the door. He got up from his seat and put his headphones onto his desk. The orc opened the door, looking at Gilik with an annoyed sigh. "What is it?"

"Some woman said she wants to talk to you," Gilik replied, and Modak glanced down the hallway. With a sigh, Modak walked into the living room, seeing Pock standing in front of the door. A bit curious, Modak grabbed the door and pulled it open a bit more so that he could take a proper look. And the person that stood there confused Modak more than just a little bit. It was Alicia, the current Mistress of the Magic Tower.

"U-Uhm . . . Wh-What are you . . . Can I help you?" Modak stuttered out, and Alicia looked back at him with a slight smile.

"Yes, you could, actually. There's something that I wanted to speak to you about that we didn't have the chance to yesterday."

Modak frowned, confused, "You wanted to . . . talk to me? Like, _me_? But . . . why?"

Alicia glanced down at Pock, smiling lightly as she turned back to Modak. "Could we speak about this inside?"

After a bit of contemplation, Modak opened the door. He wasn't entirely sure if she was trustworthy. This whole situation that Modak had found himself in was so weird and complicated, and after all of Ryan's yelling last night while Alicia was leaving, he felt a bit unsure. But in the end, he figured it should be fine to at least hear her out.

"Sorry if it's a bit messy in here," Modak apologized as he closed the door behind Alicia, who quickly shook her head.

"Nothing to worry about. You should see how Runar kept his dormitory at the tower," she laughed lightly while being guided to Modak's room. As he ushered his brothers away, the orc quickly closed the door behind him. Modak pointed toward his chair awkwardly.

"Please, uhm . . . take a seat."

"Don't mind if I do," Alicia replied, sitting down as she waved her hand around. Modak could feel the hairs on the back of his neck stand up, and Alicia quickly explained, "I just soundproofed the room. It looks like your siblings are a little nosy."

"Ah . . . yeah, sorry about that. So . . . what would you like to talk about?"

Alicia glanced around Modak's room, soon spotting the small tape placed onto the edge of the table, carefully picking it up to take a closer look. "I'm here to take a look at this."

As she did, Modak remembered something that Runar had briefly mentioned before. "So . . . you're interested in the tapes?"

"Well, if they work as Runar mentioned, I certainly am. Do you mind giving me a quick explanation?"

Modak slowly nodded. He figured he might as well. Rather, he was just unable to stop his excitement right now. No matter what happened yesterday, he was still talking to the Mistress of the Magic Tower, and she was interested in something he made. How could he not get excited about something like that?

He hurried and gave her the exact explanation, trying to go into as much detail as he wanted to. Obviously, Alicia would be able to keep up with any terminology and numbers that he threw out, and Modak was sure she was also going to understand all the projects that he used as reference. Alicia listened to everything that he was saying, asking questions to make sure she understood the whole thing properly. And then, once Modak was done, she smiled curiously.

"I see . . . I see, so this could potentially work quite well," Alicia muttered, looking at Modak. "You said you were planning on turning this process into a paper, correct?"

Modak nervously nodded. "Yes, that was the idea. I . . . I'm also using some of the things that I've worked out to help with a robotics problem my friend has, but that's separate from this."

Alicia crossed her legs, her smile never having left her lips. "I see. In that case, do you think you might want to write that paper in cooperation with the Magic Tower?"

". . . What?" He wasn't able to believe what he was hearing. "I . . . I don't even have an ounce of mana, how would I be able to work with the Magic Tower?"

"The actual ability to *use* mana is secondary to the ability to *understand* it. While we are mostly in the business of researching magic in its more classic means and uses, we have been expanding more and more into the field of magic engineering. And these tapes could be an incredible tool."

Modak was confused. "An incredible tool? What do you mean?"

Alicia raised her finger up, and a magic circle appeared in the air, just floating there without being activated. "A large portion of spells are cast through the specific aggravation, manipulation, and definition of mana. A magic circle like this only works in this specific way, because each part does its job of the larger pattern, doing what it should to define the mana in these very minuscule ways that come together into a bigger picture. And, what you are doing here with this tape is creating very particular and precise patterns of mana. Not only that, but I imagine that once the recorded audio is displayed, it has some mana infused into the sound just by its very nature, so if refined and improved, it could even replace chanting."

Unsure if he was understanding right, Modak looked at the woman in front of him. He looked at one of the most powerful magic users currently alive, who was sitting on an old chair in his cramped bedroom. "You . . . you think that my mana tape can be used as a spellcasting conduit?"

Alicia stood up and smiled up at the orc in front of her. "I think it's a possibility. Wouldn't you like to try and find out?"

CHAPTER FIFTY-TWO

Healing

After barely parking properly, Silvia jumped out of her sister's car that she had borrowed. She rushed up to the café's door, but it was locked and that SORRY, WE'RE SPONTANEOUSLY CLOSED TODAY sign that was on the door far too often just laughed in her face. Anxiously, Silvia ran around the building to get to the door leading directly into the flat, then loudly knocked on the door.

"Ryan! Runar! Open up!" she exclaimed. Silvia knew that they were here; Ryan had told her *that* much at least, but he had stopped replying at some point. Plus, Modak wasn't looking at his phone either, even after Silvia tried to call him maybe a dozen times.

That anxiety was far too much for her to deal with right now. She knew that Ryan was in the Channel, and today of all days, an overgrown giant covered in stone rampaged through that part of town? Plus, the one that took that giant down was that demon that worked for Runar, Yamada. One of the few things that Ryan had told her was that they were on their way home and would meet a healer, so she shouldn't worry. But how could she not worry when Ryan apparently needed a healer for something?

But before she knew it, the door in front of her opened up, and Runar stood right in front of her. "Calm down, will you?"

"Calm down? How do you expect me to—"

"No, I'm just saying to be quiet. The flat is soundproofed, so at least wait with that until you're inside." Runar stepped to the side and let the elf inside, and she didn't hesitate to rush past him and up the stairs, pushing open the door into the main flat. She looked around, hearing voices from the living room and quickly ran inside.

There, sitting on a chair in his underwear, was a blood-covered Ryan. In front of him, a figure completely cloaked in white was holding a golden ring in front of the ugly wound on his leg.

"Silvia?" Ryan let out, surprised, grimacing lightly as the golden ring gave off a little bit of light.

"Is that all you have to say? What the hell happened?" A wave of emotions came over her, but in the end Silvia could only feel a mixture of relief and anger. After all, Ryan kept on getting hurt over and over again. Runar stepped into the living room after Silvia.

". . . The situation is a lot more serious than I expected. The Shadows *really* want the Spirit Keeper class," he explained, as Silvia snapped her head toward her friend's uncle.

"Aren't you supposed to be the head of the family? Shouldn't you be aware of how bad things are?"

Runar slowly and hesitantly shook his head. "Just being the patriarch doesn't make me some kind of absolute, all-knowing power. There's a lot more for me to take care of than just track what the White Shadow Society is doing all the time. Plus, they have a new head, and he seems to be pretty . . . reckless."

"No shit, using a spirit core the way that they've been trying to isn't a great sign that he's got all his marbles in order," Ryan scoffed, trying to lightly shift his weight on the chair as the healer kept silently treating the gunshot wound on his leg. His flesh was wriggling weirdly and uncomfortably as it grew back together, but it wasn't particularly painful. Just something that he had to get used to.

"It's not that. He's not crazy. I mean . . . he might be, but he's just a kid that was put into a really fucked-up situation. He's maybe . . . eight years old?"

"Excuse me?" Ryan flinched as he heard his uncle's words, almost jumping up when he felt a sharp, cramping pain in his leg.

The healer pushed him back down onto the seat properly, yelling out, "Karim! Samba, ta!"

Runar sighed, "He's saying to stay still. Healing isn't an easy job."

"Mali, bora ka ji-ik . . ." the healer grumbled, continuing to move the glowing golden ring around the wound.

With an apologetic smile, Runar looked over at him. "Loria si ta porak. Idja ruti ma-lek."

". . . Ma-rik."

"Ma-sag, zhu as al." With a slight laugh, Runar retorted. Or at least, that's what it sounded like to Ryan and Silvia, who could barely even recognize the language the two were speaking. Though, as if suddenly even more motivated, the hooded healer continued his work.

"Anyway," Runar started again, "yes, he's a kid. All the leaders of the White Shadow Society are. It's a bit complicated, but . . . each leader is chosen not by the current members or the former leader, but by a curse that is passed down from one to another. It's a curse that takes the form of a class. It's kind of similar to the Spirit Keeper, where only one exists at a time. Their class is called 'White Curse's Child.'"

"Okay, so what makes that curse so special that it would make a reckless, stupid little kid the leader of a secret society?" Silvia asked as she stepped up to Ryan's side, trying to see if there was anything she could do. And as Ryan directed her toward the large bag filled with protein bars on the coffee table, Runar explained.

"Oh, I mean, reckless, yeah. Stupid . . . no. The curse is a rough one. It strips the afflicted of all physical strength, and basically makes their lifespan a fraction of what it had been. This kid won't make it to eighteen. He'll be lucky to turn fifteen, even." Runar's voice was filled with a lot of complicated emotions about this fact. And it was obvious; no matter how bad the things the White Shadow Society did were, the fact their leader was a literal child that would never reach Ryan and Silvia's age tainted everything with an air of bitterness. "But . . . in return, the White Curse's Child is gifted with intelligence beyond compare. And I say this knowing exactly how it sounds, but there's nobody more cunning, intelligent, and capable than the current White Curse's Child."

". . . You're kidding." Ryan glanced over at Silvia to make sure he heard right, as the elf was opening a protein bar for him.

Trying to sum things up, Silvia looked at Runar hesitantly. "So we're dealing with a massively influential secret society led by a superintelligent, immature little kid?"

"Mhm. Usually, the White Curse's Child was always guided by some kind of council, even if the kid would always have all the power in the end. However, that council was overthrown in the period between the death of the last White Curse's Child and the birth of the next. So now, the kid's in charge without any proper guidance," Runar explained, clearly not particularly happy about the situation. "But I guess even with the council, they've always been a bit insane. Just smarter about it. Every Blanchard's got some screws loose, to be honest."

Ryan listened as he hungrily bit into the protein bar, feeling Silvia's hand on his shoulder, not even fully registering what Runar just said. Ryan was bad with names in the first place, but the name "Blanchard" stuck out, and a moment later, he realized why.

"Runar . . . are the Blanchards a lamia family?"

Surprised, Runar nodded his head. "Yeah, they are. How did you know?"

". . . One of them goes to our school, Christopher. Actually, he was here not too long ago, while you had that phone call about Liam, and I was watching the shop," Ryan explained, and the moment he said that name, Runar's expression dropped.

"Christopher Blanchard was here? In the café? What did he want? What did he—"

"He didn't do anything, he just ordered something and went on his way. Sure, he was a bit weird, but I thought he was just being weird. Not that he was staring into my soul because he wanted to steal my class . . ."

"Wait . . ." Silvia started, putting a few things together. "Was he the one that gave Vanda the fragment?"

Ryan snapped his head toward Silvia, and then hurriedly looked over at Runar for confirmation. "Was it? Did that bastard do that to Gaia?"

Rubbing the bridge of his nose, Runar nodded his head. "Yes, or at least we think so. We don't know exactly what his class is, but it's somehow related to contracts. Hence, why that Vanda girl wasn't able to talk about him; she entered some kind of binding contract supported by the system."

"Okay, well . . . that explains it at least," Ryan muttered. "Do you think they have any more fragments or cores?"

Runar shrugged. "I'm not sure. It would surprise me, but you never know. The fact they only used Gaia's fragments to do all of this gives me hope that they don't."

With some level of relief that Runar thought so too, Ryan let out a long sigh as the healer suddenly stood up.

"Kora ga lak," he said, carefully placing the golden ring into his cloak.

"Ah, he says he's done. Get yourself cleaned up in a bit and take it easy. I think Tiar is helping you out with replenishing your blood quicker, but still, just rest for a day or two," Runar translated, and Ryan looked down a bit surprised. There was still blood covering his leg, but the pain from the bullet wound was basically completely gone. It was the same as it was with his belly earlier. No pain, just some discomfort and soreness.

"Tiar?" Silvia asked, a bit confused, trying to catch up to what was really happening. Ryan quickly held up his left arm.

"It's them, the symbiote. We decided on Tiar," Ryan explained, and the symbiote happily replied.

:D

Silvia smiled lightly. "Well, nice to meet you then, Tiar."

:) :) :)

The healer continued packing up his things, like different effigies and trinkets that were scattered around on the floor, placing them back into his cloak before walking over to Runar. "Porili-ka, mago si-ra ta por. Jhua zi gorun lumir."

Runar replied with a quick nod, "Lumir isu-ga dir maron." He slightly bowed down, as if trying to show the healer respect. "Barig unag heplan."

Turning around toward Ryan, the healer briefly nodded to him and then made his way out of the living room, leaving the flat a few moments later. Runar quickly turned toward the two. "He's going to be sticking around for a while in case we have any more . . . emergencies. But White Mages, and pure healers like him in general, are rare, so he'll have to leave in a couple of weeks. Until then, we're going to have to try and train Ryan up a bit."

"Didn't you just say I should rest?" Ryan asked with a raised brow, but Runar shrugged.

"Sure, but we do need to take some precautions. Our first priority is to get you to level 10 so that we can get the Shadows off your back since they won't be able to get your class anymore. We also need you to unlock some physical stats just as some extra insurance, but with Tiar helping you out, that shouldn't be an issue."

Ryan slowly got up, feeling much more sturdy on his legs than he expected, especially considering he had a hole in one of them not too long ago. He looked at his uncle, walking past him into the hallway. "But first I guess I should just get cleaned up and then take care of Gaia, right?"

"Right. I'll order you some food while you're in the shower. Does pizza sound good?"

"Oh yeah, pizza sounds great right now. Get the biggest you can order," Ryan immediately said as he made his way to the bathroom to take a shower. Once he was gone, Runar looked at Silvia.

"Do you want something to eat as well?"

The elf thought about it for a moment, and in the end just shrugged. "Sure. Oh, but I'm vegetarian, so—"

"I got you, don't worry," Runar replied, finishing the text that he was writing to someone. To Silvia, it didn't look like he had ordered anything, but she figured Runar knew what he was doing. He sat down on one of the chairs, looking up at the elf. "I know that this all is a bit rough to watch. But . . . this is also exactly why I didn't want to get Ryan involved. This whole world is—"

"But it's too late for that now," Silvia replied immediately. "You can't expect Ryan to just move on after everything that you've told him. And you can't expect Modak and me to just let him go through this alone."

Runar leaned more into the backrest of the chair, glancing Silvia up and down. "Why are you even going so far for him? You've known him for barely half a year."

The elf slowly moved over and sat down on the couch. "I don't know. Does it really matter for how long we've known each other? Ryan and Modak are my best friends. I don't believe that time is the most important part for that kind of connection."

The two looked at each other for a few moments, locking eyes. In the end, Runar was the one that gave in, letting out a long sigh. "Fine, you're right, I guess. Anyway . . . there's something I meant to suggest to you. You're the one that made what Ryan was wearing in the dungeon, right?"

Silvia slowly nodded her head. "Yeah, why? Was there something wrong with it? It was my first time making something like that, but—"

"No, no, nothing was wrong with it. Rather, it's the opposite; for what you were working with, it was pretty high-quality. Do you want to keep making some things for Ryan?"

Silvia seemed a bit taken aback. "Uh . . . yeah, I wouldn't mind that at all. But don't you have your own people to do that kind of thing already?"

"Well, sure, but we've kind of got people for everything already. We don't have any particular openings, but considering that you're already Ryan's aide, we could just make you his exclusive equipment designer. You would work with some others that do the actual production, though. They're Awakened and can strengthen things they make. And we would need to teach you a few more things so you know what materials we have access to . . . But it shouldn't be too much work."

Silvia thought about it for a moment. If that meant she could make something for Ryan that could actually stop him from getting hurt all the damn time, Silvia would really jump at that opportunity. It was just, ". . . Would that be the only thing I could do for him?"

Runar immediately shook his head. "No, I don't think so. It's not like he'll go through a ton of equipment anyway. We still need to show you all a bit more about what we do here. But in the end, we'll really only know what you can do to help out once Ryan's made his choice about what *he* wants to do."

CHAPTER FIFTY-THREE

Repair

Stepping out of his bedroom, properly cleaned up and dressed in new, not-blood-drenched clothes, Ryan decided to make a short stop before heading back to the living room. He knocked on the door of Runar's old office, which had now been turned into Liam's bedroom.

"Yo, it's me. Can I come in?"

For a few moments, there was silence coming in from inside. Ryan fiddled around with the small wooden box in his hands, running his fingers over the engravings as time passed. He almost thought he was going to be ignored, but before long, the boy replied, ". . . Yeah, sure."

Ryan pushed open the door; Liam was sitting in the dark room alone, the blinds having been pulled down completely, and Ryan instinctively reached out to the light switch.

"Can you keep the light off? Please?" Liam requested, and Ryan raised a brow. He figured it wasn't that big a deal; it wasn't like he was here to do gymnastics anyway. After closing the door behind himself, Ryan carefully stepped into the room, sitting down on the ground a few steps away from where the bed should be.

"You like it dark, huh? I get that, so do I sometimes."

"It's not that I like it dark, but the light is just too . . . bright," Liam explained, and Ryan remembered one of the things that Runar had explained to him about vampires. Some things that he had to know since he was going to be living with a young vampire boy. All vampires, being a people of the night, had dark vision. It adjusted a bit when they were outside, but they were generally just far more sensitive to any sort of light than most other people.

"So . . . how're you doing? Today was pretty rough," Ryan pointed out, and Liam just scoffed lightly.

"Rough? You got . . . you got shot . . ." the boy replied, and Ryan could swear that he was pushing down some sniffles.

"Meh, it could've been worse." With a laugh, Ryan leaned back onto his hands. "And hey, I even got a super cool new skill. Did you see my sick ass arm earlier?"

Liam stayed silent for a while, and Ryan just sat there, letting him think. He could feel the boy's stares digging into his skin, but that was fine. What bothered Ryan more was that he could feel some stomach gurgling closing in.

The young vampire finally spoke up again, ". . . And you're sure you're okay?"

"Never been better. I got every part of Gaia with me now. Actually, her fragments seem eager to be properly put back together, and then I'll get started building her body." With excitement in his voice that he wasn't able to hide, Ryan looked around the room as his eyes slowly started adjusting to the darkness. "Though, I'll have to figure out how to fix up Maximus first . . ."

"How can you be so . . . calm about this?"

Ryan smiled lightly as he pushed himself up, looking right at Liam, though he could only see the boy's outline in this darkness. "I'm your knight now, right? Can't come here showing my weak side to my king, can I?"

Liam stayed silent for a while again, slowly speaking up, "I'm . . . kind of tired. Do you think you could . . ."

With an immediate nod, Ryan carefully made his way back to the door, trying not to run into anything. "Of course, don't worry. I'll be headed back to the living room. I'm starving anyway. I'll probably stick around at home to take it easy for the next couple days, so if you need anything, just let me know, okay?"

". . . Okay."

Ryan pulled open the door and exited, smiling at the boy as he stepped into the hallway. It was a very short conversation, but Ryan still hoped that it helped Liam a bit. Or at least, he hoped that the boy understood that he could come to Ryan when something was wrong or when he needed to talk about what happened. And right as he closed the door, Ryan noticed something.

The smell of wonderful, oily, steaming-hot pizza entering his nose. As if drawn to it by force, Ryan rushed into the living room, where Runar was currently putting down the pizza boxes, and without hesitation, he grabbed a slice. He folded the cheese pizza in half and stuffed it into his mouth, almost moaning as the flavor spread over his tongue.

"Rude," Runar scoffed slightly, and Ryan just stared at him with a full mouth. He chewed a couple of times and then swallowed.

"Yeah, I don't really care, I'm far too fucking hungry," Ryan pointed out, sitting down at the table. He looked over at Silvia as she came over to have something to eat as well. "Oh and . . . I was wearing those clothes you made for my birthday today . . ."

The elf looked at him a bit surprised. "You did? I didn't expect you would . . . that's great! How did you find them?"

"It was comfortable as hell, really. But . . . I had to tear up the shirt to use it to stop the bleeding on my leg, and then the blood from the wound on my belly sort of soaked into the pants, so . . ." Ryan awkwardly admitted, and Silvia sighed lightly.

"Well, at least you got *some* use out of them . . . better than nothing I guess?" Silvia laughed slightly. "I can make you new ones—I think I still have the patterns at home. I kind of hoard them."

"Honestly, that would be great . . . these clothes are so fucking hot. I'm dying." With a loud groan, Ryan ran his hand over his arm. He was already sweating a ton right now. His body was running so hot at the moment, and he didn't have any other clothes that allowed him to keep as cool as the ones that Silvia had made for his birthday.

"I'll get to it when I'm home, then." With an excited smile, Silvia reached out and pulled a slice of pizza onto a plate.

"Okay, so. Let's get started." Ryan smiled, holding his hand forward. Two streams of magic flowed out of his fingertips. One of them was a mass of red wisps of light, while the other was made of deep green threads. A one-legged and one-armed Maximus stood there with the Crusader arm laying in front of him. And to his side were the three fragments of Gaia.

Ryan activated his Spirit Construction skill, quickly picking up the arm and attaching it to Maximus so that he had at least a slightly easier time until Ryan figured out how to fix the broken parts. And then, he carefully grabbed the three green fragments laying in front of him.

"Alright, let's get you fixed up first." A smile was solidly planted on his lips as he took two of the fragments, pushing them together. The moment he managed to slot the pieces together properly, the crack completely disappeared as the fragments became one. And then, the moment the third piece moved into place, some messages appeared in front of Ryan.

**[You have successfully repaired the fragmented Spirit Core
of the -Garden Golem Spirit Gaia-]**

[You have earned Gaia's Gratitude and Trust]

The moment those messages appeared, Ryan could feel something tingle in the back of his head. It was vaguely connected to the side of Gaia's domain, and curiously, he tugged on it. Though right now, it was just a shapeless sensation, he could already guess what exactly it was, stretching out his hand as he pulled it out of his mind. Before, this was provided through Maximus's quest, but this time it was a bit different.

Green threads of mana flowed out of Ryan's arm, and a massive amount at that. They slowly started to form a box in front of him. But . . . it was kind of large. Honestly, maybe a little *too* large. It didn't look like it would actually fit on the table, but he wasn't able to change where it would go anymore, as all the threads came together and formed a massive cardboard box just a few centimeters above the table-top.

The box slammed down with a heavy *thud* that Ryan could feel in his whole body, and Silvia and Runar both flinched in response as an oversized box, 150 centimeters in height, was now standing on the table. On its front was the art of an overgrown golem with moss and flowers growing on its body, surrounded by fields of crops and flowers.

"Uhm . . . Ryan?" Runar let out, peeking past the box. "What's . . . what's this?"

"Uh . . . That's Gaia, I guess?"

". . . Seriously?" With an awkward expression, Runar took a look at the box. "Was Maximus's box that large as well?"

"Nope. It was a lot smaller . . . I think this just means that Gaia's body is, well . . . massive," Ryan pointed out, looking at the writing on the box. Same as on Maximus's box, there was a small descriptive text, and within that text, the words 1:10 SCALE stuck out to him. So that meant that Gaia's true size was just absolutely enormous.

Ryan could feel the excited wriggling of Tiar on his arm, and quickly got up. He stuffed the pizza crust into his mouth and opened up the box. It was going to disappear once all the frames were taken out anyway, so he didn't need to be careful with this. And so, he quickly pulled out the first frame. It was completely made of stone. And so were all the pieces attached to that frame.

However, all those pieces were really just randomly shaped rocks the size of the last segment of a finger. Nothing that would tell him exactly where the pieces could go, nor how they could fit together. And in the end, Gaia's body was really just made of a pile of rocks.

"Are you . . . are you fucking with me?" Ryan asked with a wry smile. "Am I seriously supposed to solve an impossible puzzle like this? With a skill that I can activate for ten minutes every hour?"

With a slight scoff, Runar looked into the cardboard box. "Good luck?"

"Oh, fuck off . . ." Ryan groaned, carefully starting to pull the stone frames out of the box. Silvia and Runar both helped out until the box was almost empty, at which point Ryan took a quick photo of each of the box's sides with his phone, and then took out the last ones. The cardboard box disappeared back into green threads that were soon pulled into Ryan's arm. And then, all that was left were the more than almost three dozen individual frames made of stone.

". . . Well. Okay. So, are you going to do the whole trial-and-error thing again?" Silvia asked, and Ryan slowly shrugged.

"I might have to. But honestly, for now I'm just hoping that these parts are at least sorted a little bit. Like, at least Maximus has six different parts. Each arm, each leg, his torso, and his head. Since Gaia also has a humanoid shape in the picture, I'm guessing maybe it's the same for her? And since there's only one type of frame, and because all the parts are literally the same exact size, just shaped slightly differently . . . maybe the fitting pieces are close to each other."

". . . I think either way, this isn't going to be solved today, right?" Runar asked, and Ryan nodded without hesitation.

"Oh yeah, definitely not. This is definitely going to take a while . . ." Ryan sighed loudly. "At least it's going to help me level up the Spirit Construction skill."

"You need any help?" Silvia offered, but Ryan shook his head.

"I think it's better if I do it alone. It's not like I'm on a time crunch here, and I don't exactly have an infinite supply to work with." As he explained this, Ryan picked up Gaia's core, then spoke to her, "It looks like it's going to take a little while until you've got your body. Sorry."

The core's light seemed to respond to Ryan's words, as the light that Gaia gave off softened and brightened in joyful patterns. It looked like she was really just happy to be herself again for the time being, whether she had her body or not. Ryan smiled, carefully placing her core onto the table.

"So what, can you just understand them now?" Runar asked with a curious frown, and Ryan looked up with a shrug.

"I get a vibe of how they're feeling. Like, right now, Gaia is happy and excited. Maximus is feeling relieved, despite the fact that two of his limbs are broken. Oh, that reminds me . . ." Ryan held his hand forward, pulling the broken arm and leg out of Maximus's domain. The table was already pretty cluttered with pizza and the pile of stone frames, but these small parts didn't take up too much space.

"Wait, what the . . . what happened?" Silvia asked, looking from the broken limbs at Maximus.

"He blocked some bullets for me. The limbs were completely shattered . . . but the system message said that they 'cannot be used until repaired.' So . . . I should be able to fix them."

"Poor Maximus . . ." With a sad expression, Silvia walked up to the small knight and carefully rubbed his shoulder with one of his fingers.

Runar smiled lightly, picking up the stone frames to place them onto the ground for the time being so that Ryan had space to work. "Yeah, repairing them is part of the deal. Though exactly *how* you do it is different for everyone, just as the construction process in the first place. What kind of tools did Hayden have?"

Ryan looked over at the wooden box on the edge of the table and quickly opened it up, grabbing everything out of it. There were different types of clippers and pliers, different brushes, some needles and a small spool of thread, a handkerchief, a metal file, and that was all. Looking at some of the pieces, Ryan noticed that some parts were bent out of shape; others were cracked or fully shattered. The leather was torn, and the branches were cracked into small pieces as well.

Ryan picked up two adjacent pieces that didn't seem particularly bent out of shape. He knew that these parts belonged to each other because there was a small line running over them that seemed to connect. This part was from the upper thigh. Ryan pushed them together as he had when initially constructing the piece, seeing a small red line shining out from the crack. He didn't know how, but he could almost feel the two parts connect, but not quite. As though there was something missing. They were sticking together as if he had used glue that hadn't cured quite yet, but they weren't properly *together*.

Curiously, Ryan grabbed the other tools. He knew that the handkerchief could be used to remove scratches from Maximus, so maybe he could use it to smooth over the crack and have them properly combine again. But when Ryan actually tried this, it didn't work. Though, the scratches on the surface of the broken pieces had faded a bit. And then, he noticed the needles and spool of thread from the corner of his eye. As he reached out to it, thin lines started to glow on the needles, and the thread itself similarly seemed to glow in Maximus's red mana.

Ryan grabbed the end of the thread, then swiftly pushed it through the eye of one of the smaller needles. This one had a slight curve, so he figured it was the right choice.

"You did that in the first try? Man, dexterity really is a neat stat . . ." Silvia muttered as she watched jealously, and Ryan laughed lightly.

"My fingers just kind of do exactly what I want them to. It's pretty neat."

Once he had pushed the thread through enough, Ryan placed the tip of the needle against the metal, and as if he was trying to push through butter, the needle pierced through. And as he pulled the thread through the hole, Ryan could already tell that this was going to work. However, looking at all of these ridiculously small pieces, Ryan also understood that this was going to take a long time as well.

At least Tiar seemed excited.

CHAPTER FIFTY-FOUR

Repair (2)

Ryan carefully grabbed the pliers to bend the metal of this small piece of Maximus's broken leg properly into shape, making sure that it fit right into the spot it was supposed to go. He pressed the piece into position, quickly pushing the needle through the metal to sew the parts together.

The metal fused back into a single part, and Ryan quickly ran over the whole piece with the handkerchief to clean it up and get rid of any further scratches. The threads had already dissolved, so now, it really just looked like Maximus's leg, as though it had never been broken in the first place.

**[Knight Spirit Maximus's -Left Leg- has been
fully repaired and can now be used again]**

[The -Spirit Construction- Skill has leveled up]

A smile quickly formed on Ryan's face as he held the leg up to Maximus, who quickly hopped over. Ryan held the leg in the right position and quickly attached it before the skill's effect ran out.

"Perfect." With a relieved sigh, Ryan watched as Maximus properly moved around and put weight onto his freshly repaired leg. He still had to do the same thing with Maximus's arm, but now that he knew exactly what to do, he should be able to do it properly in the twenty-three minutes that he would now have for the next activation.

:D, Tiar seemed just as excited as Ryan had expected. He could feel them concentrating on his fingertips as he worked, as if trying to watch the whole thing as closely as they possibly could.

Just as he finished, he could hear heavy, rushing footsteps after the front door was closed. Modak rushed into the living room.

"I-I'm so sorry, I wasn't looking at my phone, I—" the orc apologized nervously, but Ryan just smiled up at him as he turned around.

"Dude, calm down, it's fine. I'm fine."

Clearly relieved to hear that and see that he was just sitting there with some pizza at his side, Modak let out a long sigh as he dropped his bag near the table.

"Oh, thank the gods . . . What even happened?"

"Some experiment to try and use the spirits in a new way went wrong, I guess? Runar says they're still trying to figure it out," Ryan pointed out, as his uncle entered the living room as well. He had gone to the door to let Modak inside, and was now catching up to the panicked orc.

"Mhm, we managed to get some images taken. Most of it was destroyed when that giant went berserk, but we're guessing that they wanted this exact sort of thing to happen. Just . . . not now." Runar sat down on the couch. "But either way, we managed to get Gaia's last fragment. Hence, all the . . . stone stuff."

Only now noticing, Modak glanced down at the ground next to the dining table. A bunch of model frames were stacked up on the ground. "Those are all for Gaia's body?"

"Mhm . . . they are," Ryan sighed loudly. "It's gonna take a while. I'll work on her body over the next couple of days, so I should be able to finish it by . . . Tuesday? Wednesday the latest."

Modak smiled lightly, glancing over at what was actually lying in front of Ryan at the moment. He spotted the tools surrounding the fractured remains of Maximus's arm. "Wait, what . . . What happened with Maximus?"

"Ah . . . he took some bullets for me, so his parts broke . . ."

Modak looked away from Ryan over to Silvia, who was just leaning back in one of the chairs. "Should've picked up the phone when I called you."

"Yeah, about that . . ." Modak hesitantly looked around at the others, particularly over at Runar. "Alicia Boreard visited me earlier . . ."

Taken aback, Silvia and Ryan looked at their friend. "Excuse me? What did she want? Are you okay?"

Modak looked at the anxious Ryan, quickly trying to calm him down. "It wasn't anything like that, she . . . she wants me to work with the Magic Tower to continue developing my mana cassettes . . ."

This time, Runar was a bit surprised. "Seriously? I figured she'd be interested, but . . . to try and scout you? Good job, I wasn't aware you were that much of a prodigy."

"What did you say?" Silvia asked, excited for her friend, and Modak just nervously shrugged.

"I guess I told her I'd think about it? I was a bit overwhelmed, so I didn't know what else to say . . ."

Ryan looked at his friend, trying to suppress his complicated feelings about that. After Saturday, he thought about how he reacted when Alicia refused to help out with Gaia's fragment, and while he did think he overreacted, he still couldn't help himself but feel iffy about her. He looked at the orc with a smile.

"You should say 'yes.' That's an insane opportunity, man. I don't think you're going to get that kind of offer very often," Ryan pointed out.

"But I . . . I promised to help you out here, so I can't just go and join the Magic Tower instead!"

"Joining the Magic Tower doesn't mean we'll never see each other again. This is something you can't let up."

Modak looked at his friend, unsure what to say. "I . . . I don't know, I'll have to think about it a bit more . . ."

Quickly, Silvia stepped in. "What's there to even think about? Just call her right now and tell her you're in! Don't worry, I'll make sure that Ryan doesn't die in the next couple of weeks," she said with a broad smile directed at Modak, who was almost tearing up at his friends' words.

"Guys, just . . . thank you so much, I—"

"Uhm . . . I don't want to spoil the mood, but . . ." Runar looked at the three with a raised brow. "Joining the Magic Tower doesn't mean you have to cut your connection with us. Plenty of the mages from our family actively work at the tower, and some members of the tower directly work with or for us. Shit, I was a member of the Magic Tower for five years. Actually, technically, I'm *still* a member, just an inactive one. You can do your research and stick around with us too. If you feel like it, of course."

Ryan, Modak, and Silvia grew silent for a moment, looking at Runar who, albeit for a very good reason, ruined the moment.

Red tendrils slithered over Ryan's skin, though rather, they were part of his skin. They wrapped around his fingers, carefully tracing exactly how he moved. Over the past few days, Tiar had gotten better and better at supporting Ryan's movements. Though Tiar didn't directly make his fingers more nimble, it felt like he had a bit more energy, and his fingers didn't feel tired as quickly.

Especially when using the Spirit Construction skill, his fingers and wrist would start to feel sore super quickly, but Tiar seemed to be doing their best to prevent that. And then, there was something else.

[Your Dexterity has increased by 0.01]

His dexterity was increasing way too fast. Sure, using related skills *did* make it easier to increase your stats, but that didn't mean that it should increase this fast. Just over the past two days, his dexterity increased by a total of 0.04. That in itself was already shocking enough, but to his even greater surprise, his intuition increased by 0.01 just this morning.

While trying to construct Gaia's body, since he didn't have anything to go off besides a drawing of what she was supposed to look like when "finished," Ryan was going mostly off his gut feelings. He'd been having a lot of those lately, and when he was relying on those instead of just what he consciously thought might fit together, he found himself actually getting through the process a lot quicker.

Though, his stats weren't the only thing that grew a good bit over the past few days. Due to him constantly using the skill, his Spirit Construction skill leveled up quite a bit.

[Spirit Construction]
[Level - 9] [Proficiency – 13%]
[Allows the user to construct the Spirits' physical bodies.]
[Effect – Spirit Construction for 28 Minutes]
[Cost – 14 MP] [Cooldown – 1 Hour]

It was only one more level until he reached level 10; though there wasn't any technical difference as acknowledged by the system, usually people could feel some kind of tangible difference when a skill leveled up to intervals of 10.

Though, Ryan couldn't feel much of an effect from the skill anyway, so maybe it was wasted excitement. Either way, the fact that he could now have the skill active basically half the time was more than useful already. At this rate, he should be able to finish Gaia's body by dinnertime.

Then again, there hadn't been much of a distinction between any proper mealtime and the usual non-mealtime. Ryan was just eating as much as he could without ever feeling properly full. Tiar was really sucking up all the calories he ate. It was to the point that Ryan's jaw was way more sore than his hands were. Even the bullet wounds from just two days ago weren't that annoying.

However, at the end of the day, the only part that really mattered now was the fact that he was almost done constructing Gaia's body. The head, arms, and legs were done first, and right now he was building the torso. Really, he didn't know exactly what to expect considering the "Garden Golem" in her name, but Gaia really just appeared like a classic golem. As if a boulder sprouted legs, or if someone pushed together rocks until they vaguely resembled the shape of a person. Technically that was what Ryan was doing, just in a very deliberate, specific way that was far too annoying. It was the hardest model he had ever built, even beyond the fact that it was the *largest* model he had ever built. How heavy everything was when put together didn't help with that either. Turning the torso around was a whole ordeal in itself.

But for now, it was time to take a break, anyway. Ryan stood up and stretched, glancing over at Maximus. He was using his fully repaired limbs again, and Ryan had swapped out the Crusader arm out for the Knight model arm, since it was the less bulky option.

"I'll head out to the balcony to water the flowers," he informed the knight, who turned away from the computer monitor, where he was once more reading some random web-comic that Ryan recommended to him.

It was getting close to a pivotal point, so Ryan wasn't surprised when Maximus immediately turned back to the screen to continue reading.

With a protein bar in his hand, unwrapping it as he walked, Ryan stepped out into the hallway. He could hear the bustling of the café downstairs as Runar took care of business on his own. Ryan told him that he was fine with helping out, but his uncle insisted that he should take it easy and focus on Gaia when he could. Maybe this would finally convince Runar to hire some more part-timers, considering how busy the café looked to be today.

Ryan stepped outside and quickly approached the small "shed" in the corner of the balcony, though it was really more of a box with a few tools in it. He grabbed the watering can from it and made his way back inside to fill it up in the bathroom. As the bathtub's faucet gurgled alive and started filling the watering can, Ryan felt a buzzing in his pocket. He stuffed the protein bar into his mouth and pulled out his phone.

There was an event that he had mostly ignored the last time he got a message about it, because he had better things to worry about, and he barely remembered to just RSVP to it at some point. And now there was a reminder.

Newly Awakened Get-Together, Reminder
Saturday, 1st Memenar 1354, 18:00 at New Riverside's Awakened Center

"Urgh . . ." With a loud groan, Ryan swiped the reminder away. There was probably nothing he felt less like doing than going and meeting a bunch of random new Awakened. He had felt sort of excited about the idea when Yanna had told him about it, but right now he really couldn't care any less about it. But at the end of the day, he figured he should do it and go, even if it was just to try and boost his sociability a bit.

As the watering can overflowed, Ryan pushed the phone back into his pocket. He poured out some of the water, turned off the faucet, and made his way back out to the balcony. He went around and quickly watered some of the other potted plants, which definitely needed a good bit of care, especially in this weather, and then approached the planter that was Ryan's main focus.

The dirt was covered in small copper-colored sprouts as the wildflowers started to push their way out. Some of them were already oxidized pretty badly, but there were a couple that seemed to be in pretty good condition. Either way, whichever the case, Ryan just had to keep on taking care of them and then see what would happen when they were fully grown.

"Maybe Gaia can do something with these," he muttered to himself. With her being a Garden Golem, Ryan figured that at least shouldn't be *too* weird an idea. And she particularly seemed to care for flowers. After Ryan had fixed up her core, Gaia's domain had quickly changed. Though it wasn't filled with any objects like Maximus's, the ground of her domain had turned into a field of grass with bright flowers planted in a circle around where the core was floating. The Spirit Domain skill also leveled up as Gaia's domain developed, so when it did, it expanded enough to reveal a small root peeking out at the edge. It seemed like if it continued expanding, some kind of tree would soon come into view. But there were still a few level-ups needed for that tree to actually come into view.

When he was done watering the flowers, Ryan put the can to the side and leaned onto the balcony's railing for a while, just looking down at the road. And just as he did, he noticed a familiar car pulling up. A moment later, a young white-haired boy stepped out of the car, wearing a small school backpack.

"Yo, Liam," Ryan said with a smile, watching as the boy looked around a bit confused before spotting him up on the balcony, "how was school?"

With a smug grin, Liam pressed his hands onto his hips. "It went amazingly! I recruited two young peasants as my servants!"

The pedestrians walking around the sidewalk looked at the boy confused, but he managed to ignore them pretty well.

"Sounds great. Come on up and tell me about it, alright?"

CHAPTER FIFTY-FIVE

Six Mirrors

. . . and then, Laram dropped the barbells straight onto the ground, and the ground *under* the platform cracked," Yanna laughed, taking a sip of her coffee, and Silvia quickly chuckled along as the two continued walking up the road to their home.

"Oh gosh, does that kind of thing happen often?"

"Oh, not at all. It was a new machine that wasn't properly installed and calibrated yet. Plus, Laram's a good bit stronger than what the school's seen in a couple years, so they might not have expected that this could happen," the minotaur explained. "But I mean, Laram's working out all the time anyway. If anyone deserves to accidentally wreck that place with a new PB, then it's him."

Silvia scoffed, "You're there just as much as he is."

As if a bit hesitant, Yanna scratched her cheek. ". . . Well, sure, but I don't do nearly as much pure strength training as he does. He's going for strength, and at this point I'm trying to refine my body to be able to properly raise my aura."

"Hm . . . I guess so. Oh, by the way, did Ryan cancel properly, or . . ."

"Yes, he did. I was supposed to properly show him around the Awakened gym at uni today, but he got hurt again. Seriously, what's that guy doing to get himself in that much shit?" With a long groan, Yanna kept sipping on her coffee as Silvia awkwardly did the same, trying to avoid the question. It wasn't like she could just say that he was shot a couple of times just two days ago. But before she could say anything, Yanna continued, "Though, I guess it kind of worked out . . . I actually met up with Modak today because I had some free time after Ryan canceled. Modak seemed kind of different, just a lot more confident and excited. He couldn't tell me what it was about, but it was great to see him like that!"

Silvia looked up at her sister with a broad smile on her face. "Come on, just ask him out already! You know he's going to say yes to literally anything you suggest. Gods, he'd even go to mini-golf with you, and he absolutely *hates* mini-golf."

The minotaur hesitantly looked down, fiddling with the straw in her coffee. "I don't know . . . it's not like I really have the time to date right now. Plus, Modak said he'd be busy for a while too, so I'm not sure if it's a good time . . ."

Though Silvia wanted to protest, she knew that it wasn't really that easy. Yanna had a lot of things going on, being an up-and-coming Awakened League star, while it looked like Modak was going to take Alicia up on her offer and work with the Magic Tower for a while.

"I get that . . . but just because you're busy doesn't mean you don't get to give this a try. At the very least, you two should talk about it!" Silvia pointed out. "Look, Fae and I spoke about things as well, and we're going on a proper date this Saturday! And if we had both kept on being weird and avoiding talking about it, that wouldn't be happening. I know you're worried it's going to be weird, but you just need to give it a shot, or nothing's going to change. And that would . . . suck. You two are, like, perfect for each other!"

Yanna looked at her younger sister hesitantly. "You're sure?"

"Oh, of course I'm sure! Now, stop being so scared of a single nerdy orc! You'll literally be taking punches, swords, and blasts of magic to the face for a living!"

"Yeah, but I don't have to be scared about ruining my friendship with those punches, swords, and blasts of magic . . . Plus, if things don't work out, wouldn't that make things weird for you too? Or rather, even if it *does* work out, your sister dating your best friend? That . . . isn't that weird?"

"Hah, as if! It's like, the best thing ever! If you two are endgame, he'll be family! Too bad we don't have another sibling . . . but . . . hmm, do you think Modak's sister is Ryan's type? If we could get those two to hook up, we'd at least all be family somehow, right?"

Yanna thought about it for a moment, but when she caught herself considering it in a serious manner, the minotaur couldn't help but let out a laugh. The two continued chatting as they approached their home. As Yanna climbed up the stairs to the front door, Silvia's phone started ringing.

"Ah, go ahead! It's Fae, I gotta take this," Silvia said excitedly, and Yanna grinned lightly.

"Alright, little lovebird. Just don't stay out for too long."

"Shush!" Silvia replied immediately, answering the call with an excited expression. As Yanna made her way inside, Silvia sat down on the steps.

"Wait, seriously? And then, what? He just picked it all up like nothing happened?" the young elf asked with a gleeful joy in her voice, feeling her cheeks turn a bright pink as she heard the other girl's voice talk about some random things that happened to them today.

The conversation continued for almost too long, to the point where the sun was starting to glare into Silvia's eyes as it was setting. "Hey, I gotta go, alright?

I'm pretty sure my mom should have finished dinner right about now. Yes, it's those spinach cannelloni, I don't know how she does it, but my mom makes them taste divine! Mhm, yeah! Yeah, you . . . you should come over sometime and give them a try . . . I'm sure my parents would love to have you over for dinner," Silvia pointed out nervously, but soon, a broad smile appeared on her face. "Yeah, alright! That sounds great! Okay, I really do have to go now. I'll talk to you soon! Alright, bye-bye!"

Biting her lower lip excitedly, Silvia jumped up onto her feet, ready to sprint up the stairs. That was when a voice entered her ears and made her freeze up completely.

"I-I see you finally like spinach, huh?"

Silvia flinched at the source of the voice. In front of her stood a young elven woman. Actually, Silvia knew exactly how old she was. She had turned thirty-four this year, though she definitely didn't look it. She looked more like a human her age than an elf. The smell of her thick hibiscus perfume almost made Silvia want to vomit, as did her bright red lipstick.

Silvia froze in a cold sweat as she looked at her birth mother standing in front of her.

Six mirrors were lined up in a half circle. Mellow green runes were glowing on their frames as the figures of different individuals were revealed in each of them.

"Alright, we're all here, then." Runar crossed his leg, standing in front of those mirrors.

The person in a mirror to Runar's left spoke first. The elderly cyclops was wearing intricately decorated robes like you would have seen from nobility a few centuries ago. His rough, disgruntled manner of speaking came in clear contrast to his fashion choices.

"What's this about? This about that vampire boy? Something go wrong already?" he asked, and before Runar could reply, the person displayed in the mirror farthest to the right replied.

"That's why we shouldn't have used a child, especially not one with his sort of personality problems." The mustiar carefully stroked her long whiskers that were almost invisible against the mouselike woman's graying fur. "I've been against this from the beginning!"

Runar let out a long sigh, before the other elders could throw in their opinions. "No, this isn't about Liam. He's doing well, he seems to be making friends at school. It has been fully announced that he's a vampire, and I even spoke to some of the parents at his school, and they seemed more curious than anything. Some seem a bit apprehensive, but since Liam is such a lively boy, even if a bit weird, they seem to be a lot more open than I actually expected."

The human in one of the two middle mirrors leaned back in his chair, interlocking his fingers. "So then what is this about? I assume it's not to chat and report on your new kid's achievements."

"Hah, when have I ever reported anything to you guys?" Runar scoffed, shaking his head instantly. "No, this is something else. As some of you might be aware, my nephew has been living with me for a while now."

". . . Against our wishes, yes. What Hayden has done was nothing less than a betrayal of everything our family stands for," the human elder pointed out, and Runar couldn't really say anything against that. It was true; it was to the point where some factions within the Aglecard family even advocated to imprison Hayden, but Runar's father decided that he would be completely "banished" and blocked from any contact with the family. When Runar himself then became head, he could circumvent that without anyone being able to say anything, and even lifted the inherited banishment on Ryan.

"Yes, but that was Hayden, not his son. Is our family not about openness and acceptance? Why try to push out a boy who was not even a concept when his father betrayed us," the lizardman in one of the mirrors, with scarred, matted scales all over the exposed parts of his skin, pointed out. Runar smiled lightly at him, but before he could speak, the cyclops responded.

"Blood means something! The kid of someone that could commit such a sin is capable of the same, if not worse!"

"Blood does not carry morals, words do. And Hayden's words were never able to reach the boy. Hayden died long before any memories could be formed."

"Then what about his mother? Someone that'd get with a heinous criminal like Hayden can't be any better! A broad like her—"

"Shut your mouth, Orion." Runar's voice carried a weight that startled all the elders. He was usually a calm-minded man and didn't often raise his voice, after all. "Mary is a good, kind, and loving woman. She raised Ryan into a man of upstanding character, who doesn't hesitate to help those in need. When's the last time you took a bullet and threatened to jump to your death, just to—"

Realizing that he was talking about things that none of these people knew about yet, Runar stopped himself. First and foremost, he had to explain one thing.

"Ryan was chosen as the Spirit Keeper."

The six elders grew silent, but their expressions spoke volumes. There were only a few things that could really be passing through their minds right now, and Runar quickly continued, "He came into contact with two spirits already. The first was Maximus, the Knight Spirit. Later, while exploring a dungeon, he destroyed a dungeon heart and found a fragment of one of the spirits that was lost back then, Gaia the Garden Golem Spirit."

"Wait, hold on." The mustiar leaned forward. "A dungeon? Why was a spirit's fragment in a dungeon?"

Runar closed his eyes with a long sigh. "Well, why do you think? It's 'cause of the White Shadow Society."

"Of course it's them," the human elder scoffed, annoyed. "Have you found other fragments?"

"We found all the fragments. Ryan is currently constructing Gaia's body. However, each one of the fragments was being used for a very clear reason. The first was in a low-level dungeon with an easy-to-find core room and acted as the trigger of the dungeon being born. The second was placed inside of some kind of small robot, and later on was corrupted to cause the robot to go berserk. And the third was apparently being used for some kind of experiment. I'm sure you all heard about the giant in the Channel the other day."

Orion, the cyclops, crossed his arms. "So they're trying to tap into the spirits' powers? What for?"

". . . From my point of view, there only seems to be a single good reason," the lizardman pointed out. "Those were clearly all very obvious cases. Too obvious for how the White Shadow Society usually operates. Are they aiming for the spirits themselves this time?"

"That's what it looks like, yeah. If they can turn the tide of public opinion against *spirits* . . . then other magically influenced species will follow pretty quickly." Runar tiredly pushed his hand through his hair, trying to get it out of his face. "We're keeping an eye on them right now, but for the time being, it looks like they won't be able to abuse spirits like that anymore. But we should still be careful. Bruno, please tighten the search for the lost spirits. We'll send over some of the data we've gathered from the lab where they were doing the experiments; that should help you out."

Bruno, the rottweiler canir who had been keeping quiet this whole time, slowly nodded his head. "Got it. That reminds me, I *was* wondering why you requested the cores we had collected so far."

"I figured it made sense to keep them safe with Ryan. He's doing a pretty good job, and he's ridiculously protective over them. Even after just finding a single fragment, helping out Gaia was his top priority. Plus, the more spirits are with him, the faster he can level up. Bluesky is after him right now. Ryan . . . registered."

"Excuse me?" the human let out. "How the hell did you let that happen?"

". . . I was on a trip the day after he awakened. Dealing with that kobold hole that popped up a bit ago, remember? And it looks like Maximus, the Knight Spirit, found out that there was a trace of another spirit somewhere. Ryan immediately registered so he could go into that dungeon," Runar explained. "I've dealt with the guys going after him for now, but I want to push him above level 10 as soon as possible so that the Bluesky guys can't try to steal the class anymore."

The last of the elders, the old gnome woman who had kept silent this whole time, finally spoke up, ". . . Is there anything different about the class? It was inactive for twenty-five years, that in itself is abnormal. Is it safe? Are the skills the same?"

Runar thought about it for a while, but in the end decided that it was best to just fill them in for now. It seemed like the elders were generally receptive enough. Plus, they would find out sooner or later anyway. "Mostly everything seems the same, with two exceptions. One, because his flesh was infected with corruption, I brought him to the nearby symbiote nest. There, he bonded with a variant called a ruby symbiote. Tiar, the symbiote, seemed to have connected to the system somehow, giving Ryan a skill that allows him to recreate parts of the spirits' bodies as armor for himself. I hadn't seen that skill in any other records, so it seems to be a unique case through Tiar's assistance."

"A symbiote, eh?" Orion let out, clearly a bit annoyed. "A lucky fellow, ain't he?"

". . . Yeah, maybe. In some ways," Runar sighed awkwardly. "But I think the most important part is the form that his 'construction' type took. It's the same as his father's, that model-building method. He found Hayden's old tools and they respond to his ability perfectly fine."

"Did the class get stuck on that method, or was Ryan also an active model-builder?" the gnome asked.

"The latter. Actually, he seems more hard-core about it than Hayden ever was. But that's not why I'm bringing it up. Hayden's version was plastic; very, very strong plastic, but all of our analyses said that it was the same material as any other model-building kit. But in Ryan's case, the models are constructed with metal, leather, fabric, and even wood. Gaia's body that he's constructing right now is made of actual stone. And I don't know why either. It's not like he's ever built models that use those materials, only those classic plastic ones."

The gnome cupped her chin curiously. "So either it is a unique sort of adaption, or the class *did* undergo some changes over the past two decades."

Runar looked at the gnome hesitantly. "Actually, it does look like there was a change that we can tell for sure. I always kept a line to that Spirit Keeper–seeking spell. It didn't respond, even though we know for a fact that the Spirit Keeper is back," he explained, and though the others weren't sure exactly where Runar was going, the gnome did seem to understand.

"You don't mean . . ."

Runar nodded his head. "Yes. I think it's possible that there was another Spirit Keeper between Hayden and Ryan."

CHAPTER FIFTY-SIX

Gaia

With anxiety running through his veins, Ryan pushed the green gemstone into its place inside of the center of Gaia's body. It fit in perfectly and was solidly held in place by the rock around it. Once Ryan felt confident in pulling back without the gem falling back out, he grabbed the last plate of stones that he had laying next to him. It was about a dozen of the rocks, already fully put together, so that he only had to do this one last thing.

He pushed the stones onto Gaia's chest as the green glow of her mana lit up the stone around her. All of the small individual rocks that Ryan had pushed together to form Gaia's body were starting to grind against each other as a wave of spasms flowed through the spirit's new body. Her thick fingers were pushed to their furthest angles and her stout legs bent in unnatural ways. If her body weren't made of a bunch of stones, this would look incredibly uncomfortable, just as it did with Maximus before.

However, it didn't take long until Gaia's body went completely limp. The rocks were still properly attached to each other, but Ryan almost felt worried that they were about to fall apart as the gap between each small rock was "widening," as if they were only held together by a thin, invisible thread. Really, he had no idea how their bodies were held together. He was just happy that they were.

"Gaia?" Ryan asked, as the golem's body slowly came to life. She took control and slowly sat up, pushing up against the rug below her. Since there wasn't a ton of space on Ryan's desk, he was only using it for the individual parts, and was instead putting Gaia's body together on the ground. She was pretty big, after all, about a meter tall when standing up properly.

The spirit carefully got up onto her legs. For a few moments, she was incredibly unsteady, but before long, as her magic continued spreading through her body, she was able to properly move her body. Without hesitation, she nodded her head toward Ryan. Truly, he didn't fully understand why she even had a head, considering that she didn't have eyes or a mouth, just a mass of rocks coming together like the rest of her body. But he appreciated it, anyway.

Before anything else could happen, Maximus stepped up in front of Gaia. The two looked at each other for a moment, before Gaia moved down onto her knees, leaning toward the knight. Maximus pressed his forehead against the golem's. They stayed like this for a few moments, until Maximus pulled back to turn toward Ryan. He bowed with a grateful demeanor, happy to have his friend returned to him.

"Don't worry, I'm glad that it all worked out in the end." Ryan smiled, looking at the large model golem in front of him. "But that means at your 'regular' size, you should be ten meters tall? If the packaging is to be trusted, at least . . . I guess you should fit into your domain properly, but will you be okay? You wouldn't be able to move a lot, if at all."

Gaia seemed to look up at Ryan, before taking a step toward him. As she did, her body broke apart into green threads that were quickly pulled into his arm, traveling up his veins, through his heart and into his head. Inside of her domain, Gaia's body now reformed. She was kneeling on the ground, staying still like a statue. The grass around her was waving around happily, as if excited to see her.

As Ryan thought, her body took up most of the domain. Ryan didn't even know if she would be able to stand here properly, considering that the dirt below her feet took up about a bit of space as well. Though, she didn't seem to mind all too much, simply sitting there happy and serene. But even so, she still quickly came back out of the domain, having just gone in there to show Ryan that it was fine.

With a smile, Ryan watched her body come back together, and a system message appeared next to him.

[The -Spirit Domain- Skill has leveled up]

Maximus's and Gaia's domains expanded slightly into all directions, though not particularly much, after the skill reached level 6. But more importantly, this message *did* remind Ryan of something else. He had to take a look at Gaia's status window. It hadn't been available until now, but it should be ready for him to access at this point.

Just as he thought so, a deep green system window popped up in front of his eyes.

[Gaia]
[Garden Golem | Level - 1]
[MP - 30.5]
[Stats]

-[Intuition - 0.71]
-[Mana - 0.81]
-[Naturalism - 0.76]
-[Sociability - 0.64]
-[Spirituality - 0.83]
[Skills]
-[Garden Golem's Division | Level - 1]
-[Garden Golem's Eye | Level - 1]
-[Golem's Garden | Level - 1]

Ryan looked through the information in front of him. The first thing he noticed was how high Gaia's MP was—it was higher than both Ryan's own MP or even Maximus's AP, and this was just her state at level 1. But then, the next surprising part was that Gaia had no physical stats at all. Actually, most of them, besides one, were the exact same as the ones that Ryan had, so the Garden Golem was a magical class.

But there was also the naturalism stat, an incredibly rare one that appeared only in a specific type of known classes. It referred to how close one was to nature and how well the world around you reacted to your presence. It was thought that it related to the concept of the "green thumb," and that those with a higher naturalism stat could raise healthier plants more easily.

That being the case, Ryan was more interested in those three skills right now, and he pulled up the first in the list.

[Garden Golem's Division]
[Level - 1] [Proficiency – 0%]
[Allows the user to split off parts of their body
to act independently to a degree.]
[Effect – Create up to two sub-Golems]

"Huh . . . this is a passive skill? That . . ." Ryan looked over at Gaia, a bit surprised. "Could you show me what that means?"

Gaia didn't hesitate for even a moment, as some of the rocks on her torso started rumbling and moving around. Two lumps of rock fell off her body onto the rug and, before Ryan knew it, stood up. The lumps shaped themselves into smaller versions of Gaia. Though, they were a bit thinner and had proportionally longer arms and legs, even if not by much. And each of them was just a little shorter than Maximus was. Looking at Gaia, she now had two lumps missing from her body, but considering her size, it didn't seem to make all too much of a difference right now.

With a light smile on his face, Ryan moved closer to the two "sub-golems" as they were just standing there. They were almost cute standing next to Gaia and

Maximus liked that. Curiously, as the two sub-golems climbed back onto Gaia's body, Ryan looked at the skill window.

Considering that the Effect section specified the word *two*, it was possible that this would increase as the skill's level went up. But either way, that was something that they would have to see in the future, and for now, Ryan pulled up the info of the next skill.

[Garden Golem's Eye]
[Level - 1] [Proficiency – 0%]
[Allows the user to see the information of applicable plants]
[Effect – Gardener's Eye]
[Cost – 2 MP] [Cooldown – 1 Minute]

This one seemed more straightforward. It was an appraisal-type skill. At this level, it wouldn't be able to show much information, but then again, Ryan had never seen this specific skill before, and appraisal skills were pretty rare so, ironically, there wasn't a ton of specific data about them. Either way, it was exciting and fun, so Ryan couldn't wait to ask Gaia to try it out on the balcony later. But before then, he had to figure out what the last skill did.

[Golem's Garden]
[Level - 1] [Proficiency – 0%]
[After establishing a space as the user's Garden,
it will receive benefits according to this skill. At the same time,
the user's body will be affected by what is grown in said garden.]
[Effect – +5% Growth Speed]

"Oh!" Ryan wasn't able to hold back his surprise and curiosity. This one was a caretaker-type skill! After specifying and choosing a valid space, people with this type of skill could exert some kind of control. The exact type of control was different depending on the class and exact skill, but usually, like in this case, the space would receive a number of benefits based on the user, and the user would receive benefits in return.

And before he was able to make the suggestion, Gaia reacted first and a window appeared in front of Ryan.

[You have received a new Quest!]

[Gaia's Garden]
[Gaia needs a Garden in order to use her abilities to the fullest.
Please find her an adequate space.]

[Conditions – Find a Garden that Gaia is satisfied with]
[On Success – Random Selection of Seeds for the Garden]
[On Failure – Gaia's Disappointment]

With a smile on his face, excited to see the quest, Ryan got up from the ground. He looked at Maximus and Gaia, smiling at them both.

"Well, in that case, let's check out the balcony first."

Richie walked through the roads of the Channel, pearls of sweat dripping down his forehead. He was called here by the company he got a job offer from for some sort of orientation meeting. Being an Awakened, and a Technomancer at that, probably meant that they wanted to put him to work as soon as they could. Though, of course, he didn't really mind. That just meant he could get paid sooner.

But the annoying part was that a ton of the roads around the building were locked down. During that villain attack last weekend, there was so much damage done that it messed up basically all public transport. There would be construction going on here for months. The fact it was so hot right now really wasn't helping either.

"Oh gods, I thought it was supposed to be kind of chilly today," Richie groaned, loosening his tie to let some air into his button-up. Under his jacket, half his shirt was completely drenched in sweat. And he was even seeing things; he could swear there was something moving under his shirt. He tried to grab at it, but there was nothing.

"Uhm . . . sir?" Someone stepped up in front of Richie, and the gnome looked up at them surprised. "We found that the structural integrity of the nearby buildings has been compromised. Could we ask you to vacate the area?"

"Hm?" Richie stared at the person, for some reason taking a while to register what they were saying. They were looking at him with an almost disgusted expression, and Richie awkwardly nodded his head. "Oh . . . oh yeah, right, for sure . . ."

Moving along, he continued walking on the sidewalk. Was it getting hotter? Richie took off his jacket, then folded it over his arms. At the edge of the area that he was supposed to leave, there was a small convenience store. Richie still had plenty of time, so he rushed into the store and headed straight for the fridges. He pulled out one of the chilled bottles of water, then opened it and chugged the contents.

It didn't take long until the bottle was empty, and he grabbed the next. It was helping, but it wasn't even close to enough. The freezers caught his eye, and he quickly grabbed one of the cups of crushed ice, holding it against his forehead. That was much, much better.

"Yo, dude, be careful," the pimply teenager behind the counter called out to Richie. "If you bleed on those, you gotta pay for 'em. You need some paper towels?"

Confused, Richie turned over toward them. "Huh? Bleed? What are you . . ."

As he spoke, he started to feel a slight coppery taste in his mouth. Richie put down the cup of ice and touched his finger to his nose, still holding his jacket in his other hand. When he pulled his fingers back, he saw dark red blood on there. Actually, it was a bit too dark for blood: black. Just then, he noticed an almost rotten taste accompanying the blood's copper, as his stomach began to churn.

"D-Do you guys have a restroom?"

The teen slowly nodded his head, pointing to the corner of the store. Quickly, Richie rushed over and stepped into the small single-person restroom. He placed his jacket onto the closed toilet seat, and then stepped up to the mirror.

The dark blood flowing from his nose only stuck out more on his sickly pale skin. But it wasn't just the blood; the veins on his neck and forehead were dark and bulging. Along with his heartbeat, they were pulsating. No, they were *writhing*.

As if triggered by the realization, a deep, visceral pain coursed through his body, starting from his chest. It was like something had burrowed its way into his body, like dozens of worms digging their way through his veins. Anxiously, Richie pulled open his button-up shirt that had already gone translucent from sweat. Same as on his face and neck, dark veins were bulging all over his chest.

Before he could even react properly, he felt a stinging in his eye. Glancing back at the mirror, he noticed blood flowing down his cheeks like pained tears.

"Wh-What the hell is . . ."

The sentence was interrupted by an animalistic retching, as if he had bitten into a piece of rotten meat, and maggots were now spreading around and filling his mouth. Though Richie was fighting against it with his whole body, Richie vomited into the sink. It was a black, viscous liquid, like some kind of thick ink. But what was even worse was that it looked like that whole ink was made of disgusting, thin black worms. As he grabbed his cheek, he could feel some of those moving threads still clinging to his cheek.

Richie lost the strength in his legs and fell down onto the ground. He vomited again, covering the ground in those rotten black threads. They clung to his fingers, trying to climb back up. Pulling back, Richie tried to get back, but the threads were faster than him. Moving along underneath his shirt, dyeing it in a foul black, they climbed back up onto him. Instinctively, Richie knew what was about to happen. The tendrils climbed up his neck and forced their way back inside his throat.

Richie could feel them force their way down his throat.

He grabbed at the threads, trying to pull them back out, but when he did, it felt like he was tugging on exposed nerve ends, feeling a disgusting pain that made him shrivel back completely. But not all of the threads were making their way back inside. In general, the dark, inky mass was growing larger, as if the threads were becoming longer and intertwining farther with every second.

It didn't take long until they covered the whole ground, and when he glanced at the sink, the parts in there were already climbing up the mirror and walls. Richie watched as the entire small restroom was covered in these threads, as if he was about to be devoured by a black hole.

And then, when not an iota of light could be seen, everything went silent. The singing pain all over Richie's body was getting worse and worse.

The blackness was closing in on him.

He was scared and exhausted. Richie barely clung to consciousness.

As his eyes went blank, and the tendrils forced their way into him even if it meant digging their way through his skin and muscles, the blackness won.

And then, Richie stood back up.

He pushed himself off the ground, straightening his tie. After checking his face in the mirror a few times, Richie picked up the neatly folded jacket off the toilet seat and put it back on.

As he practiced his smile, Richie's eyes glanced down at his chest, and the silver sparrow pin that adorned it.

He should hurry. At this rate, he would be late for the orientation meeting.

About the Author

Quinn Rivers is the author of the Totally Spiritual series, originally released on Royal Road. When they're not busy playing or creating indie games, they enjoy reading comics, sewing plushies, building figurines, and tending to their plants. Rivers resides in Cologne, Germany, among many loving friends.

RESPAWN YOUR CURIOSITY

follow us on our socials

 podiumentertainment.com

 @podiumentertainment

 /podiumentertainment

 @podium_ent

 @podiumentertainment